THEY
DID BAD
THINGS

Also by Lauren A. Forry

Abigale Hall

THEY DID BAD THINGS

A THRILLER

LAUREN A. FORRY

ARCADE
CrimeWise

An Arcade CrimeWise Book

For Dad, who taught me to love a good mystery

First Edition

This is a work of fiction. Names, places, characters, and incidents are either the products of the author's imagination or are used fictitiously.

Arcade Publishing books may be purchased in bulk at special discounts for sales promotion, corporate gifts, fund-raising, or educational purposes. Special editions can also be created to specifications. For details, contact the Special Sales Department, Arcade Publishing, 307 West 36th Street, 11th Floor, New York, NY 10018 or arcade@skyhorsepublishing.com.

Arcade Publishing® and CrimeWise® are registered trademarks of Skyhorse Publishing, Inc.®, a Delaware corporation.

Visit our website at www.arcadepub.com.

10 9 8 7 6 5 4 3 2 1

Library of Congress Cataloging-in-Publication Data

Names: Forry, Lauren A., author.
Title: They did bad things: a thriller / Lauren A. Forry.
Description: First Edition. | New York, NY: Arcade CrimeWise, [2020] | "An Arcade CrimeWise Book." |
Identifiers: LCCN 2020000508 | ISBN 9781950691449 (hardcover) | ISBN 9781950691630 (ebook)
Subjects: GSAFD: Mystery fiction. | Horror fiction.
Classification: LCC PR6106.O777 T48 2020 | DDC 823/.92—dc23
LC record available at https://lccn.loc.gov/2020000508

Cover design by Erin Seaward-Hiatt
Cover photograph: © JannHuizenga/Getty Images (sofa); © Vladimirovic/Getty Images (texture)

Printed in the United States of America

EVIDENCE

Recovered/Seized from (Person or Location):
Wolfheather House, Isle of Doon

Remarks:
Diary located immediately upon entrance to house, on
doormat. (Footprint on cover belongs to first officer on scene.)

Missing pages not yet recovered.

To Whom It May Concern

You're not afraid of doing bad things. You're afraid of getting punished for doing them.

No, not me, you say.

Really?

Okay, think about it like this.

It's your lunch hour. You're thirsty, but you forgot a drink. The vending machine is broken, and the nearest shop is a fifteen-minute walk. You've already lost ten minutes because Sheila from accounts wouldn't shut up about free-range chicken salad, so by the time you reach the shop, you only have forty minutes left. Even if you hurry, that will only give you twenty-five minutes to eat once you get back to the office. Wouldn't it be easier to grab a bottle of Coke from the shelf and walk out of the shop rather than wait in line while some old biddy pays the cashier in 1p and 2p coins and the young mother after her remembers she has to grab one more box of nappies and the schoolgirl who's next and should probably be in class right now is too busy reading <u>Heat</u> magazine to move up in the queue?

Wouldn't it be ten times easier to take what you need and leave the shop? 'Course it would. But you don't.

Why?

Because store security would chase after you, give you a warning. Maybe even phone the police, who might give you a pat-down just to make sure you weren't nicking something worth more than 90p. Might even ban you from the shop or arrest you.

So you don't do it. But you would if you could.

That's only a bit of light shoplifting, you say. That's not a serious crime. That's not like murder. You'd never murder anyone.

(Everyone thinks they'd never commit murder.)

And I'd say, even if you wouldn't get in trouble?

And you'd shake your head and talk about morals or throw in God for good measure.

And I'd say, isn't fear of getting in trouble with God fear of getting in trouble? And maybe you're an atheist so you care fuck-all about God, but still, you say, you wouldn't do it.

Why?

Because, you say, you'd feel guilty. And that guilt would eat you up until you were so desperate for the pain to end, you'd turn yourself in because then it wouldn't be a punishment. It would be relief.

The police will tell you it's not your fault. They want you to believe that. You're young and attractive and the whole world is in front of you, so they say it right to your face. *It's not your fault about Callum.* Like they want to believe there's good in people. They should know better.

But what if you could kill someone *and* not get in trouble *and* not feel any guilt? What if you could take a life as easy as taking that Coke from the shelf?

Think about it.

Really think about it.

I'll wait.

You've got a specific person in mind, don't you? A celebrity, a politician, a coworker. Maybe a friend. That one person that makes you think the world would be so much better off without them.

Yeah.

That one.

See, I knew what you were thinking because at their heart—and the police know it—people care about nothing except themselves. Given the choice, they'll always take the easy way out. The way without guilt. Without pain.

Face it. People aren't really very nice.

(Except Callum. He was a nice person. Maybe that's where he went wrong. Maybe if he hadn't been so nice, he'd still be breathing.)

I've always known that people were shit. However, it wasn't until I got older that I realized there are three different kinds of shit. I learned it from a ghost story. Well, not a ghost story per se.

More like monsters.

The story goes that there was once a Scottish laird, an owner of a manor in the Highlands, who bred a pack of wolf-dogs to protect his property. These were large, terrible beasts with coarse gray fur that got matted with blood whenever they ate. But they could be playful and loving so long as they got their way. One night the laird had a guest and, to honor him, a fine cut of venison was prepared. To appease the pack, the laird gave each dog some of his meal. The guest, famished from the long journey, refused to relinquish a single morsel of his own meal despite the laird's request.

At the end of the night, the guest retired to bed, only to be woken a short time later by someone breathing in his ear. He opened his eyes to admonish the maid for disturbing him, but it was not the maid's eyes he saw. Before he could scream, the pack leapt and tore what was theirs straight from his belly.

And that's people.

People are the tired guest or they're part of the pack or they're the laird. The laird I've always thought was the worst because he knew what the pack might do, but did he try to contain them? Distract their attention? Make provisions to protect his guest's life? No. In the story I was told, he hid deep in the manor. More concerned with what might happen to him than what might happen to another.

So that's what I know about people. People hide and people cheat and people lie and people only look out for themselves because people are shit and very few deserve better.

And Callum should've known this. This was the story he used to tell. But now, I guess, it's mine.

This is, word for word, what I had sent The Inverness Courier. They never printed it. Apparently, they felt it was "inappropriate" for an obituary. But I put it here, at the beginning, because this is what I wanted you to read first. Before I tell you what they did to him. Before I tell you what I did to them. I want you to understand that I know which of the three I became. What I want you to think about is very simple.

Which one are you?

FRIDAY

1

Hollis

A sudden onslaught of rain splattered the windshield, drowning out Bon Jovi. Hollis Drummond swerved back and forth on the single-lane road, fumbling to find the wipers on the unfamiliar car. Refusing to stop living on a prayer, he turned up the volume and belted the chorus as he finally hit the windshield wiper lever. But unlike Tommy and Gina, he had no clue if he was halfway there because his phone was no more than a black brick. Hiring a car without GPS for a five-hour drive to the Isle of Skye, followed by a thirty-minute ferry ride, followed by another thirty-minute drive on a mostly uninhabited island, thinking he could rely on said phone, might not have been his most brilliant idea, he decided as he jiggled the cables.

The charger was attached to the phone port, the other end plugged into the car, but his mobile was not charging. Probably hadn't been since he picked up the car in Inverness. Disconnecting and reconnecting the cable did nothing. He thought about ringing Linda for the directions, then remembered the dead phone was the reason he needed the directions in the first place. Timing his movements to the percussion, he tossed the useless thing onto the passenger seat. The road led only one way anyway.

The headlights illuminated the rocky landscape as he continued north, highlighting a patchwork of browns and dull greens, the vibrant purples and yellows of heather and gorse now out of season. Hollis liked the colors as they were. They reminded him of the brown and gray streets of Manchester, those he'd plodded up and down for so long and which, come Monday, he would see from a new angle. No uniform pressing for PC Drummond this weekend. A new pair of suits awaited him along with polished black shoes and a red tie with a subtle Manchester United watermark logo—a gift from Linda. It might've been thanks to his blind luck with the Marcus case, but he'd finally done it. The lads had taken the piss, of course. Hollis Drummond—mid-forties, the phrase "pushing fifty" just around the bend, his dozens of exams taking up a whole drawer in the filing cabinet—had finally made detective. He'd pretended it wasn't that important, joked that some people needed to age like fine wine (or stinkin' cheese, someone had blurted out). They tried to embarrass him by taunting him about his new partner, Khan, being ten years his junior and already a DS. If Hollis were lucky, they said, he'd be promoted to DS right in time to be pensioned off. Hollis shot back by saying Khan's success had something to do with him being Asian.

"*Dad, that's so racist!*" Linda would've said, so he hadn't told her that bit, even though Khan was always saying the same thing himself. Unlike Khan, Hollis was never that good at laughing at himself. But he had gone along with the "old man" jokes to cover up how excited he was. And nervous.

Here he was on his last pre-CID holiday with a bottle of Dalmore and a few cheap paperbacks. A whole weekend to kick his feet up while the anticipation for Monday built like the final days before Christmas. And he still wasn't sure he deserved it. The promotion. The trip. Any of it. Part of him thought he should be at home. Seeing Dr. Bevan one last time before his new Monday shift. But Linda had been so proud of him. And so pleased she had pulled off this surprise. He couldn't disappoint her, even if instinct had been needling him to turn around since Inverness. He turned the stereo up another notch.

It was dark now, but Hollis still wondered if he'd see one of those orange cows Linda loved before the weekend was out.

"*Coos,*" she had said. "*They call them Highland coos.*"

Keeping his eyes peeled for a *coo*, Hollis almost missed the silver SUV blocking his path.

He jerked the car left and slammed on the brakes.

"Shit."

As Bon Jovi yowled about steel horses and six strings, Hollis let out a slow breath, then switched the stereo off. The sudden silence was deafening as he lifted his gaze to the rearview mirror. The only reason he and the SUV hadn't collided was because the SUV wasn't moving. He could see it lifted up on a jack, but, from his vantage point, he couldn't see anyone changing a tire. Using the keychain torch he kept in his pocket, he hopped out to check for signs of the driver, turning up his collar against the rain.

Mud and cow dung wafted in the air as needles of rain pricked his face. Wet gravel lodged into the soles of his boots. Though he was hundreds of miles from his own jurisdiction, he couldn't switch off the part of his brain that urged him to help, holiday or not. After all, hadn't he found Catherine Marcus on a day like this? A dark night, heavy mist, no other passersby.

There was no one inside this car, though, tied up or otherwise. The doors were unlocked and the driver had left the keys on the seat. There were no personal belongings and the registration indicated that, like his, this was a hired car. Nothing to indicate who had driven it here, or who had abandoned it. Hollis had been the only car on the ferry. Hadn't passed anyone on his way in, saw no pedestrians in the distance. Out of habit, he checked for signs of blood or a struggle but found none. The tire iron was missing, but no body lay in the ditch. Not as far as he could see, which albeit wasn't far.

He cupped his hands to his mouth and called out, listening to his voice carrying over the rain, then waited for a response. None came. The longer he stood there, the more the rain soaked through his jacket. He shouted one more time.

Back in his car, he shook his head like a wet dog and dug through his bag for the reservation confirmation.

Wolfheather House, The Bend, Isle of Doon, IV55 8GX.

The little square map showed the area ten kilometers around, but the last he'd looked at his phone before it died, he was still fifteen out. Hollis tossed the confirmation aside and restarted the car, scanning the horizon for any sign of the missing driver. The phone chirped—the red battery icon glowing before going black. Three minutes later, it held enough charge to power up, and he reentered the address into Google Maps.

"Now, stay that way, mate." He gave the phone an encouraging pat, taking one last glance at the abandoned car as he drove off.

Though the music continued, he stopped singing along. Leaving a car like that in a place as isolated as this, it didn't feel right, especially when the only problem seemed to be a flat. Each time he thought he glimpsed movement, he slowed, but there was never anything to be seen.

A few minutes later, the turnoff for Wolfheather House appeared on his right.

The main road disappeared in the rearview as he accelerated down a bumpy gravel path that, according to Google Maps, did not exist. The blue arrow that represented his car hovered in a tan abyss. After a few minutes, he had started to think this was all a practical joke orchestrated by Linda and the lads at the station when a sharp turn in the drive brought the well-lit house into stark view. Hollis slammed on the brakes.

"Fuck me."

He grabbed the confirmation page, but the sole picture showed his guest room, not the entire cottage. Or rather, what he had assumed would be a cottage.

Last time he'd been on holiday, it'd been a basement room in the El *Something* Hotel in Benidorm that smelled of stale lager and flop sweat. Music from the club upstairs had reverberated through his mattress like an unwanted massage. He'd been expecting something on par, if maybe moderately better, but even if Wolfheather House had a cellar, it was probably nicer than his own flat. The three-story brick and stone manor was smaller than the mountains surrounding it, yet presided over the landscape like the lord who must've once owned it. The only time he'd seen a house this gorgeous was on *Midsomer Murders*. But his admiration faded as he continued down the drive. The longer he stared at the once-beautiful Wolfheather

House, the more faults he found. Chipped brickwork and broken sashes. Overgrown hedges and weeds nesting in the flowerbeds. Cracked urns flanking the doorway like decorations for a funeral parlor.

As he pulled in next to a banged-up Vauxhall sedan, the bad feeling he'd had on the main road returned. It was the same feeling he'd had when he made Frank Landry pop the boot of his Ford Fiesta, knowing he'd find Catherine Marcus tied up but breathing. It wasn't instinct alone that had caught Landry, but Hollis's eye for detail. "Poirot minus the OCD" an old partner had once described him. It helped Hollis remember traits and faces so that Landry's attempt to conceal his features had looked poorer than a child dressing up for Halloween.

Hollis got out of his car and stared up at Wolfheather. With the sunlight near gone, darkness enveloped most of the house. Unlit windows gave the façade the look of a spider's many black eyes. Maybe he did deserve this place after all.

Hollis made himself laugh. Adrenaline and exhaustion were getting him worked up. That was all.

He hoisted his kit bag over his shoulder and made his way inside.

The lobby of Wolfheather House warded off the chill outside. In the grand entranceway, a wide staircase laid a red-carpeted path to the next floor. Exposed beams crossed the elevated ceiling; to the left of the main entrance, a peat fire burned in a stone fireplace, filling reception with a welcoming scent that reminded him of his Irish great-gran's cottage. Two overstuffed armchairs sat in front of the fireplace like a pair of old friends. A forgotten red carryall left a puddle on the floor.

A series of closed doors lined the wall to his right, and muffled voices permeated through one of them—a hushed argument like his parents would have before his father stormed off to his mate's for the night.

"I don't care why. What matters is that . . ." A sweating, red-faced young man, a cordless phone pressed to his ear, emerged from a different door on the right and closed it behind him. Tall and lanky with a shock of ginger hair, he looked like a scarecrow that had descended from the fields, a scarecrow wearing a designer suit.

"Hang on. Checking in, aye? Drummond?"

"Yes, sir. How'd you know?"

"I'm a bloody psychic. No, I was being facetious," he said into the phone. "Look, get your affairs in order and . . ." He rolled his eyes and pointed to the paper register. "Sign here. No, I don't need *your* signature," he said down the phone. "Are you a complete monkey's ass?"

Hollis scribbled his name in the book, but the young man swept it away before Hollis could read any of the other names. There were at least four others here, though, if none had been recorded on the previous page. Perhaps one of them belonged to the disabled SUV.

Hollis pointed to a wooden nameplate on the desk. "Are you Mr. MacLeod? Back on the road there's a—"

"Do I look like a fucking Dugal MacLeod? Yeah, I am referring to you," he said into the phone. "Your fans are asking after you, so you better get your ass up here by the last ferry or I'll say more about you besides." He chucked the phone onto the desk. "Let me find your key. It's around here somewhere . . . fucking paperwork. There is a filing cabinet right bloody—" He swept some paper onto the floor.

"Do you need to see some ID?"

"You say you're Hollis Drummond?"

"I am."

"Good enough for me. Everyone else for this weekend is already here."

"Did one of them have car trouble? There's a disabled vehicle—"

"They're all in the dining room if you want to ask, waiting on the dinner that I have to prepare like some fucking housewife because the fucking hired help—" He held up his hands, closed his eyes, and took a deep breath, which only made him look more like a toddler having a tantrum. "Apologies. Sir. Bit of a staffing problem. Here's your key. Room six, top floor."

"Room six." A little chill ran through Hollis.

The sound of glass breaking echoed from the dining room, and the indistinguishable voices rose.

"I suppose I have to see to that now, too." The young man hurried to the dining room, giving Hollis enough time to glimpse a blonde woman with her head in her hands before the door shut. He didn't see her face, but something about her posture, the crystal-blue color of her blouse, triggered a memory. Sticky green carpet and the smell of fried chicken. He stared at the key in his hand, then at the door. But he was being paranoid. There were other guests here, clearly, but no one he would know. He started up the stairs.

His back, stiff from the long drive, ached as he walked up to his third-floor room. Plush red carpet continued to line the hallway on his left, where dark maroon walls surrounded closed doors stained a deep brown. To the right, a sagging, frayed rope blocked off a darkened hall, the floor bare and lined with sheet-covered furniture. A misspelled handwritten sign pinned to the rope read: CLOSED FOR RENAVATION. Hollis followed the carpet.

All that distinguished his door from the others was the brass 6 gleaming in the yellow light of the wall sconce. Before unlocking it, he imagined feeling a rush of cold air escaping from within, bringing with it black dust and a smell of must. But the door opened soundlessly to a clean scent Hollis traced to a Glade PlugIn by the bed.

The interior matched what he'd seen in the website's photos. The walls suffered the same maroon color as the hall and the paisley-patterned bedspread spoke of years of use. A desk, high-backed office chair, and bedside table completed the furniture but nothing matched, as if the pieces had been scavenged from throughout the house. Stepping between the bedroom and bath, however, was like traveling through time. The small bathroom had been renovated with a modern waterfall shower, white ceramic sink, and water-efficient toilet. Black tile lined the walls and gray slate the floor.

Back in the bedroom, he wanted to text Linda and tell her he'd arrived safely, but his phone, which had died again, didn't have enough power yet. He unplugged the air freshener, plugged in his phone, then searched through his bag for some paracetamol, finding the Dalmore first.

"Don't drink it all in one weekend, mind." Linda had laughed as she handed him the bottle.

With his pocketknife, Hollis sliced the gold ribbon from the neck of the bottle and flattened the gift tag out on his knee. Her cheery scrawl—*Congrats, Dad!*—smiled up at him. Linda was so proud of him it hurt, especially when he didn't think he deserved such admiration.

He tossed the bottle back and forth in his hands and considered pouring a drink, but stopped himself. If he started drinking now, he might not stop. He would try it later, when he had a full stomach and a clearer head. He'd send Linda a picture of himself with a glass of it. Maybe use one of those silly filters she'd installed on his phone. He tucked her note into the breast pocket of his shirt.

The wind battered the building as Hollis made his way down the cold hall, which held a damp whiff of wet dog. He straightened his shirt cuffs, eager for the warm fire downstairs, when a thump sounded from behind him. Nothing but closed doors, and the weight of a presence.

"Oi!" he shouted, hoping to startle anyone who might be there. Nothing save the wind responded.

He waited a few seconds more, then shook off his paranoia. Maybe he should've had that drink first, he thought.

Reception was empty, so he warmed his hands by the fire and breathed in the smell of burning peat, enjoying the quiet he never got to have in Manchester.

Until the heated voices from earlier erupted into a full-fledged argument. Hollis dropped his hands. Just what he needed. Some domestic spat where he'd have to play peacemaker. He slipped into his policeman's persona as he paused at the door.

"Trouble follows me, Linda," he once told her.

"Dad, you only say that because you're a copper. What you think is trouble is normal to everyone else."

But when he opened the dining room door, he knew they'd both been wrong. This wasn't normal. And it was worse than mere trouble.

The shouting ceased once he stepped inside, the four other guests looking far less surprised than he. He logged each of their faces, their names popping into his head as if he'd last spoken to them yesterday, not twenty years gone.

Maeve Okafor, wet frizzy hair enveloping her head like a bird's nest, jeans a size too small and a jumper two sizes too big, her ballet flats caked in mud.

Eleanor Hunt, body thin and sharp as a knife, her long blonde hair chopped off to a line so straight it could cut.

Oliver Holcombe, his black leather jacket with sweatshirt hood meant for a man a decade or two his junior, a beer gut and an almost—but not yet—comb-over.

Lorna Torrington, sensible skirt and a turtleneck that concealed her large chest, the same black bob framing her face.

Lorna flipped her fringe out of her eyes, and suddenly he was back—back in that room in that house with these people and the black niggle in his stomach that told him to run.

Run now, as fast and as far as he could.

Pp. 6–15

to tell you something. It's from memory, this story. Mine and theirs. So I may not have everything right. It's possible I may have got some things confused. But I've done my best. I swear.

This story begins with a house. Or rather a roundabout. One particular roundabout on one particular day in early September 1994.

Read carefully.

Five ordinary streets protruded from the concrete central island of this roundabout, known as Manor Circle, a roundabout which loitered on that side of the Thames only ever discovered by accident. None of these streets contained anything resembling a manor. Chiltern Drive led to a chip shop and off-license, open when they weren't needed and closed when they were. Sandal Road curved toward the train station, where tourists disembarked to visit the failing high street and purchase overpriced goods at half-stocked housewares shops. The Byeways contained a pub which on Saturdays doubled as a nightclub and closed monthly when the police had to investigate the latest stabbing. Berry Avenue wound around to Cahill University's back entrance, which students never knew existed and so never used.

Caldwell Street led nowhere.

On either side of its buckling tarmac squatted semi-detached, three-story family homes purchased decades ago by young pregnant couples hoping to get in on the up-and-coming regeneration area of Moxley Gardens. The children had since been born and grown and were now sitting university exams while their aging parents continued waiting for Moxley Gardens to up, come, or regenerate. However, most of the Caldwell Street houses remained acceptable enough for a crowd with a certain ironic sensibility.

This was not the case with house number 215. The façade of number 215 sagged more than its neighbors. Damp warped the window frames. The fence leaned as far as a fence could without falling over. In fact, all that made number 215 special was that the weed-infested front garden had yet to be paved over for off-the-street parking. However, what made number 215 Caldwell Street a poor excuse for a family home made it a fantastic student house. (Until a fire of unknown origin would destroy it some years later, but we're not there yet. Don't jump ahead.)

Because of its proximity to the university and its excellent transport links to London (which were excellent so long as the weather was neither snowy, rainy, windy, nor sunny), number 215 held great appeal for students. Over three narrow floors it contained six bedrooms, one full bathroom, a downstairs toilet that sometimes worked, a spare room, a kitchen, and a communal front room. There was also a private back garden, lovely for barbecues except during the spring and summer when it was prone to flooding with sewage. The landlord had not set foot on the property since his wife left him and the mortgage fifteen years ago. He allowed it to be let and managed by Jameston Estate Agents, where it became the charge of a man called Yanni who no one was certain even worked there anymore. As the landlord chose not to remove any of the shit furniture his ex-wife had bought from her alcoholic brother, the house also came fully furnished. Over time, it filled with the various abandoned items of previous tenants, including but not limited to coffee pots, teakettles, three microwaves (one of which worked), a *Learn Spanish Now!* VHS tape, and a vinyl recording of the *Grease* soundtrack. No student was entirely sure what belonged in 215 Caldwell Street and what they would be required to bring, as Yanni was the only person with the move-in and move-out checklist and his coworkers were beginning to think immigration had returned him to Ukraine.

And yet every autumn, number 215 was fully let because the university kept attracting students and students needed a place to live. House shares were the ideal alternative for those who preferred private accommodation with no privacy and the constant odor of a pot-smoking wet dog. In return, letting agents loved students because students never complained when their door wouldn't lock or the smoke detector didn't work or there was something suspiciously close to a bloodstain smeared on the wall of bedroom 2. As long as they had running water and a working microwave, they would chalk anything else up to life experience before returning to the ever-providing arms of the family unit following May exams. The cycle would continue and by September, six new young adults would claim 215 Caldwell Street as their own, pretending its faults were charms as they suffered within its walls.

The beginning of the end of communal living at house number 215 began in the afternoon of that one particular September day when a Ford Escort bumped against the curb and rattled to a stop. The engine wheezed and a clicking under the bonnet continued as the car wound down.

"This it then? Hollis. Hollis!"

His mum elbowed him in the side. Hollis jerked awake, grabbing his knapsack before it slipped to the gum-encrusted floor. He glanced out of the window, confused as to why trees were no longer passing in a blur.

"This it?" he asked, sitting up.

"What I asked you, innit?" She lit a cigarette, and Hollis held out his hand. "Where are yours?"

Smashed in the back pocket of my jeans, he thought, and flung open the car door. His mum popped the boot, and he gave it the extra thump it needed to open. He withdrew his canvas duffel and the cheap pink polyethylene zip bags Gran had given him, which he would torch as soon as possible.

"Hurry it up, love." The cigarette dangled from her lips as she grabbed a plastic Tesco bag from behind her seat. Caldwell Street, number 215, his home for the next nine months, looked as dumpy as the letting agency had warned. A good lick of paint could've at least brightened it a bit, but whether or not the house wanted to be brightened was another matter.

Hollis unlocked the chipped green front door as his mother lagged behind.

"Don't understand why you couldn't have gone to the polytechnic like your brother. Good enough for him, and your father." She wheezed, out of breath from the short walk.

"Dunno." Hollis stepped into the darkened hall. "Hello?" No one answered.

"This is nice," she said as she waddled ahead of him. "Look at this front room. Bigger than Gran's. Where's the kitchen? Never mind. I see it." She continued down the narrow hallway. "And there's a garden! Didn't tell us 'bout the garden, did you, Hollis? Could do with a bit of work. Wonder if they'd let you do some DIY in exchange for rent?"

Hollis went upstairs. A musty smell emanated from the carpeted staircase, and a layer of sticky black dust clung to the banister. He couldn't blame the letting agency, though. They hadn't actually promised it would be professionally cleaned, only hinted that it might be.

Each bedroom came with its own lock, but the agent hadn't known which key went to what door and had handed Hollis one at random from a Quaker Oats box. Hollis's key opened bedroom 6 on the third floor—a square white box with yellow patches on the ceiling and hardened Blu Tack marring the walls. On one side, a wardrobe took up half a wall and half the floor space. On the other, a thin pillow and even thinner duvet were spread across a simple box spring bed. Hollis dropped his knapsack and looked out onto the overgrown garden, where he saw his mum repositioning the mismatched furniture to mimic the arrangement they had at Gran's. He tapped on the glass. She didn't hear him.

After carrying up the pink bags, he wandered into the narrow kitchen as she came in from the garden.

"Nice place this," she said. "Could be real nice. When are the others coming?"

"Dunno. Today or tomorrow. Freshers' Week starts Monday."

"You ain't no Fresher, are you?" She winked.

"Technically, suppose I am." A red splotch stained a square of brown floor tile. Dried bolognese, he hoped.

"None of that now. Chin up." She straightened his shoulders and lifted his head. "That other place weren't good enough for you. Didn't respect you, did they? You'll be good here. Better."

"Yeah."

"Let me see a smile. There's a good lad. Wait here a mo." She left Hollis in the kitchen. The yellowed fridge clicked on, vibrating the Ziggy Stardust magnet that held up a pizza takeaway menu with coupons three years out of date.

"Here we are." She handed over the plastic bag.

"What's this?"

"Open it and see."

Hollis set the bag on the laminate countertop, wincing as its contents clanked, and pulled out a brand-new frying pan and electric kettle.

"Couldn't have you going without your morning fry-ups, could I? Best thing for a hangover, ain't it?"

"Mam, you didn't . . . there's a kettle here." He pointed to the plastic one on the counter, lime scale visible through the blue measuring window.

"You deserve your own. Now, keep 'em clean. I don't want to see mold growing over the sides. And after you wash 'em, they go right back in your room. They're not for anyone else, all right? They're yours." She hugged him, her head barely reaching his chest as he wrapped his arms around her wide shoulders.

"There." She pulled away. "Enough of that now. Best be off. Dad needs the car for bingo. Saw a chippy down the road, off that roundabout. Get yourself a good meal tonight."

"Yes, Mam." He walked her to the door.

"Oh, and here." She pressed her cigarette pack into his hand. "Don't spend it all in one place." She winked again, then waddled to the Escort, breathless by the time she reached it. "Call us tomorrow!" she shouted, voice hoarse. "Let us know how you're getting on."

"Aye!" He waved her off, watching her lopsided three-point turn and listening to the engine's rattle as it sputtered into the distance. The street fell into a silence made worse when he closed the front door, the house filling with the type of quiet unfamiliar to a teenager with three brothers, a mam, a dad, and a gran squeezed into a two-story, one-bath maisonette.

He brought up the new kettle and pan, tucking them on top of the wardrobe. From the outside pocket of his knapsack, he pulled out the wrinkled Freshers' Week pamphlet and plopped onto the bed, resting his head against the wall. There were plenty of things to keep him busy—parties, pub crawls, picnics. Enough so he wouldn't get bored. So it wouldn't be so quiet. Hollis took out his lighter and opened the half-empty cigarette pack Mam handed him. Only then did he notice the £20 note stuffed inside.

It was later in the day, but not long after Hollis slipped the note into his wallet, that Lorna Torrington paused before house number 215. Sweat rolled down her back, plastering her fringe to her forehead and producing a faint odor from her armpits. Though exhausted after walking from the train station, her arms and back sagging from the weight of her luggage, it was the sight of the building itself that made her drop her things.

"Shit."

The pictures from the estate agent hadn't depicted the water-stained roof, cracked front steps, or clogged gutters. She leaned against a pillar box and considered returning to the agency and demanding to be let out of her lease, but as the feeling returned to her shoulders and arms, she decided it was better to be stuck in this near-condemned pit than homeless for the night or taking the convoluted train route back to her parents'.

"Might be better on the inside."

She took it in trips to carry her bags up to the front door, which squeaked open without the need for a key.

"What an exceptionally good start." She kicked the door in and dragged her first bag over the threshold.

Lorna had requested a bedroom on the highest floor, preferably in the corner where it would be quiet, so of course her bedroom key opened a room one floor up across from the bathroom. Perhaps if one of her housemates were particularly gullible, she could convince them to swap. For now, she was stuck with scratched white walls, a metal-framed bed, and a flimsy fabric wardrobe. The beat-up desk sported a pink Post-it proclaiming DON'T WORRY, BE HAPPY! Lorna crumpled up the note and tossed it in the bin.

When she made her second trip downstairs, she peeked through the kitchen, not sure if she was prepared to learn of its condition, and spotted someone in the garden. She watched as a guy in a baggy hoodie and torn jeans sat on a three-legged lounger and held a flame to a pink bag. She crossed her arms and leaned against the door jamb.

"What are you doing?"

"Naught." The boy dropped the lighter. "I'm Hollis."

"Do you have a habit of setting things on fire, Hollis?"

He shrugged.

"Right. Keep it outside. I haven't bothered to get renter's insurance, and I don't want all my things going up in flames."

He shrugged again. Lorna decided that was the extent of his communicative abilities and turned to go inside.

"Hey! What's your name?"

Lorna kept walking.

Having carried all her belongings to her room, she locked her door and pulled out her books and word processor. She tried the small television, but it wouldn't turn on. In fact, all the outlets in her room were dead.

"Is everyone here completely useless?"

Lorna called the agency from the house phone but received no answer.

"Yeah. Of course."

Back in her room, she opened the letter her mum had handed her before she left. Sixty pounds and a photograph of her Spitz-mix, Alfie, dumped into her lap. Mum had scribbled on the back of the photo: *He misses you already!*

Lorna stared at his smiling face and her chest tightened. *Alfie would love that back garden*, she thought, but pets weren't allowed. For their own safety, most likely. If the boy outside was any indication, her housemates were liable to set Alfie on fire or feed him beer and crisps. No, he was better at home without her. She could trust Mum and Dad to take decent care of him, even if it meant he couldn't be here, snuggled up at the end of her bed or sitting at her feet as she finished an essay.

Unable to sit still, Lorna tried the electrical outlets again, flicking the switches off and on. No power. She unlocked her door, ready to handle this in person at the estate agent's office, when a flurry of chirpy voices rose from downstairs. Lorna retreated and locked the door. As the voices escalated, she sat on her bed and stared at Alfie's photo, willing the house to quiet.

Lorna could've had her quiet if it weren't for Eleanor Hunt. She was squealing as soon as her father parked the Rover. The house, to her, was absolutely marvelous. Everything. From the little painted fence to the decorated sashes.

"Are you certain this is it, poppet?"

"Caldwell Street, number 215," Ellie read from her notes. "Oh, Daddy, isn't it wonderful?"

"It's certainly something."

Her sandals flapped on the pavement as she ran through the front door.

"Hello?"

Light trickled in from the back of the house, but the front room remained dark until she flung back the faded red curtains, allowing the sun to pour in. Dust motes danced in the air. Bathed in light, the sunken pink sofa looked like a smile, and the pale yellow paint a sunrise. She ran her fingers across the mantelpiece above the bricked-up gas fireplace despite the dust. When her father entered with the first of her bags, Ellie skipped across the carpet and clung to his arm.

"It looks just like the photos!"

"So it does." He kissed the top of her head. "Go find your room, poppet. We don't want to leave your things in everyone's way."

Ellie hurried upstairs to the narrow second floor, knocking on doors instead of trying her key.

"*What is it?*" a girl's voice barked from a room across from the bathroom.

"Hi! My name's Eleanor but you can call me Ellie. I'm your new housemate."

"*I'm busy.*"

"Sure, sure! Sorry to bother you. We'll chat later! Daddy, there's another girl here!" Ellie hesitated to see if the girl would open the door after all. When she did not, Ellie followed the staircase up to the third floor, which stank of fried chicken and chips. The source of the smell came from a room halfway down the hall, where a boy with headphones jammed on top of his ears sat on his bed, flipping through a magazine and eating from a takeaway box between his legs. A Bon Jovi poster hung at an angle above his bed. When he noticed Ellie, he wiped his hands on his jeans and slipped off his headphones.

"Hey," he said.

"Hi! I'm Ellie."

"Hollis."

She lingered in the doorway, twisting her foot into the carpet, unsure of what else to say. The boy, Hollis, chewed a mouthful of chicken, waiting for her to speak. Her father's panting breaths broke the silence as he arrived on the top floor, a piece of luggage in each hand.

"Did you find it, poppet?" He spotted Hollis. "Ah, hello."

"Here, let me help." Hollis rolled off the bed and took a suitcase from her father. She could see the sheen of grease on his fingers but said nothing.

"That's very kind of you. Eleanor, dear, find your room, please."

"Oh, yes. Sorry, Daddy." Her key opened the door to the left of Hollis's. "Look! We're neighbors."

Hollis shrugged. Her father frowned. Ellie clapped her hands. The room was bigger than she imagined, with a beautiful view overlooking the back garden through dirt-streaked windows. Various stains marred the cream carpet, but she could find a rug to cover them.

"I think you brought too much," her father said as Hollis brought the first suitcase inside.

"Don't be silly, Daddy. I'll get some under-the-bed boxes and a few crates. And we packed a fabric wardrobe, didn't we? That can go right there, and if I ask, I'm sure the agency will let me hang a shelf or two, don't you think?"

"Yes, well"—he checked his watch—"let's get the rest then. Your sister's play is tonight. Mother will be cross if I'm late."

Ellie followed her father downstairs to see him off.

"You have everything?" he asked. "Keys?"

"Yes, Daddy."

"Credit card?"

"Yes."

"Which is for . . ."

"Emergencies only."

"Call your mother or me if you need anything."

"I will, Daddy."

"All right then. Study hard. Be a good girl."

"I will."

With a honk of the horn, he drove away, and she waved to the car until it was no longer in sight. Alone on the unfamiliar street, goose-bumps rose on her skin. She rubbed her arms to keep them warm, then stepped back into the house.

Upstairs, Hollis had closed his door. She raised her hand to knock but let it drop and returned to her room. Before, it seemed so large. Now, filled with suitcases and bags and boxes, it had become incredibly small, and with every item she unpacked, it continued to shrink. She could find no home for any of her belongings. Half her things were in the wrong spot. The other half were in the way. In frustration, she kicked her teddy bear across the room and let out a muffled scream into her pillow. Then, with a deep breath, she sat on the edge of the bed, smoothed a loose strand of hair, and stared at the catastrophic mess around her, unsure of what to do.

As Ellie waited for someone to save her from her loneliness, a BMW pulled up with a screech alongside the sidewalk. Oliver Holcombe had barely switched off the engine before he was out of the car. He looked the house up and down and flicked his cigarette end into the road.

"This is fucking brilliant." He grabbed his bags, ready to mark his territory, but two steps inside, the stench of fresh lemon and bleach assaulted him. A fit blonde bent over a crap sofa, wiping down the skirting board.

"They didn't mention maid service."

"Oh!" She dropped her rag. "No, I got bored waiting for people. And whenever my mum gets bored she cleans, so I guess I'm turning into my mum, which will be a terrible surprise to her I'm sure and—"

"Hey, it's cool. Oliver." He watched her melt.

"Ellie."

"So, Ellie, now that you've fixed the place up, how do you feel about hosting a little party tonight?"

"I don't—"

"Excellent. We'll say ten, so expect people around eleven, eleven-thirty. If you could grab crisps or beer or something, that would be brilliant. There a toilet upstairs?"

Ellie nodded. "One floor up. It's the first door on the right. And if you continue to the other end of the hall, there's another set of stairs and that will take you to the top floor and that's where my room is. Along with another boy. His name is Hollis, and he helped me carry my luggage—"

"Brill!" He silenced her with a wave of his hand and jogged up the stairs, wondering if Princess Chatterbox's obvious insecurity was worth the potential pursuit. He would have to check out the other housemates first. There was one now—a short-haired brunette with a decent rack emerging from the bathroom.

"Hey." He leaned against the wall. "I'm—"

"I know exactly what you are. Keep your eyes off my breasts." She disappeared into a bedroom across the hall.

"Lesbo." Oliver kicked the bathroom door shut, pulled down his zip, and released the piss he'd been holding in since the A25. Tilting his head back for maximum arch, he stared at the black mold clusters on the ceiling and let out a relieved sigh. He shook the last few drops free then zipped up, kicking his toe at the white-painted plywood that covered the side of the tub.

"Cheap shit."

To his dismay, his bedroom was located next to the bathroom near the Bitch with Breasts. The carpet was so thin it might as well have not existed, and the light blue curtains made from old bed sheets did little to keep out the light. As for the bed, there was none, only a mattress on the floor. The room proudly said "fuck you," and Oliver said it right back. Dropping his bag by the door, he tossed himself onto the mattress. Black mold speckled the corners here, too. If he squinted, it almost looked like wallpaper. Maybe it'd be all right, he thought, lighting a cigarette. He could sell the no-bed thing as new-wave free-love bullshit to the pretty young things he'd be pursuing over Freshers' Week. Cover the mold with some posters. Yeah, the mold he could handle, but this mattress would be bad for his back. That's what his physical therapist would say, he thought, trying to straighten his right knee. He'd call Mum, tell her what size and style he needed and when he needed it by. Right about now she'd be napping by his half-sister's crib, but the call would wake her. Oliver kicked his bags toward the wall with his good leg, then changed into fresh clothes. He had plenty to do before the party, mainly finding people to invite. He grabbed his wallet and headed out.

In the hall, he met a hoodie-wearing bloke who smelled like fried chicken. *And what council estate did you come from?* he thought.

"Oliver."

"Hollis."

They shook hands.

"Party tonight?" Oliver asked.

"Yeah, cool. Carling?"

"Sure."

With a nod, Hollis continued downstairs, lighting a cigarette on the way. Council Estate could be all right then, Oliver decided. From the house phone in the hall, he rang home. No response. He hung up and tried one more time. Nothing.

"Whatever."

He had better things to worry about, he decided, trotting out of the house. He didn't need a fucking bed.

As day dragged into dusk, two bedrooms remained empty. Oliver's party, however, prevented anyone from sparing a thought for their absent housemates. By the time the next to last arrived, no one even remembered that they were expecting anyone else. But reaching the house was all Maeve had in mind.

"Here. Here! No, turn here!"

"Which way is here?"

"The way I'm pointing!"

They circled the roundabout twice, Maeve gripping the instructions so tightly she thought they might rip. In the back seat, her little brother moaned, threatening to be sick.

"There. Caldwell Street. There!" She pointed. Her mother jerked the car to the left. "Careful!"

"This street's not very well lit, is it?" Mum said.

"If we would've left on time, it wouldn't matter."

"I told you to finish packing last night, not wait till this morning."

"I was standing by the car waiting to go. You were the one tottering about inside."

"Is this it? Doesn't look very safe." They could hear the bass thumping through the house's windows.

"This is it. I'll get my things and you can go." Maeve unbuckled her seat belt.

"Well, I have to come inside."

"No, you don't."

"Maeve."

Her brother gripped the seat-back. "I need to pee."

"Your brother needs to pee. We're coming in."

"There's a petrol station back there!"

"Hurry up, Max."

"Seriously?" Maeve slammed the door and grabbed her things from the back. Carrying one bag and a box, she hurried to the front door ahead of her mum and brother. She knocked. No one answered. She knocked again. A stunning white girl with long blonde hair opened the door.

"Hi! Are you here for the party?"

"Uhm, sort of. I'm supposed to live here?"

"Oh, that's wonderful! I live here, too!" The girl threw her arms around Maeve, then pulled her inside. "I'm Eleanor but you can call me Ellie. Oliver—he lives with us, too—he thought we should have a house-warming." Ellie dragged her to a crowded front room. Maeve could barely hear anything over the music but saw the smoky haze generated by the hookah on the floor.

"Everyone! This is Maeve! She lives here!"

A few hands rose in greeting. Someone was passed out on a crappy pastel pink sofa. Empty beer cans were stacked in front of a disconnected gas fireplace.

"Are you going to leave us out here?" Mum entered the hall, carrying more things.

"Mum, wait."

"I need to pee!"

"Your brother needs the toilet. Where . . . oh. Hello."

The same hands rose again, greeting her mum.

"Hi! I'm Ellie!"

"I. Need. To. Pee!" Max stomped his foot.

"Hi there, poppet." Ellie smiled. "The working toilet's right upstairs."

Max took off. Her mother looked away from the cluster of drunken students.

"Maeve, I'll start carrying up your things."

"There's an empty bedroom on the top floor across from mine," said Ellie.

"Thanks." Maeve hurried after her mum.

"Well, that girl seems nice."

"It's just a party, Mum."

"I didn't say anything."

"I can see it in your eyes."

They trudged up the second set of stairs.

"First thing tomorrow you go and get your keys from the agent."

"Yes, Mum."

"Need to be able to get in and out of your own home."

"I know, Mum."

"Do they really need that music so loud? When I was in . . ."

Max chased after them, almost tripping Maeve.

"Watch it!"

"A girl by the toilet hissed at me," he said.

"You probably deserved it."

"Be nice to your brother. Now where is this room?"

Room 4, located on the third floor, was massive. Maeve couldn't believe her luck. It was twice the size of her room at home and overlooked the street. She could see Mum's car below, the boot and passenger door open. Mum clucked her tongue.

"I hope no one steals anything."

"Who's going to steal something? There's no one out there."

"It's too dark to tell, really. Let's get the rest of your things."

The car was empty in ten minutes, but it took her family another twenty to leave. Her mum couldn't stop organizing things, rearranging the minimal furniture, complaining about the noise. Despite Maeve's insistence that it was all fine, her mother wasn't content to leave until Maeve promised to come home next weekend.

Once she and Max were gone, Maeve stood in her room, listening to the music thumping downstairs. The room was comfortable, private, and all hers. It told her to relax, that she was free and independent now, and a bright year lay ahead, but Maeve wouldn't listen. She decided to change clothes before going back downstairs but couldn't find an outfit she liked. This dress was too formal. This, too casual. This she hadn't worn in three years. Why had she even packed it? After settling on the jeans she was wearing and a top that didn't smell of McDonald's, she decided to freshen her makeup but couldn't find the bag she'd packed it in, so she reapplied the toffee lip gloss she found stuffed in the bottom of her purse and examined herself in her little compact mirror.

"You can do this. You'll be fine. They're just like you." She gave herself a thumbs-up.

Downstairs, Ellie patted the seat next to her.

"Maeve! Come sit over here."

The cushions on the sofa gave as she sat, and she sank toward the floor like she was being swallowed whole. She blushed, thinking she had broken it, but then relaxed when she saw that the thin blonde had sunk to the same level. Ellie pointed to the boy on Maeve's other side.

"Maeve, this is Oliver."

Maeve sat up and shook his hand. Floppy hair. Deep brown eyes. He looked like Thomas Kinsey and she was over Thomas Kinsey because he was an asshole who never gave her the time of day and she swore never to be such an idiot again. She was a strong, independent young woman who didn't need the attention of boys, so she spoke to Oliver with casual reserve, answering his questions politely with no hint of flirtation. Then she said something silly. Only a little thing about her family, but it made Oliver laugh, and it was too late. Maeve was in love.

The party dragged on until the beer had gone. The guests stumbled away from 215 Caldwell Street, their first—but not last—time hoping they remembered the way back to their temporary homes, while the house's newest residents made the shorter trip to their bedrooms upstairs. Except Lorna, who, that night, never left her bedroom.

They woke the next morning to the sound of crinkling aluminum cans and the smell of bacon. When they opened their doors, little presents—Oreos, tea, Pringles—wrapped in brown paper greeted them, each with the same typed note on blue stationery.

> Don't be fooled. The day's not done.
> Happy Wednesday's just begun!

They cracked their sleep-crusted eyes and stumbled downstairs.

That's where they saw him for the first time.

Backlit by the morning light, a tall, lanky outline was cleaning up their mess, cooking enough bacon to feed an army. A camera hung around his neck. When he noticed them, he waved the spatula, flinging drops of grease onto the wall.

"Oh! Sorry." He winced. "I hope you don't mind? I got in this morning. You were all sleeping, so I thought I'd cook us some breakfast?"

Almost every sentence ended like a question, as if he were always asking for permission, even when giving his name.

"I'm Callum? You found your notes! Sorry, I didn't know what each of you liked? Happy Wednesday's something a teacher of mine did for us in sixth form. You know, keep us motivated to get through the week? I thought it'd be a nice way to introduce myself? It's lame, isn't it? Sorry." He held out the pan. "You guys want some rashers?"

They did. And as they ate, they got to know one another better, the awkwardness of being strangers melting away as Callum filled any gaps in the conversation with a funny anecdote. That morning, he became the glue that held them together.

Nine months later, Callum would stumble down the stairs, slamming his knee so hard on the bottom step it would leave a bruise. It would be the most drunk he had ever been in his life, or ever would be, for his life would only last a few minutes more. But he wouldn't know that, just like he wouldn't know there would be someone watching him as he made his way to the house phone. That he would be watched as he put his hand on the receiver. That he would be heard as he muttered, "I'm gonna do it. Got to. Have to. Have to turn them in. It's wrong. What we did is wrong."

And someone—someone who had been sitting at that wobbly table nine months prior, sharing that crispy, greasy bacon—would come forward as he picked up the receiver, and would ask him, "What are you doing, Callum?"

2

Lorna

Hollis eyed them up in turn, like he was running through a checklist in his mind of what they each should look like in order to confirm they were who he thought they were. Unlike the rest of them, he wore his age well, his stocky body a better fit for a man in his forties than a boy of nineteen. Lorna was trying to reconcile the grown man in front of her with the young man she once knew when Hollis turned his analytical gaze on her, and there he was. The Hollis she remembered. The look of a troubled boy out of his depth, trying his best, wanting only to do what was right.

"Lorna." He spoke her name as if brushing the dust off a long-forgotten book. "What the fuck is going on?"

She couldn't tell if the question was meant for her. Her clarity had vanished the moment Ellie entered the dining room, and it hadn't come back upon the appearance of Oliver and Maeve. No less than five minutes ago, she knew Hollis's arrival was imminent, but that had done nothing to lessen the shock of actually seeing him. Of having all four of them in the room with her. If his question was for her, she couldn't answer it. She would do what Lorna had always done. Stand back quietly and let the others hash it out.

Hollis slammed a whisky bottle down on the nearest table. The bang echoed through the room.

"I said, what is going on? What are you all doing here?"

"We … we don't know," Maeve offered. Yes, of course Maeve would go first. Try to smooth things over. "We were trying to figure that out when you …"

And of course Maeve would utterly fail.

"Trying to figure it out? You mean this is all a surprise to you? None of you knew the others would be here? Well, that's complete and utter shit. Go on then. Which of you was it? Who put this together?"

Oliver leaned forward, going for one of his chummy "man to man" speeches. "Hollis, mate—"

Speeches that Hollis had never fallen for. "I am not your mate!"

Like Lorna, Ellie knew talk was useless, but unlike Lorna, the tension showed in her body. She rocked back and forth in her chair like a branch caught in the wind. Lorna couldn't help but remember how quickly that dry branch could catch fire.

"That's it. I'm going." Hollis spoke so softly that only Lorna, who was standing closest, could hear.

She did nothing to stop him as he picked up the whisky bottle.

Maeve—always interfering Maeve—asked, "What did you say?"

"I said I'm leaving!"

His intention was what shook Lorna. The house felt more dangerous with him here, with them gathered altogether, yet also safer. Hollis's presence, his clarity over the danger they were in, returned to her the strength she thought she'd lost, that had been drained first by Ellie, then Oliver, then Maeve. Hollis could leave, but Lorna needed him. By the time she spoke, he was already at the door.

"Hollis, you can't," Lorna said. "There's no place else to go on the island, and Mr. Caskie told us the road might wash away in the storm."

"And the last ferry's already left," Maeve added.

"Oh, leave it, Lorna." Oliver kicked his feet up on the chair. "Let him run. It's what he's good at. I mean, I'm surprised he's stuck around this long. It's been, what? At least five minutes."

Hollis re-gripped the neck of the bottle and removed his free hand from the doorknob. "What would you have me do? Stay for a drink? Or seven? How many have you already tucked away, Oliver? By the slur of your speech I'd say at least five. That's a healthy belly you've put on, too. It can hold, what, at least half a dozen more? You know, I'm glad you're sitting there smoking all casual-like while several mounds of shit are clearly hitting the fan. I'm not sure I would've recognized you otherwise. Getting your haircare tips from Prince Charles nowadays?"

"Really, Hollis. Insults?" Oliver said. "Can't we at least try to be adults about this?"

"I don't know what *this* is, but I have to say, that advice is rich coming from the person who coined the nickname 'Hunt the Cunt.'"

Ellie gasped.

"Oh, you didn't know that, Ellie?" Hollis asked as Oliver's face went red.

"I always assumed it was Maeve," she said.

"I may have said it, but I didn't start it," Maeve said. "And I didn't even say it that often! I swear."

Maeve apologizing, Ellie feigning ignorance, Hollis and Oliver fighting. How quickly they'd each fallen into their old roles, herself included. Good ol' Lorna—keeping silent, trying not to let them draw her into their argument. But it didn't take long for them to fling questions her way. She had blocked out the conversation after Maeve's comment and didn't know which direction the argument had gone when Hollis asked, "What about you, Lorna? Anything to add?"

"No." She squeezed the single syllable out like the last drop of water from a dry tap.

"That's just typical, isn't it?" Oliver laughed. "Switzerland over here refusing to get involved while bombs are going off around her. 'But it's nothing to do with me!' If it's nothing to do with you, sweetheart, why are you here?"

"Why are any of us here?" Maeve asked.

"Don't be thick, Maeve. If it's possible." Oliver rolled his eyes.

"There's only one reason someone would get us together," Hollis said. But no one wanted to say what that reason was.

"It wasn't our fault," Ellie whispered. "We didn't do anything wrong."

"We didn't do anything right, either," Hollis said.

Lorna closed her eyes and pretended she didn't know what Hollis was talking about. Pretended she could leave. But Lorna had no place to go.

2 hours prior

The Vauxhall sedan kicked up dust as it sped down the drive. Lorna gripped the steering wheel, her vision narrowed on the horizon, watching for the house that was to appear at the end of this drive, and missed the pothole. The car bounced in and out, landing so hard that the boot scraped the ground. She hit the brakes, and her head smacked back against the headrest. A squeaky belt chirped louder than the ping of the rain on the car. The steering wheel vibrated in her hands.

"Don't die here. Don't die here."

She pressed down on the accelerator. The Vauxhall inched forward, then picked up speed.

"Thank you."

A warning light dinged.

Hatch open.

Glancing in the rearview mirror, she saw the open boot bobbing up and down.

"Shit."

If the universe wanted to stop her from exiting the car, it almost succeeded. The seat belt almost strangled her as she fumbled with the latch. On the drive, her shoes slipped on the wet stones as she stumbled around the car. Twice she slammed the boot down, but it refused to latch.

"Shit shit shit."

Rain gathered at the nape of her neck and dripped down the back of her shirt to her bra strap. She rested her hands on the car and took several breaths, letting the water travel along her spine.

"I'll be fine. Everything will be fine. I will make sure everything is fine."

She pushed down on the boot a final time and heard it click shut.

"See? Fine. Just like I said." When she returned to the car, she didn't bother with the seat belt.

Viewed from the crest of the drive, the lumbering red brick manor that was Wolfheather House looked like a redcoat soldier standing at the edge of a long, thin loch. Cast in the shadow of the surrounding snow-capped peaks, a single plume of smoke rose from one of its six chimneys. An inconsonant glass conservatory protruded off its backside, an unnecessary addition that made the house even more of an eyesore.

Lorna parked at the base of the drive, facing away from the house. Rain peppered the quiet loch and she remembered how, as a child, the water could calm her. Despite the weather, she left her suitcase by the Vauxhall and went down to wet her hands. It eased the pain on her scratched hands but failed to provide the calm she'd hoped for. The towering mountains made her feel trapped in a large cage, the gray cloud a heavy tarp pulled across the top. But wasn't a cage what she wanted? She skipped a single stone, rippling the loch's surface, then dried her hands on her jeans and made her way to the house as an unseen dog barked.

A fire burned in the empty reception hall while dishes clattered in a room to her right. Lorna followed the sounds of clinking porcelain and saw the back of a man laying out plates and cutlery in the large dining room. The room comfortably fit ten round tables, each surrounded by four chairs. No two tablecloths were alike—some lace, some polyester, some plain blue, others patterned with spring flowers. A hodgepodge of candles, two or three to a table, acted as centerpieces. The mismatched décor helped hide how the heavy red curtains clashed with the pea green carpeting and yellow walls. If she had her way, she would redecorate the entire place so that it didn't remind her of her great aunt's drawing room and the uncomfortable evenings spent there. She could almost smell the Jean Patou Joy perfume. Lorna rubbed her cold arms and cleared her throat.

The young man spun round, a dinner knife clutched in each hand.

"Bloody hell! You shouldn't sneak up on people like that. Give them a heart attack, you will. Sneaking around like a bloody ghost . . ."

"Sorry to interrupt. I'll go wait till you're ready."

Lorna happily exchanged the coldness of the dining room for the warmth of the fireplace and debated sending a text as she waited. Her mother's voice rang through her head.

Always let someone know where you are, at least one person, please, Petal, please. In case of an emergency. In case something should happen . . .

But who would care where she was?

"You're the—"

"Bloody hell!" She jumped at the sound of the man's voice.

"Now you know what it's like to be frightened."

"I wasn't frightened."

"'Course you weren't."

She stuffed her phone in her pocket and followed him to the front desk, signing the book.

"You're the first one here," he said.

As he handed over the key, he looked as if he wanted to say something more, but the phone rang. He answered, and she started for the stairs.

"Wolfheather House. James Caskie speaking . . ."

At the top of the stairs, her first instinct had been to turn right, but a rope blocked that direction along with a frayed roll of pulled-up carpeting. So left it was, down a hall with dark brown side tables adorned with silver candlesticks and geometric paperweights to a room with a brass *1* inelegantly screwed into the door.

She withdrew her phone and sent a quick text to the one person she thought might care. Then, before changing out of her travel clothes, she collapsed on the bed, eyes closed, arms outstretched. For the first time in months, she lost the feeling of being watched and, for a few brief minutes, became herself again.

Ellie

Ellie was not yet certain of what she was seeing. She could identify the images—Hollis yelling, Maeve rubbing her arms through the wet sleeves of her jumper, Lorna staring into her empty wineglass, Oliver with his cigarette burning down—but it was like watching a show on television. A show about their lives, dramatic reenactments portrayed by actors who resembled them but didn't quite match with her memory of them. Hollis's hair was never that short, and his shoulders were too wide. Maeve looked several pounds heavier, some of the fat rounding out her face. Lorna had a somewhat smaller chest, and wasn't her nose stubbier? Oliver she could barely look at. He was all wrong. Like Oliver's father had dressed in the real Oliver's clothes. So yes, they were all here, but these weren't the people she remembered. And although the prospect of spending the weekend with complete strangers sounded exciting, in reality she thought it would be better to follow Hollis's original intent and vacate the premises as soon as possible. As soon as no one was looking. And yet, could she?

Possibly the best option was to wait and keep an eye on everyone. See how this all played out.

She thought of texting David and asking his advice. But she dismissed that thought with the blink of an eye. She couldn't text David. Not about this. Not right now. Not until she could return to her room. She drank some of the wine, tasting nothing as it passed through her lips. Then she clapped her hands together.

"Right," she announced, interrupting Hollis's argument. "I'm here because of Avon."

They all looked at her, confused, as if they'd forgotten she was there.

Hollis came so close, she could feel his breath on her cheek. The wrinkle on his forehead that had once been a slight line had deepened to a crevasse.

"You're here because of what?"

She adjusted her bracelet. "Avon. I sell Avon. You know, soaps, lotions, beauty products. We have an excellent men's line that would do wonders for those worry lines, Hollis." She uncrossed and crossed her legs. "Anyway, my regional supervisor held a sales contest to promote our new Highland fragrance line. I won."

"Did you get to choose where to stay?"

"No. They arranged everything."

"They?"

"Avon."

"How did you know you won?"

"They sent me an email."

"And you're sure that email came from Avon?"

"Who else would've sent it?"

That terrible laugh, the one she never thought she'd hear again, sprang from Oliver's throat.

"That's the question, isn't it, love? That's why Hollis here is playing detective. He thinks he can catch you out in a lie, or figure out who's been lying to you."

Oliver's voice drew Hollis like a lure to a greyhound.

"Playing detective?" Hollis slapped Oliver's feet off the chair.

The heat of interrogation lifted, Ellie hadn't realized her hands were shaking until they stopped.

"Playing detective?" Hollis repeated. "I *am* a detective, Holcombe. Manchester CID. What have you been up to? Any of your big plans come through? Your business investments? Saw *Dragons' Den* by the way. Loved the suit." Hollis's face remained grim, but there was a smirk in his voice. "So, because I am what Oliver says I'm *playing* at, I'm going to ask you all questions, and you're going to answer them. Because, one, I'm the most qualified person here to do so. And, two, I won't trust any of you until I do. Ellie's already volunteered. Do I have any others?"

Ellie held her wineglass to her lips and cast her eyes around the room. Each of them gave away so much on their faces. They didn't know how to keep their emotions bottled in, not even Lorna, who kept fidgeting with the ring on her forefinger. No, there would be no leaving. Not until she saw more.

1.5 hours prior

"Talk to your father. He can make that decision. I'm sorry but . . . I'm sorry but . . . Well then, if that's Daddy's decision, I'll stand by it. I'm sorry *but . . .*"

The world outside the windshield sank under water, rivulets blurring the gray road. Ellie scrambled to find the windshield wipers in the hired Land Rover while holding the phone to her ear.

"Poppet, I'm sorry. If Daddy said . . . if Daddy said . . ."

She switched her phone to her other ear, taking in a deep breath of the floral scent of her Avon car freshener.

"I do understand, poppet, but if Daddy— All right . . . All right . . . I'll talk to him . . . Yes, I'll talk to him. Yes, I'll— Yes . . . I love you, too."

She set the phone in the cup holder and located the correct lever. On high blast, the wipers distracted as much as the rain itself, but she could at last make out the twisting road ahead.

"What did I do? What?"

"In five hundred meters, turn right."

"Haven't we given her everything she's asked for? God forbid her brother turns out the same way."

"In two hundred meters, turn right."

"I blame myself. I really do. You're too nice, Ellie. That's exactly how you get into these situations."

"Turn right."

"David's right. You need to grow a backbone or you'll never—"

"Missed turn. Make a U-turn."

"What? How did I? Of course I did." She spun the Range Rover around, slipping on the wet road but managing to save the car before it tipped into a ditch.

"In one hundred meters, turn left."

"Where? There's not even a— Oh, there!"

Her frustration shifted to a new target as the car bounced down the unpaved drive.

Why hadn't there been a sign to mark the house? Why couldn't they have done this on Skye itself? Why make her take a ride with a ferryman who wouldn't stop leering at her? Why make her drive out into the god-forsaken middle of nowhere?

She smacked the steering wheel, then took a deep breath. Tried to see the positives. For example, when was the last time she had been on her own? No David, no children, no anyone? It must have been before their wedding, so at least fifteen years. She looked at the passenger seat. So strange to see it empty. Yet freeing, in its own way. She was alone, and she was doing something for herself. Something that had nothing to do with her family.

The manor house, when it appeared, looked more like a child's drawing than the real thing. Uneven lines and too many windows. Ellie would've laughed, except it seemed inappropriate, like laughing at the child who came to school in dirty jumpers and too-small shoes.

She parked near a beat-up little Vauxhall and tapped her fingers against the steering wheel, debating whether or not to wait out the heavy rain that patterned the glass, obscuring the house's façade. Through the rain, the house looked like a watercolor painting, one she might see hanging in a café on the King's Road. She could be there now with a mug of black coffee, cooing over the babies in prams that clogged up the seating area. But that thought retrieved a memory, one she thought she'd shaken once her plane had taken off at Heathrow. One that now made her shudder. She unclipped the air freshener and stuffed it into her trench coat, pulled the trench over her head, and exited the car, only to step right into a mud puddle that splashed up her leg. She swallowed down a scream and ran into the house.

Hoping the staff wouldn't notice the messy trail she left on the carpet runner, Ellie rang the bell at reception until an attractive young man hurried down the stairs.

"Yes, yes. I'm here. Let the bell rest." His immediate frown conveyed his frustration at her mess, but he left it unmentioned as he checked her in.

"Such a lovely place you have here," she said with a smile after giving her name, twirling her hair on her finger. "It must be so much work to maintain."

"It keeps me busy. Your room is on—"

"And what an enterprising young man you are"—she laid a hand on his arm—"to run it all by yourself."

He withdrew his arm with a closed-lip smile and held out her key. "I do what needs to be done. Now, your room is on the third floor. If you—"

"Could you be a lamb and help me with my suitcase? It's been just a terrible drive, you see. I'm not usually this exhausted, but I haven't traveled this far by myself in such a long time."

He cupped the key in his palm. "Of course, Mrs. Landon. I'd be happy to assist. My mother is about your age, and she also tires easily."

He carried the suitcase toward the stairs. Ellie frowned, wiped her muddy shoes on the carpet, then followed.

Once they reached the top floor, he handed her the key. "By the way, Mrs. Landon, if you happen to hear a wee knocking in the middle of the night, don't let it alarm you."

"Just the pipes?"

"No. It's not the pipes."

Without another word, he returned the way they came. Ellie stared at the shining 5 on her door, then leaned her ear toward the wall. Silence. She shuddered, then laughed it off and unlocked the door.

Once in her room, Ellie stripped out of her wet clothes, purposely leaving them in a pile by the bed. David would yell if she left damp clothes on the hardwood floors in their bedroom.

Water spat from the showerhead in fits and starts before the flow evened. She was lining up her own bath gel, shampoo, and conditioners on the soap dish, humming to herself, when her phone chirped. Expecting to see Jilly's name, she returned to the bedroom. But it wasn't Jilly. She read the text three times, now reminded of why she'd come all this way.

Oliver

"What about you, Oliver?" Hollis asked. "Did you win a contest, too?"

Of course Hollis would choose him next. Unfortunately for him, Oliver already had his answer ready.

"You think I'd fall for a stupid trick like that? Like I'm that naive?" He turned toward Ellie. "No offense, love."

"Well, either you were that naive or you knew the plan all along. So which is it?"

It took every ounce of self-control not to pop Hollis one. That would only put more suspicion on him, so instead he finished off his whisky, let it burn all the way down. The others waited, watching. He plopped the glass onto the table.

"Fine. A mate. Said he'd booked the place but something came up and he offered me his reservation."

"How well do you know this mate?"

"Worked with him once or twice. We have the same local and spot each other for drinks now and then."

"And would this mate need money?"

"Yeah, suppose so." Oliver lit a cigarette. "You think someone paid him off?"

"Easiest way to manipulate people, isn't it?"

"If that's true, then I'm going to beat Gerald's ass into the ground." He propped his feet on a chair.

"Happen to have Gerald's surname and phone number?"

"Fancy a date?"

"More like evidence."

"For or against my word?" Oliver met Hollis's stare, took a long drag of his cigarette, then exhaled. "Sorry, we're not that close. First-name basis kind of thing."

"Convenient," said Hollis.

"Or just the opposite." He held Hollis's gaze as he tapped ash into the empty whisky glass, daring Hollis to challenge him.

But Hollis gave in first and shifted his attention to Lorna, who had been pacing slowly since Hollis started his interrogations. Oliver watched the proceedings carefully, wanting to be ready if Hollis tried to catch him out.

"Go on, Lorna. How did you end up here?"

Lorna stopped pacing. Oliver watched her rub a scratch on her hand. "Similar to Oliver, really. A colleague. I needed a last-minute holiday. It's a long story. But she offered me her stay here. Said I could pay her back."

"How long have you known her?" Hollis asked.

"About two years."

"And does your colleague have a full name?" He looked at Oliver as he asked the question.

"Jennifer McAllister."

Hollis looked back at Lorna, another question on his mind based on the confused expression on his face, the one Oliver remembered from Hollis's study sessions in the front room, but Hollis shook it off and turned his attention to Maeve.

Lorna caught Oliver staring at her hand and shoved it in her pocket. She toed a piece of broken glass on the carpet with her shoe.

Oliver bit the end of his cigarette to keep from jumping in with a well-timed insult. It had to be a lesbian thing, he thought. A girlfriend, the kind Lorna never admitted to having. She looked more like a dyke than ever, wearing that big black turtleneck that did her chest no favors.

"That leaves you, Maeve," said Hollis. Oliver swiveled in his seat so he could watch Maeve stammer out a response.

"I thought . . ." She looked away. "I thought I was meeting someone."

She wiped sweat from her forehead, then chewed the cuff of her jumper, the same way she used to act whenever she and Oliver had been alone in a room together. Out of all of them, she looked the most like her younger self. Almost pretty, if she could ever fix that hair and lose about a stone. When Hollis asked another pointed question about her missing companion, Maeve flinched and stammered out an incoherent response. It clicked then, and Oliver couldn't stop laughing.

"Something to add?" Hollis asked.

"You haven't figured it out, *Detective*? Maeve thought she was meeting a man here. That she was coming for a romantic getaway. You got catfished, didn't you?"

She hid her hands in her jumper and wrapped her arms around herself, unable to meet his eye. It was too easy with Maeve. Like riding a bike that had hung in a garage for years. She might be a little rusty, but he remembered how to pedal. Twenty-odd years gone, and he remembered how to play them all.

1 hour prior

"God damn piece of . . . god damn!"

The jack lifted the tire, the tire iron cranked the jack, but for some reason the lug nuts refused to budge. Oliver's fingers slipped on the wet hubcap, and he fell back into the road. Water seeped into his clothes from new angles.

"Fuck cars. Fuck tires. Fuck Scotland!"

Mud clinging to his hands and face, Oliver grabbed his phone and bag from the car, stuffed the pamphlet into an outside pocket, and continued on foot, carrying the tire iron out of spite, the long walk exacerbating his limp. If there was beauty in this barren landscape, he didn't see it. Even a stupid hired car didn't want to make this trip. Why should he have come? It was stupid. He'd known that all along. What would this solve? *Fuck all, that's what,* he told himself.

By the time he reached the house, he held nothing but contempt for it. A spare parts house, that's what it looked like. Cobbled together from bits and bobs nobody wanted, and poorly done at that. He was tempted to throw the tire iron through a window but flung it into the hedges instead.

After kicking the door shut behind him, he dropped his wet things and rubbed his hands by the fire. What he needed was a way to warm himself from the inside out. To his surprise, he found his favorite method in a room to his left. A large, Victorian-themed study lined with bookshelves and a long leather chesterfield sofa housed a full bar complete with tin counter and, most importantly, a healthy selection of spirits stacked in front of a mirrored wall.

"They must be having a laugh."

He dug the damp brochure from his jacket pocket and glanced over it. But this was definitely the right place. He looked around, expecting a trick, but when no one appeared, he helped himself to a fifteen-year-old Glenlivet single malt.

"Five pound fifty."

Oliver choked on the whisky.

At the other end of the bar, a young man in a suit wiped down the counter with a flannel. Oliver couldn't see where he had come from.

"I can start a tab or add the cost to your bill."

"The bill's fine." He wasn't paying anyway. He finished the glass and poured another. "Oliver Holcombe. This your dad's place, then?" He looked out the windows. The falling rain made it difficult to discern the edge of the car park and the wilderness that lay beyond.

"James Caskie. And it's my place, actually. You might want to take it easy on those." Caskie checked his phone and, face pinched, dropped it back into his pocket.

Oliver hadn't checked his since the tire blew. She'd probably left three or four voice mails by now, he thought, but when he checked his notifications, there was a single email: Groupon Getaways.

"I didn't hear you pull up," Caskie said.

"My car copped it on the main road. Transmission, I think," he lied. "Had to walk the rest of the way in."

"Glad you made it in before nightfall."

"My phone doubles as a torch."

"Not the dark that should concern you."

A shutter flapped against the window.

"Shit." Oliver grabbed a cocktail napkin and blotted spilled whisky off his hand.

"Care to see your room before you have another?"

Oliver bit his tongue and followed Caskie into reception, wishing he still held the tire iron instead of this glass.

Maeve

Maeve's good jeans, soaked from the rain, chafed her thighs. She never had the chance to get changed. Not even Hollis had asked if she wanted to get out of her wet clothes before he questioned her. The worst part was feeling like she'd wet herself, and she pretended this was why she was uncomfortable as Hollis explained what catfishing was to Ellie.

"Oh, you poor thing!" Ellie cooed.

"It's not a big deal, god," Maeve snapped.

"Do you have his email or phone number?" Hollis asked. "I can have someone try and track him down."

"His email. And his Skype username. Kit_Snow0273." She reached for her phone, praying for her hands to stop shaking. Her phone case was damp from being in her pocket and she went to rub it on her jumper, but this was just as wet. "Sorry. Sorry, I—"

"Here." Hollis handed her one of the cloth napkins from the table.

Maeve wanted to thank him, but he had already turned away. They were all drifting away from one another. Lorna toward the windows. Hollis toward the door. Ellie leaned against a far wall. The table behind Maeve kept her from drifting all the way back to the kitchen entrance. Only Oliver remained anchored to his chair in the center of the dining room, but Maeve got the impression he would sink through the floor if he could. Having embarrassed her, Oliver had shifted his attention once again, leaving Maeve to roil in a mix of relief and disappointment. She stayed nearer to him, both hoping and not that he would notice her again.

"Go on then, Drummond," Oliver said. "Storytime. Who lured *you* here? Or maybe you're the one who brought us all together?"

Hollis's confidence slipped like a glove from a pocket. Pain creased his face, but Maeve could see he was going to answer. Lorna interrupted before he could.

"Someone's leaving." She stared out the window.

"Who else is here?" Maeve asked.

Everyone answered at once. "Caskie."

Hollis led the charge into the front hall. By the time he flung open the front door, Caskie was nothing more than a pair of red taillights cresting over the hill of the drive.

As the others lingered in the rain, sharing shouts and curses, Maeve retreated inside, taking the warmth of the fire for herself. The burning peat sounded like soft wind through the trees, and she enjoyed that brief peace for all of a few seconds before the others joined her in the foyer. All four argued at once among each other, seeming to forget Maeve was there.

So Maeve remained the only one by the fire and the only one to see the letter propped on the mantel.

As soon as it was in her hand, they noticed her again. Noticed that she had found something.

"What's that?" Hollis asked.

"I'm not sure."

He took it from her and opened it himself.

"Dear guests," he read. "Due to a private family matter, I must return to Skye tonight. Prepared food is available in the kitchen refrigerator. See note for reheating instructions. Apologies that the normal caretaker is unavailable. Once on Skye, I will arrange for a housekeeper to arrive via private boat tomorrow morning. Thank you again for choosing Wolf-heather House. Yours faithfully, James Caskie. Note: In the earlier confusion caused by Mr. MacLeod's absence, I neglected to distribute the gifts from your benefactor."

"Your benefactor?" Lorna peered around Hollis's shoulder to read the note.

"He must mean those." Ellie pointed to the reception desk.

On the floor by the desk was a pile of brown-wrapped paper packages, each tagged with a name. No one said anything. No one wanted to.

"Those look like—"

"Shut up, Maeve," said Oliver.

Hollis crossed the room first and grabbed the package with his name. He wasted no time in tearing off the paper. A two-liter bottle of Strong-bow Cider. Lorna went next. A cassette tape of Take That's *Everything Changes*.

"I haven't listened to that in ages," Ellie said. "Not since . . ." But she paled and didn't complete the thought. Oliver went next.

"Smallest of the lot," he muttered. He tore the wrapping off in small pieces: a purple Sharpie.

When neither Ellie nor Maeve approached, Hollis handed them their packages. Maeve waited until Ellie went first: a joint.

On their own, each of these items was innocuous. But seeing them together filled Maeve's mouth with a bitter taste. A memory echoed in her mind—thumping music, sticky glasses, sickly sweet alcopops, the smell of pot, and the haze of low lighting. By the looks on their faces, she could tell the others shared the same memory.

"Open yours, Maeve," Hollis said.

Something rattled inside. Maeve's clumsy fingers struggled to pull the string and tear the paper. An unmarked black box. She took off the lid, and they waited for her to reveal what was inside. After a long breath, she held it up.

"It's a key."

But the key mattered less than the Scottish Rugby keychain hanging from it.

"Well, it can't be—" Maeve started, but a gasp from Ellie interrupted her.

"Of course not," Lorna said. "It's impossible." Her words lacked their normal conviction.

"We should find the door that goes with that key," Hollis said.

"The house is so big," Ellie said. "It could be any door."

"Two," Maeve said. "It must be Room 2."

"But why . . ." Then Ellie looked again at the gifts. "Oh yes. Of course."

By silent agreement, they made their way upstairs.

Maeve hung back, letting the others lead her down the hall with its dark walls and carpets. She kept imagining the dim lights might flicker to reflect the mood, but they remained steady and sure.

Room 2 was near the end of the hall. She gathered with the others behind Hollis. The key was in her hand, but he didn't ask for it. He knocked, and they waited.

"This is Detective Constable Hollis Drummond."

Silence.

Oliver rolled his eyes and snatched the key from Maeve, his fingers brushing against hers. She stuck her hands in her wet pockets.

"Just open it," he said.

"Wait." Hollis knocked again. "I said this is the police. If you don't answer, we're going to let ourselves in. We're giving you fair warning."

He pressed his ear to the door, then took the key.

"All right. I'm unlocking the door." He pushed the key into the lock but did not turn it. "Stand to the side."

Maeve and Ellie moved immediately.

"Why on earth should I?" asked Oliver.

"We don't know what's behind that door. Or what might come out."

"You think it's booby-trapped?" asked Lorna.

"I have no bloody idea, but I'm not taking any risks."

Lorna joined the other women. After a dismissive huff, Oliver did the same. Maeve smelled his aftershave—the same after all these years—and took an extra step back as Hollis turned the key. With slow, deliberate movements, he opened the door and looked inside. Maeve could not see his face, but his shoulders sagged. He ran his hand over his hair, and Maeve remembered the time Hollis had found one of Oliver's friends passed out in the middle of the front room one Sunday morning. He'd made the same motions.

"What is it? Who's in there?" asked Lorna.

"Come and see."

Lorna pushed past Oliver, who went in next. Ellie's shoulder bumped Maeve as she followed. Maeve heard no conversation, but no shouting either. Were they waiting for her? She approached, one careful step at a time.

They stood in a semi-circle, their backs to her, blocking the view of what Hollis had uncovered. The shortest of them all, she stood on tiptoe to peek over Ellie's shoulders, seeing little until Hollis finally stepped to the side.

A worn brown armchair, the fabric on the seat worn down to a thin grayish patch, sat on the right side of the room, but what held their attention was positioned on the left: a pink sofa pressed against the wall, its sunken cushions bulging outward like a fat lower lip. Maeve recognized the stain on the left armrest, the splotch in the shape of France caused by a cup of tea she had spilled twenty-odd years ago.

"It's not the same," Oliver's voice sounded hoarse. "Obviously, it isn't the same one. It's too old. Thing looks like shit."

"No, just older," Maeve said. "It's the same. It's just older. Like us." But she wasn't looking at the sofa so much as the note card of blue stationery that rested in the middle of it. Stamped in a typewriter font on the front were the words:

```
The Residents of Caldwell Street
```

Maeve wondered what would happen if none of them opened that envelope. Would they stand here forever, staring at that sofa?

Or would they be able to leave? Pretend they had never come here. Had never unlocked this door.

"That's—" Ellie choked on the words. "That's his stationery. He used to leave us notes in that stationery. And the gifts, oh god, the gifts. Brown paper. The Happy Wednesday Elf?"

"It's not him," Oliver said. "We know exactly where to find that fucker, and it's not in this bloody house."

Despite his bravado, Oliver distanced himself from the sofa. Ellie looked to the others for support, but Lorna kept glancing around the room, avoiding eye contact. Maeve, too, looked away when Ellie caught her eye. Hollis's gaze never wavered from the sofa. The rustling of his clothes was as loud as a roar as he reached forward and plucked the envelope from the cushions. He looked it over, each corner, each edge, as if searching for some clue. Then he opened the envelope and removed the card inside. Unlike Caskie's letter, Hollis read silently.

"Come on, Drummond," Oliver snapped. "Out with it."

Hollis cleared his throat. "It's a rhyme. *Trade one secret for another. Admit what happened to your brother. No one leaves until it's done. Come on, friends, won't this be fun?*"

Oliver grabbed it from Hollis's hand. "That's it? That's all there is?"

"This is wrong," Ellie said. "This is all wrong. I don't even have a brother."

Lorna rolled her eyes. "He's not talking about biological family."

"But I don't get it," Ellie said. "What is it we're supposed to do? Trade secrets? What secrets?"

Hollis examined the brown armchair. "If this really is the same one . . ."
He ran his hands over the armrests, shoved them down the side of the
cushion.

Oliver flicked the note card to the floor. "I'm not standing around
while Hollis feels up a chair."

"Do you lot really not remember?" Hollis asked. Something clicked
inside the chair. "Ah ha! This armchair, or as Lorna lovingly referred to it,
the poop chair, had a faulty armrest. Which could pop open." He flipped
up the left armrest, revealing the vacant space inside. "And is where you,
Oliver, used to store your drugs."

Hollis stuck his hand into the hole and rooted around.

"That . . . that really is the same chair then," Lorna said.

"Or one designed to look like it." He clutched something inside the
armrest. "But I have a feeling it is the same. Why bother to replicate the
cigarette burns?"

"They could be different burns," Oliver said.

"They're not. I remember." Hollis pulled out his hand. In it were more
blue envelopes—larger than the other. Padded with more paper.

"That means . . ." Maeve glanced at the sofa. "That means that's really
the same sofa."

She closed her eyes, waiting for the tears to come, and backed away,
bumping into Oliver, his body soft and warm. Until he stepped away.

"You may want to stay here," Hollis said. "Until you read this."

He handed Maeve an envelope stamped with her name, then gave out
the rest. They all looked at one another, waiting for someone else to start.

"Were we supposed to find these?" Lorna asked.

"I think he was counting on it," Hollis said.

"It's not him," Oliver muttered.

Maeve looked Oliver's way. Wanted to reassure him, to hold his hand
and squeeze it. But every time she inched nearer, he leaned away. She
shrank back into her jumper.

"Well, if no one else is going to." Hollis opened his envelope as
carefully as the other. Lorna clenched her jaw and followed. Maeve

looked at Oliver and Ellie, waited to see what they would do. When Ellie tore into the paper, Maeve did the same. Oliver followed with a reluctant sigh. At first, Maeve was too busy watching the others to read hers. Lorna covered her mouth with her hand and closed her eyes. Ellie became very still, except for her face, which drew more lines as it hardened. Veins bulged in her hands. Oliver kept muttering "Bullshit" to himself. Hollis became very pale, and all his strength seemed to leave him.

Maeve finally read what she had been gifted. Photocopies of credit card statements in her sister-in-law's name. Credit cards near maxed out. Line by line reminding Maeve of different purchases, including the jumper she was wearing right now. And the red suitcase downstairs.

Hollis folded up the papers he'd been given and slipped them back into the envelope.

"So." He tapped his envelope against his palm. His voice was steady but sounded higher. Twenty years younger. "My guess is, if we admit what really happened that night, in exchange, none of this, whatever your *this* is"—he held up the envelope—"gets out."

"Well, my *this* isn't a problem." Maeve tried to fold up the paper the way Hollis had, but it wouldn't go. She couldn't make it bend. Her hands shook. "I had permission. She said I had permission. Why would . . . he, why would he think he could blackmail me with this? He's wrong. He's made a mistake."

Oliver ripped the papers from her hand. Waved them in her face. "Stop saying *he*. It's not him! And there is one really good fucking reason. You remember that, right? He's dead. Callum's dead!"

The name transported them. Now that it had been spoken, it could not be taken back. Now there was no pretending there was the slimmest chance that this was about anything other than him. They were no longer adults standing in a bed and breakfast but teenagers in the front room of a grimy house share.

Maeve stumbled and caught herself on the doorframe.

"Maeve?" someone asked. Lorna, she thought, but she couldn't see because her eyes were closed, and she was trying to show them how hard she was trying not to cry.

"I'm fine. I'm fine. Don't touch me! I'm fine." She wasn't sure if anyone had reached out to her or not, but it was easy to imagine they had. And easier to know they hadn't. "I'm tired. I drove for hours. And as soon as I got here I was roped into whatever this is and I'm bloody soaked and freezing and all I want is to shower and change and deal with whatever all this is in the morning!"

When she braved a look, she saw they were staring at her, but there was no pity. Only annoyance. They were pissed off to be putting up with her again. Just as she knew they would be.

"Maeve," said Hollis, "we should probably talk about—"

"No! I'm too tired for talking. Not tonight." She stopped herself. She couldn't completely break down. They wouldn't listen to her then. "So you do whatever you want, but I'm not thinking about this right now. I'm getting a shower and I'm going to bed and we can discuss this in the morning."

She gathered the papers—her papers—that Oliver had dropped to the floor and left without waiting for their response, found her way downstairs, and grabbed the handle of her red suitcase. The warmth from the fire felt good, though, and she stood there, wondering what it would feel like if she could stick her hands into the flames without getting burnt. But like so many things, this was impossible.

When she returned upstairs, she saw them dispersing. Oliver ignored her and slammed the door to Room 3 behind him. Lorna met her eye and tried to smile but did not and continued on to Room 1.

Up the next flight of stairs, she caught sight of Ellie before Ellie slipped into Room 5. Maeve found her own room—Room 4—as Hollis called her name.

"If you want to talk, I'm right here across the hall." He looked at his door. "Just like old times."

"Thanks, Hollis. Really."

She stood alone in the hall, imagining Callum waving goodnight and disappearing behind a door just like the others. But that was impossible. And the reason it was impossible was the reason they had all been brought here.

45 minutes prior

The wipers streaked back and forth at full speed, unable to keep up with the relentless rain. Maeve drove with her chest leaning over the steering wheel and stared through the waterlogged windshield, trying to piece together a vision of the road. She had wanted to get to the island earlier, when there was still some daylight left, but needed to take a later ferry instead. The darkness amplified her terror, so much so her anxiety made her shake, even though she knew she should be happy. This was what she'd wanted for years. At least half her life. Everything was going to be perfect. Everything was going to be fine.

Unless, of course, it wasn't. Because when did she ever get what she wanted?

"No," she said. "This weekend is about change. Remember? Positive thoughts. Positive thoughts. Positive thoughts."

Her phone chirped and she fought the urge to check it.

It chirped again. Her fingers tapped the steering wheel.

"You're almost there. You can wait another five minutes before you check your bloody phone." She resolutely kept her eyes on the road, counting the seconds. "See? Nothing's so urgent that it can't—"

It chirped a third time.

She grabbed the phone and checked the new text message, looking up in time to see the disabled SUV ahead. She yanked the steering wheel hard to the right, hydroplaning past the other car and spinning 180 degrees. Several seconds passed when all she could hear was her own breathing. When she could finally move again, she looked down at the phone and tried to type *ok!* but messed up the letters as her hand shook. It wasn't canceled.

"See? Positive thoughts."

She smiled, then kissed her phone and tossed it onto the passenger seat.

The turnoff welcomed her, and the house lights beckoned, promising warmth, companionship, change. It was all there. All for her. But once she parked the car and the rain fell harder, she couldn't make herself open the door.

"It's okay." She closed her eyes as if in prayer. "You're a good person. People like you. You have nothing to prove. You . . ."

She forgot the next line. From her pocket, she pulled out her laminated index cards.

"*You're a good person*," she read and flipped to the next card. "*People like you*. Well, some people, some of the time. I suppose. *You have nothing to prove*. Which isn't really a nice thing to say, is it? If you don't have anything to prove, doesn't that mean you have nothing worthwhile that needs proving? I should talk to her about that one. Here we are. *You can achieve whatever you set your mind to*. Whatever you set your mind to."

She looked up at the house as if its sturdy countenance could somehow be passed on to her. She drank it in—every window, every shingle. It would shelter her. Protect her.

"You're a good person. People like you. You have nothing to prove. You can achieve whatever you set your mind to." She tucked the cards into her pocket. "And if you can't, you can lock yourself in your room and not come out until the end of the weekend."

Suitcase in one hand, phone in the other, and her jacket draped over her arm for the short dash to the house, she hopped out of the car into the pouring rain. In her rush to get inside, she dropped her bag, then dropped her keys trying to get her bag. She managed to hold onto her jacket until it caught on a plant near the front entrance. Then it fell from her arm into a puddle. By the time she made it into the empty foyer with all of her belongings, her hair and clothes were soaked from the heavy rain.

"Hello? God, I'm so wet. Hello? Mother of . . ." Her bag slipped from her wet hand, and she let it drop. "Hello? I'm here to check in. I hope I'm not too late. I got lost. Missed the turning probably five times."

The silence felt expectant, as if it were waiting for her to say more. Hearing noises from a room to her right, she approached the door, clothes dripping and shoes squelching. *What an impression to make*, she thought and opened the door.

"Hi hi hi. Sorry to interrupt! I'm—"

But when she saw them all standing there, all she could think was, how could anything this weekend possibly go right?

FRIDAY NIGHT/

SATURDAY MORNING

3

Hollis

The end of the bed sank under Hollis's weight while he stared at the rectangular glow of light from his phone. Fully charged, but no messages and no signal. The little bars said he was connected to the Wi-Fi, but he couldn't access his email or the internet. Was it a blessing, he wondered, if he couldn't ask Linda what was going on? If he let this weekend play out, then questioned her later? His little girl—had she tricked him or had she no idea? Could he make it another hour without demanding an answer? He knew she kept her phone on at night. He could ring and ring and ring until she answered. He could already hear her crying, asking why he was treating her like a suspect. Telling him she had only wanted to do something nice. She hadn't known.

Hadn't known what?

Because Linda didn't know anything about Caldwell Street or Cahill University. He'd made damn sure of that. Hollis shoved his phone in his pocket. The black void in his room matched the stillness of the house. The others slept now, or at least pretended to.

He wanted to go home, forget this weekend ever happened, forget that Linda had somehow got involved. Wanted to start work on Monday in his new suit and tie. Solve cases that had nothing to do with him. But the envelope sitting on the desk reminded him that if he left now, that future was impossible. He stood up and paced, typed out a text he hoped didn't come across as accusatory.

Hearing Callum's name had opened a box in Hollis's brain, one that he'd taped up and filed away on a dusty shelf, like the forgotten evidence of a cold case. Now it was open, he couldn't stop sorting through the contents.

The way Callum could appear in a room and no one noticed how he got there, despite him being over six feet. How he would volunteer to help with the dishes the night after, even if he hadn't been at the party. The day Gran died and Hollis had to rush home, Callum had been the only other person in the house. He'd pulled Hollis into a hug, told him he'd contact his lecturers for him, get any notes he might need. It wasn't just talk. When Hollis returned the next week, Callum had placed a stack of notes, organized by course, on his desk.

In the silence, Hollis kept trying to recall the sound of Callum's voice, but it hid in the patter of the rain, the hiss of the radiator, the scratch of mice in the walls.

His texts again failed to send. He almost threw the phone against the wall, but thought better of it and shoved it in his pocket as he left the room.

The fire in the lobby glowed red, the peat burning without flame. A small lamp on the reception desk gave off a weak light. Hollis's footsteps provided the only sound. He paused, unable to remember the last time he'd occupied a building that seemed so empty. His block of flats in Manchester had so many people coming and going no matter the hour, he sometimes felt like a train conductor. Here he felt like a ghost.

He slipped into the study and sat at the bar with a bottle of Glenlivet that had been left out, pretending, as he often did, to be an adult. He tapped his pen against his notebook, his trusty aid when he'd been a patrolman. The boys had bought him a new one for his first day as detective. That one sat, wrapped in plastic, on the counter at home, awaiting Monday like the suit and shoes in his closet. This old one still had the scuffs from when he and Landry fought. A few unfilled pages remained inside, plenty of space to jot down his thoughts on what had happened at Wolfheather House so far. He'd worry about Linda later. What mattered now was unraveling the web that brought him here.

So focused was he on writing that he didn't notice that the door had opened. The hairs on the back of his neck stood up and he turned around sharply.

"Sorry." Lorna clutched a book to her chest. "I didn't think anyone was down here. I can go somewhere else."

"It's fine." He nodded to the bottle. "Want a drink?"

She hesitated, then sat down, setting her book on the bar. "No point in lying. It's what I came for."

For several minutes, they drank in silence. Almost as if they were waiting for someone. Maybe they were, Hollis thought.

"Anything interesting?" She nodded toward his notebook.

"Just some notes. Trying to pick all of this apart, so I can piece it back together." He tapped the pen against the paper.

"Don't do that. Please." She pressed her fingers to her temples.

"Sorry. I know the noise is annoying."

"No. It's not that. It reminds me too much . . . It makes me feel like we're back there. You and me sitting quietly in the front room. Me with a book. You studying your notes, tapping your pen. It's too much." She looked into her drink. "Do you think we have PTSD?"

"Don't know." He thought of the nightmares that came to him at least once a year. "Probably."

He set his pen on the bar, picked up her book. "Truffaut's *Hitchcock*. Didn't you read this at Cahill?"

"It's even the same copy. Not as interesting as it was, though. I got rid of most of my things from that year, but I still haven't been able to part with a book. You should see my flat." She took the book back and ran her thumbnail down the spine.

"You folded down the corner of the pages," he said.

"Yeah, I guess I did."

She looked younger in this light, with her hair in that same blunt cut, like she was using it as a helmet to protect herself against the world. But he couldn't quite picture her as the girl she had been. Like she was a pho-tograph damaged with age. The years had scarred her too much. But then again, he saw the same when he looked in a mirror.

"Hollis, do you think we deserve this?"

As a policeman, he was used to being asked such questions. But not by Lorna. Lorna always had answers, right or not. Not questions.

"I think we were young and stupid. The worst kind of stupid. And given the chance, I'd go back and change everything that happened."

"But you can't."

"No. I can't," he said. "So maybe all the bad things that have happened to us since are some kind of karmic retribution."

"And maybe we're just very good at doing bad things." From the back of the book, she pulled out the folded papers. They were missing their envelope now, but he recognized what they were. "You tell me yours, I'll tell you mine."

She held them out, but Hollis didn't take them.

"Keeping secrets is what got us into this mess," she said, "and secrets will only make everything worse. The more light we shed on ourselves, on everything, the less power he has over us. This person. Whoever he is."

"It's a short list of people who knew Callum wrote those Happy Wednesday notes," he said.

"And an even shorter one of who knows what really happened that night. I trusted you back then, Hollis. After I felt confident you weren't going to set the house on fire. That hasn't changed." She slid the folded papers across the tin bar. "I slept with a student. A potential student. Allegedly. One I was recruiting for the university."

"Was he the age of consent?"

"Yes. *She* was." Lorna sipped her drink. "But that sort of thing is frowned upon. Except I didn't do it. We may have flirted a bit, but that's as far as it went. Her dad, though, has been after me for weeks. Thinks I, and I quote, 'corrupted her sexuality.' Someone must have paid or pressured her to say it happened. But it's the excuse they'll need. The new administration's been begging for a reason to let me go. I guess I'm still not very good with people."

He pushed the papers back without reading them. She returned them to her book, and he spat out what he needed to say before he changed his mind.

"I planted evidence on a suspect so that I would have probable cause to search his car."

"Allegedly?"

In response, Hollis downed the rest of his drink.

"Jesus. Was it worth it?"

"It saved a life."

"Well, at least what you did could be construed as noble. I just come off as a horny lesbian wench."

The humor was wrong for the situation, and Lorna knew it.

"Sorry. I'm shit," she said. "Here I am thinking this would be the end of the world for me when you . . . God, you'd lose everything, Hollis. Wouldn't you?"

"Don't be sorry. The end of the world looks different for different people. We all have our tipping points." He finished his drink and slid off the barstool, suddenly desperate to be on his own.

"No, you stay," she said. "You were here first."

"That's all right. I'm done anyway. Enjoy your book."

Her thumb fiddled with the spine again. "I won't tell the others. I promise."

"I thought you didn't want any more secrets," he said.

"Yours isn't mine to tell."

He looked at her once more, the battered book in her hand, the black jumper and blunt haircut. So much the Lorna he remembered. She was right. It was too much.

"Goodnight, Lorna."

He left her in the study as his brain began to work. Sometimes he couldn't control it. It attacked a mystery automatically, like an anti-virus. He needed to be alone, to give himself space to parse out these fragments of thought. Something Lorna had said tonight had set his mind off, but he didn't know what it was or why. He was still trying to sort it out when he realized his feet weren't carrying him all the way upstairs to his room but down the second-floor hall to Room 2. Callum's room.

Lorna and Oliver were also staying on this floor, but Lorna remained downstairs and Hollis heard nothing from Oliver. They'd left Callum's door open, the key dangling in the lock. Hollis closed it behind him.

It was after he'd sat in the armchair a few minutes, running through his thoughts, that he spotted it. The edge of a photograph caught in the cushion of the sofa. He slipped it free.

There they were—all six of them—seated on that very couch in their old house on Caldwell Street. So young then. So stupid. He ran his thumb over the background of the picture. Examined the image in detail. And then he knew. Whether this picture had been left accidentally or on purpose didn't matter. It filled the gaps of his memory, the missing pieces from his evidence box.

"Shit."

He shoved the photo in his pocket and pulled out his phone, but there was still no signal. Of course. There wouldn't be.

Oliver

Oliver stumbled through the kitchen, desperate for something to soak up the whisky in his stomach. Fucked up. That's what this whole situation was. *People should be allowed to make mistakes*, he thought. They should be allowed to move on with their lives. They should be allowed to leave this house. But with his car out of commission on the main road, the only way he was getting out of here was by hitching a ride. Or taking someone else's. He found the dry goods in a walk-in pantry and tore open a bag of crisps. Some fell and crunched under his shoes. Ellie's car keys. He should've nicked them when he had the chance. They'd been sitting right there on her desk, on a fuzzy pink keychain. The salt and vinegar burned his lips. God, she looked gorgeous. He might've put on a pound or two, but Ellie, he'd seen the shape of her beneath her clothes. He'd barely been able to keep his hands in his pockets. But he had some self-control. And the knowledge that he needed her on his side. It used to be so easy to win them over. A smile for Ellie, a handshake for Hollis, a wink at Maeve. Lorna, just leave her alone. Callum, though, had been a riddle. Oliver must have done something right, because why else would Callum have brought Oliver Lucozade and paracetamol after his birthday rager? Or loaned him a tenner whenever Oliver asked? But Oliver never quite figured out what Callum needed. He had been the lone child watching through the window as the other kids played together outside. With greasy fingers, Oliver pulled out his phone. No signal, but that comforted him. Maybe she'd been texting him after all and the messages weren't coming through. Good. For once she could be the one at home worrying. After all, he hadn't told her he was traveling to a possible dead zone. Hadn't told her he was leaving at all. Only one person knew he was going away this weekend. Only one person knew where to find him.

Maeve

Goosebumps rose on Maeve's naked skin as she shivered in the bathroom. Even her bra had been soaked through. That, along with the rest of her useless clothes, was piled on the floor. Lines ran down either side of her nose. The dark circles beneath her eyes were permanent thumbprints. Her hair, frizzy from the rain, at least showed no signs of gray, but only because she dyed it. When did she get so old? She couldn't be in her forties. She hadn't done anything yet. No job. No career. No family. Not even a dog. Nothing to drown out the memories of the awkward, gangly boy who used to hover around her like a lost puppy. She'd come up with plenty of excuses as to why they weren't right for each other. He was too tall. Obsessed with his camera. He couldn't play guitar and he couldn't sing, so how would he ever propose to her by playing an original song about their love in front of strangers at the Hyde Park Winter Wonderland while a light snow fell? He'd had a stupid crush on her. That was all. She hadn't loved him, didn't even like him that way, no matter how many times he went out of his way to ask her how her day was or leave a note in blue under her door. Back then, it wasn't about Callum. It was about survival. And for so many years, she never thought she'd survive them again. Yet here she was. Perhaps it was foolishness, or adrenaline, or a vitamin deficiency from living off Doritos and Fanta, but as she towel-dried her hair, she realized she didn't fear them now.

Lorna

Lorna couldn't make sense of the words on the page. Each sentence got jumbled up in her head, like she was trying to read in a foreign language. In the background, a single question pulsed, growing louder until it was the only thought in her head: *What are you really doing here?* It was harder than she thought sitting in the room next to Callum's—the room they'd designated as his—and not think about house 215. Lorna and Callum had shared a wall there, too. She remembered the gray carpet with the brown stain and the Monty Python poster hanging above his desk. Pictures, too. Lots of pictures. Of home, of London, of family, of them. He would stick them up with Blu Tack even though Ellie had warned him it would ruin the walls and he might not get his security deposit back. Closing her eyes, she imagined she heard music from his stereo seeping through the house. Grunge, usually. Nirvana. Bush. Stone Temple Pilots. To her, the music fitted the band names—shabby, dirty—the opposite of Callum. He showered twice a day, never re-wore a piece of clothing without washing it. Kept his auburn hair clean and cut short. The only time his appearance matched his choice in music had been his death. And thinking of his death reminded her of where she was and why. She hated it here. Hated this place and hated Caldwell Street and hated them and hated everything so much. But she needed it all to end. Needed to stop hearing his voice inside her head. Needed stop the feeling that, despite the empty room, Callum was always just on the other side of the wall, waiting for her to save him.

Ellie

Ellie thought about flipping on a light, but she liked the room as it was. The outside spotlights cast the study in strange shadows. The remaining darkness softened the corners, hid the cobwebs. Created anonymity. This could be any room in any house. Perched on the edge of the sofa, a drink in hand, she listened to the wind and rain. It was better down here, away from the others. At some point, she had heard someone leave their room—Hollis or Maeve, she wasn't sure—but paid them no mind. All that mattered was creating a space where she would be able to sleep tonight because every time she closed her eyes, she could see him. Callum. Who never once mocked her for being forgetful or asking a stupid question or needing help with something the others might see as trivial, like putting the sliding drawer back into her desk. He'd done it because she'd asked him, a favor for a friend. But when he'd asked her for a favor, had she been as kind? Ellie jumped from the couch, rubbing her hands. She hadn't had a flashback in a long time, not since Jilly was a baby and Ellie had panicked that she'd stopped breathing. It had taken David half an hour and two gin and tonics to calm her. He thought she was overprotective about the baby, but that wasn't it. That wasn't it at all. In a sudden fit, she downed her entire drink. Callum had been a giver, this was true, and she was not. But that didn't mean she would let him take from her now. She would see to that. Ellie went to fix herself another drink but spotted something on the floor—a small, square piece of paper. She wandered from the study into the glass-walled conservatory, listened to the rain ping off the glass. The house's outside light shone through the glass room like the beam of a spotlight, illuminating her find. It was a piece of sparkling gold cardboard, a bit of ribbon stuck through a hole. The words *Congrats, Dad!* written in proper cursive.

A splotch of red marred the final letter.

Hollis

The cold wind woke Hollis like a shock. He zipped his jacket all the way to the top, ducking his chin into the collar. He'd hurried from the house as soon as he'd found the photograph. It had all clicked then, what Lorna had said, what had bothered him about the whole evening. She hadn't been in the study when he returned, but he didn't want to waste time looking for her. He needed to get them help. Fast. The outdoor lights of Wolfheather House guided him up the rocky drive as he kept one eye on his footing, the other on his phone. Drops of rain beaded on the screen, and he tried to remember if his phone was water resistant while his boots crunched on the wet gravel.

"Come on. Can't I have one bar at least?"

A metal ping echoed in the air behind him.

Hollis scanned the area, using his phone as a torch. Seeing nothing, he continued up the drive. When the lights of the house were mere specks in the darkness, not one but two bars emerged. Hollis fist-pumped the air.

"Yes! There we are." He rubbed the screen dry on his jeans. As he tried to open the phone app, a long series of email alerts popped up faster than he could dismiss them.

"Come on. Quit it! I don't care about my bloody *Men's Health* subscription."

Then he saw the texts from Linda.

19:32 *Hey Dad u there?*

19:40 *Dad ring me when u c this*

19:43 *Srsly Dad need u to answer*

19:47 One new voice mail.

Hollis pressed play. He had to listen to the voice mail twice before understanding it.

"Shit."

He dialed 999. The bright screen blinded him to all else, including the tire iron swinging at his head.

Pp. 23–30

promise there's a reason behind everything. I swear on Callum's grave. And you might think I'm skipping a whole bunch of time, but honestly there's really nothing else you need to know about the rest of September 1994, or even October. In fact, if everything could have kept going like it did in those months, then none of us would be in the situation we're in now. But things did change, and that change started early in November, when the weather still felt like October and most people thought it too soon for Christmas decorations.

That November morning, Lorna made a resolution. She was going to be more sociable. For two months she had avoided long conversations in the front room and flat-out refused to participate in the near weekly house parties. She wanted to focus on her schoolwork, get her degree, and move on from this temporary phase in her life. But excluding herself hadn't given her more focus. It had turned her into a ghost, benign but unwanted. Whenever she entered a room, she sucked the life out of the conversation. People avoided eye contact so as not to set her off. She didn't want to be that person anymore.

That morning, she pulled her short hair into a ponytail and nodded to herself in the mirror. She could do it. She could be a normal university student.

When she opened the door, she met Callum as he exited his room. Years later, Lorna would recall him ducking his head to fit through the doorway as he examined the Minolta Maxxum 9000 that hung around his neck by a black and red woven strap. She remembered that the strap resembled a seat belt. When he walked, he would keep one hand braced against the camera to prevent it from bouncing against his chest. When he held it to his eye, it blocked most of his face. When not in use, the camera remained in a padded black nylon case with a Scottish Rugby keychain attached to the zipper pull. The case would sit on the back left corner of the desk in his bedroom, which was pressed against the wall that formed the border between his and Lorna's rooms.

"Morning, Lorna!" He winced. "Sorry. Too loud?"

"No, you're fine."

"Sorry? Were you headed to the bathroom? You can go first." He cradled the camera as if protecting an injured bird and waited for her to pass.

"It's fine. I was headed down for breakfast. Actually, I'm glad I caught you. You know that paintball thing you were telling me about? Friday, right?"

"Yeah, but I'm not sure I'll go. I asked Maeve and she didn't seem keen, so . . ." He fiddled with a button on the camera.

"Well, I was going to say, if you wanted, I'll do it with you."

"But you said you had no interest in getting shot at by total strangers who only wanted to see women humiliated in the field of sport."

"I was having a bad day."

Callum raised his eyebrows.

"Or month. But it would be fun to get out some aggression."

"Really? Okay! Sign-ups are in the student union. I was going by there today. I could put us down as a team or—"

"Yeah. That'd be great." Lorna winced at her own cheerfulness, but Callum's face brightened.

"Brilliant! I'll see you downstairs. I've got to, uhm . . ." He pointed at the bathroom.

"Right. Have at it."

I did that, she thought, making her way downstairs. *I did something that made someone happy.*

When she reached the kitchen, her pride at her newly discovered propensity for cheer caused her to call out Maeve's name so loudly, it struck the girl like a bullet. Maeve's head snapped around in a panic.

"Sorry. Didn't mean to scare you. Breakfast?"

"If someone didn't eat my Frosties again." Maeve kept her distance, like a skittish child afraid of the dog that once bit her.

Lorna's chipper mood withered, but she pressed on, determined to coax it back to life. "Did you hear about the paintball? Callum and I are signing up."

"Yeah, he asked. Paintball's stupid, though. I don't want to go. And I have to study anyway. This maths course is killing me." Maeve chewed on the cuff of her jumper and resumed looking out the window.

"It would be good exercise."

Maeve winced, and Lorna realized she'd screwed up once again. She'd meant exercise for herself. She used to take Alfie on walks every day but now barely left her room. If she could explain that to Maeve, she could smooth things over, but the words jammed in her throat along-side all the other apologies she felt she needed to make today. She really tried to make those apologies that week, she said, but she could never seem to find the right time.

That particular morning, it was Callum who interrupted.

"Did someone eat your Frosties again?"

Callum sounded genuinely concerned, but his voice reached Maeve as if through a filter. She couldn't feel the impact of his words as all her attention was fixed outside where she watched Oliver and Ellie play-fighting in the back garden. Oliver held something in his hands that he hugged to keep from Ellie, who kept tugging at his arms and leaping on his back.

"There's a surprise." Lorna rolled her eyes, but Maeve coughed and belatedly answered Callum's question.

"Nope. There they are."

Callum leaned against the counter and continued trying to talk to her as she got her breakfast, but whatever he said, she was oblivious to it. All she could hear were Ellie's giggles and Oliver's laugh.

Maeve knew her schoolgirl crush was stupid. That didn't stop the fantasies that helped her sleep at night, the dreams of Oliver sneaking up to her bedroom when everyone else was asleep and knocking on her door. They didn't even do anything but snuggle and talk through the night. She imagined Oliver telling her his opinions on which of the Brontë sisters was the best writer and her contradicting him and him saying, "That's a good point, actually," even though she had no idea if he'd ever read anything by the Brontës and this part of the fantasy was a carryover of the nightmares she used to have about her English A-levels.

"Maeve?"

This time she heard Callum.

She had dumped cereal all over the counter. As she brushed the extra flakes into her hand, Oliver and Ellie stumbled through the door. Ellie laughed and poked Oliver in the shoulder with a cassette tape.

"And don't make fun of my music again!"

"I wasn't making fun. I swear. Morning, ladies. Gent."

Lorna grunted. Callum waved a cheerful hello. Maeve's reply caught in her throat and came out as a cough.

"All right there, love?" Oliver asked.

"Yep," she managed. "Fine. Morning."

She avoided eye contact, which prevented her from seeing what he was doing. As she reached into the fridge for the milk, he reached for the juice. Their arms touched.

"Sorry." She pulled back. "You go ahead."

He took his orange juice first, then pressed the carton of milk into her hand with a wink. The warmth of his arm on hers lingered long after he'd pulled away. She ran her fingers over the spot, hidden by her sleeve, pretending his hand was still there. Callum handed her a spoon and she took it with two pinched fingers, not wanting to make contact.

Oliver never recalled bumping Maeve at all, and he wouldn't have cared either way if he did. That morning, he bounced from foot to foot as he unscrewed the cap on the juice carton, waiting to share his news. "I'm glad you're all here. You'll never guess what I found out."

Lorna peeled an orange with the same disregard with which she spoke. "You found out why Hollis was expelled from his last uni."

Oliver choked on his juice.

"So I was right, then?" She flicked a piece of orange peel out from under her fingernail.

"What do you do all day in your room, lesbo? Spy on us?"

"Hey," Callum jumped in. "There's no need for that. Someone's sexuality is none of your business, and it should never be used as an insult."

Oliver saw Lorna blushing and wanted to dig the knife in further, but Callum remained firm, and no one else was contradicting his defense. Oliver held up his hands.

"Sorry, Lorna. I apologize." He overemphasized each word, then plopped himself down in the seat next to Ellie.

"Go on, then," Ellie said. "Tell us what you found."

"One of my mates from back home has a mate who has a brother who goes to Exeter."

"Wow, a reliable source, then," Lorna said. This time he ignored her.

"He did some asking around and you know what he found out?"

"We would if you'd just tell us."

"Jesus, Lorna! Fucking eat your bloody orange somewhere else if you don't care."

"Language, please," Ellie whispered.

"Sorry, princess. Anyway, turns out Hollis is a total nutter. A bona fide psychopath!"

"He sleeps in the room next to me," Ellie gasped.

Callum laughed. "Hollis? Our Hollis? The Hollis that helps every little old lady cross the street?"

"It was one lady, and she wasn't even that old! Look, Charlie says this comes from multiple sources." He stared at Lorna. If he could convince her, he could convince them all. "Story goes Hollis took this tame fox one of the biology lecturers kept as a pet, right? And he tortured it. Then when he was done having his fun, he strung it up from a tree by its neck and let it hang there till it died. Rumor is he got off on it, but I'll admit no one knows for sure what his motive was. The facts, though, were printed in the school paper."

"Where's this paper?" Callum asked, not as sure as before.

"Charlie's getting me a copy. But it makes sense, doesn't it? Why he kept holding his hand over the candle flame at the last party . . ."

"You were all doing it," Callum said. "You were off your heads."

"That time we were leaving the Byeways and he threw a rock at the fox rummaging through the bins."

"It was the paper from his kebab," Lorna said.

"Whatever. Come to your own conclusions. But word is you go to Exeter University and say 'Hollis Drummond,' the first thing they'll say is 'the fox fucker.' I'm telling you, the bloke is mental."

"Mental, eh?"

Despite the sun streaming through the windows, Hollis cast a shadow over them as he leaned in the kitchen doorway. Lorna stopped fiddling with her orange. Maeve shoved a spoonful of cereal into her mouth. Callum stared at his feet. But Oliver looked at him dead on. Hollis only ever pretended to be intimidating. He was no more than a custard cream donut. A softy. No spine in the middle. All it took was for one person to stand up to him, and Hollis would give in. Crumble.

Gossip generally turned Ellie's stomach. Over the years, she would become more impervious to it, but that morning, still so young, she felt absolutely awful getting caught out like that. However, if Hollis had done something terrible, didn't they have a right to know? As an adult, she could've posed the question, but back then she didn't want to get involved, and the long silence stretched between them all. She knew Hollis wanted them to say something, but she had no idea what would remedy this and so waited for someone else to fix it.

"Hollis, mate—" said Oliver.

"I'm your mate now, am I? Thought I was mental."

Oliver laughed like he'd been caught cheating on an exam. Hollis waited.

"If you didn't want us to be so curious, maybe you should've just told us."

"Maybe I didn't tell you because it's none of your fucking business. Ever consider that?"

Oliver stood, the legs of his chair scraping against the linoleum floor.

"I think we all have a right to know if we're living with a fucking psycho, yeah."

Ellie whimpered but no one held any concern for her feelings when a match hovered this close to a fuse.

In their minds, they took bets on who would do more damage. Oliver because he was taller or Hollis who had more muscle? Hidden deeper was their desire to watch the violence happen without a care for why or who would get hurt.

"Hey guys? How about that photo?"

And so Callum reentered the conversation, deescalating the tension.

"Remember? We agreed last night? The group shot. You said this morning would be a great time to take it since we'd all be here . . ." He left the sentence trailing, hoping someone would pick up the thread, but the tension that had inched them toward violence receded into an embarrassment that crippled them. "I guess if it's not a good time, we could scrap it? I have to go see Yanni anyway about sending someone to fix my door before new job orientation at the uni admin office, so . . ."

Oliver held his hands up. "Sorry, Tripod. We did agree. And if that's important to you, we'll do it right now."

"I mean, it's not like it's *that* important." Callum shrugged.

"No," said Lorna. "It is. You've been talking about it for ages. And isn't the light perfect right now?"

"Yeah, I guess."

"I should go study," Maeve said. "But a picture would be fun."

Ellie hopped up from the table. "Tell me where to pose! I love taking pictures. Daddy always says how photogenic I am."

"Come on," Oliver said. "Out in the front room. That'll make for a nice shot."

Once the shutter clicked, their smiles faded along with the glare of the flash. Crammed into the confines of the dirty pink sofa, sharp elbows and knees jabbing soft stomachs and thighs, they couldn't wait for this ordeal to be over only to hear . . .

"Wait. If I could just get one more."

This was what they would remember of Callum all those years later. They couldn't recall his surname, but the nickname, Tripod, was ingrained in their memory. Along with how he could turn their eye-rolling and exasperation into laughs and friendly ribbing. They posed for shot after shot, making up stories about what had happened on this sofa prior to their moving in, having no idea what they would do to Callum in six months' time.

Because in six months, in that very room, the phone would be knocked from Callum's hand, and he would be held down on that same sofa while a hand was pressed over his nose and mouth. He was tall, yes, but so skinny. No muscle on him at all. And he was very, very drunk. Too drunk to put up much of a fight.

If you could travel back in time and warn them about what they would do, about how they would lie about what they had seen, they wouldn't believe you because it would mean acknowledging a part of themselves that they could not accept existed. The part that emerged when Hollis and Callum almost came to blows. They would never believe you because they thought themselves good people, more or less.

And, more or less, they were.

Once.

Good, decent people who thought they remembered everything about Caldwell Street but never remembered the front door opening as they sat on the couch, waiting for the final click of the shutter, never remembering the person who entered as the timer went . . .

SATURDAY

4

Lorna

Cocooned in an old knit jumper, Lorna stopped halfway down the main staircase to double-check her watch. Half past nine, but the house looked as dark as it had when she went to bed. She listened to the rain all around her, watched it through the large windows above the front door. She hugged the jumper tighter and continued down. Though she couldn't say she had slept well, surviving the night had given her a fresh perspective on the morning. Callum's memory remained but had retreated to the darker corners of her mind, no longer suffocating her with its presence. The calm silence of the morning made her believe she could be the cool, measured Lorna Torrington they remembered.

Down in the foyer, fresh blocks of peat burned in the fireplace, but all she could feel was the draft.

"Hello? Good morning?"

She checked the study—empty—then the conservatory where rain sounded like gunshots against the tall glass walls.

Clouds obscured most of the mountains and fog further limited visibility, making Wolfheather House feel even more isolated from the rest of the world. Lorna thought of a snow globe her grandparents used to have, thick with glass that protected a wintry scene. She used to imagine a family lived in the house inside. Had even given them names. When she shook the snow globe, she pictured furniture flying, their bodies toppling over one another. She imagined, once she stopped, how they worked together to rebuild their rooms. And then she would shake it again.

A door slammed.

"Hello?" she called.

Back in the foyer, Lorna saw nothing. No sign of who had come or gone. The dining room door remained open, as it had been last night. A little farther down the same wall was another half-open door, revealing a junk room. Across from it a closet built beneath the main staircase. She made her way through the narrow hallway that ran between these walls to the very back of the house, where large sash windows gave her the same foggy glimpses of the Highlands as the conservatory. Cans of paint flecked red and white were stacked beneath the windows, along with a plastic drop sheet, rollers, and stirrers, all caked with paint. A spider had woven a web from the handle of the paint roller to the windowsill and now dangled in the corner, waiting for a meal.

All was silent.

She closed the junk room door as she returned to the dining room, checking over her shoulder, just in case.

In the kitchen, there was no food or drink to be found. No sound of anyone.

"All by yourself now, aren't you?" she whispered to herself.

Then she turned. And screamed.

Ellie had appeared like a phantom. Face pale. Hair and clothes soaked in rain. Mud up to her ankles.

"Jesus! Why are you sneaking up on people like that?" Lorna asked.

Ellie said nothing.

"Are you all right? Ellie?"

Ellie looked down at her clothes as if having forgotten she was wearing any. Then words poured out of her mouth like a running tap. "I went for a walk. There's no gym. I needed some exercise. Is there tea? I hope there's tea. I really need tea. A great deal of tea because we can't go to the shop because there is no shop and there's no way to get to a shop, even if there was a shop, or even a neighbor, because all of our cars have been vandalized and if I don't get some tea and I'm going to lose my mind!"

Ellie

The suitcase spilled open as she closed the bedroom door. Ellie fell to her hands and knees, scrambling to collect her fallen bras, socks, shirts, toiletries. She couldn't leave any sign she had been here. Not a trace. Her suitcase left tracks in the carpet as she wheeled it down the hall. She was tempted to go back and rub out those marks, but there wasn't time. If she wanted to leave, she had to go now. Before the others woke. She cupped her keys in her hand to prevent them from clinking and descended the stairs to the second floor. No sight or sound of Oliver, or anyone else. Just the cracklings of the warm fire. She adjusted her grip on the suitcase and continued down the main stairs. Like crossing a swimming pool in a single breath, Ellie rushed through the foyer and out into the rainy morning.

Keeping her head down, she pressed the buttons on the key fob with every step, causing the Land Rover's lights to flash. She climbed into the driver's seat, tossing the suitcase beside her. Only once the door closed did she let out a breath.

Once on Skye, she would ring David. No. Text. She'd text him, say she wasn't feeling well, say she missed the children, say the guesthouse wasn't up to her standards. She'd say something. Or maybe she'd call Gordon. Gordon always did as she asked. Although wasn't Gordon partially responsible for this mess to begin with?

Through the rearview mirror, she watched the house watching her with its long, dark windows. This would be another day Callum's favors went unpaid. She turned the key in the ignition.

A wheezing sounded from underneath the bonnet. She tried again, pressing the pedals, but the engine sputtered. Ellie knew nothing about cars, but she did know a two-year-old Land Rover shouldn't break down like this. She looked out at the loch then, in the mirrors, at the house.

No one had come rushing out. Maybe no one had heard. They could all be asleep yet. They were always fond of a lie-in, except Lorna. And if Ellie could find where they'd left their keys . . .

As she hopped out of the car, the clasp on her bracelet gave and slipped from her wrist. When she reached down to retrieve it, a hole in the punctured tire gaped at her like an open wound. The back tire was the same. And the two on the passenger side. All four destroyed beyond repair. She looked at the other three cars. All of them sat lower than they should. All of them bore flattened tires. All of them were useless.

Somehow, she made it back to the house. She didn't know how or for how long she'd been standing in the foyer, her wet clothes dripping on the floor. When she heard sounds coming from the dining room, she went in to find Lorna there. In her mind, she calmly explained what she had discovered outside, but when she opened her mouth the words tumbled out.

Before hearing Lorna's reaction, Ellie escaped to the kitchen. Tea, she'd mentioned. Tea sounded like an excellent idea. She took her time choosing a mug from a rack by the sink and a tea bag from a glass canister. She filled a kettle with water, placed it on the stove, and waited for the water to boil.

She wouldn't be leaving. She was trapped. With them. For at least the weekend. Possibly longer. Trapped. When she hadn't even wanted to come here at all.

She slammed her fist into the wall. Bits of white plaster dusted her knuckles. She watched her hand bleed, waited for it to sting, and, when it finally did, felt somewhat calmer.

"It will all be fine," she whispered and ran cool water over her hand, rinsing away the blood and plaster. "You've done nothing wrong."

The floor creaked behind her. Ellie turned, but there was no one there. "Hello?"

She listened.

The kettle whistled.

Once her tea was done, Ellie took one last glance around the kitchen, then returned to the dining room. Just in time to see Oliver kick a chair.

"That fucking son of a bitch!"

She wanted to cover her ears but couldn't bear to put the warm mug down even as the heat from it burned her palms.

"We don't know it was Caskie," said Lorna.

"Of course it was! Must have done it before he left, which is why he scarpered out of here as fast as he did. Should've chased his car down last night instead of watching him drive off. Bet he knows all about our blackmail-happy little friend."

"Then we should let Hollis snoop around," Lorna said. "See if he can find a way to track Caskie down."

Oliver snorted.

"He *is* the detective . . ."

The door clicked open.

"Speak of the devil," said Oliver, but it was Maeve, looking like she'd rolled out of bed and all the way down the stairs. "Morning, sleeping beauty. Where the fuck have you been?"

Ellie's eyes flashed at Oliver. He caught her glance and rubbed a hand over his head.

"Sorry," he muttered. "Rough morning."

"No, I'm sorry. I didn't mean to sleep in." Maeve rubbed her eyes. "I thought I set an alarm. Where's the coffee?"

"Hollis up yet?" Oliver asked. "Seems we have a little job for him."

"I thought Hollis was down here," Maeve said.

"Sleeps in later than you." He fished a cigarette out of a pack.

"If he's sleeping, it's not in his room. Is there a pot of coffee or is it a make your own sort of thing?"

"How do you know he's not in his room?" Lorna asked.

"'Cause the door's open and he's not inside. What about breakfast?" She shuffled halfway into the room, then finally noticed something was bothering them. "What is it? Did you find more notes or something?"

Lorna explained what happened to the cars. Maeve shrieked and ran to the windows.

"You can't be serious! I just paid it off."

Oliver laughed around the end of his cigarette.

"It's not funny! Maybe you can afford a new car every other year, but it took me ages to save for the down payment."

"I wasn't laughing at you," he said. "I was laughing at the situation."

"What on earth is funny about this?" Lorna asked. "Please explain."

"He wasn't saying it was funny. He was only laughing," Maeve said. "It's a normal reaction for some in times of stress."

That was enough to stir up another argument. Their three-way squabbling scratched at Ellie's brain, this out-of-tune symphony playing like a repeat of a long-forgotten record. When she closed her eyes, she could remember a similar argument from years ago—Oliver standing in a kitchen doorway, Lorna across from him, shouting, Maeve cowering by the closet under the stairs, Callum silent on the old sofa . . .

"That's it!" Ellie silenced them. "No more shouting. No more arguing. We are adults now. Yes? So we will handle this like adults instead of little children. Is that clear?"

She breathed in the scent of her Earl Grey tea, keeping her eyes fixed on Oliver. From the corner of her eye, she saw Lorna fold her arms. Maeve mumbled a sarcastic, "Yes, Mum."

Oliver broke their gaze first and stomped into the foyer to shout for Hollis. Lorna and Maeve followed, leaving Ellie alone in the dining room. She watched them from a distance as someone entered the room behind her. The presence was so tangible, she thought it was Hollis and turned to say hello. But there was no one there.

She scanned the dining room, seeking out the corners and curtains, anywhere someone could hide, and saw no one. No longer willing to be alone, she abandoned the mug on a table and joined the others in the foyer.

"We think Hollis went for a walk," Lorna told her. "Maeve said his jacket's not in his room."

"What were you doing snooping around his room?" Ellie asked.

"For the love of—I wasn't snooping! The door was wide open. And it's not like it's a big room. It was easy to see his jacket wasn't in there. It's bright yellow, for god's sake."

Ellie remembered then what she had found last night and retrieved it from her pocket. "Does Hollis have a child? I found this in the study."

Lorna took the little card that read *Congrats, Dad!*

"I saw him in there last night," Lorna said. "We both had a drink. It was late, sometime after midnight. He must've dropped it then." Lorna paused and tilted her head to the side, examining the corner of the tag, and tensed. "That's blood."

"Are you sure?" Oliver asked.

She handed over the card. He grimaced and passed it to Maeve, who pinched it between her forefinger and thumb. No one said anything until Maeve handed the card back to Ellie. Ellie didn't need to read it again. Instead, she watched Maeve, who was staring at the fireplace.

"Do you think it was Hollis who relit the fire?" Maeve asked.

No one answered.

"Did any of you do it?"

No one answered.

Oliver

A small key rested in the lock of the door beside the main entrance. The rest of their search had turned up nothing. This was the last place he and Lorna had left to check. Oliver twisted the key and, expecting a closet, grimaced as he looked down the wooden steps.

"Of course. A cellar," he sighed. "I don't see a reason to go down there, do you?"

He ran his fingers through his thinning hair, hoping Lorna wouldn't notice how anxious he was. It used to be so easy to cover what he was really feeling. But the years had made it harder for him to hide behind his bluster.

"We've already checked the dining room, the kitchen, and the study," Lorna said. "Nothing. Ellie and Maeve obviously haven't found anything upstairs yet. Let's just finish the job. There's a light switch right here." A single bulb sprang to life. "See? Not even a flicker. You're not scared, are you?"

"When have you ever known me to be scared?" But he could think of at least one time. By the look on Lorna's face, so could she. He motioned to the stairs.

"Ladies first."

"If you push me, I'll murder you."

He held up both hands.

The steps creaked under their weight. Oliver plodded along behind. True to his word, he let her go unmolested all the way down the stairs. He hesitated on the middle step.

"Well?"

"Oh yeah," she called up. "It's a total nightmare. You might want to stay where you are. Could hurt yourself on an errant bath towel."

The steps groaned as Oliver joined her below. "You know, Lorna, you're just as funny as you were at school."

"By that you mean not at all?"

"Glad to know some people don't change."

They stood side by side listening to the rain outside. A small cracked window at the top of the wall opposite revealed weeds driven sideways by the wind. The only cellar he knew was his grandfather's, filled with vegetables and jars of pickled foods and jams, and an old bomb shelter Grandad refused to get rid of in preparation for "the next big one." This cellar was as unremarkable as Lorna had implied. A few metal racks held a hodgepodge of items—old sheets and towels, extra wastepaper bins, mini-bottles of shampoo—but stacks upon stacks of cardboard boxes took up the majority of the space. Instead of dirt and onions and a broken jar of strawberry jam, this cellar smelled of wet cardboard, sawdust, and petrol. It reminded him of the junk room in Caldwell Street, the one stuffed with random bits of broken furniture and kitchen equipment, previous tenants' junk mail, the bag of dirty laundry. He and Callum had tried to sort through it once early on and managed to pull out enough scraps to jerry-rig Callum a desk. Oliver had even sanded it down and restained it for him, and Callum had bought him several rounds at the Byeways in return. They spent the night being miserable at darts.

The memory put him on edge. As Lorna headed for a pile of disused furniture in the corner, he followed like a toddler dragged through a store by his mum. Yesterday, he couldn't wait to reach the house after abandoning his hired car. Now, he calculated how long it would take him to walk back there, and if he could change the tire once he did.

"Jesus, look at this." Lorna picked up a green Koosh ball and bounced it on her finger. "Callum had one of these on his desk. He used to throw it against the wall whenever he was studying. Drove me so mad I hid it from him once. He got so sad when he couldn't find it, I didn't have the heart to keep it from him." She looked at it for another second, then placed it back into a box and continued farther into the cellar.

"What do you remember about him?" she asked.

"Not much." Oliver nudged a box of wood blocks with his toe. "I mean, he was quiet, wasn't he? Didn't get in the way much. Not until . . ."

He crossed his arms and glanced at an empty bird feeder.

"But haven't you been thinking about him? All of us here, that horrible sofa, hasn't that brought anything back?"

"Nothing to bring back. We weren't mates. Barely said hello to each other."

"You know that's not true. Maybe he didn't go to your parties, but you two hung out now and then. And he got you that ticket for George Michael at Wembley."

"If you tell anyone I went to a George Michael concert, I'll cut your balls off."

"So you do remember."

Oliver pushed past her to a deeper corner of the cellar. Of course he remembered. Each minute he spent in her company brought back another memory of Caldwell Street. They were collecting like drips from a leaky faucet. No matter how much he twisted the taps, they kept getting in. He even remembered that stupid Koosh ball, except Callum's hadn't been green but pink. He remembered because he'd made a gay joke about it that made Callum wince so badly Oliver had wondered if he *was* gay, despite the hard-on he'd had for Maeve. He wasn't going to tell that to Lorna, though. Let her guess what he did or didn't remember. What had he done with the tire iron?

He kicked aimlessly at a stack of crates. A black cardboard box fell into his path.

"Hello there. Hey, Lorna . . ."

But she was staring up at the ceiling.

"Where are we?" she asked. "What's above us?"

"I don't know. The dining room? Son of a bitch. Lorna, look at this." He turned the box over in his hands. "Lorna? Oi. Big tits."

She snapped out of it and wiped a hand across her forehead.

"Knew that would get your attention. Here." He shoved the box into her hands. "Know what that is?"

"A box."

"Don't be thick. What's it a box for?"

Lorna tipped it toward the light. "JF100 Wall Mounted 2G, 3G, 4G, Wi-Fi Jammer. Are you fucking joking?"

"One of these babies can block all cellular and Wi-Fi signals for over a hundred meters."

"I know what 'jammer' means, Oliver. How do you even get one of these?"

"Easy. Amazon. Where else?"

"Why do you know so much about them?"

He snatched the box back. "Don't be suspicious of me, love. Out of all of us, I give the least shit about any of you."

"So you keep saying." She looked again at the ceiling. This time Oliver followed her gaze.

"Why do you keep looking up there?"

"I thought I heard something."

"Well I haven't heard a thing."

A thump, like something falling, rattled the ceiling.

"Except that." Oliver ran up the stairs, box in hand.

When he reached the foyer, he stopped, Lorna bumping into him from behind. The door to the dining room stood open. Lorna looked at him, waiting for him to do something. Of course he needed to make the move. That's what he did. That's who he was. The guy who made the decisions. At least, that was who he used to be. He could fall back into that role if they needed him to. He cleared his throat and approached the door.

"Hollis?"

No answer.

Lorna nudged him. "Go."

"I'm going!"

But when he got to the door, there was nothing to see. He ushered Lorna over.

"We did hear something, didn't we?" she asked.

Oliver left the empty box on the nearest table and walked to the windows.

"Did someone come through the window?" she asked.

He tugged at the sashes. "These are shut up tight."

"Maybe the kitchen?"

They both looked across the room. Was his mind playing tricks or had the door just moved, like it had fallen back into place after being pushed? He blinked. The door was still. At least now. Oliver approached the kitchen. Nothing. No movement of shadow between the door and the floor.

"Hollis, is that you?" he called. Again, no answer.

He felt someone watching him and turned, but it was only Lorna, keeping near the door to the foyer. She nodded, urging him on.

Oliver curled his hand into a fist and pushed in the kitchen door.

Maeve

Maeve dragged her hand over the bumps in the wallpaper as she and Ellie walked deeper down the hallway that housed their guest rooms. The same pattern repeated everywhere, on each floor, like they weren't really moving at all. Like she and Ellie kept returning to the same place. She thought of her nephew's gerbil and the little plastic tubes attached to its cage. Hours it would run, keeping her up at night, never moving an inch from the place it started.

"Do you really think we'll find anything up here?" Maeve asked, glancing over her shoulder at the staircase they had just left behind. The higher they climbed within the house, the more disconnected she felt, like the air was somehow thinner up here. Or maybe it was the result of being stuck with Ellie.

Ellie opened a door, took a perfunctory glance, and shut it again. "It's better than sitting around waiting for something to happen."

"What do you think will happen?" Maeve asked.

"I don't know. Hollis? Are you in there?"

They stood in front of his open door. His room had the same old furniture as Maeve's, the same grandmotherly bedspread. Maeve tried to spot anything special about it, anything that could give away where he had gone. Ellie giggled.

"Remember how our floor always smelled of fried chicken?" Ellie asked. "He ate it almost every night. It was like living in a Chicken Cottage."

"Why is that funny?"

Ellie frowned as if she realized she'd been laughing at a funeral.

"I suppose it's not. I was just . . . just remembering."

"Yeah well, I'm not in a mood to reminisce." Maeve stepped into the room to get away from her, but no matter how far apart she got, it was like she was tied to Ellie with an invisible string. She felt the tug as she searched through Hollis's bag. Clothes neatly folded: shirts, socks, trousers, trainers. A paperback novel, its bookmark a folded newspaper clipping. Something about a kidnapping.

"Maybe we're overreacting," Ellie said. "Maybe Hollis did go for a walk."

"Like you?"

"What's that supposed to mean?"

"Lorna told me you went out this morning."

"When did she tell you that?"

"When we were downstairs. God, do you get this defensive with David?"

Maeve returned to the hall, feeling Ellie's eyes on her, the giggles gone.

"How do you know my husband's name?"

"Because you told us about him." With every step she took, Ellie took two, like a trailing yo-yo, until Ellie was close enough to grab her arm. Maeve yanked it free.

"It's just I can't remember saying anything about David since you've been here."

"Well, you did. There's nothing up here. Let's go." The lights in the hall were giving her a headache. Maeve wished she could unscrew each bulb and crush it against the floor.

"You may not think so, but I pay attention to every word I say."

"Because you're totally obsessive-compulsive that way." Maeve pinched the bridge of her nose, hoping to keep the migraine at bay. "We came up here to look for Hollis. We can't find him. Let's go downstairs. Who cares about your stupid balding husband anyway?"

"How did you know he was balding?"

Maeve bit her tongue. "Isn't that what happens to all old men?"

Ellie folded her arms like a disappointed schoolmarm. "Is it really so hard to tell the truth?"

"When has either of us ever told the truth?"

In that moment, Maeve found herself back at Caldwell Street arguing in the front room, instinctively avoiding Callum's gaze. Even though Callum wasn't here, the old anxiety crept up her throat like a spider in its web. When she saw Ellie tugging at the cuffs of her shirt, biting her upper lip, she could tell she felt it, too.

"Fine," Maeve said. "I saw it on Facebook. Happy?"

"But we're not friends on Facebook."

"I looked you up. Can we leave it now?"

Ellie, now with the upper hand, stopped chewing on her lip. "I guess Jilly was right about my privacy settings. Jilly's my daughter, but I suppose you know that, too."

Maeve chose not to reply. If only she could pull her quotations from her pocket. Read her reassurances. But that would have embarrassed her further, so she fiddled with the nearest doorknob instead.

"I'm sorry I ignored your friend request," Ellie said.

"No, you're not."

"Wait. You sent that a few years ago, didn't you? But David didn't start going bald until last summer."

Maeve walked to the door that marked the end of the hall, trying to put distance between them. Perhaps from farther away, Ellie would see her less clearly.

"I look you up sometimes. And Lorna. And Hollis. Oliver now and then. It's not a crime."

"I suppose not, but I certainly don't see the point."

"Because I have nothing better to do! There. Happy now, princess?"

"Don't call me that." Ellie furrowed her brow.

"Why not? That's what we always called you. And it's what you are. Isn't it? Princess Ellie with her perfect life? You sell your soaps and lotions and live in a massive house that's a registered historic landmark. Then there's Lorna who gets to work at the University of Edinburgh, where I could never have got accepted even if I tried, and Hollis is an actual police detective, and Oliver was on *Dragons' Den*, even though he didn't get an investor, and do you know what I am? Nothing. Unemployed. On the dole. You have a mansion in Richmond? I live in my brother's spare room. To make me feel better, he pays me to watch his kids like a live-in nanny. It's everything you've ever wanted for me, isn't it?"

A long silence stretched between them. Somewhere downstairs, Lorna and Oliver searched similar rooms, perhaps sharing similar arguments, but Maeve could not hear them. Last night, she had sworn she would be different around them. Stronger. A few pithy comments from Ellie, and already she was crumbling. She had to hold it together.

"I didn't mean to upset you. I'd always hoped you'd do well."

But she couldn't.

"Don't lie, Ellie. You never thought of me at all." Maeve rattled the handle of the door to the attic. "I'll go downstairs and find the key."

"Shouldn't I go with you?"

"I'd really rather you didn't."

Tears blurred her vision as she hurried away from Ellie, and she hated herself for it. She hugged her arms to herself and tried to squeeze the anxiety out. Why did she always cry when she was stressed? Why couldn't she get angry or haughty? Why did it have to be sadness? This was all Callum's fault. If he hadn't died, she could be living a normal life. Maybe even a successful one. But she knew this was stupid even as she thought it. It wasn't Callum's fault she was here, just like it wasn't his fault when she failed her maths exam or broke the teakettle or didn't budget properly and ran out of grocery money. How many times had he paid for her lunch or got her dinner at the pub? She'd lost count, but she knew how many times she'd returned the favor. Zero was an easy number to remember. But this weekend, it was a chance to fix that, wasn't it?

Lost in thought, she didn't see the rope until she bumped into it. She'd wandered past the main staircase over to the wing of the house closed for renovation. The thin rope blocking off the closed wing swung limply back and forth from her touch. She grabbed it to steady it, but then smacked it in frustration. Why had she told Ellie about looking her up on Facebook? Why couldn't she keep her mouth shut? She hit the rope again. No. No more tears. There was no reason to cry. She smacked the rope once more, and the weak catch that secured it to the wall broke. One end of the rope dropped to the floor.

"Of course," she muttered and bent down to retrieve it, thinking she could somehow re-secure it.

As she lifted the end, she heard a sneeze.

She looked down into the darkened wing.

"Hello?"

Silence.

She looked behind her, but there was no one there. She didn't expect there to be. The sound had come from the closed wing. No one was supposed to be down there.

"Hello?"

No answer. She let the rope fall. She couldn't see far down the hall. The doors to all the rooms were shut and there were no windows to let the daylight in.

She listened. More silence.

And then, a faint creak, like a door being shut very softly. She'd heard that creak before. Last night.

Maeve hurried back to the main staircase and ran all the way down to the lobby. Lorna's and Oliver's voices carried up from the cellar as she turned at the bottom of the stairs and followed the narrow hallway that led to the back of the house. The windows back here looked out onto the distant hills, the bitter gray sky dampening the day.

If she followed this hall to the right, she would be walking underneath the closed wing above, wouldn't she?

A scream echoed through the house.

Maeve froze.

"Ellie," she whispered.

Ellie screamed again. Maeve rushed back to the lobby, running into Oliver and Lorna, who were coming out of the dining room.

"Where is she?" Ollie asked.

"I don't know. Upstairs?"

Oliver ran for the stairs. Maeve followed alongside.

"You two were supposed to stay together!" he yelled back at her.

"I thought I saw someone!"

Lorna grabbed her arm. "Who did you see?"

"No one. I mean, I thought I heard someone."

"Hollis?" Oliver asked as they reached the second-floor landing.

"I don't know."

"But you heard them downstairs? Why did you leave Ellie?"

"I didn't! I mean I did but—"

Ellie screamed again and this time didn't stop.

They reached the top floor, and the narrower hall condensed the sound. Oliver tracked it to a closed door on their right.

"Ellie? What's happening? What's wrong? Ellie!"

The knob rattled. The door held firm.

"Ellie, let me in!"

Oliver landed a kick to the door.

"Ow! Fucking hell."

The door didn't move, but Oliver limped back. "Who installed these fucking doors? What did they do? Cement the fucking hinges? Ellie!"

"Hush," said Lorna. "Listen."

Maeve noticed, too. The screaming had stopped. In the quiet, she heard the lock unbolt. Then Ellie stood before them, holding her left arm as if wounded but otherwise apparently unharmed. She forced her way through them and staggered down the hall.

"Ellie, love," Oliver said, going after her. "Calm down. It's all right. I'm here. Calm down. Tell us what happened."

He tried to take her arm, tried to hold her, but Ellie kept turning away, passively resisting as she stopped and started down the hall, Oliver trailing after her. She paused at a wall sconce and held her arm under the light, examining a wound—red marks that looked like scratches. *What could have done that to her?* Maeve thought. Who could have done that, when Lorna and Oliver had been downstairs?

Ellie crumpled to the floor, her face shining from tears.

"What happened?" Lorna asked Maeve.

"I don't know. I told you I thought I heard someone. I mean, I went to find a key for the attic, and that's when I thought I heard someone, so I went downstairs and that's where I was when I heard her scream."

"You heard someone up here, so you went downstairs?" Oliver snapped. "What the fuck sense does that make? You were running away, was that it?"

"I wasn't—I got my words jumbled. I went downstairs to find a key for the attic, and then I thought I heard someone, and then—"

"Stop. Look." Ellie's whisper silenced them. She shook her head back and forth, like she was having a seizure, and pointed at the room. "Just look!"

"Okay. Okay." Oliver rubbed Ellie's shoulder, then went to look into the room.

His face went gray and he staggered back, stricken by the same shock as Ellie. Maeve exchanged a glance with Lorna. Then they viewed the room together.

The walls were the same pale shade of yellow as those of Caldwell Street and were specked with hardened Blu Tack. A large wooden wardrobe, angled to the right from a missing leg, leaned against one wall, and empty Chicken Cottage boxes littered the floor. A Bon Jovi poster was taped above a box-spring bed.

This was Hollis's old bedroom, a near-exact replica. The only difference was the position of the opened window, the curtain wet and blowing from the rain. But this wasn't what had Oliver dry-retching or Ellie muttering to herself. It was what lay on the bed.

They didn't need to check if he was alive. Half his skull was caved in. Blood drenched the entire left side of his face down to the collar of his yellow jacket.

"Hollis," Maeve whispered. His clouded right eye stared at her, and Maeve couldn't look anymore.

Lorna stepped closer.

"What are you doing?" Oliver asked from the hallway.

But Maeve didn't need to ask. By Hollis's head was a card in one of Callum's blue envelopes. Lorna plucked it from the mattress, then pulled Maeve out into the hall and shut the door behind them. Both of them sank to the floor, where Oliver and Ellie had already found themselves. When Oliver saw what Lorna had, he started shaking his head.

"Don't," Oliver said. "Don't open it. Lorna."

But she did anyway.

> You try to leave when it's too soon,
> you'll die like Hollis in your room.
> Someone murdered Callum dear.
> Till they confess, you're all stuck here.

Pp. 35–45

but they had to go and make things harder than they needed to be. Honestly, I shouldn't have been surprised. I mean, this is how they've always been. I just had to keep telling myself it wasn't my fault. Because it's not. They're here because of their choices, even if they didn't see it that way. They've never been able to see things for what they were. That was never more obvious than in December 1994, and what happened after.

The pale blue envelope lay flat on the dark green carpet in front of the closed door. From Maeve's position—sprawled belly-down on the bed, the side of her face pressed into the scratchy pillowcase—it looked like someone had taken a penknife and cut a perfect square from the carpet.

Maeve didn't need a note to remind her of last night. Every time she closed her eyes, the memories played back as clearly as watching a rerun on TV. Her empty stomach protested her inaction, but moving remained impossible. The rooms around her were as quiet as her own. An apocalypse morning, she called it, when long moments passed without the sound of another human being and she could imagine she was the only person left alive. The last had occurred over the summer, when Max had been at a sleepover and her parents visiting friends in Leeds. Maeve used to love the peace and quiet of apocalypse mornings, but having one at a house like Caldwell Street was unnatural.

Brisk footsteps sounded up the stairs and disappeared behind the click of a door—Ellie's or Hollis's. Though quiet, they were enough to break the morning's spell. Or afternoon's, rather, for when she looked at her clock, the hour hand pointed almost to the one. She shot out of bed. She never slept this late, and it made her feel even more lazy and useless than usual. But Caldwell Street did that. They all knew it. It drew you into this world where every fault was amplified and every feeling—good or bad—became thrice what it would be elsewhere.

Maeve slid out of the low bed, one foot warm in its sock, the other bare and cold. She ignored the envelope as she threw on an old hoodie and hunted for a fresh pair of socks, but the envelope would not let her be. She wanted to step on it as she walked to the door, even hovered her foot over it, but she couldn't bring herself to do it. Sitting cross-legged on the carpet, she opened the flap.

I had a great time. You looked really fine. (That's a bad rhyme.) But I had a lot of fun. What do you say to another one?

Maeve read it a few times, then slid the card back into the envelope, sick from her memories of last night. There had been drinks, laughing, his thumb sweeping over the back of her hand as they huddled together in the booth at the club. She tucked the envelope into the front pouch of her hoodie. She needed breakfast. Or lunch. Once she had some food in her, she'd be able to think about this more clearly. But when she reached the first landing, she collided with Callum as he was leaving his room.

"Maeve! Sorry!"

"Hi." She cringed when she saw they were dressed alike: plaid pajama bottoms and red hoodies.

"Sleep well?" he asked.

"Oh yeah. No problem. You?" She bit her lower lip at how awkward the question sounded.

"Sort of? Actually, I had this really weird dream that I was doing an internship for some botanical gardens or something out in the country? And we had no power and I kept having to fill in these holes with cement?"

"That's weird."

"Yeah. Do you think it means anything?"

She shrugged. "You're not meant to be a gardener?"

He laughed, and her face got hot because it was a sweet laugh. An honest one. And then she was laughing with him, and some of the weight from that morning lifted away.

"Are you hungry?" he asked. "I was going to grab a quick shower then get something to eat? That café by the train station has surprisingly good fry-ups, and they don't charge for refills on coffee. Want to give it a go?" He fiddled with the cuff of his sleeve, his pale skin turning a shade of pink, which became darker when his eye caught the corner of the blue envelope peeking out from Maeve's pocket. Maeve's doubt crept up inside her, but she swallowed it back down.

"Yeah, sure. You're going to shower first? I'll have time to get changed."

"Or we could go like this?" He laughed, then stopped. "That's a joke. It was a joke. I really do need to shower. I stink from last night." He blushed. "You don't. Just me. You're fine. You look fine." He glanced at the envelope and winced.

"I'll meet you downstairs," she said.

"Great!"

"Great."

They nodded like two strangers who'd been discussing the weather and had run out of things to say.

"Right. Shower." Callum hurried to the bathroom.

"See you."

The bathroom door closed, and Maeve winced again at how stupid she sounded before retreating back upstairs to her bedroom.

Maeve's heavy footsteps might have been what woke Oliver. Or perhaps it was Callum turning on the shower. Either way, one moment he'd been in a dream. The next, he was lying on his mattress, staring up at the water-damaged ceiling. The waking had been so abrupt, he couldn't recall anything about the dream other than an impending sense of dread, and he knew then why he'd woken.

She was going to call.

He listened to the shower running in the bathroom next door, the groan of the pipes the loudest in his room, and told himself this time it would be different. This time when she called, he'd stick to his word. He wouldn't come running.

The phone rang. He fumbled down the stairs and picked up the receiver on the fifth ring.

"Yeah?"

He heard her voice, the baby crying in the background.

"Mum, I can't . . . Mum, I have a final exam . . . Then get your husband to—"

Her answer did not surprise him. He rubbed his thigh, pain springing from his knee and traveling the familiar route to his hip.

"I'll see what I can do . . . Yeah, you too."

The phone's shrill ring stirred the rest of the house. Once he hung up, a steady cacophony of footsteps, random thumps, drawers opening and closing echoed between the walls like an orchestra warming up. When Oliver returned upstairs, the shower had stopped. He ran his fingers through his hair, rubbed his itching eyes, and knocked on Callum's door. No one answered, and he tried again. The third time, the bathroom door swung open, and Callum appeared in only a towel.

"Callum! Exactly who I wanted to see."

"Oh! Oliver. Um . . . Let me get dressed and I can—"

"Don't worry about it, mate. Come on. Let's go to your room. I have a quick question for you. You work in the records office, yeah?"

Lorna remembered this day as the first—and, she pledged, the last—she ever experienced a hangover. Her head pounded, her mouth was dry, and her stomach couldn't decide if it wanted to intake food or expel it. Little comfort could be taken from the knowledge that she hadn't done or said anything ridiculous, but she was an idiot for not sticking to her own golden rules: three drinks max, a glass of water before bed, no befriending strangers at Oliver's parties. But the stress of her courses, particularly her incompetent media prof who detested anyone who detested Ayn Rand, had made her let her guard down.

She stumbled down into the front room, kicked over a stack of empty Carling cans, and woke a red-eyed stranger crashing on the sofa. The boy muttered something about his mum as Lorna got him to his feet and shoved him out the door. As she started collecting the cans, she remembered the girl she'd been flirting with. God, had she been flirting? She'd put a hand on the girl's knee and leaned into her side. The girl hadn't even been that pretty and all she talked about was Oasis. Lorna dumped the cans in the metal bin out back where they clattered like a broken wind chime. She wanted to pour a big glass of juice and sneak back up to her room to work on one of the three papers she had due on Thursday, but by the time she filled her cup, she only had strength enough to sit.

A muffled argument sounded upstairs, but before she could discern anything more, Maeve shuffled into the kitchen, an envelope in her hands. She looked surprised to see Lorna but recovered quickly.

"Some night last night, was it?" Maeve asked.

Lorna took a sip of orange juice and grimaced. "I wished you would've been there. You would've stopped me from that fifth . . . what was it? Vodka and Coke?"

"Pepsi, looks like." Maeve picked up an empty two-liter bottle from the floor and set it on the counter. "But it does you good to act like a normal person every once in a while."

"I am a normal person." Lorna eyed the card. "How was your night then?"

Maeve hid her face. "Fine."

"What time did you and Callum get in?"

"Later. God! It was nothing. Neither of us wanted to go to Oliver's stupid party, so we went to a film and stopped for some drinks afterward and why are you looking at me like that?" The envelope crinkled in her hand.

"Looking at you like what?" Lorna hid her grin behind her glass.

"It wasn't a date. Nothing happened. Stop making a deal about it."

"I'm not making a deal about anything."

"Yes, you are. And I don't want to talk about it."

"Then why are you carrying around that card for everyone to see?"

Maeve glanced at her hands as if surprised to see the card there. She waffled a bit, looking out the kitchen doorway, then to the card, then to Lorna. With a sigh, she sat down at the table and handed over the card. "Why would he write a note? What kind of guy does that? It's like last night was one of his stupid Happy Wednesday gifts for . . . for fuck's sake."

"Is this supposed to be a limerick?"

"It's not funny!"

Lorna slid the card back across the table. "It is sweet, though."

Maeve looked at the card as if it might leap off the table and bite her—or worse, kiss her.

"Maeve, do you really not like him?"

Before she could answer, Ellie appeared in the doorway, and Maeve swiped the card off the table.

Maeve needn't have worried. Ellie hardly noticed the pair of them, let alone what was on the table. She slipped into the kitchen like a wisp of lace blowing in the wind, one hand pressed to her stomach as she searched the fridge. Though she stared into it, she could not see what she was looking for. Lorna's voice jarred her.

"Hey, Ellie. Want some juice?"

There on the table was the juice carton, and sitting at the table were Lorna and Maeve, who looked at Ellie as if she had something on her face. Ellie wiped a hand across her cheek in case she did.

"Oh yes. Thank you."

"Did you have a good time last night?"

Why couldn't they leave her alone?

"Yes, I had a lovely time, thank you." She chose a clean glass from the cupboard, poured half a glass of juice, and drank it without stopping. She hoped it would fill her up, but it disappeared somewhere into the vacant space that had taken possession of her body. She didn't want them to speak, but nor could she bear the silence. Noises upstairs brought her peace—shouting and the slamming of a door.

"*Some friend you are!*"

Oliver's voice made her hand tremble. She poured another glass to distract herself.

"All right, ladies?"

Ellie was proud of herself for not choking on her juice when Oliver appeared. Lorna and Maeve each muttered a greeting as he stepped around Ellie to grab a can of Pepsi. This was silly. She was being silly. All she had to do was ask. What harm was there in asking? She picked at a loose thread on her shirt and tried to keep her voice cheerful.

"Oliver, could I talk to you?"

He yawned and wiped his nose with the back of his hand. "Hm? What? Oh, sorry, got to pack. Mum's expecting me home by five." He cracked open the can and took a long drink. Ellie wanted to ask again, but Maeve's voice overtook hers.

"Don't you have one more exam tomorrow? You said I could help you study. *Hamlet* is so my thing, remember?" She twirled a single lock of frizzy hair.

"Maeve," Lorna snapped and nodded to the front room.

"What?"

"I need you in the other room, please. Now."

Chairs squeaked as Lorna and Maeve pushed themselves away from the table. Ellie watched them go, torn between wanting them to stay and never wanting to see any of them ever again, including Callum, who had appeared from nowhere to greet them outside the kitchen door, his camera around his neck. He glanced at Oliver, then hurried through the kitchen and out into the back garden without a word.

Ellie smoothed her shirt and tried again. "Don't you have that exam?"

Oliver shrugged. "I'm skipping it."

"Can you do that?" she asked.

"I'll work out a deal. Just have to grease a few palms, and uni is smoother sailing than a hot dog in a whore's vagina. You should try it."

"Um . . . No, thank you."

"Suit yourself." He finished the soda and left the empty can on the counter. Ellie, after some hesitation, followed him upstairs.

Clothes and empty beer cans were strewn all over his floor. Sticky tissues and empty soda bottles filled the wire bin in the corner. If the room had a distinct odor, she could no longer tell. In four short months, they'd become accustomed to it. Though the door was open, Ellie knocked. Oliver continued shoving clothes—dirty and clean—into a gym bag. She kept her toes at the carpet line, as close as she could stand without entering.

"I don't want to bother you."

He didn't say anything.

"I was wondering if we could talk."

"I'll have loads of time when we're back from Christmas break."

"But . . . no. We need to talk. Now."

He laughed.

"It's not funny, Oliver."

He dropped a shirt and stalked to the doorway. "You think because we fooled around a bit, suddenly you own me?"

"No! No, that's not it at all."

"Then what's your problem, love?"

Her hands shook, and she smoothed her shirt again, though there were no wrinkles. "I only wanted to know what happened last night."

"If you were too drunk to remember, that's not my problem, is it?"

She tried to say something more, but no words would come. She ran back downstairs in tears.

Out in the garden, shivering in the December air, Ellie took a seat in the broken lawn chair, feeling it creak and sink under her weight.

"All right?"

Callum startled her. She hadn't noticed him standing in the corner by the house, camera in hand. He looked so calm, the concern in his eyes eating away at her resolve. Ellie's smile kept faltering, like a radio station you couldn't quite tune in.

"It's nothing. Really. I'm being silly, as always."

Callum crossed the patio and sat in the chair beside her. "Not my business, but Oliver can be an ass sometimes. He really isn't worth getting upset over."

"I know. Stupid girl. I, well, all I want to know is sort of exactly what went on last night and then I can—"

"Wait. What do you mean what went on?"

"Oh, I can't quite remember, that's all." Her laugh was a harsh and brittle thing. "I was drinking. A lot, I think. And last I remember we were on the couch, and then this morning when I woke up in his . . ." She shook her head. "I'm sorry, Callum. If I hadn't been drinking so much . . ."

Callum stormed into the house in time to see Oliver hefting his kit bag out the front door. He grabbed the bag and pushed Oliver into the wall.

"What the—"

"Did you take advantage of her?"

Oliver eyed Ellie across the room and tried to laugh it off. "Take advantage? What is this, the 1950s?"

Callum slammed him into the wall again. Other faces appeared as witness, but no one approached.

"Tell the truth."

"Fine. The truth is we were both drunk."

"But you remember, don't you?"

"Callum." Ellie spoke from the corner by the closet under the stairs, slipping in when no one had seen. "It's okay, Callum. Leave him alone. It's not a big deal."

"Yeah, Callum." Oliver smiled. "It's not a big deal."

Callum glared, then released him with a shove.

"Cheers, mate. Happy Christmas." Oliver scooped up his bag and skirted out the front door, leaving behind the tension he'd created.

In the hall by the spare room, Maeve sighed and rested her head on the doorframe. "I wouldn't mind Oliver taking advantage of me."

"Are you fucking serious?" Lorna asked. "You think it's fine for a guy to feel you up—or worse—while you're drunk?"

"Depends on the guy."

"You mean depends if it's Oliver."

"Don't get so defensive, Lorna. I only made a comment."

"I'm being defensive? Do you even know what the word means?"

"Why do you always have to be so rude?" Maeve stomped into the now vacant kitchen and tore into the fridge, desperate for something to eat.

"I'm not being rude. I just don't condone sexual assault."

"Please don't shout." Ellie appeared in the doorway, rubbing her hands together. "It was nothing, Lorna, really."

"See?" said Maeve.

"It wasn't nothing! God, why can't you all see that?"

"I don't know why you're so upset," Maeve said. "Nothing happened to you. Or maybe you're just cross because you never get any."

Lorna tossed her used glass into the sink. Orange juice splattered the wall. "I thought you . . . never mind. Okay? Never mind." She pushed past Ellie into the living room, her path blocked by Callum.

"Lorna," he said, "I'm with you. What Oliver did—"

"This isn't about you, Callum."

Once upstairs, Lorna slammed her door and turned on her music, though it didn't fill the bloated silence that formed between Maeve and Ellie.

"Uhm," Maeve stuttered. "There's one more slice of pizza, if you want it. If you're hungry."

"Hm? Oh. No, thank you."

Maeve should have asked if Ellie was all right, but Maeve never said what she should have. On that day, at that moment, she should've apologized and said Lorna was right, her comments were crass and inappropriate. But the words were trapped in her head, unable to find a way out. Or maybe she didn't try hard enough. What she did do was heat up the leftover pizza.

In the living room, Callum fiddled with his camera strap, his face blushing red from anger, fading into blotches like wine stains. "So, Maeve, we headed for that fry-up?"

"I don't want a stupid fry-up, Callum. God." Her heavy footsteps pounded up the stairs.

Ellie passed through soon after.

"Hey Ellie, if you need anything . . ."

"I'm fine, Callum." She continued up the stairs without stopping. "Have a happy Christmas if I don't see you." But the words were remote, robotic, like her movement up the stairs.

Callum returned to the back garden where Hollis had now appeared, leaning against the house, smoking another cigarette. Callum stood beside him, and they stared out at the leaning, rotted fence, listening to the traffic in the distance and a dog barking nearby.

"Did I miss something?" Hollis asked.

A bitter wind sliced through the clear day, and Callum shuddered. Hollis didn't seem to notice the cold.

Callum nodded to the cigarette. "At this rate, you'll have cancer by your thirties." He laughed. Hollis stared at him. "Sorry."

Hollis offered the pack. Callum reached for one, then withdrew his hand.

"No, I shouldn't. Mum will smell it on me a mile off. So, last night. Some party?" Callum asked.

Hollis shrugged. "Yeah, suppose."

"Shame I missed it."

"Not really." Hollis stubbed the cigarette out in the overflowing bowl-cum-ashtray by the back door, then disappeared into the house, leaving Callum alone outside with the wind and the returning bark of the dog.

Months later, when they found Callum's body, Maeve would say it wasn't her because she didn't remember anything after Oliver and Callum's fight. She didn't stumble out of bed in the middle of the night to use the toilet and hear Callum crying in his bedroom.

Hollis would say it wasn't him because after he helped Maeve to her room, he went straight to bed. He didn't see Callum in the back garden by the fence, wobbling on the broken chair, drinking straight from the bottle.

Ellie would say it wasn't her because she never went downstairs for a glass of water. She never heard Callum vomiting in the front room and never stepped over it to return to her bedroom.

Oliver would say it wasn't him because he had passed out in bed once the music stopped. He hadn't used a purple Sharpie to draw a penis on Callum's face while Callum was passed out, the bruise from their fight swelling to close his right eye.

Lorna would say it wasn't her because she had stayed in her room for the rest of the night. She hadn't been woken by a crash in the hall- way and didn't open her door to see Callum stumbling down the stairs.

Twenty years later, after they found Hollis's body, they remembered how Callum often embodied the emptiness of Caldwell Street, like he some- how became the physical manifestation of the house itself, absorbing their pain and their disagreements as if he could get rid of them or turn them into something better, all of which never happened. What they failed to notice was that this emptiness had found a home in them, and that it had begun to consume them from the inside out.

5

Lorna

Hollis was dead. They had suspected it this morning when he couldn't be found. They had feared it. But they didn't want to believe it. Now, they all knew it. Hollis was dead, and they would have to deal with the consequences. Hollis was dead, and if Hollis could die, any one of them could be next. Lorna stared at the card in her hands and listened to the others.

Maeve, closest to her, kept muttering, "We have to ring the police. We have to ring the police. We have to . . ." Oliver was doubled over, head between his knees, groaning like he had a stomachache. Ellie remained the farthest from them, sitting with her back to the wall and knees pulled to her chest, running a hand over her arm, muttering something only she could understand.

"We have to ring the police," Maeve repeated yet again, her voice bordering on hysteria. "There's been a murder! We *have* to ring them. We have to get them involved. We—"

Oliver crossed the hall and slapped Maeve across the face. She cradled her cheek, apparently too stunned to say more.

"Stop saying that!"

"Oliver!" Lorna cut in.

"We can't contact the police!"

Maeve took a step back, palm pressed to her face. "Why? Because you're the one who killed him?"

Maeve flinched when he raised his hand again, but he did not strike.

"No. I mean we won't be able to reach them. Have you tried using your phone lately? Ellie, what about you?"

Ellie continued her silent conversation with herself.

"I haven't had a reason," Maeve answered. She looked to Lorna for support, but Lorna didn't know what she could say.

"No texts? No emails? No chats with your online boyfriends?"

"That's enough, Oliver. Tell her."

With the air of a father at his breaking point, Oliver explained about the empty box he and Lorna had discovered in the basement.

"We didn't find the jammer," Lorna added. "But my phone's not working and neither is Oliver's."

Maeve pulled out her phone and tapped at the screen. "You're right," she said. "It says the last time my email updated was 5:32 last night."

Oliver folded his arms, his anger giving way to the smug satisfaction he used to wear so well. Trim a few pounds, add a few hairs, and he could be the same cocky son of a bitch he once was. Almost. Age had done too much damage. And there was too much fear in him now, despite how he tried to cover it up with his voice.

"Caskie must have thought we'd ring the police the first chance we got," he said.

"Caskie?" Lorna asked. "You think Caskie killed Hollis?"

"Contrary to popular opinion, Lorna, I'm not as thick as a slice of French bread. Of course I think Caskie did it. This is his house, yes? He has access to every room. Knows the house inside and out, which means he knows where to hide stuff. For example, a dead fucking body. That fucker ruined our cars and murdered our mate and now he's after us."

"Language," Ellie whispered, rising from the floor. Shock had settled on her the longest, and she was only now beginning to shake it.

"Sorry. Look, we all agree we saw a car driving away last night, right? But none of us saw who was in it. And even if it was Caskie, who's to say he didn't come back in the night when we were sleeping? It fits. He crept back in the night, damaged the cars, killed Hollis, and is hiding somewhere waiting to finish us off. Maeve herself said she thought she saw someone."

"I thought I heard someone," Maeve said. She looked again at Lorna, then down at her feet, whatever she wanted to say left unspoken.

"We heard something in the dining room just now, which obviously wasn't Hollis," Lorna added.

"You did?" Maeve asked. "Was it in—"

"Ellie," Lorna interrupted, "can you tell us what happened? Did you see who hurt you?"

"She was by the attic," Maeve said. "We were about to search the attic."

"Thank you, Maeve," Oliver said, "but I think Ellie can speak for herself."

Ellie looked as if she were about to contradict him, but after several shuddering breaths, she managed to speak.

"Maeve's right. I went up to the attic. The door was unlocked, so I went up there to search. But it was very dark. And I couldn't find the light." She closed her eyes and swallowed. Lorna leaned in, as though willing Ellie to speak faster. "I'm not sure what happened next. I bumped into a stack of boxes and then something—someone—leapt at me. Almost pushed me down the stairs. I ran."

"You didn't see what—who—it was?" The anxiety Lorna had felt last night upon her arrival returned. She glanced up and down the hall as if Ellie's attacker might suddenly appear. "Was this before or after Maeve thought she heard something?"

"It must've been after," Maeve said, "Because I heard it before Ellie started screaming. That's why I—"

"And you ended up in this room?" Lorna asked Ellie, interrupting again. Oliver held out a hand, indicating Lorna should take it easy, but she ignored him.

"It was the first door I could open."

"But it wasn't unlocked when you first searched this floor?" Lorna asked.

"I . . . I don't know. Maeve was checking the doors on that side of the hall."

"And Maeve," Lorna said, turning to her, "you were where?"

"Down the hall there." Maeve pointed.

"And that's where you thought you saw someone?"

"Heard someone. And I did hear them. I'm sure of it now."

"But when you first passed this way," Oliver said, "you didn't realize the door was unlocked? You didn't check this room?"

Maeve shrank back, hugging her arms around her waist. "No. I mean, I don't think the door was unlocked. I mean, it could've been. I guess I wasn't really paying attention."

"Convenient, that, don't you think, Lorna? Ellie just happens to be attacked while Maeve's off somewhere else, and Maeve just happens to think she saw someone, and Maeve just happens not to notice an unlocked room with a dead fucking body?"

"This doesn't matter! None of this matters!" Ellie shouted. She grabbed the note card out of Lorna's hand and tore it into pieces. "It was an accident! Callum's death was an accident. Why are we being punished?" She shouted to the ceiling as if someone in the attic would hear her. "It was an accident!"

"We all know that's not true," Lorna whispered.

The silence after she spoke was deafening. She might as well have shot off a gun. The truth they'd blanketed safely beneath so many years of lies had now been aired. Spoken aloud for the first time. They might have all been culpable for some of what happened that night, but only one of them had done the act. Lorna looked at the pieces of the card now scattered on the carpet.

You try to leave when it's too soon, you'll die like Hollis in your room. Someone murdered Callum dear. Till they confess, you're all stuck here.

"Hollis died because he tried to leave," she said.

"Hollis wouldn't do that," Ellie said. "He wouldn't have . . . He's a detective. If he was leaving, it was probably to help us."

"Was a detective," Oliver corrected.

"Shut up!" Lorna took a breath and lowered her voice. "Sorry, Ellie, but Hollis must have tried to leave and that's why he's dead. Not because the blackmailer thought it was him. That he was the one who . . ." She couldn't finish the sentence.

"We don't know either," Maeve said. "We've never known."

Wind gusted against the house, flapping a shutter somewhere nearby. They looked at one another. Lorna knew what they were thinking. Which of them was it? Who had done it? And would that person finally break now that over twenty years had passed? Would they confess? Or would they cling to their secret ever more tightly? Try to throw someone else under the bus? Mistrust flickered from face to face. Then, by some unspoken agreement, they decided now was not the time to cast blame. That might come later, but not now.

When the storm was quiet again, Oliver spoke.

"Let's tell him it was Hollis. It can't do Drummond any harm. Not anymore." He paled, like he knew it was a crass thing to say, even if it was practical.

"Hollis was the one who found him," Ellie said. "And isn't it normally the person who finds the body?"

But Lorna couldn't let Hollis take the blame for something she knew he had not done.

"It wasn't him, though, was it?" she asked, knowing that shifting the blame from Hollis meant she was suspicious of the others. "I mean, I never really thought . . . not him."

No one said anything, but from the looks on their faces they all thought the same.

"Hollis had been in trouble before Caldwell Street," she said, "but he didn't harm anyone to get out of it. There's no reason to think a boy who rescued baby birds and little old ladies and cried when one of his rugby heroes was injured would suddenly escalate to murder."

"It might've been someone else," Ellie said. "Someone else who was there that night. At the party."

Not one of us was left unspoken.

"There's always a chance," Oliver agreed.

They all left it at that and stood there in silence, trying not to glance at one another. Trying not to send an accusatory look in the wrong direction. Right now, there was a bigger enemy to fight.

"Is there a landline?" Lorna asked. "This is an old house. It has to have a landline, doesn't it?"

"I don't know," Oliver said. "Maeve, did you *happen* to see a landline while you were wandering around the house by yourself?"

"Enough." Lorna warned. "I think there's one downstairs at the front desk, near the hotel register. It's possible whoever installed the Wi-Fi jammer also cut the wires, but we should check anyway."

They all agreed with the suggestion, but no one moved. The threat of leaving this hallway was too great. The house had become a giant mousetrap, filled with hidden dangers. The narrow walls on either side gave the illusion of containment, of safety. There was nothing to harm them in this hall. Yet their time here was limited. Eventually, they would have to move, and that time was nearing. The rain and wind picked up. The lights flickered, the house winking at them.

Oliver grabbed a heavy candlestick from a sideboard in the hall and handed it to Lorna, then gave the matching one to Ellie. He pulled open a drawer and rummaged around until he extracted what looked like a stone paperweight and tossed it to Maeve, who jumped back in fright, then bent down to pick it up. For himself, Oliver chose a smaller metal candle holder that had a bit of weight at the base.

"We'll go downstairs together," he said, looking each of them in the eye. "Slowly. Keep your eyes open for anything. Don't hesitate to strike. But try to keep Caskie alive. I have a few questions I'd like to ask first."

"God," sighed Lorna. "When did my life turn into a game of Clue?"

The comment slipped out before she could stop it. No one laughed, and she knew she shouldn't have spoken. Like too many other things in her life, she couldn't take it back.

Ellie

Their shoes against the hallway carpet sounded louder than shattering china. Several times, Oliver stopped and pressed a finger to his lips. He'd cock his head to the side and then wave them forward. The curves of the silver candlestick dug into Ellie's palm as the sleeve of her jumper rubbed against the scratches on her arm. This would be heavy enough to crack open the skull of whoever had attacked her. She could still feel the nails on her skin. The hot breath on her cheek as she'd torn herself away. One false step down those attic stairs and she would've become like Hollis, her head bleeding out on the floor. She pictured Mr. Caskie standing over her, smiling as he watched her die, and wished she could scratch his eyes out.

Approaching the great red staircase was like walking into an open wound. Ellie stared across the upper landing to the other wing, watching for Mr. Caskie to appear.

But no one came. What was visible of the foyer remained empty.

They hesitated at the top of the stairs for what seemed too long a time, no one saying a word. Their panicked selves from moments ago had been left outside Hollis's door. If they retraced their steps, Ellie knew they would see themselves trapped in time, crying and screaming. They were hollow copies now. Empty shells propelled onward on nothing more than some primal instinct to survive.

Oliver finally moved them onward. Two by two they traveled down the two flights of stairs, Oliver and Ellie in front, Lorna with Maeve behind, every step taken with caution. When they reached the foyer, they huddled together like a pack of frightened animals. Oliver scanned the room's corners, then placed his hand at the small of Maeve's back and pushed her forward.

"Go on, then. Check it," he said.

"What? Why me? Why can't we all go over there together?"

While the front desk was visible, someone could easily be hiding behind. Maeve looked to Lorna and then Ellie for help, but they said nothing. Oliver had singled Maeve out, and Ellie wouldn't interfere. The group meant safety, and Ellie would do whatever was necessary to remain safe.

Maeve, realizing she wasn't receiving any support, detached from their huddle, gripping her stone paperweight above her head, ready to strike. Her feet stumbled on the final steps.

A shout.

Ellie flinched, but Maeve lowered the paperweight.

"He's not here," she said. A little laugh escaped, a shudder of nerves.

"Brilliant," said Oliver. "The phone?"

"Right." Maeve reached for it with the same hand that held the paperweight, winced, and set the weight aside.

Ellie held her breath. Caskie couldn't have forgotten about the landline, could he? As Maeve lifted the receiver, hope wedged its way into her like a sliver of glass. If the landline worked, it wouldn't matter that the Wi-Fi and cellular signals had been blocked.

Maeve set the phone down and frowned, an expression reminiscent of Ellie's mother-in-law's French bulldog.

"No dial tone," she said.

"Did anyone notice any other phones in the house?" Lorna asked.

"Probably wouldn't matter," said Oliver. "More likely than not he cut the main line."

"How far does the jammer block the signal?" Lorna asked. "Didn't the box say a hundred meters? We can walk that far, get a signal."

"If there's a signal to be had," Oliver said. "The moment I drove off that ferry, I lost service. I think there's one cell tower that serves this entire bloody island, and in this weather?"

As if on cue, a gust of wind blew against the house. The lights flickered again.

Maeve threw up her hands. "So we can't phone the police or anything. And our cars are buggered so we can't go anywhere."

"Who says we can't go anywhere?" A rain jacket hung on a coatrack by the door. Oliver grabbed it and slipped it on. "We've got legs, don't we? Lorna was right about the walking. Even if we can't catch a signal, maybe we can catch a boat."

"You want to walk to the quay?" Lorna asked. "That's miles away. We'll never make it there before the last ferry."

"We'll make it there in time for some ferry. If not today then tomorrow."

"You'd stand out there all night? In this?"

Rain lashed the windows.

"It's better than staying here with a fucking psychopath! You think Caskie hasn't planned this all out? He's probably waiting, just waiting, to do us like he did Hollis."

"You saw the note," Ellie said. "We're not supposed to leave. If we leave, he'll kill us."

"And maybe no matter what we do, he'll kill us anyway because that's been his plan all along."

"But I still don't understand," Maeve said. "Mr. Caskie is half our age. What could he possibly have to do with Caldwell Street? With us? With any of it?"

"I don't plan on sticking around to find out," Oliver said. No one moved. "Come on. A stormy night? A creepy house with a psycho killer? I've seen this film, and I'm not keen to stick around for the ending."

The rain marked the time as the fear they thought they'd left upstairs wove its way down to them. Oliver looked at each of them, and Ellie knew that no matter how much he wanted to leave, he wouldn't go alone. He needed a group, a following. For all his talk, someone else needed to give him the final push, like they had with Callum all those years ago.

"Caskie has what he needs to blackmail us," Ellie said. "If we leave, maybe he can't kill us, but he'll hurt us in other ways."

"So that's it then?" Oliver asked. "You want to give in? Ruin the rest of your life?"

"No. I don't know." She closed her eyes and shook her head.

"Because I didn't do anything wrong that night. I have nothing to confess."

Ellie cleared her throat. "You hit him first."

Oliver's eyes raged like the storm outside. He pointed at Ellie.

"Fuck you."

He pointed at Lorna. "And you."

He pointed at Maeve. "And you. What Caskie's got on me, it's not as bad as a murder charge. Maybe you can't say the same, but I'm willing to take my chances."

He threw up the hood of the raincoat, his steps like thunder across the floor. He turned the doorknob and yanked.

And yanked.

And yanked.

"Open up," Oliver whispered fiercely. "Open. Up."

He kicked the door. "Open up!"

It held firm.

"Caskie, you fucker!"

He beat on it—Ellie remembering the damage his fists could do—then stormed into the dining room, where they heard him smashing chairs and clawing at windows. He returned to reception, knuckles bloodied, and then he was gone, across to the study.

"We have to get away from him," Lorna whispered. "You know happens when he—"

"Piece of shit!"

The sound of splintered wood exploded from the study.

Maeve ducked, though there was nothing to avoid.

"Where are we supposed to go?" Maeve asked. "We're locked in a house with a bloody tornado."

"Fuck you! Open up!"

"Lorna's right," Ellie said. "Even if we can't get out, we need to find a safe place to hide until he calms down."

"God fucker piece of—"

Another crash.

"I'm not going back upstairs," Maeve said.

"The back of the house. This way." Ellie pointed to the passage that led beneath the main staircase. "Maybe there's a place back here we can use."

Oliver's anger was tearing apart the group that had protected Ellie. Now Caskie seemed the lesser of the two evils. Maybe she could find a way to say what he wanted her to say. Or at least give him enough of the others so she wouldn't have to give herself. After all, she must've been special, or else the others would know as much as she did, wouldn't they?

"I'll kill you, you fucking bastard!"

While Lorna and Maeve hurried down the back passage, Ellie lingered by the staircase. Caskie was probably somewhere upstairs. She could find him before the others. Make a deal. Return to David and the children before anyone realized she was missing. Return while Caskie did to them whatever needed to be done. She placed one foot on the staircase.

Oliver

"I'll kill you, you fucking bastard!"

Oliver threw one last barstool, then staggered back against the wall. His chest burned and a hoarse cough wracked his chest. He spat a glob of mucus into a potted plant and rested his hands on his knees, examining his bloodied knuckles as he tried to regain his breath. His anger—at Hollis, at Caskie, at Wolfheather House—continued to rage inside his head, but his body could no longer keep up. The anger turned inward, at his own stupidity for coming here in the first place. But before self-pity could overtake him, the girls screamed.

Oliver ran into the foyer, face red and flushed, wondering which one would be dead, but all three of them were alive, standing and staring at something on the floor. Ellie noticed him first and stepped aside.

It didn't register at first, what it was. When he tried to speak, he was out of breath and had to take a big gulp of air before he could ask.

"Who the fuck is that?"

Ellie, paler than usual; Lorna, shaking hands betraying her steely glare; Maeve, chewing on the cuff of her jumper—none answered. And neither did the body on the floor.

The dead old man wore a green parka, mostly dry. His eyes were open, glassy and tinged red from broken blood vessels. His mouth gaping, a glob of dried spit on his chin.

"Any of you seen him before?" Oliver asked.

Each shook her head no.

"Just what we need. Another fucking body." What remained of his chaotic rage narrowed to a pinpoint of focused anger, spurring him to action. Oliver knelt beside the man and pulled down the collar of the plaid shirt underneath the parka. A red-purple ring circled his neck, but whatever had been used to strangle him had been taken away. Oliver placed the back of his hand against the man's cheek.

"He's cold." He lifted the arm and set it back down. "But not stiff. And he doesn't smell. So rigor mortis hasn't set in yet. He's been dead less than two or three hours."

"And what makes you a forensics expert all of a sudden?" The waver in Lorna's voice belied the courage in her words.

"Mum watches a lot of *Forensic Files*. Like, a shit ton."

"He's right," Ellie said. "My daughter was studying the stages of decomposition for her GCSEs. Jilly was asking her tutor all sorts of morbid questions."

Oliver checked the man's pockets but found no keys. There was, however, a driving license.

"Dugal MacLeod," he read.

"Caskie's missing caretaker?" Lorna asked.

"Not missing anymore. His jeans are damp. It can't have been that long ago that he was outside." Not wanting to touch the dead man again, he tossed the ID onto the floor.

"Caskie seemed genuinely angry yesterday that the caretaker wasn't here," Lorna said. "What if he's innocent after all? He left like we thought and MacLeod came back here to take care of us for the weekend."

"The fire," Ellie said. "Mr. MacLeod must've relit the fire this morning. And why would he do that unless he really was here to look after us and the house?"

"This where you found him?" Oliver pointed to the open room beside them.

"He fell out," Ellie said. "He just . . . fell out when the door was opened."

What might have once been an office now served as a large storage area. Cardboard and plastic boxes. Mops and buckets. Tins of paint. Bins. There was another door on the opposite side of the room. Oliver tried to open it, but it was locked. He left the junk room and returned to the others, who had started arguing.

"Maybe Hollis killed him?" Ellie asked. "Or he and Hollis killed each other?"

Lorna shook her head. "And then what? Hollis staggers up the stairs with half his head missing, somehow not leaving any blood trail? Then places a note card on his own chest—again without leaving any blood on it—before he dies?"

"There's only one thing we can be certain of," Oliver said. "If Hollis killed MacLeod, then someone else killed Hollis. And if it was MacLeod who killed Hollis, then someone else killed MacLeod."

"Either way," Ellie realized, "it means there's someone else in this house."

"Caskie's letter," Lorna said. "Remember? In the letter, Caskie said those gifts were left by our benefactor."

"But who is that?" Ellis asked.

"Maybe someone who's been hiding here the whole time," Oliver said. "Or someone standing here, who hasn't been telling the truth."

The distrust returned and rippled through them all. He saw it in the way they moved away from one another. In the way their eyes darted from one person to the next. In the way they tensed their muscles and folded their arms. Where upstairs they had been united, now they had splintered apart.

"Who opened the door?" he asked.

He watched them as he waited for an answer. Waited to see which way the wind blew. And he couldn't say he was surprised when Lorna and Ellie both turned toward Maeve, who, Oliver realized, had yet to speak.

"Why did you open the door, Maeve?"

Maeve's hand fluttered to her neck, and she blinked several times before answering. "I was looking for another way out. We all were."

"Tell me again why you were down here when you were supposed to be upstairs with Ellie."

"I don't know how many times you want me to repeat it. I was looking for the attic key. I mean I heard something. Someone." Maeve backed away.

"Which was it? You were looking for the attic key or you heard something? And how did you hear something down here from all the way on the top floor?"

"I didn't. I mean I did hear something. But I was mostly looking for the keys. Why are you asking me all these questions?"

"Why are you getting so defensive?"

"I'm not being defensive! You're . . . you're being aggressive. I swear I had nothing to do with this. With him. Lorna, you believe me, don't you?"

"She admitted to Facebook stalking me," Ellie said. "All of us."

They circled Maeve, corralling her against the staircase.

"Wait. You're twisting my words. I never said I stalked you. I said I looked you up sometimes. That's all. And what does that have to do with a body that just fell on me?" Her voice pitched higher on each word. Lorna stepped close and squeezed Maeve's shoulder.

"Take a breath, Maeve. I know you're upset. Just tell us what really happened. We'll understand. I'll understand."

Maeve looked as if Lorna had stuck her with a knife. "What do you mean, what happened?"

"If this was self-defense . . ."

Maeve jerked away from Lorna. "I didn't kill that man! Why are you accusing me, Lorna?"

"You left me alone," Ellie answered.

"You were downstairs when you weren't supposed to be," Oliver said.

"And you found this poor man's body," said Lorna.

"And you were so mad at Callum that night," Oliver continued. "Madder than the rest of us. You were the one who—"

"Don't. Don't you dare bring Callum into this. I never hurt Callum. You know I didn't. And this man? I've never seen him before in my life. Besides, if I had killed him, why would I open that door in the first place? That's insane. I would try to hide it, not . . . not . . ." She wiped away tears with the back of her hand.

"Why don't you tell us more about why you came here this weekend?" Oliver asked.

"Oh, so you can humiliate me further? I told you all last night. I thought I was meeting my boyfriend."

"Right. Your online boyfriend. A believable story coming from you. Maybe a little too believable? Fits you a little too nicely?"

"It's believable because it's true. His name is Tom. He's fifty-one, and he lives in Inverness and—"

"Then why not meet in Inverness?"

"Because he thought this would be more romantic. He said he knew this house. He'd stayed here before." She was blubbering now, tears falling too fast to wipe away.

"And you fell for it? Come on, Maeve. Isn't there something else? Something you don't want to tell us?"

"That I'm an idiot? A gullible forty-year-old fat lady who tried online dating and got screwed?" She wiped her sleeve across her eyes. "Do you really think I could strangle a man? Me?"

"Why not ask Callum what you're capable of? Oh, that's right. He's dead."

Her wet cow eyes fixed on Oliver. "Oliver, I wouldn't hurt you. I wouldn't hurt any of you. You are, you were, my friends. I care about each of you. That's the only reason why I looked you up. I missed you. Lorna, you know I—"

He grabbed her by the arm.

"Please! Oliver, I swear I wouldn't hurt you. I couldn't. I—"

Oliver tightened his grip, but in the struggle, Maeve's oversized jumper caught on the corner of the banister. As she fought to free herself, a stack of cards fell from her pockets. Oliver scooped them up before she could get them.

"What do we have here?"

"Give those back! Those are personal!" She grabbed for them, but he held them out of reach.

"We know how much our benefactor loves note cards. Oh, and these are laminated! How posh. Let's see what they say. *Accept the kindness of others. Be strong, stay strong.* Oh, this is a good one. *You're a good person. People like you.* What kind of self-help bullshit is this?" He laughed. "So what else do you have in your pockets, eh?"

"Nothing!"

He grabbed her again.

"Stop touching me!"

And pulled a long, thick piece of twine from her pocket.

"What's this for, Maeve?"

Then he saw the specks of red where the rough twine had cut into MacLeod's neck as he was strangled. As Maeve had strangled him.

He looked at Ellie. He looked at Lorna. Then they all looked at Maeve.

"I . . . I don't know," she said. "I've never seen it before. I don't know how it got there, I swear."

Oliver took three steps back and knelt by MacLeod's body. He held the twine against the marks on the neck. It matched.

"So," he said. "Did you suffocate Callum, too?"

But Maeve was already running up the stairs.

Maeve

The smooth cards slipped from her fingers, leaving a trail like breadcrumbs. Maeve knew she should let them go, but she couldn't. Not yet. She managed to stuff the ones that were left into the pocket of her jeans and keep running. She wasn't sure where she was in the house. She had gone upstairs, but one flight or two? All the halls looked the same. It hadn't been far, but her lungs were burning. When was the last time she'd gone jogging? Sometime in her thirties with Bev, who lived next door during that brief stint in Birmingham.

Their voices sounded on the stairs.

This wasn't the time to be thinking about Birmingham.

She tried the door nearest to her, which turned out to be a linen closet. She shut it and tried another. A guest room. She slipped inside and closed the door as quietly as she could. Her first thought was to hide under the bed. And maybe she could have when she was younger, but the years had added another layer of padding barely concealed by a John Lewis jumper. So she went into the bathroom and hid behind the door. The floor was cold and hard beneath her, but she didn't dare move, not until the sounds quieted outside. She tried to calm down, tell herself this was like playing hide-and-seek with her niece and nephew. All she had to do was sit very quietly until those searching got bored and forgot about her. But she wouldn't emerge to find this pack of animals watching *Teletubbies*.

That's what they had transformed into again: the pack. Ravenous, rabid animals that would do anything to protect themselves, including attacking one of their own. Someone had called them that to their faces once. It had been in the spring because she could remember the rain and the green leaves outside. Who had said it, she couldn't recall. Possibly Lorna or one of the hundreds of girls Oliver brought around during those months. Or had it been Callum? It didn't matter. The pack had returned and singled her out as the weak link, the easy target, and they would stop at nothing until they had trapped her, and once they had . . .

Maeve lowered her head to her knees. She didn't want to think about what would happen, but now that the thought had entered her mind, her anxiety wouldn't let it go. Nervous energy filled her like bubbles in a shaken soda bottle, and the breathing exercises her therapist taught her weren't working. She pictured Hollis's body—his head split open, a piece of his skull missing, the pink-gray color of his exposed brain—and imagined her own cracked head lying beside his. How had a piece of twine she'd never seen before ended up in her pocket? How did a man who wasn't supposed to die turn up dead?

Crouched in the bathroom, she bit her knuckle to muffle the sound of her crying as footsteps ran back and forth in the hall. Doors slammed. Once someone shouted, but the shout came to nothing and eventually Maeve heard nothing more. How long she'd been sitting there she couldn't tell. Minutes? Hours? Long enough that her bum had gone numb and her right foot had fallen asleep. Pins and needles shot up her leg when she stood, but she stopped herself from crying out.

She hopped from the bathroom to the bedroom on one foot, shaking her leg as she went. With some relief, she lay back on the firm mattress. Her body wanted sleep, and she wanted to give in, but how long would this room remain safe? If she were at home—at Max's home—she would be in bed, watching an afternoon documentary on the little television Max and his wife moved in for her from her nephew's bedroom. Maybe with some popcorn and a glass of wine, the taste of which she was teaching herself to enjoy because that was what adult women were supposed to drink.

Her eyes closed against her will, her body sinking into the mattress, and she wondered if it even mattered if they found her. Why not let them take care of things once and for all? Twenty-three years was a long time. Twenty-three years Callum had lain in his grave. She remembered how they used to lie next to each other on the floor of her bedroom, staring up the ceiling, pretending the stains were stars. They'd talk about how much of a dick Oliver was being that day, plans for the weekend, where they saw their lives headed after university. It used to calm her before an exam or after an argument with her mum. Callum would reach out his hand. Sometimes she'd take it. More often, she didn't.

Her chest rose and fell, the tears drying on her face as the memory passed her by, and she took a deep breath.

Lavender.

Maeve opened her eyes. She hadn't imagined it. The room smelled strongly of lavender. Bottles of perfumes, lotions, and air freshening sprays lined the back of the desk. A silk nightgown lay folded on the seat of the armchair. A silver suitcase stood in the corner of the room. Maeve read its tag:

Eleanor Landon

"Shit."

She slapped a hand over her mouth and hoped no one had heard her. Of all the rooms she could have stumbled into, it had to be Ellie's.

Shit shit shit, she mouthed and tugged at her hair. If they got tired of the hunt, if Ellie said she needed to lie down for a little while . . . At any moment that door could open. But was it safe to move? Maybe they'd given up searching. Maybe they were drinking. Maybe they were searching the house for weapons they could use to beat her to death. Buckets to put her different organs in after they tore her apart like a pack of dogs. She bit her cheek to stop the thoughts whirring around her brain and imagined her therapist's words:

Don't overthink. Find a way to relax.

"Relax," she whispered. "Relax, relax, relax. They think you're a murderer and probably want to kill you, but relax."

Something down the hall thumped and Maeve threw herself to the floor. She lay down with an ant's-eye view of the room, afraid to move, and spotted a square white box leaning against the wall beneath the bed with a long cord that was plugged into the electrical outlet. Maeve didn't have Ellie's skinny arms, but she could reach the cord and used it to pull the box toward her. The plastic was warm to the touch, and she turned it over in her hands, trying to figure out what it was. It had no markings or product name but looked sort of like a large Wi-Fi router. Had there been one in her room? Then she remembered the signal jammer.

"Yes!"

If she had time to explain before they attacked, this could be the proof she needed to make the pack turn from her to Ellie. But could she take that risk? Ellie might return to her room at any time. With her anxiety on the rise, Maeve reached for her cards. Only one remained, the most recent from her collection: *Be the shark, not the minnow.*

"Okay," she whispered. "Okay."

She left the jammer plugged in and tiptoed to the door to press her ear against the wood, listening for any sound. Hearing nothing, she opened the door inch by inch.

She peeked into the hall.

Empty.

She left the room, not bothering to close the door.

They probably were in the study, debating what to do next. She would approach them with hands raised, ask for permission to explain, then tell them what she had found in Ellie's room.

From the top of the main staircase, she could see down into reception.

When she listened, she heard voices coming from the study. They were all so predictable.

Two hands shoved her from behind.

The world somersaulted as she tumbled down the stairs. The fall seemed eternal until she stopped, eyes on the undulating ceiling. Her arm hurt, and her neck, and she couldn't stand. One by one their faces appeared above her, Ellie, dusting off her hands, the last.

Maeve tried to say, "No, it's her!" but garbled "Noooser" as Oliver grabbed her under her arms and dragged her across the floor. She clawed at his hand and arm but couldn't get a hold of him. They passed the armchairs by the fireplace, and somewhere near a door opened. A cool gust of air stroked her face. Oliver released her, but she remained too terrified and in too much pain to move. He pushed her into the cellar. She managed to grab the railing and stopped herself from tumbling down the wooden stairs, but before she could get to her feet, the door closed, shutting out the light.

6

Lorna

Light strands of dried blood traced the lines between Lorna's shaking fingers, her skin cracked from the cold. She pulled down on her sleeves, the comedown from the rush of adrenaline plus the lack of food and caffeine giving her the shakes, making her act nervous. The morning had been spent in a rush, each event blurring in her mind like someone had pressed fast-forward, then rewind, then fast-forward, unable to land on the right spot. Her body a crumbling VHS tape, her image blurred and distorted. One more rewind and she would break. They were all being rewound, turned back into past selves. While she found her confidence slipping, Oliver bounced on his feet, a shadow of the ball of energy he used to be. Ellie, the wide-eyed princess, fretted.

"Was she hurt? I didn't mean to push her so hard." Ellie looked up and down the stairs as if by standing there long enough she, too, could rewind recent events.

Oliver stuffed the cellar key in his pocket, then flung his arm around her shoulders. "She's fine, love."

"So that's it then, isn't it?" Ellie asked. "We've got her. We can leave. Get the police."

"Absolutely. Except they're probably going to need proof. Which is why we need to soften her up a bit before the interrogation."

"Interrogation?" Lorna asked.

"Well, there's two things we need, isn't there? One, the keys to get out of this house. And two, her confession. Who knows if she's left behind enough evidence to prove she killed Hollis and MacLeod? And there certainly isn't any that she killed Callum. Her confession will make the case airtight. I say we leave her there five, maybe ten minutes. Then we yank her out. Tie her up in, maybe, the kitchen? Plenty of tools there to scare the truth out of her."

"What do you even know about interrogation?" Lorna asked.

He hung on Ellie like a drunk at a club. "It's only Maeve. It can't be that hard. What is it? You've got your weird thinking bitch face on."

Lorna tried to relax her face. "Nothing. It was nothing."

She turned on her heel.

"Where are you going?" Oliver asked. In Lorna's mind, she saw the younger version of him calling to her. The full head of hair, the cocksure grin. "Oi! I asked you a question."

"To get some food." But when she looked, it was the older Oliver who stood there.

"Right. Good time for lunch, is it?"

"I haven't eaten all day. I'm starving. And we've been running around this house like a bunch of wild dogs looking for Maeve. So yeah, it's a good time for lunch."

"I can certainly see your point. Nothing like finding two dead blokes to work up an appetite. Might as well make it a picnic, why don't we? Relax away the afternoon. Great idea, don't you think, Ellie? Let's while away the hours in a house of murder. I don't need out of this place. I don't need to get back to my life."

"Because it's such a stellar life to get back to, right?"

Lightning flashed and a roll of thunder echoed. The sky darkened.

"I don't want to stay here any more than you do, but who knows when we're going to get out of here, with or without Maeve's confession. I would like to have some energy for whatever else we have to today. So can we not do this on an empty stomach, please? That's all I'm asking."

Oliver blinked once, twice, then shrugged. "Well, since you said please. Five minutes. Nothing you need to cook. And bring something back for me and Ellie."

He returned his arm to Ellie's shoulder and herded her into the study. Lorna watched them go, her shoulders sagging in relief when the door closed behind them. Her hands trembled worse than ever while her mind tore itself between different images. Hollis's body. The dog barking. Maeve in the cellar. She pressed her hands against the sides of her head, trying to put it all back together, slow the tape. For the first time, she doubted her ability to handle herself. Deep breaths slowed her thoughts and her pulse. After a final, silent count to ten, Lorna smoothed her hair and returned the armor that had protected her for so many years. She stepped over MacLeod's body and made her way to the kitchen.

After grabbing a mishmash of snacks, Lorna joined her companions in the study. Oliver and Ellie, already drinking at the bar, had also taken the time to settle their nerves. Oliver's excess of energy waned and Ellie no longer resembled a deer in flight. Lorna passed out the snacks while Oliver poured her a glass from a bottle of Dalmore and added a splash of soda. Lorna didn't drink whisky, but asking for something else seemed too much effort. She watched the gold ribbon around the neck of the bottle as Oliver refilled their glasses. Drinking someone else's liquor too early in the day and eating crap food while none of them knew what to say—time really had rewound itself.

"Five more minutes," Oliver said, making a show of checking his watch. "Then we drag her out of there."

"And what?" The whisky lingered on Lorna's tongue. "Beat her up?"

"If it comes to that."

"Are you forgetting it's your fists that got us into this mess in the first place?"

He slammed his glass onto the bar, making Ellie jump. "That had nothing to do with it. And are you forgetting that your poor little Maeve killed Callum?"

"She's not my Maeve." Lorna downed the rest of her drink, then grabbed a handful of crisps. "And we don't know she killed Callum."

"We know she killed MacLeod."

"Yes, but . . . Never mind."

"No, go on. Do tell, Lorna. Clearly something's on your mind." Oliver leaned on the bar. "Share with the class. You were happy enough earlier to lock her up. What makes you so quick to defend her now?"

"You want to interrogate Maeve? Want to go beat it all out of her? Fine. Come on, let's go now." She poured herself another whisky, drank it in one, and slammed the glass down beside Oliver's. "You think I won't do it? That I can't? That maybe I'm having reservations because I know Maeve is innocent? And I know she's innocent because I'm the real killer? That's what you and Ellie were talking about while I was gone, wasn't it? Thought you could press my buttons. See if I'd confess to something? As if I haven't been thinking the same about both of you. You said it yourself, Oliver. There's no evidence of what happened that night. It could have been Maeve. It could even have been Hollis after all. It could've been any of us. Callum. Or MacLeod. So if we're going to do what I think you want to do, then I want more proof than a piece of string."

A flash of lightning was followed by a crack of thunder, loud as a tree bursting to pieces. Oliver held up his hands and licked the liquor from his lips, and Lorna knew what he was going to say. It was all happening again. A remake rehashing the plot of the original. As if by being together they could never stop this endless cycle.

"What I think is that we'll all trust each other a little more," he said, "if the three of us stick together."

The lights shut off. The room dimmed like a cinema, spared total darkness by the benefit of the sun hidden somewhere by the storm clouds in noon sky.

"Seriously? Seriously?" Oliver said. Ellie was on the verge of crying again.

"Maybe there's a generator somewhere," Lorna said.

"Yeah, probably outside where we can't get to it. Unless we had the keys."

An electronic chime interrupted Lorna's answer. Ellie pulled out her phone.

"I have a signal!" Ellie squeaked. "One bar : . . oh, it's gone."

Lorna and Oliver's phones followed suit, beeping and buzzing like they'd been switched on after a long flight.

"I have one bar. Two. Now one," Oliver said.

"The signal jammer," Lorna said. "With the electricity out, that means the jammer's lost power, too."

"Oh." Ellie took a long drink from her glass. "I suppose Maeve hadn't thought of that."

A faint glow shone from underneath the sofa. Without a word, Lorna crossed the room, crouching down on all fours to retrieve it. She sat back on her knees as she stared at the screen until Ellie asked what she had found.

"Hollis's phone. This is him with I guess his daughter on the lock screen." Lorna looked toward the window, then back to the phone. "Hollis was wearing his jacket. Which means he probably went outside before he was killed. Maybe he was trying to get a signal."

"Do you think he contacted the police? Are they on their way?" Ellie asked.

"I don't know. It's locked, so I can't check the call log. He's had some emails since he last unlocked it, though, and a few missed calls from Linda. Whoever Linda is," she added.

"It's an iPhone, right?" Oliver asked. "What model?"

She turned it over, running her fingers over the Manchester United case. "I don't know. Not the newest, I don't think. The screen doesn't go all the way to the edges."

"It's new enough to have fingerprint ID," he said.

"But how do we unlock it if—" Ellie's eyes went wide. "Oh." She finished her whisky in a single drink.

"What's the point, though?" Lorna asked. "Our phones are working now."

"Because then we can check the call log," Oliver said. "Check his texts. See if Hollis did manage to reach one of his detective mates. He said Manchester CID, right? Say they left last night, they'd reach us by the end of the day. And we could check his emails, too. Maybe he has it synched to his work account. I don't think Hollis was trying to run out on us, either. I think he was piecing this together, and I want to see what he came up with. Then we can ring the police from our phones if he hasn't already."

"But I don't understand," Ellie said. "Why don't we ring them now?"

"Because," Lorna answered, seeing where Oliver was heading. "If Hollis has—had—a theory that Maeve was responsible, then that backs up why we threw her in the cellar. But also, if he decided to pass on any new information about what happened to Callum that night, anything that doesn't back up our original story, or point to Maeve, then we'll know about that, too."

"After all," Oliver said. "What's the point of jumping out of the frying pan and into the fire, eh?"

Ellie

Very little light penetrated the windowless halls upstairs. Ellie and Lorna held up their phones for light as they turned the corner that led to the guest rooms, while Oliver carried the whisky bottle. The alcohol and crisps had smoothed the rough edges of their anxiety, but it was no easier entering this room knowing what to expect than it had been before. Ellie waited to see if what they had witnessed earlier had been an illusion. But the recreation of Hollis's Caldwell Street bedroom remained, along with his body.

Oliver nudged Lorna toward the sofa. "Go on then."

The room didn't smell. It was too soon—and too cold—for that, but Ellie imagined it did, and that was enough to churn her stomach.

"Ellie, give me your jumper."

She toyed with the top button. "It's quite chilly in the house. And with the power off—"

"Give her your jumper, Ellie."

Ellie took her time peeling the pale blue jumper off her shoulders and handing it to Lorna, who cast it over Hollis's face.

"Was he right- or left-handed?" she asked.

"Right, I think," said Oliver.

Lorna dropped his hand the first time she touched it, and Ellie jumped, thinking Hollis had moved.

"Come on, Lorna. Don't be so squeamish." But Oliver spoke the words to the floor, unable to look at the body.

Lorna slipped the phone into Hollis's crooked hand and pressed his thumb down. As soon as the phone unlocked, she pulled back.

"Well? Did he ring anyone?" Oliver asked.

"Hang on. I want to disable the security features first because I am not doing that again."

Ellie craned her neck to watch the phone screen as Lorna found the call log.

"No. No, he didn't make any outgoing calls." She searched through his recent messages. "Someone left a voice mail last night, though. Linda, again."

She put it on speaker.

"Hey, Dad. Sorry to bother you on your weekend away and all. But something a bit weird happened. The police came by, which isn't all that unusual for us, yeah, but they weren't local. Came from down south and said they needed to ask you questions about something. There was a fire at some house on . . . hang on. I wrote down the name. Coldwell Street? No, Caldwell. Can't read my own writing. Anyway, I said I didn't know what you'd have to do with a fire last month when you were being the big Catherine Marcus hero up here, and I said they could check that with DI Thompson and DS Khan, but then they said it wasn't so much the fire itself, but that they have reason to suspect the fire had something to do with a death that happened there in the nineties when you lived there as a student? Which I said didn't sound right 'cause you went to Nottingham. Anyway, I think it's probably the lads playing a joke 'cause of your promotion and all. But the whole thing felt really, I don't know, weird. Anyway,

hopefully it's just your phone being wonky up there in the Highlands. But give me a call when you get this. And remember to take a picture of a coo for me! Okay, love you! Bye bye bye."

"She sounded nice," Ellie said. "His daughter sounds very nice."

"So Maeve burned down the Caldwell Street house?" said Oliver. "Probably took out all the furniture beforehand. Had it shipped up here. How long has she been planning this?"

Lorna tapped the phone against her palm. Oliver drank straight from the bottle and wiped his chin with the back of his hand. Neither of them noticed Ellie as she inched toward the doorway.

"I want to see what else Hollis has on that phone." He reached for it, but Lorna pulled it back.

"I can look."

"Then shut up and do it."

Ellie stood in the hall now, waiting for them to yell at her to come back. But their argument took up all of their attention.

"Didn't you listen to that voice mail?" Oliver was saying. *"If the police are suspicious enough to travel up to Manchester to interview Hollis, it must be because Maeve already sent them something. And we don't know what it was or what else he has."*

"But what if it wasn't Maeve?"

"Then who else . . ."

"I . . . I think . . ."

A roll of thunder drowned out the rest of Lorna's reply and covered Ellie's footsteps as she back-stepped down the hall.

Bad things happened when Ellie drank. Alcohol reminded her what she was capable of. Revealed the side of herself she worked so hard to hide. The side these people brought out in her. She'd only had two small glasses downstairs, but on an empty stomach that was enough.

The house creaked and groaned in the storm, and Ellie turned around with every step, expecting someone, perhaps even Callum, to appear behind her. She rubbed the scratches on her arm and hurried upstairs to her room.

She reached under the bed and grabbed the jammer. Held it in her hands, torn between cradling it to her chest and throwing it out the window. Her phone beeped, and she welcomed the distraction. A text from Jilly.

if u dunt let me go 2 Kevs party ill h8 u 4eva

Ellie laughed. How had she never noticed how innocent her daughter was? Kevin Barlow's party—a life or death situation. If only Jilly knew.

Ellie tied back her hair in a stiff ponytail and reread the last text she'd received from the Unknown Number:

Is it done yet?

Ellie tightened her ponytail again, letting the hairs pull at her scalp. She was good at following instructions. She could accomplish each task like a checklist no matter how difficult—come to Wolfheather House, bring a cellular signal jammer, feign surprise when the others arrive. But no matter how many times she checked her phone, no further instructions seemed forthcoming.

When she first got that text last night, as she ran the water for the shower to cover the sound of her movements, she had immediately retrieved the signal jammer from her suitcase and plugged it in underneath the bed. She thought it was safest to get rid of the box somewhere and had managed to hide it in the cellar before entering the dining room for the first time. How was she supposed to know Lorna and Oliver would go looking down there? And how had they found it behind those dusty old boxes anyway? It was almost as if they had known what they were looking for. Or at least Oliver had because didn't he say he was the one who found the box?

She wondered now if Maeve had been given instructions, too. And if the two of them had known what they were really getting into this weekend, what about Oliver and Lorna? How much of what they said was the truth, and how much of it was an act?

Ellie stuffed her phone in her pocket, then took the signal jammer to a different room, sliding it underneath a random bed, and returned to the hall, where she heard Oliver and Lorna arguing in the room with Hollis's body. But as she prepared to return to them, she noticed an open door. One in the closed wing, just on the other side of the rope. One that had not been open when they'd last been together on this floor. Ellie looked over her shoulder, then ducked under the rope.

Enough light filtered through the window that she knew what she was seeing had to be real. The wire-framed bed and crate of cleaning supplies. The framed photos hanging on the walls. The paperboard desk that took up too much space. Like the room that housed Hollis's body, this room had been turned into a replica of her Caldwell Street bedroom. A memory came to Ellie, long buried underneath years of purposeful forgetfulness, and she yanked open the drawer to the desk, but there was no folder. No notebook. No diary. Only a blue envelope with her name typed on the front. She pinched it with two fingers and extracted it from the drawer.

```
There once was a girl named Ellie,
Who faked being good and jolly.
She always thought it not her fault
Whene'er she committed assault,
So her brain's now about to be jelly.
```

Oliver

"Let me get this straight," Oliver said. "You don't think Maeve killed Callum *because* she killed MacLeod?"

"Yes. I mean no. I mean . . ." She pressed her palms into her eyes and let out a frustrated groan. "I mean I don't think it's as simple as we think it is. Something's not quite right."

"Dunno. Seems pretty straightforward to me. Maeve murders Callum. Decides she doesn't want any witnesses, so she lures us all here to finish us off. Old man MacLeod isn't supposed to show up but he does and she takes him out, too."

Lorna threw up her hands. "But why? What's her motive? You said you watch *Forensic Files*, right? The murderer always has a motive."

"I told you. We're witnesses."

"And if Callum had been killed last week, I'd buy that. But it's been over twenty fucking years, Oliver. I didn't feel like the police were suddenly closing in on me. Did you? They never even investigated his death as a murder. This"—she waved her hands at the house—"only reopens something that had been shut tight, nice and tidy. If Maeve killed Callum, she wouldn't be thick enough to restart something that would get the finger pointed at her."

Oliver ran a hand over his head and sighed. "Say you're right. Maeve didn't kill Callum. But since she's the one behind this, then why does it matter who did do him in? We don't need to answer that question for our 'benefactor' because we have her locked in the cellar. All we need to do is take care of her and go our separate ways. Leave the past in the past."

Lorna dug her toe into the carpet, then kicked aimlessly at the air. "Do you really think she's capable of pulling off something like this on her own?"

Oliver shrugged. "Why not? All it would take is a little planning. We know Maeve's unemployed, so she's got plenty of time on her hands. Although this would also take a fair bit of cash, and I'm not sure where she'd get that from. Course, she could have a rich dead uncle or something. Anyway, it would have to be someone who knew what life was like in Caldwell Street. I mean, Callum never did those Happy Wednesday notes for anyone other than us. And like you said, the police never investigated his death as murder. So other than the five of us, no one else knows what happened that night. That makes it a short list of people who . . ."

Lorna glanced suddenly at Hollis's covered face.

"What is it?" he asked.

"Hollis said the same thing last night. The last time we spoke. He said it's a short list of people who would know all these details." She approached Hollis and tentatively patted his pockets. Oliver's lip curled at the thought of touching the body. "Hollis *was* making notes last night, but he wasn't using his phone. He wrote them in a notepad. If he'd figured anything out before he . . . it would be in his notebook, not his phone."

Oliver's phone buzzed. All of her messages suddenly came through, at least one every half hour since 4 p.m. yesterday when he hadn't returned to the house as usual.

Traffic bad?

Long line @ shop?

If @ shop get extra bottle. It is the weekend!

Why aren't u answering?

Are u ok?

Useless. Your dad never this bad.

Do u hate me? Is that it?

Like your sister now? Never talk to me again?

I don't need u. No one does.

He should delete the lot. But he couldn't. Many times his sister—half-sister—had begged him to leave Mum to her fate. What was the word his sister had used? Codependent. Enabling. Easy enough for her to get away, though. She didn't need their mother. She had a dad who adored her. A dad with money. Last time Oliver got the nerve to look up his dad, the old coot was on a fishing trawler somewhere near Alaska.

"It's not here," Lorna said.

"Huh?"

"Hollis's notepad."

But Oliver wasn't listening. Mum had texted, so Mum had his attention. Callum had noticed, back in the day, the effect Mum had on him, after another phone call left Oliver scrambling to get home. Callum said it was good to love your parents, but you had to set boundaries. You couldn't let them get away with disrupting your life, especially when it was hurting you. He'd had that look, one where Oliver could tell he was speaking from experience, but Oliver couldn't remember if he'd said anything else. Oliver had never taken Callum's advice.

When he looked up again, Lorna was gone. Ellie, too, was nowhere to be seen.

"Shit." He hurried into the hall. "Lorna? Lorna!"

He turned and bumped right into her.

"Ow!" Lorna rubbed her shoulder. "Calm down. I'm taking a look in

Maeve's room. If your theory's right and she killed Hollis, she might have hid his notepad there."

"Don't you mean *our* theory?" Oliver asked, but Lorna didn't answer, already caught up in her search.

Flashes of Caldwell Street returned to him as he observed the mess in Maeve's room. Her belongings had expanded to fit the available space like scum on the surface of a pond. Clothes scattered on the floor and furniture. Various face washes and lotions and cotton balls littering the bathroom. Papers scattered on the floor. Her suitcase closed but not zipped, the sleeves of shirts and legs of jeans sticking out like tongues. Oliver picked up the loose papers while Lorna made her way across the room to the desk.

"Credit card statements? Who brings those on a romantic holiday?"

"It could be what was in her envelope last night. The blackmail."

He flipped through the pages. "None of these are in Maeve's name. And they're all maxed out. Cash advances." He whistled. "Well, we wanted to know how Maeve could afford an evil plan like this. Mystery solved! She decides to use this as her 'evidence' that she's being blackmailed, too, but like everything Maeve does, it's backfired 'cause now we know she had the funds to book this place. What else did you think you could hide, Maeve?"

Oliver tossed the statements on the bed and picked through the suitcase while Lorna looked at a paperback book on the desk: a shirtless, long-haired, chiseled man in a kilt embracing a buxom woman in a tight-fitting green dress. Oliver was ready to make a joke about Maeve's large cotton panties when he found a lacy red bra and panties.

"Oh, sick." His lip curled. "These are Maeve's? I do not want that image in my head."

Lorna rolled her eyes and turned a page in the book. A cream envelope fluttered from the pages to the floor by Oliver's knee. The creases and skin oil stains showed that it had been read and re-folded multiple times.

"What a surprise. Another envelope. Let's see what this pathetic riddle says. 'My dearest M Doll . . .'" His voice slowed as he realized what he was reading. "'I can't wait to finally meet you in person. I feel like we know each other more intimately than any two other people on earth, but it won't be until I can entwine my legs with yours and taste . . .' Nope." Oliver dropped the letter onto the suitcase. "I'm not reading any more of that."

Lorna picked it up and skimmed to the end. "It's signed 'Yours Forever, Tom.'"

"Who's Tom?"

"The online boyfriend she said lured her here. Shit." Lorna ran a hand through her hair. "All these body lotions. The lingerie. You pack all this for a dirty weekend, not for murder."

"She could've staged it."

Lorna raised an eyebrow. "You mean Maeve would've anticipated that we would suspect her and search her room? Maeve? A woman who couldn't even predict it was going to rain when the sky went black and the wind picked up?"

"You have a point. What website did she say she met him on?"

"I'm not sure. SingleMingle, I think?"

Oliver pulled up the website on his phone, dismissing the notifications that asked him to download the app. "And his username. It was Kit something?"

"Kit_Snow0273."

A few seconds later he had found it. Oliver showed Lorna the photo on his phone: a balding white man with a beer gut and the kind of smile that could make up for a less than attractive body. The kind of smile Oliver had perfected in his teens. But there was something off about the picture. The resolution was a little too clear, the lighting a little too perfect, for a candid selfie down the pub. He dropped the photo in Google. The image appeared multiple times. The fictional Kit_Snow0273 was part of a group shot of middle aged men in a stock photo, raising pints in a generic pub.

"She was telling the truth," Lorna said. "Someone catfished her."

"I'll concede a 'maybe.' Happen to see Hollis's notepad anywhere?"

He tapped the phone against his palm as Lorna shifted a few more of Maeve's belongings but soon quit. They both knew it wouldn't be here.

"So . . ." he drawled. "You're saying I was wrong?"

"I'll also give you a 'maybe.' We did find the twine in her pocket, and it does look like that was what was used to strangle MacLeod." Lorna bit on her fingernail. "What if MacLeod is somehow connected to Callum? Unlike Caskie, he's old enough to have known him. Maybe he was behind this? He's the one who catfished Maeve? She finds out he tricked us and strangles him?"

Oliver nudged the suitcase with his toe. He needed a drink to sort this all out. Puzzles were Hollis's thing, not his.

"Another maybe," he said.

"You don't sound convinced."

He remembered Maeve following each of them around the house, trying to impress them with a new outfit, a good exam score. Offering free beer or food. Telling them about how she almost bumped into Noel Gallagher at the grocery store. Any scrap she could offer she waved in front of them, even though none of it ever helped.

"If it's true," he said, "I don't understand why she wouldn't tell us. We've all been wondering how we got played. If she found out who it was—and not only found out but killed him?—she'd want the credit. Maeve's always been worried about status. And what better way for her to raise our esteem of her than by saving us? It just doesn't make sense that she wouldn't have told us."

"No, you're right," Lorna said. "She would've told us. She would've woken the whole house to tell us. So then why did she kill him?"

"Maybe the better question is, how did that twine end up in her pocket?" Oliver asked.

"She was always a deep sleeper. What if someone snuck into her room this morning and planted it there? She was the last one up."

Wind struck the house, and Oliver stood up straight, cocking his ear toward the hall. "Was that a door?"

"I didn't hear anything."

He held up his hand, listened.

"What do you—"

"Footsteps." He listened to the movement of someone below.

"Maeve," Lorna said. "If it's not her . . . She's on her own down there.

Whoever locked us in will have a key to the cellar, and we left her alone. Shit. We've left her alone."

Oliver took Lorna's arm and held her back. "Where's Ellie?"

Maeve

During the day, the flat was hers. She'd pop open the curtains, put her books on the coffee table and her shows on the TV, move the potted plants to where she liked them best. She'd make a coffee and breakfast, sit down at the table with a paper, and pretend this was her life. Pretend every morning was a Sunday morning, and that this was the one day a week she needn't go to her artsy job in the West End, or the BBC Studios, or the National The-atre. She often pretended that she had a little dog—a terrier mix rescued from Battersea Dogs Home—that slept by her leg while she ate her eggs and toast. She'd speak to him some days—Duncan, she called him—comment on articles in the paper, pretending she knew the people involved. Some mornings she got so entrenched in her daydream, she would offer him scraps from the table and become confused when he didn't take them. On these days, she burst into tears and had to scrub her face an extra five minutes before heading down to the unemployment office.

Whenever she had an appointment, she always came with a detailed list of the places she'd applied to or had interviewed with. Sometimes she really would have applied to one or two of them. She never had an interview. Afterward, she'd run errands, do a little cleaning, and watch her imagined life drip away as she restored Max's flat to its original state. One by one he and his family would return, bringing reality with them. When the kids got home from their after-school clubs, they commandeered the television to watch their programs and eat their snacks on their sofa. Max's wife was the next to return. She'd talk to Maeve about her day as she changed clothes and removed her jewelry, helped Maeve set the table. Unless he was working late, Max usually arrived home in time for dinner, the kids screaming his name, the conversation shifting away from Maeve as if they'd exhausted everything they had to say to her. Like they'd filled their daily quota of being kind to the strange spinster auntie who had taken over their spare room.

That was why Maeve disappeared to her room after dinner—to spare them the pain of having to tolerate her for the rest of the evening. To let them pretend it was only the four of them, the happy family, no fifth wheel. And Maeve would turn on her little television and eat a bag or two of M&M's and pretend the sounds echoing throughout the rest of the flat were only neighbors.

It was on one of these nights, when she had already retired to the spare room—eating some stale Pringles she'd found under her bed and watching reruns of *The Simpsons*—that she got the text.

See you soon.

She sat in bed, the phone in one hand, a Pringle in the other, and wondered if it was too late to back out. Her thumb hovered over the phone, ready to reply. To decline. But her hand shook. So she got out of bed and opened her desk drawer. There on top was the picture she kept of Callum. The picture of the two of them, smiling, his arm around her shoulders at some party. The last time a man had touched her with kindness. She typed a reply.

Ok

That simple two-letter response had led her to a cold dirt floor a thousand kilometers from home.

Grit coated her tongue. She tried to spit it out, even licked the back of her hand, but as the taste of dirt retreated, fear advanced.

"I can't see. I can't see!"

She remembered reading something online about a man who got hit in the head by a falling sign and lost his vision. What if she would never see again? Her last image would be Oliver at the staircase. And not even Oliver in his prime. Middle-aged Oliver.

"Oh god."

Tears fell, and she punched herself in the thigh.

"Stop. Fucking. Crying."

She brushed the dirt from her fingers, then wiped the tears from her eyes. Shapes emerged from the darkness. She hadn't lost her vision. The cellar was simply that dark. Grasping the wooden railing, she made her way up the stairs one by one, her right ankle smarting with each step. The door at the top was locked, but she found the light switch. She pressed it. Nothing happened.

The darkness crowded in around her. Panic crept in at the edges of her mind. How had that old man, MacLeod, died? How had the murder weapon ended up in her pocket? Maybe she had done it in some psychotic state. Perhaps she'd been sleepwalking. Run into him while she slept. But no. Oliver said he could only have been dead for at most three hours, and she'd been up longer than that. But Oliver was hardly a coroner. He could've been wrong about the time of death.

"No. Stop it."

She gripped her hair and pulled on it to stop her racing thoughts.

"You didn't strangle that old man. You didn't strangle anyone. It was Ellie. It must've been Ellie."

Oliver had been too surprised when he saw the body. And it was Ellie who had the signal jammer. Ellie who, with a smile, had pushed her down the stairs. She must've put the twine in Maeve's pocket.

"But they'll never believe you. They'll kill you before you get the chance to explain. Ellie will make sure of it, and Oliver will follow her lead. Lorna won't be able to stop them."

She pulled harder on her hair.

"They're going to kill you, Maeve. Let you die like Callum. One less problem to worry about. They're going to kill you and let you die. Kill you and let you die. Kill you. Let you die."

She squeezed her eyes so tight, she saw bursts of color as thoughts beat in her head like a drum, building to a crescendo until finally she shouted, "No!"

She stood in the darkness and dropped her hands to her side.

"No. Maybe you deserve to die, but you're not going to let them do it. And you're not going to wait for them to do it. You're a good person. People like you. You can achieve whatever you set your mind to. So, Maeve

Okafor, you can either bang on that door until they let you out, or sit on that step until they come for you, or you can find your own damn way out. Who votes for option number three?"

Maeve raised her own hand.

"All right. Get moving then."

She used the railing to guide her back down.

"Torch, torch, there must be a torch," she sing-songed, pretending her heart wasn't racing. "Or maybe even a candle."

With arms straight out in front of her, she walked until she collided with a metal shelf. Like a blind woman, she ran her hands over every object she found. She imagined cutting her hand on broken glass or some misplaced gardening equipment. Severing a tendon. Hitting an artery. Slicing off a finger. She could feel every injury before it happened. See blood dripping down her arm despite the darkness that squeezed her tighter and tighter. Her pawing became more frantic. A plastic bottle fell onto her hand as her palms pounded the shelf, encountering a mix of round and sharp edges, bits of metal and plastic. A glass or ceramic object shattered to the floor. A heavy piece of metal hit her in the foot.

"Please, a torch. Please, something. Please please."

She slammed her hands on the shelf. An eerie green glow entered the room, and the numbers 04:19 stared back at her. Maeve grabbed the digital clock before the Indiglo light faded. It couldn't project far but created what seemed like a world of sight in the pitch-black cellar.

As the light died, she pressed the Indiglo button again and pointed the glowing display at the shelves. It cast everything it touched in a strange aquamarine glow, like she was seeing in night vision. Even with the rain, she could hear the high little buzz made when the light was active and listened to it fade away with the light. She held the button down, hoping she wouldn't drain the battery, and made her way through the shelves. At the end of the row, she tripped over a camping lantern. Fuel sloshed inside when she shook it, and she searched the shelf for something to light it with.

"Why did I quit smoking?"

Her luck turned. Among a roll of cord and some loose nails sat a small box of matches. Unable to strike a match and hold the clock at the same time, she sat cross-legged on the dirt floor with the lantern in front of her and the alarm clock beside her. She hit the button and struck a match. It didn't light the first or second time, and the clock's whine petered out as the green glow faded. She slammed her fist on the Indiglo button and struck the match again. It lit on the fifth try, but the short matchstick burned quickly. The flame bit her fingertips, and she yipped and dropped it into the lantern, where it burned to nothing without lighting the tallow.

Maeve pulled the lantern closer and tried again.

"Always give up too easily. That's what Max says. Now's your time to show him."

She pressed the Indiglo button and struck another match. It lit on the first try.

"Ha!"

She stuck the matchstick inside the lantern and held it to the wick.

"Come on, come on."

The flame grabbed hold.

"Tada!"

Maeve shook out the match and experimented with the wick, turning the flame up and down before setting it at a good height and stuffing the matchbox in her pocket. Her field of vision expanded, and with no one to mock her, she danced in triumphant circles despite her ankle.

"I have the power of flame! I am the Master of Darkness. I am . . . Jesus fucking Christ on a bike!" Maeve grabbed the shelf to steady herself.

Her brain told her it was nothing. Only a shadow on the wall. A shadow that resembled a person.

"Hello?"

Wind battered the window.

"My name's Maeve. I didn't mean to disturb you. I don't want to be down here at all, actually. They put me down here and I—"

A faint smell of orange, cedar, and balsam seeped into the room.

"Drakkar Noir?"

She stopped rambling. That smell took her back to a dark cinema watching *Stargate* and being utterly confused by both the film and Callum trying to hold her hand when she was reaching for the popcorn.

"Callum?"

Holding her breath, she turned around and faced the blank wall.

There was nothing there. She tiptoed to the end of the row and swung the lantern right and left. Maybe she had seen an old dress form or coat rack, but there was nothing down here like that. Nothing that would've cast such a shadow.

"You were imagining things, Maeve. Of course Callum's not here. Just light and shadow. And I mean it's already a creepy house to begin with."

Something fell to the ground.

Maeve jumped so high, she thought she touched the ceiling. Her heart pounded, about to burst. She listened, but heard nothing more. She walked toward where the sound had originated. On the ground was a fallen cardboard box, its contents spewing out.

With the lantern in one hand, she sifted through the spilled contents with the other. They were personal items, knickknacks like what one might find at a flea market—dragon figurines and empty photo albums, a Koosh ball, random Happy Meal toys, a pewter mug. Then, in the middle of it all, she found a photo of a couple. She held it close to the lantern. A familiar man and woman in Aran jumpers in an unfamiliar sitting room on a couch, holding hands. The woman's hair reminded Maeve of her mother's in the eighties.

Maeve shuddered in the draft. Then paused. It wasn't a draft. It was a breeze. Air was coming through the wall. She moved the remaining boxes.

"No bloody way."

There in the wall was a door.

She pressed her hands against it to make sure it was real. The rusty knob wouldn't turn, but a panel of the door had rotted away. She reached through and found a key inserted in the lock on the other side. She expected it to give her trouble, but it turned with ease. The door opened onto a tall but narrow passageway. Maeve shuffled from foot to foot. She heard nothing in the passage, nor could she see where it went.

She hesitated, then took a step forward. But as soon as she crossed the threshold, she panicked and staggered back. She needed a way out, but no good could come from exploring dark, unknown passages. She reached to close the door.

And another door slammed above.

Maeve crouched down in case she could somehow be sensed above by the heavy footsteps that paced the foyer and paused above her head. Footsteps from someone who had entered the house through the locked front door. Footsteps that approached the cellar door.

Pp. 51–60

so fucking complicated. They had to come up with their own solution to the problem instead of just doing what they were told. Yeah, well, how did that work out? About as well as how they tried to "solve the situation" with Callum.

So in January 1995 a deep chill had settled over Caldwell Street. Christmas cheer kept many of the houses there warm, but the memory of New Year's soon faded and dutiful husbands and wives and housemates returned to their dreary commutes in a world made barren by winter. Even the sky embraced a gray pallor which it refused to shed no matter how the winds changed. Under this sky, the wind making her nose run and whipping her hair into her eyes, Maeve returned to house number 215, dragging her dad's old rucksack behind her like a disobedient dog. Placing a foot on either side of the crack in the pavement that led up to the door, Maeve brushed her hair away with a gloved hand and let the rucksack slip from her fingers. Since she last saw it, the house looked like it had been beaten and left for dead. The door's green paint against the gray walls resembled a bruise. The roof sagged like a crushed skull. A smell of rubbish, like spoiled milk, drifted down the street from uncollected bin bags. A nagging tug pulled behind her sternum, and she pressed a hand there, hoping to push the feeling either away or at least deep enough inside herself that she would no longer notice it. In the end, it was not the cold that made her enter, or the promise of her large private room, or the new electric teakettle she'd received for Christmas now clanking in the rucksack. She carried her bag to the door because Oliver's car was not there.

Inside, a wall of warm air struck her. Hollis had promised to turn down the thermostat before he left. She supposed he could have forgotten, although that didn't seem like him. Her fingers, frozen inside her thin gloves, warmed as she set the new kettle in the kitchen and carried the rest of her things upstairs. The heat of the house matched the burning shame she carried within. At least a quiet house meant she had time to decompress before the others returned. Time to pretend she felt perfectly normal. She was shedding her winter coat when she stopped outside the door to her room. The open door.

"What are you doing?"

Ellie spun round, Maeve's package of Oreos in hand, crumbs on her lips, and red rims beneath her eyes.

"Oh! Maeve, I'm so sorry. I was really hungry, but I didn't get to the shop yet. I promise I'll buy you more." She spoke too quickly, even for Ellie, and they both knew it.

"I didn't think anyone else was back." Maeve dragged her bag into the room, pulling it in a half-circle around Ellie who did not move.

"I got in earlier this morning. Daddy dropped me off." She kept standing in the way as Maeve unpacked her clothes, reminding Maeve of a character in one of Max's video games—stuck in a useless loop, repeating the same action as the hero maneuvered around it to complete a mission.

"Did you have a nice Christmas?" Ellie asked.

"Yeah. It was all right." The natural response would be to ask Ellie how her Christmas was. She didn't want to. Ellie told her anyway.

"Mine was very nice. Daddy took us to Edinburgh for Hogmanay. It was so wonderful. I'd been to Edinburgh before but never then, and we drank coffee and ate sweets at this little café that was right beneath the castle and there was the tiniest bit of snow on the ground, enough to make it look magical, and it was so beautiful and almost European and Daddy said that if I'm very good maybe next year he and Mummy will take us to Paris for New Year's."

At the word *magical*, Ellie had started crying, and now she'd run out of words. Maeve didn't want to look at her. It wasn't her fault Ellie was homesick, and she wasn't much in the mood to comfort anyway. Besides, Ellie cried all the time. Maeve cried, too, but no one knew it because she kept it private like she was supposed to, locked in her room at night, under the covers, with a pillow to muffle her so no one would hear. But everyone knew when Ellie cried because Ellie made a point of letting everyone know and they would rally around her and hug her and tell her everything would be all right. When Maeve cried, no one even looked at her until the next morning when, even after she'd washed the tears from her face and brushed her hair and teeth, one of them would inevitably tell her, "You look like shit."

Maeve ignored her and stuffed clean socks into her dresser drawer, hoping Ellie would take the hint, but the sniffing and whimpering continued.

"Forget about the biscuits," she said. What did she care? They were 25p. Then she glanced in the plastic crate where she kept all of her non-refrigerated food. There was no other way to keep it safe from these vultures. All that remained were a tin of baked beans and the stale, half-eaten pack of Oreos she'd forgotten to take home with her.

"What the hell, Ellie? Where's my food?"

Ellie pressed the Oreos against her chest as if protecting an infant, tears on her cheeks. Maeve pushed past her and headed across the hall. Ellie called after her then, but Maeve didn't stop. A mess of food packaging littered the floors of Ellie's room.

"You said you just got back."

Ellie looked at her feet.

"How long have you been here?"

Her lower lip quivered.

"Christ, what is it? Are you having some kind of mental breakdown? The university has counselors, you know."

Ellie's voice was a whisper. "They're not back until tomorrow."

Below them, the front door opened and shut. From the sound of his footsteps alone, they both knew who it was.

"*Hello? Anybody home? Fuck, it's hot as hell in here. Hollis, if you forgot to turn down the thermostat, I'm not paying for it!*"

"Don't tell him I'm here. Please don't," Ellie said. Maeve bit the inside of her cheek. What did it matter if Oliver knew who was here? It would be nice to see Little Miss Ellie squirm, let her face her own awkward situations instead of using someone else as a buffer. But then she saw Ellie's eyes and they reflected the same panic Maeve had seen when she'd woken up New Year's Day in a strange bed, in a strange house.

"Hell-oooo?"

"Go to my room."

Ellie did so as Maeve intercepted Oliver at the top of the stairs. He'd cut his hair and wore a new designer jacket that hugged him in all the right places. Maeve dug her fingers into the cuffs of her sleeves.

"Hey!" she said.

"I knew someone was here. What's with the fucking sauna?"

"The house was freezing when I got in, so I thought it would heat up faster if I turned it all the way up."

"Well, Jesus, it's hot enough now."

"Sorry. I'll fix it." She hurried down to adjust the thermostat, and he trotted after her.

"Anyone else back yet?"

"Not yet. It's just us!" She laughed because she was nervous, but it sounded like she was flirting and why did she always have to embarrass herself? She coughed, then tried to cover her tracks. "But Hollis is due back soon. I think Lorna might not be back until tomorrow? Her classes start a day later."

"No Lorna? Excellent!" He slipped off his jacket and tossed it over the brown armchair. "Perfect night for a party."

Maeve followed him to the kitchen. "A party? Tonight? Everyone's going to be tired from traveling."

"I can find a few things to boost everyone's mood. This is nice." He fondled her new kettle and then filled it, dripping water down the sides that marked up the stainless steel.

"We don't want a party!"

He dropped the kettle onto the plastic base and flicked the switch. "We? I didn't think anyone else was here."

"They're not. I meant. Me. And Callum. And Lorna. Me and Callum and Lorna. We were talking earlier. On the phone. Not all at once. We spoke at various times. And I thought you might suggest a party, and we'd rather not. Any of us."

"You and Callum, eh? Naughty Maeve. Didn't think he was your type." Oliver stuck his finger into the sugar bowl, then licked it clean.

"How's your mother?"

His smile dropped, and he pointed the wet finger in her face. Maeve flinched but kept her feet planted.

"You know fuck all about my mother." He clenched his fingers into a fist, and she wished he would hit her. Smack the shame she'd brought back right out of her.

"I know what I read in the paper. You and I don't live that far apart, you know."

But then the front door opened and closed. Callum, camera case looped across his chest, struggled to herd an unwieldy suitcase through the door. Maeve called out and hurried to him, like he was a knight come to defend her. His expression brightened when he saw her.

"Hey, Maeve."

"Hey! Remember what we talked about the other day? On the phone? About having parties?" With her back to Oliver, she stretched her smile, winked, tried to get him to play along.

"Uhm, having a party when?"

"About not having a party. Here. At all. For at least two months?" *Please*, she mouthed through her smile.

Callum nodded. "Oh, right. Yeah. No parties. Two months. Yeah, that was a great idea. I'm all for that." He looked over Maeve's shoulder. "You're all for that, too, right Oliver?"

Oliver rolled his eyes and stomped toward the stairs.

"Pathetic," he muttered as he headed up to his room.

As soon as he was out of sight, Maeve relaxed and squeezed Callum's arm. "Thank you."

"Anytime." He looked as if he wanted to say more, but Maeve started back for the kitchen.

"Are you making tea?" he asked, following. "I'm dying for a cuppa."

"Sorry. It's my new kettle." She unplugged it from the wall. "Maybe later."

"Well, are you going to be around today? I . . . Christmas holiday was . . ." He ran a hand through his hair. "Anyway, it'd be really nice to catch up. It's been a month since we saw each other."

"I don't know. I might be. Sorry."

She left him there and hurried up the stairs, eager to tell Ellie how she had stood up to Oliver. Pride coiled within her as she knocked on her own door, not eradicating the shame, but at least putting it in the corner for a time out. No one answered, and when she entered, the room was empty. She left the kettle on her desk and went across to the hall. Ellie's door was locked.

"Ellie, it's me."

When she knocked, Ellie said nothing. The pride slinked away, and Maeve returned to her room, locking herself inside. She thought she heard laughter from downstairs and knew it was directed at her. Oliver making fun of her stupid grandstanding. Maeve flopped down on her bed, the motivation to unpack gone, and lowered her hand into the crate for those stale Oreos. They were gone, along with the remaining tin of beans.

"Stupid fucking princess." She pressed her hands over her eyes, trying to block out the light and keep in the tears.

Oliver had not, as a point of fact, laughed. Though Maeve would never know this, what she mistook for a laugh was an angry bark as he kicked the baseboard beneath the tub in the bathroom. His fingers gripped the soiled sink that now reminded him of the cheap, utilitarian washroom in the police station where he'd tried to hide until Mum had been released. He wanted to punch a hole in the wall, then he remembered his security deposit and the anger slithered out of him.

Callum appeared in the hall, dragging his suitcase after him. Oliver rearranged his face in the mirror and hopped out of the bathroom.

"Hey, mate! I tried ringing you a few times over break. I left a message with your . . . mum? Sister?"

"Yeah, I know."

"Why didn't you ring me back?"

"Can we not talk about this right now?" He entered his room and Oliver followed, shutting the door behind them. Callum plopped the suitcase on the bed, pretending he was alone as he clicked open the latch and tossed back the lid. He stared at the contents, then removed them one by one as Oliver leaned against the door.

"It's a golden opportunity I'm offering, mate."

Callum piled the clothes onto the bed, the camera bouncing against his chest. "And I said I was fine."

Oliver crossed the room in two steps and slammed down the suitcase lid, catching Callum's fingers. "This isn't about you."

A red line appeared across the tops of Callum's knuckles. He stared at it as if he couldn't feel the sting. "You're right. Like everything else in this house, it's about what *you* want. What *you* deserve. Isn't that right?" Callum flipped the suitcase back open. "I'm not playing this game. We might be stuck in the same house for the next five months, but I'm not feeding your ego anymore."

Oliver let silence surround them, the atmosphere like water about to boil. Callum's reddened fingers gripped an old Aran jumper as if waiting to tear it in two.

"Sorry," Callum said. "I'm sorry. It's been a long trip."

"Okay." Oliver backed off. "No need to freak out. I was only offering a business opportunity, but you want to decline? I can respect that. How about this? I'll make it a standing offer. No pressure. You decide to change your mind, then come and see me." He opened the door. "Happy New Year."

He fumed as he pulled the cigarette pack from his jeans pocket. First Maeve, now Callum. What was it? Beat up on Oliver day? Fuck that, he thought. He'd get this house back in line. He barreled out the front door, leaving a trail of smoke in his wake.

* * *

Lorna followed that smoke trail as she returned to Caldwell Street and her room upstairs, a photo album of new Alfie pictures under her arm and a tin of homemade shortbread her mother insisted she share, which she intended on hiding under her bed. She glimpsed Callum standing over his bed and flexing his fingers as she unlocked the door to her room. He looked lost, like an alien trapped in a human body, unsure how the different parts worked. Lorna decided she could spare a few pieces of shortbread.

"Hey, Callum."

A moment of fear crossed his face.

"Hey," he said.

She held out the tin. "Do you want some?"

"Sorry." His voice was rough, and there were tears in his eyes. He took a deep breath and didn't acknowledge them. "Sorry. Long trip. I'll talk to you later."

His door closed with a bang that echoed in the hall.

"Happy New Year to you, too."

She closed her own door and, after a thought, locked it behind her. That's what she got for trying to be nice.

Anger. It seethed through the house that January. Resentment pooled in the corners. In addition to the shortbread and the teakettles and the new clothes and new cassettes, they had also brought back anger in all its various forms. Anger amplified by that house on that street and the lives of those with whom they shared this place. Unbeknownst to them, the moment Callum closed his door, a clock began to tick. A clock they could not see or hear but felt, buried deep in the heart of the house. A clock that counted down. And just like the clock that had marked the time to Callum's death, another had started the moment they threw Maeve into the cellar of Wolfheather House.

7

Lorna

"Footsteps," Oliver said.

Lorna soon heard it. The movement of someone below.

"Maeve," Lorna said. "If it's not her . . . She's on her own down there. Whoever locked us in will have a key to the cellar and we left her alone. Shit. We've left her alone."

Oliver took Lorna's arm and held her back. "Where's Ellie?"

Ellie was gone, and she hadn't even noticed till now. How stupid was she? How could she let herself lose track of any of them?

"What is she doing downstairs?" Lorna asked.

"I'm not downstairs."

Both Lorna and Oliver jumped.

There Ellie stood in the hallway, silent and pale. A wild look stained her face.

"Where have you—" Oliver started but Ellie pressed a finger to her lips and pointed down.

Footsteps again crossed the floor below.

Lorna's first thought was that Maeve had somehow found a way out, but then a voice followed the footsteps—a man's. Lorna waved the others back into Maeve's room and closed the door. They listened and waited.

Ellie kept glancing over her shoulder even though she was standing with her back to the wall. Oliver drummed on his thigh.

"Did you see him?" Lorna whispered to Ellie. "Do you know who it is?"

"I told you I haven't been downstairs. I didn't even hear him until just now."

"Well, where were you then?" Lorna asked.

Ellie looked her in the eye but said nothing. But Lorna knew Ellie had been somewhere. Had seen something. Or had done something.

Lorna laid her hand on the doorknob.

"What are you doing?" Oliver whispered.

"I'm going to see who it is."

He grabbed her wrist.

"He'll find us," Oliver said while at the same time Ellie said, "You can't do that."

Lorna tossed up her arms. "And what's your alternative? Stay here? Does the phrase 'sitting ducks' mean anything to you? Not to mention Maeve's down there on her own. Do you really want her to end up like Hollis? No matter what she's done, do you really truly want that for her?"

Oliver lowered his hand.

"Why should we care about Maeve?" Ellie asked.

Lorna had to stop herself from striking Ellie right then and there. Instead, she channeled her anger into yanking open the door.

Silently, she hurried down the hall and the first set of stairs. The others followed. Oliver's breath blew hot against the back of her neck, and Ellie kept stepping on the heel of her shoe. Lorna wanted to tell them both to back off, but they were too close to the main staircase now.

The man was in the foyer, opening and closing doors, pacing back and forth. Twice he cursed to himself in between a string of other sentences. Although Lorna could make out words here and there, she couldn't piece them together into anything sensible. Her first thought was that somehow MacLeod wasn't dead. That he'd merely been unconscious. Had Oliver checked for a pulse? She couldn't remember. But then from the top of the great staircase, she caught her first glimpse of him as he went into the dining room—a long, jeans-clad leg, an arm in a navy-blue coat sleeve. MacLeod had been wearing a green parka. Lorna looked at the others. With a nod of agreement, they crept down the stairs.

There would be no place to hide if he returned to the foyer. He would spot them, rats huddled on the staircase. With every step down, Lorna expected him to fly from the room. But the dining room doorway remained unmoving, unchanged. Any moment now, she thought. And yet the silence remained.

They reached the half-shut door unnoticed. Lorna mouthed, "On three." And held up her fingers: one, two . . .

The man barreled out of the room, knocking into all three of them. Everyone fell, a tangle of arms and legs and screams. Lorna tried to knee someone in the stomach. Her nails found a face. And then, with a grunt, the struggle stopped. Ellie lay on her right, shaking. A weight held them both down. Lorna pictured MacLeod's body falling on top of her, suffocating her.

But this body rolled away. Or rather, was rolled. Oliver stood over her with the silver candlestick Ellie had carried downstairs earlier.

"You all right?" he asked.

Lorna looked to her left, and there the man was, unconscious. It was Caskie. What struck her was how young he looked compared to them. A baby, in jeans and his ratty knit jumper, dirt on his clothes, scratches down his cheek.

Oliver helped Lorna up, then Ellie, and handed Ellie the candlestick. After finding some duct tape and rope from a cupboard near the front desk, he bent over the unconscious form.

"Well maybe now we can get some real answers."

Ellie

They waited in the study as the rain fell steadily outside. Lorna on the chesterfield sofa, watching out the windows. Oliver pacing the short distance between the chesterfield and the bar. Ellie watching the melting wax of a burning candle.

Mr. Caskie remained motionless in the center of the room, tied securely to a chair.

Until he woke, there was nothing to do but wait. Now was the perfect time for Ellie to tell the others what she had seen upstairs—the room, the note. But no matter how many times she imagined the conversation in her head, she held back. Lorna and Oliver would not help her. If she had been marked as the next victim, the others would be only too willing to hand her over. But why should she have to die? A mother and a philanthropist? Why not the unemployed alcoholic or the childless shrew?

She watched Caskie breathing, his bloodied head slumped forward. In those old jeans and flannel shirt, he looked nothing more than a child, and Ellie knew how to handle children. If he was the one who had sent her those texts, she was going to find out—one way or another.

Lorna got Oliver's attention the next time he came close to the sofa. She spoke too softly for Ellie to make out what was said, but she heard "Maeve."

"Are you kidding? She'll be hysterical. She can stay where she is for now."

Ellie wanted to ask them why they were considering freeing Maeve at all when Caskie groaned. They ran to face him.

He squinted up at them. When he tried to speak, the duct tape over his mouth obscured his words. Oliver tore it free.

Caskie ran his tongue over the sore spots left by the tape and swallowed, his Adam's apple bobbing up and down.

"Could I have a glass of water?"

Lorna made a move toward the bar, but Oliver held up his hand.

"What you can do is tell us the truth," he said. "And then maybe we'll let you have a drink of water. If we're feeling generous."

"What's the truth matter to you?" Caskie muttered.

Oliver backhanded him. Lorna jumped at the blow, but Ellie kept her feet planted and dug her fingernails into her arm. Caskie coughed once and spat blood to the floor, a red mark rising on his smooth chin.

"Look, I'm sorry, all right? I didn't mean to frighten you. I was looking for Mr. MacLeod and . . ." He looked at Lorna. "This wasn't meant to happen."

"So why did it then?" Oliver asked.

"Why else? Money. Grand house like this goes to waste most of the time. Could be used year-round if MacLeod would ever finish the renovations, but he keeps putting it off. Keeps finding something new to fix. Should do it all at once and be done with it. Not like he doesn't, didn't, have the money. Certainly doesn't spend it on my salary. Didn't. Could you loosen these, please?" he asked Lorna. "I'm not going to hurt anyone."

"Hang on. Salary?" Oliver asked, but before Caskie could answer, Ellie was asking her own questions.

"So who was it?" she asked. "Who paid you to lure us here?"

Caskie blinked a few times as if uncertain how to answer. He looked right at her when he spoke.

"You did."

The weight of Lorna's and Oliver's gaze shifted to her, but before she could deny it, Caskie continued.

"All of you did. You answered the ad I put up on Gumtree. All of your names were on the email. Said you were planning some sort of reunion. And you sent those gifts on ahead. Said it was some sort of inside joke. I thought it was stupid but—"

"You're saying you don't know who we are?" Lorna asked.

"Am I supposed to?"

"This is bullshit!" Oliver grabbed Caskie's shirt collar, smacked him again. "You brought us here on purpose!"

"I didn't!"

"You thought you could blackmail us into staying!"

"I swear I—"

Oliver punched him. Blood sprayed the floor. "Your plan all along was to kill us one by one!"

"I don't want to kill anyone!"

"I almost let you off the hook. You should have never shown your face again." Oliver raised his fist again, but Lorna placed a hand on his arm.

"Wait!" she said. "Please. Ellie, water."

Ellie went behind the bar as Lorna whispered, "Wait," to Oliver again. Caskie was crying now, his cheek swollen. Mucus and blood hung from his nose.

"Please," he begged Lorna. "Please untie me. Make them let me go."

Ellie handed the water glass to Lorna, who crouched in front of Caskie and held it to his lips. He took a sip, wincing at his split lip, and Lorna asked her question.

"I want you to tell us why you came back." Her voice was calm and firm.

Caskie muttered something through his tears. Lorna placed a hand on his shoulder.

"I know you're scared. Just take a deep breath. You did leave last night, didn't you? So why did you come back?"

Caskie took not one but three shuddering breaths and calmed himself enough to speak, but he spoke only to Lorna, wincing whenever Oliver or Ellie moved. He was pleading with her, and it made her want to pull away. "I wasn't going to come back until Monday morning. You'd paid me . . . I thought you'd paid me . . . to stay away for the weekend. Give you all privacy. I promise that was what I was going to do. I promise. But Mr. MacLeod. He was supposed to be in Glasgow this weekend. He wasn't. I found out he'd got back early and was headed straight for the house. He was going to find you all here and I didn't . . . He knew I let the house out again. He's had his suspicions before, but I always got away with it. This time, I don't know how, he knew. He found out. Someone told him. Someone must have told him."

Lorna allowed him another sip of water, and he continued.

"I thought I could make it back here. Head him off and, I don't know. I figured I'd think of something."

"So," Lorna said, "it's really Mr. MacLeod who owns Wolfheather House. You work for him and let the rooms without him knowing. Pocket the cash. Is that right?"

Caskie nodded.

"Then tell us this, *Mister* Caskie," Oliver interrupted. "Why have you been skulking about all day?"

"I haven't. I just got here. I left Portree as soon as I got wind of MacLeod, but the storm made the sea too choppy. I couldn't cross safely till late this morning."

"Did you take the ferry?" Lorna asked.

"I have my own boat. Docked at the quay. Won't be another ferry until Monday, not with the weather the way it is. Please, I don't know what's been going on here or what you think I've done. But I've told you everything, I swear. Please let me go. Whatever it is you're after, I'll help you. I know this house inside and out. Or I can take you to Skye. My boat can hold everyone. Please. I can take you all away from here, and whatever's happened . . . we can get away. I'll help you get away."

"Mr. Caskie. James," said Lorna. "Look at me. Thank you. But I'm sure you saw him. Out there in the foyer. Mr. MacLeod. There's no getting away from that."

Caskie shut his eyes and shook his head. Started crying again.

"James, did you kill Mr. MacLeod?"

Caskie could only cry. Lorna offered him more water, but he turned his head away.

"Look, James. Something's happening here that we have to see through to the end. If you help us, it won't matter what you did to . . . It won't matter what happened to Mr. McLeod. But we can't leave until we're done."

Lorna tried again to coax him into calming down, but he wouldn't say anything more.

Oliver nodded to the doorway and they followed him into the foyer, leaving Caskie to his tears.

"What do you think?" Oliver asked, his anger waning.

"I don't know," said Lorna. "He's practically a kid. And he's a mess. I could see someone bribing him to get us here, but honestly, other than money, what motive would he have? He's half our age. He couldn't have been more than an infant when we were at university."

"Well, of course he didn't set it all up," Ellie said. "Maeve did, and she used him to help her." Now that they'd spoken to Caskie, it was obvious. Maeve had finally got her revenge for that night. For what they did to her at the party. For what happened to Callum. "Women can manipulate soft-headed men like Caskie into anything. Including murder. You might have trouble believing that, Oliver, but I'm sure Lorna understands."

Caskie was no different than her Gordon, she thought, just a little younger.

But instead of backing her up, Oliver and Lorna exchanged looks. Then Lorna explained that they thought Maeve had been telling the truth about the catfishing. If Maeve was telling the truth about that, she couldn't possibly be responsible for what was happening, they thought. Ellie could see how they would make that assumption based on the information they had. But they didn't know what Ellie knew. They didn't know Ellie had been contacted before coming to Wolfheather House, and that the same was probably true of Maeve. That someone could have told her to pack that lingerie as a cover. She could have told them all of that. Now was her chance. But she knew how angry they would be with her, and it was still possible she could get out of this without either of them ever knowing what she'd done. If she could just speak to Caskie alone.

"Didn't you notice how he didn't ask about Maeve?" Ellie said. "Or Hollis? He knows he checked in five people. But he hasn't asked where they are. That's because he already knows."

"Or he's scared shitless and it hasn't crossed his mind," Lorna said.

"Then get Maeve up here. If you're so certain she's innocent, let her in to see Caskie. If he's lying, maybe he's the one who catfished her. I bet we could get it out of him with her help."

"I told you earlier we should let her out," Lorna said to Oliver.

"Yeah, all right. Fine. I guess we can deal with her now that we've got a better handle on Caskie."

"Then it's settled," Ellie said. "You two fetch her while I watch Mr. Caskie."

Lorna shifted her stance. "Ellie, we shouldn't leave you alone with him. What if—"

"Nonsense, Lorna. I'll be perfectly fine. Hostessing is my specialty, after all."

She smiled and watched them walk to the cellar while anger bubbled inside her like champagne. If they truly no longer suspected Maeve, their suspicion would fall elsewhere. And if they discovered Ellie played a part in this, no matter how small, that suspicion would fall on her. Ellie couldn't have that. Not when she hadn't done anything wrong.

Lorna might believe young James Caskie, but Ellie knew better than to fall for a younger man's words. He had to be hiding something, and Ellie knew how to find out. She removed her hair from its ponytail and shook it out with her fingers, then undid the top three buttons on her blouse and pinched her cheeks. With her sweetest smile, she returned to the study.

"Hello again, Mr. Caskie. Would you like some more water?"

Oliver

The stairs creaked as they descended. Oliver flashed his mobile phone's light in different directions, but the cellar looked much the same as it had that morning. It felt different, though, in a way he couldn't explain. Like it had witnessed something that left a mark.

"Maeve," he whispered. "Maeve! Where is she?"

"Hiding because she's afraid you're going to beat her to death."

At the bottom step, he stopped and cast the light around the room.

"Maeve," said Lorna. "We need to talk to you. We wanted to apologize."

"Yeah, Maeve. We're sorry we pushed you down the stairs. Although that was Ellie's idea."

Lorna slapped him on the arm. "Give her a chance to respond."

Several more seconds passed without an answer. They began a circuit around the room.

"What if she's unconscious? That could've given her a serious head injury," said Lorna. "Or if not unconscious—"

"Don't. Last thing we need is another body."

But he'd been thinking it before she said it. He hadn't been himself when they'd put Maeve down here. Ever since he was a kid, whenever he got angry—really angry—a second person seemed to take over. He'd scream and hit and rage. Sometimes, once it was over, he couldn't really remember all that he'd done. It would come back to him later, like the memory of an old television show. Sometimes that memory would make him ill, and other times he could ignore what he'd done. But he couldn't ignore Maeve. Not because of who she was or their shared history, but because he didn't want to be responsible for anyone's death. To see her curled in a corner, unmoving, with a bloody head wound, no breath left in her body, and to know he did that? He'd start drinking more than Mum.

Oliver tripped and stumbled against the wall.

"What the fuck was that?" he asked, afraid it was Maeve.

"A big, scary lantern," Lorna picked it up by the handle.

Oliver pointed the light down. "By a puddle of blood."

He'd stepped into the stain unawares but now saw the pattern of blood all over the dirt floor. Drops here and there. But no sign of a body.

"Shit," Lorna whispered.

"Right then, Maeve," he said, a tremor in his voice. "Come on out. We really do want to talk."

But Maeve didn't come out, and the more they searched the cellar, the fewer places there were for her to hide, until none were left.

"I don't like this," he said. "You don't lock someone in a cellar because you want them to disappear. Shit. Caskie killed her, didn't he? That's what he was doing before we came down. He's killed her and put her in the dining room or the kitchen. And we caught him in the act."

"And now he's alone with Ellie," Lorna said.

"Shit." Oliver raced up the stairs, Lorna close behind, and flung open the study door.

Lorna screamed first.

Oliver thought the shadows were playing tricks on him, but the longer he stared, the more he understood what was happening.

James Caskie, one arm untied, was staring at a dark stain spreading across his stomach while blood dripped from the corkscrew in Ellie's hand.

Pp. 75–82
The five of them, they were animals. James Caskie's death proves that. You couldn't trust them at all. I've been saying that for years. Ever since I first met them. Or not then. That's a lie. Sorry. A few months after I met them. After Callum did something really stupid. When, in the middle of this ticking time bomb, he put himself in the most dangerous position of all—the center of their attention.

The precipitation falling that day in February wouldn't be classified as snow by anyone outside of England. Most would have called it a flurry, yet within the confines of the capital and her suburbs, the light white dusting that coated the ground like sugar was enough to halt public transport and close most local shops. The inhabitants of 215 Caldwell Street had been trapped within their rented walls for eleven hours, low on supplies and bereft of amicability.

From the top floor, Hollis's music thumped into Lorna's room, vibrating the walls. As she tried to complete her course readings, she found herself reading the same lines over and over, the yellow highlighter growing warm in her fingers. She had failed her last essay thanks to a lecturer who refused to acknowledge feminist perspectives of film theory. She had never failed an assignment before, and was not going to again even though she'd been stuck with the same lecturer for the new term. But Hollis's music made it impossible to concentrate. A break at the end of a song allowed her a moment's respite and she reached for another piece of shortbread from the tin at the side of her bed. Her fingers brushed crumbs and smooth metal and she stared down at the shining empty container. Her stomach grumbled. A proper dinner would involve going downstairs and making conversation with those there, so she licked the crumbs from her fingers and tried to will the hunger away. But Hollis's music started again and she couldn't focus on the words in front of her, which seemed more content to dance to the heavy beat than stick inside her brain.

The half bag of Smarties in the bottom of her backpack helped stave off the hunger for another few minutes but replaced it with a sugar rush that made her giddy and even more irritable. She put a bookmark in *Men, Women, and Chain Saws: Gender in the Modern Horror Film* and opened Truffaut's *Hitchcock* but couldn't get past the table of contents. The call of the spinach and ricotta cannelloni microwave dinner waiting for her in the fridge became stronger than her desire to read more cinematic theory.

Descending to the front room felt akin to entering a stranger's house. Lorna drew as little attention to herself as she could. Oliver was stretched out on the sofa and laughing at some inane program on TV while Callum sat in the armchair flipping through a stack of photographs. Neither spoke to Lorna as she passed, and she thought perhaps her anxieties had been unfounded. Perhaps she could heat up her meal and return upstairs without anyone saying a word to her. Then she opened the fridge.

"What the fuck?" She stomped back into the front room. "Who ate my cannelloni?"

"Dunno." Oliver yawned and scratched his stomach. "Are you sure you even had any?"

"Of course I'm sure. I bought it yesterday, put it in the fridge, and now it's gone."

"Well maybe you ate it yesterday and forgot."

"Yeah. Definitely. That's exactly it."

"Sorry, Lorna," said Callum. "I remember seeing it in there."

"That's really helpful, Callum. Cheers." She thought of saying more but knew it would be pointless, and so focused her energy on finding evidence of the theft. She dug through the rubbish bin but couldn't find any of the packaging, even after sifting all the way to the bottom. She went out into the garden, shivering in her thin jumper, and checked the bigger bin out back, but there was nothing there, either. Whoever ate it had either hidden the packaging in their room or disposed of it elsewhere.

Back upstairs, she went into the bathroom to relieve herself of the three cups of tea she'd had so far that day, trying to figure out what else she had left for dinner, and there in the small wastebasket under the bathroom sink was the empty plastic container and cardboard sheath of her missing microwave dinner.

"Un-fucking-believable!"

She grabbed the packaging, intending to wave it in Oliver's face—because of course it must have been Oliver—when something else in the bin caught her eye. She had just cottoned on to what it was when someone ripped it out of her hand.

"Whoa-ho! What do we have here?" Oliver, who had snuck up behind her, turned the small cardboard box over in his hands. "Well, well, Lorna, have you been keeping a secret from us?"

She jumped to snatch it back, but he held it out of her reach. "I was looking for this"—she held up the food packaging—"and I found that alongside it."

"Riiiiight." He paused, then a smile crept over his face. "Actually, coming from you, I do believe it. So let's find out whose this is, shall we?"

"Oliver, maybe we shouldn't . . ."

But for Oliver, this was better than Christmas morning. He bounded out of the bathroom, shouting "house meeting" as he knocked on doors. The house atmosphere had been spiraling down the toilet for a while now. Maeve's "no-fun" referendum in January had led to the Berry Avenue student house becoming the party spot of the spring term, and while they always invited Oliver, rather than host, he had to play second fiddle to that fat bastard Jabba. With another week left until the party ban would be lifted, another week before Oliver could return any semblance of normality to this dull place, this find represented the change in fortune that was due him.

He gathered them downstairs—Hollis leaning against the closet under the stairs, Ellie on the sofa, Maeve in the kitchen doorway, picking at a hangnail, Callum in the armchair, and Lorna on the bottom step of the staircase, ready to beat a hasty retreat. Oliver stood in the center of them all, the box hidden in the front pocket of his Cahill University hoodie.

"I suppose you're wondering why I called you all here."

Hollis raised his hand. "Did someone let the squirrels in again?"

"What? No. Turns out we have a little mystery brought to my attention by the lovely Lorna."

She folded her arms. "Don't bring me into this."

"But aren't you the one who discovered it?"

"Get on with it," Hollis said.

"Very well. Upstairs, hidden in the bottom of the bathroom bin was none other than . . ."

"I did it!"

Everyone turned to Maeve.

"I ate your cannelloni. I'm really sorry, Lorna. I'll buy you two to replace it as soon as the shops open, I swear. I have a can of ravioli, if you want it."

"It's fine, Maeve. Thanks."

The group shifted as if accepting the mystery solved. Oliver was losing them, so he spoke louder to recover.

"How noble of you to confess, dear Maeve! But Lorna's missing dinner isn't the mystery." He whipped out the box and held it high in the air, turning about so everyone could see the image of the pregnancy test on the front.

"Now Lorna says it isn't hers, and I'm inclined to believe her."

He watched their eyes fall away from Lorna and shift to Maeve and Ellie, who kept throwing glances at one another.

"All right then, ladies. Time to fess up. Which one of you is going to be a mummy?"

"Did you find the actual stick?" Hollis asked.

"No, just the box," Lorna answered.

They usually sided with Oliver, but if Hollis was firm enough, they would shift allegiances. But Hollis said nothing more, leaving Oliver free to continue.

"Come on. Don't keep us in suspense! That's how rumors get started. Isn't it better if we're all open and honest with one another?"

Maeve sucked in her lips the way she always did when she had something to say but wasn't sure she should. Usually, it was better if she didn't. At best, it would be something inane and toothless; at worst, offensive and inconsiderate. Ellie stared at her lap, her fists clenched tight enough that her already pale knuckles turned a lighter shade of white. The seconds ticked by, marked by the snowflakes spotting the windows.

Despite the chill outside, the temperature inside increased, the room like an underground bunker with the oxygen running out. They knew that wasn't true. They each knew they could walk out a door or up the stairs at any time, and maybe things would be different now if they had, but they didn't. Something held them there, and they didn't want to admit what it was. To admit that they wanted to know.

Time stretched, slower than when their English lit lecturer had asked that wafer-thin girl in the back row something about Hamlet and the girl had sat there unable to utter a sound as her skin grew redder and redder and the lecturer had waited, tapping his foot, folding his arms, and the girl started to cry until finally someone in the front row shouted out the answer and spared her.

They didn't know who they were right now. If they were the lecturer or one of the dozens of students hunkering down in their seats. They certainly weren't the student in the front. They never would be.

Like the earth completing its rotation, Oliver finished another turn, the empty pregnancy test box held high in the air. Then several things happened at once.

A car drove past. Hollis sneezed. Maeve started to speak. Ellie spoke louder.

"It's Maeve's!"

They thought a glass had shattered. But it hadn't. That was only what it felt like.

"It is not." Maeve's voice cracked.

"She told me when she got back from Christmas break that she'd slept with this boy from home and she was worried that she might be pregnant because they hadn't used protection."

"That's not . . ." Maeve closed her eyes and shook her head. "I told you that in . . . That's yours. I know you bought it. Tell the truth!"

"I did buy it. For her. Because she was too scared to get it herself."

"I wasn't too scared! I never needed it in the first place."

Oliver spun the box. "So you're not pregnant?"

"No!" Maeve shook her head again. "I mean I never thought I was! It's hers. It's Ellie's." She pointed as if they might need reminding who Ellie was. Or perhaps she wanted to redirect their eyes away from her, but Oliver's gaze held firm.

"And why would Ellie need a pregnancy test?"

Maeve looked at Oliver. Everyone else looked away. None dared say it, Maeve least of all. She would rather let herself be slaughtered. And when it seemed the final knife would stab Maeve's heart, her denials and accusations disregarded, prepared to become the detritus of an unfair joke dug up over the next several months, a cataclysmic shift occurred.

Callum stood up.

Callum, his thin arms hidden in the padding of an oversized gray sweatshirt, Callum, a good stone lighter than Oliver, grabbed the box from Oliver's fingers and walked it out to the garden. In the silence formed by their shock, they heard him deposit it into the big bin. He returned with hands again stuffed into the front pocket of his hoodie.

"It doesn't matter," he said. "It's none of our business."

Without meeting anyone's eye, he crossed the circle of bodies and walked up the stairs. The tension that had held them there like the grip of a spider's web unraveled. Hollis grabbed his coat off the hook and left through the front door. Oliver let out a single confused laugh that fell on empty air, muttered to himself, and scurried upstairs. Lorna went next, leaving Ellie and Maeve alone. Neither would look at the other. If either spoke, the force of their words would've been enough to crack the foundations of the house. So it was in silence that Ellie ran upstairs, leaving Maeve shaking in the kitchen doorway until she, too, gathered enough strength to move.

The light in Lorna's room shifted from gray day to gray dusk. Her hunger had grown, but leaving her room wasn't an option. The last time she'd left she'd caused near disaster. So it was better to stay locked away where no one could trouble her. Where she could trouble no one. She read the same passage of *Hitchcock* over and over, underlining the same sentences, her highlighter leaking through the page, until a new distraction emerged in the form of voices on the other side of the cold wall that partitioned her room from Callum's. Callum and a girl. Maeve, she thought, based on the conversation.

"*I told you. I really don't care.*"

"*But I want you to know the truth.*"

"*I meant what I said. It's none of my business.*"

"*But it was . . .*"

"*I don't want to gossip!*"

Something thumped against the wall, and Lorna jerked away. Had that been a hint to stop eavesdropping? No, they couldn't have known, but their voices dropped to an indistinct hum rather than words. She pressed her ear to the wall but heard nothing more than mumbles. In her distraction, her book slid off the bed and thudded to the floor, waking her from her trance. This was ridiculous. She would never behave like this at home. Never.

A sudden knock sounded on her door. The voices in Callum's room went quiet. Lorna bookmarked her page and opened her door to find Maeve in her woolen winter jacket, snowflakes coating her shoulders like a heavy layer of dandruff, eyes puffy from crying. She held out two containers of microwavable cannelloni.

"The off-license down by the pub was open. Not sure how good they are but they're within the expiration date, so . . ." She held them out.

"Thanks." Lorna took only one. "You need dinner, too, right?"

Ellie appeared at the opposite end of the hall, ready to turn into the bathroom, but when she spotted Lorna and Maeve, she hurried back upstairs.

"I'm not really hungry." Maeve handed Lorna the other container. The words Lorna wanted to say caught in her throat, but she managed to speak before Maeve walked away.

"I believe you."

She also wanted to say she was sorry, but she couldn't get it out. Maeve hesitated as if she wanted to say something in return, but she dusted the melting snow from her hair and then shuffled to the staircase.

Maeve watched the water bead on her jacket and wished she could stay downstairs with others, but no one wanted her in their presence. Not even Lorna, whose door had once again closed. As she retreated upstairs, Callum emerged from his room, and she paused, thinking he might welcome her, but he made no acknowledgment that he saw her, even though he had to know she was there. She wasn't trying to hide. It was like he wanted her to watch, to bear witness as he knocked on Oliver's door and asked, "Can we talk?"

All doors closed to her, Maeve went to the only one over which she retained any control. The spacious double had never before felt as empty as it did now, even cluttered as it was with her suitcases and clothes and posters and textbooks. She curled up on her bed because she wanted to feel small, contained, manageable.

Why the fuck had she told Ellie about Thomas Kinsey? What moment of utter weakness had caused her to sit cross-legged on the floor and spill her guts about losing her virginity to her secondary school crush over Christmas break? Thank god she hadn't told Ellie everything. She had left out the bit about how Thomas Kinsey had gained a stone and an acne problem since the last she saw him and now smoked so much that his breath always stank and his teeth were the color of weak piss. Because those were the only reasons the once-beloved golden boy had deigned to sleep with her. The freedom of university life had wrecked him, and Maeve, who'd always been a wreck, was finally in his league.

But she'd never feared pregnancy, never told Ellie she had. Her period had come two weeks later, right on schedule. In fact, the arrival of her period remained the only reliable thing in her life. None of that mattered now, not with what Ellie had said. Though they both lived on the top floor, in the house hierarchy, Ellie remained firmly above her. The others would always believe her lies over Maeve's truth.

At some point she'd begun crying again, her face a soggy mess, and she wiped it across her coat sleeve, unable to motivate herself to get out of her wet things, and swore she would never forgive Ellie for this—not tomorrow or in a month or in a year or in twenty years—and her crying became more fierce, a mix of anger and shame, and if she was grateful for one thing that night it was that Hollis turned on his music and she could not be heard.

A mere four steps away, in her own room, perched on the edge of her bed, Ellie also appreciated Hollis's music, but for a different reason. She did not know the artist or even the song, but the deep, pounding base-line mixed with the jarring chords spoke to a part of her she didn't know existed, mimicking a feeling she kept buried beneath her smiles and graciousness and cleanliness. A feeling that made her want to rage and scream and smash. That music wound its way inside her, wrapped itself around every nerve, and before she knew what she had done, all of her framed pictures were smashed on the floor. Like a wicked fairy, the feeling flew out of her when the song ended, leaving her ashamed and trembling, surrounded by her destruction.

I watched Ellie from the stairwell that day. There was a mirror on the back of her door, and I saw her reflection, and I prayed and prayed she would cut her hand. But the first time her hands would become covered in blood did not happen until just a few hours ago.

8

Maeve

She wished she had her cards, pretended to feel their comforting touch, and tried to visualize their words, the typeface, the colors, but a clear image wouldn't form in her mind. It was like trying to grab hold of a stray dog, running out of reach when she thought she had it cornered. Anxiety always took form of a dog: her dog as a child, slipping its collar and dashing away from her, never to be seen again. But she had to let it go. Let it all go. If she wanted to get out of here alive, she had to let go of everything in the past. Let herself become someone new. Close the door on everything that had once hurt her.

"You're a good person," she whispered. "You're a good person. You're a good person. You're a good person."

The footsteps retreated from the cellar door. Maeve emerged from the stack of crates she'd used for cover, slicing her hand on an open pair of shears.

"Shit! Ow!"

She covered her mouth with her good hand and stared at the ceiling. The footsteps didn't return. Quietly, she found the stack of old towels and wrapped one around the cut. Whoever was up there was not someone she wanted to meet. She turned back to the dark passage. Not wanting to be followed, she concealed the door behind her, then started down.

The stone floor and walls, illuminated by the old torch she'd found hanging on the wall, were supported by wooden beams that reminded her of the uni-sponsored trip to the Parisian catacombs, when she got separated from the group and was later found, crying of course, by a tour guide as her coach was about to leave. The memory didn't help. Nor did the memory of Callum sitting next to her on the ride back to the hostel, giving her a warm croissant he'd bought for her while the group had waited for her to be found. In the catacombs, her only company had been the skulls lining the walls and the whispering she swore that she'd heard and confessed only to Callum.

The passage was short and ended in a set of stairs that led up to a door similar to the one in the cellar. A terrifying thought formed in her mind—what if she was still in the cellar after all? What if the door and passageway had been an illusion brought on by stress? Her panic worsened when she found the door locked. It was true. She'd lost it. A full-blown hallucination. Even her newfound strength was only an illusion. Then she remembered the key in her pocket, the one that had been in the door on the cellar's end. She stopped hyperventilating and stuck the torch under her armpit. Then, with her uninjured hand, she fumbled the key into the lock. The door opened.

The room was an empty shell of a once grand ballroom. A row of boarded-up windows spotted the wall to her right while drop cloths lay on the floor, giving the impression the dancers' bodies had disappeared, leaving piles of clothes behind. Her footsteps echoed to the high ceiling as she crossed the floor. She found another door to her left, but when she tried it, it was locked. Further down, she tugged at the boards covering one of the windows, but they were nailed tight. She reached the end and turned around, which was when her light caught a flash of white. When she'd first entered, she hadn't looked behind her. Now she couldn't look away.

From this distance, it was difficult to make out what she was seeing—something covering the back wall, like peeling wallpaper. As she stepped closer, she noticed images. They were pictures. Pictures tacked to the wall. At first she didn't recognize what they were of. Another few steps, and they came into focus.

It was them. Pictures taken over twenty years ago: Hollis, Ellie, Oliver, Lorna, her. Some contained Callum. Others did not. And then she noticed other pictures. Ones from not so long ago. Pictures she recognized from her Facebook page and Ellie's. Pictures of Hollis in his police uniform. And pictures that were not from online. Pictures that could only have been taken by someone on the street. Ellie walking out of Top Shop. Oliver smoking against the side of a pub. Hollis leaving a football pitch with a young woman who shared his stocky frame. Maeve kneeling in the park, talking to strangers' dogs.

"Holy shit."

On the floor below, what she had mistaken for another drop cloth was a sleeping bag. Alongside it, empty tins of food. A broken bottle of Drakkar Noir. That's what she'd smelled from the cellar. Plus dirty clothes. And notebooks. Notebooks of all shapes and sizes scattered around the floor. She picked one up. A journalist-style Moleskine, mostly filled in small, blocky handwriting. Some of the words were in a shorthand she didn't recognize and there were names, too—Landry, Catherine Marcus—that meant nothing to her. She dropped the notebook back onto the pile and chose another, spiral bound with lined paper. This was filled with a completely different but also unfamiliar handwriting, a slanted feminine script. The font was so narrow, she could only make out a word here and there. But two that leapt out at her began with big, looping C's that appeared over and over.

Caldwell.

Callum.

Lorna

A bubble of blood escaped Caskie's lips.

"Don't . . . don't do it. Juh-juh . . . en—"

His body slumped forward. Blood dripped onto his jeans. Lorna waited for his head to bounce upward. For one final gasp of life. For his breath to pierce the air. But it was over. He had choked on his final words.

Ellie stared at the corkscrew in her bloodstained fist. With her clean hand, she brushed a loose strand of hair from her cheek, then placed the corkscrew on the bar. Exchanged it for a wineglass.

"Mind if I have a drink?"

Her hand shook, the red wine slopping up the sides of the glass. The rim trembled as she pressed it to her lower lip.

Lorna pictured herself flying at Ellie, knocking her to the ground, the glass shattering against the floor. But her brain had disconnected from her body. It shouted commands, but she remained as still as Caskie.

Ellie tipped the glass back as she finished the last of the wine. With a cocktail napkin, she dabbed the corners of her lips, ignoring the blood drying on her right hand.

"What. The. Fuck," Oliver said.

Ellie twisted the napkin in her fingers.

"He knew my name." She pinched her eyes shut, adding lines to her forehead that hadn't existed twenty years prior.

"My maiden name. He knew the nickname 'Hunt the—' You know. And he knew the Caldwell Street address."

"He didn't say that. I don't believe you." The words floated from Lorna's lips before she had the chance to stop them. Her body was rebooting, but not all the processes were working.

"He said he was trying to help. That he knew what happened at 215 Caldwell Street. About what happened to Callum. He mentioned Callum by name and said that was why he'd come. He'd been lying to us all along."

"You killed him," Lorna said.

"He was planning on killing us! Look. Look at his hand. He'd got one free, see? I turned my back to him when I couldn't bear to listen to him anymore, and when I turned back around the ropes were coming undone and he was going to run at me, so I . . . I . . ." She waved her hand, then resumed tearing the cocktail napkin to pieces. "It was self-defense."

"You can't prove any of that!" Lorna said. "So his hand got loose? So what? There's no sign that he was about to attack. Just your word for it. Fuck. Do you ever think at all? Someone's been trying to prove we're murderers, so what do you do? You murder someone!"

Lorna wrapped her arms tight around her chest, afraid she might fall apart. She needed to think, but she couldn't. She needed to run away, but she couldn't. She needed to cry, but she couldn't. All she could do was stand there and try not to lose it until she could figure out what to do next, which she couldn't do until she could think.

Oliver leaned on the bar, staring at the corkscrew. "Lorna's right. Forget going to the police."

"But it was self-defense." The whine in Ellie's voice made Lorna want to scream. Oliver did it for her.

"Shut up, Ellie! You stupid— Even if Lorna and I lied and said we saw everything you just described, and I mean everything, it's too suspicious. And even if we untied him now and said he got completely free, they'd do all this forensic shit to prove he was tied up when he died. The long and the short of it is we tied a man to a chair and you stabbed him to death. And—here's another *even if*—even if we could sell it, which is a fucking big if, they'd want to know more about what he was doing to us. Why we were so desperate to silence him. Too many questions I don't want to answer. This isn't like Callum. We can't cover this one up." Oliver paused and drummed his fingers on the bar. "I suppose, though, that there is an upside to all of this."

"Please," said Lorna. "Share with the class."

"Ellie got info. Caskie really was our mystery benefactor. No more Caskie means no more someone trying to kill us. We can take our time figuring out what to—"

Maeve burst through the study door.

"Someone's been living in the closed wing!" She saw Caskie's body. "Shit!"

"You're alive?" Oliver asked. Lorna couldn't tell if he was pleased or disappointed. She felt nothing. She hadn't expected Maeve to be dead, so to her, Maeve's return felt expected. They were all together again, the way it should be, but Lorna felt nothing.

"Of course I'm— Who the fuck is that?"

"What do you mean, someone's been living in the closed wing?" Lorna asked. The words tasted like cardboard against her tongue. "Where have you been?"

Maeve couldn't draw her eyes away from the body. "There's a passage down there, in the cellar. To the other wing. The door opens onto a ballroom, or what looks like one. There's not much furniture, but the walls are covered in pictures. Of us. And a sleeping bag. Old clothes. Tins of food. It's pretty creepy to be honest. Is that . . . is that Mr. Caskie? Is he dead?"

Oliver rubbed his hands together. "That's it then. Further proof, if you needed it, Lorna. Caskie hid in the other wing, waiting for the right moment to pop out and surprise us. I bet there are other passages like the one Maeve found. Servant's entrances. Old houses are full of shit like that."

"If it was him living there, he wasn't alone," Maeve said.

"Give us a break, love! I thought even you could put two and two together and get four. Let us have a win."

"Yeah, well, here's some math for you, Oliver. If Mr. Caskie was the one living in that ballroom, then tell me what he needed a bra and a box of tampons for."

Normally Lorna loved seeing Oliver taken down a few pegs, his confidence draining away, the slouch in his shoulders showing he was beaten. But she couldn't muster any schadenfreude as her own world tilted beneath her feet. She gripped the bar counter to keep herself steady.

"You're lying," said Oliver.

"Go see for yourself."

"Why would she lie?" Lorna asked.

Ellie laughed, and the others stared. It was high and nervous, like someone embarrassed at being scared. "How stupid are we?"

Lorna couldn't tell if she was somehow referring to Maeve or to something else, but Ellie wasn't looking at Maeve as she lowered herself to a barstool, holding a freshly filled glass with both hands.

"I can't remember her name. What was her name?"

"Ellie?" Oliver asked.

"The pregnancy test wasn't mine."

Lorna didn't understand what she was talking about, and neither, it appeared, did Oliver. But Maeve grimaced.

"And I know it wasn't yours," Ellie admitted, looking at Maeve. "You've waited two decades for me to say it, so there it is. It wasn't yours. But I swear it wasn't mine."

"What pregnancy test?" Oliver asked.

"The box Lorna found in the bathroom bin," Maeve said. "The night of the snowstorm."

"We are such idiots," Ellie said. "We forgot about *her*. I don't remember her name. Can't even picture her face. But I remember thinking she was too pretty for him. Sometimes I'd see her coming in and out of the house. Don't you remember? Callum's girlfriend."

Lorna watched Oliver and Maeve's reactions, wondered what her own face showed, while in her head she looked at Caskie's body and did some math.

"Shit. I remember. I would hear them arguing," Oliver said. "Even though they didn't shout, the sound would travel across the hall into my room."

"I did, too," Lorna chimed in. "From my side of the wall."

"Terrible insulation, Caldwell Street." Ellie sipped her wine. "Maeve, don't cry. We all forgot things about those days."

Maeve wiped a sleeve across her eyes. "It's not that I forgot. I really never knew."

"So," Oliver said, his brain ticking slower than the rest. "Callum had a girlfriend. She's the one who used the pregnancy test and . . ." He looked at Caskie's body. As Lorna had already done, he now did the math on Caskie's age. "Fuck. Oh, fuck me!"

"We were wondering what Caskie's motive was," Ellie said.

"They . . ." Maeve stammered. "They have the same hair."

Oliver kept cursing. "Some crazy bitch went to all this trouble because she thinks we killed Callum, and Ellie's gone and gutted her *son*?" He threw a barstool across the room. No one flinched. "We're so fucking dead!"

"Unless we get out of here," Ellie said.

"You want to run?" Maeve asked.

"As fast as I can. We can figure out the rest later. But first we have to get out of this house. Get to the quay. Caskie said he left a boat there. Even if that was a lie and we have to wait a day for a ferry, we'll have the water at our backs and a clear view of the land in front. She can't sneak up on us. Out there in the open, four against one, those are chances I'd take. Oliver's right. If we stay here another night, we're dead. No matter who killed Callum, she'll hold us all responsible for this. I checked him already, and he didn't have the keys on him. Maeve, did you see a way out through the other wing?"

Maeve was chewing so hard on a hangnail, Lorna thought she might tear her whole thumb off. She took her finger from her mouth and wiped it on her jeans.

"No. I don't know. It was dark. There are windows, but they're boarded up. There might be other rooms we can get into. I didn't search the whole place. Like I said, it was creepy."

"Right, then." Oliver took the glass from Ellie's hands and placed it on the bar. "No time like the present. Let's get the fuck out of here."

Ellie followed him to the door, while Maeve and Lorna lagged behind. "We're just going to leave him here?" Lorna asked.

"You want to stay here alone and keep him company, be my guest. Come on, Ellie. Maeve, show us the way."

Oliver and Ellie left the study. Lorna spared James Caskie another glance, then followed. At the doorway, out of the others' earshot, Maeve tugged on her sleeve.

"Lorna ..."

But she shrugged Maeve off and kept walking without looking back. The only way out of here now was to keep moving forward.

Ellie

It had all started innocently enough, of course. A glance at one another during an Avon party she was hosting at Bethany Stone's house. He was the only man there, meant to be watching the children while Ellie hosted and Bethany and the other women played little parlor games and oohed and aahed at the free samples. But the children kept screaming in the back garden, disrupting Ellie's concentration. None of the women acknowledged the flaws in her performance, but she knew they noticed. As soon as she packed up her kits and drove off without a sale, her awkwardness would become the hot topic of conversation among Bethany and her friends, and Ellie would be back to spending hours at home, staring at the walls, pretending to care about linen selections while David worked fourteen-hour days.

She had left the women smelling samples of next spring's fragrance line and excused herself to the kitchen, where she helped herself to a glass of water. Outdoors, the children—seven or eight of them—wrestled on the ground, pulling each other's hair, a football forgotten by the fence.

He stood inside the garden doors, looking out at them with the same exhaustion she felt inside. He noticed her then, smiled and shrugged. The women in the front room burst into a laughter that pierced Ellie's ears. She winced, and he saw it. So she smiled and shrugged. To her amazement, he'd laughed. She couldn't remember the last time she'd made David laugh, and suddenly she didn't feel as tired and distracted as before. She returned to the party with renewed vigor and pulled out her biggest sales of the year. Bethany, who received a commission for hosting, was well pleased and held her back after the other women and their children had left. The man, whom she had assumed belonged to one of those other women, remained. Bethany introduced them as she prepared some tea.

"Ellie, dear, have you met my brother, Gordon?"

He was tall and muscular, with thick, dark hair, white teeth all in a row like a Hollywood movie star. And nothing like David at all.

Gordon texted her two days later. He'd swiped her number from Bethany, he said, and wanted to meet her for a drink somewhere, and soon. Ellie, a good girl, immediately replied that she was flattered but also that she was married. His response had been simple: *I know*. That should have been enough of a warning, but Ellie had never learned to heed warnings.

Sex followed quickly—the first time a hurried affair in the back of her car. Then later his flat, a hotel, even Bethany's house when she and the family were away in Majorca, on the same table where she'd so carefully presented samples of hand lotion and perfume.

But as quickly as it had begun, it turned sour. As with many things in her life, Ellie got bored. She thought she could cast him off as fast as she'd led him on, but the text messages continued. She didn't respond. Then came the phone calls. Then showing up on her doorstep. David had chased him away with a broom handle. After failing to convince David that the handsome young man had been some religious fanatic, Ellie crumbled under the weight of this new lie and promised to break it off. Promised she'd never do anything like that again. David promised to be a better husband, more loving, more attentive. And he was. But then Jilly was born several months later, and Gordon came back to her life. Whenever David slipped in his attentions, Gordon was there to entertain her. Sometimes it was only for a single day. One day spread out over years. Sometimes it lasted a week. A month. But she always broke it off again and she never told David.

After fourteen years, Gordon had become as familiar as an old handbag. One of sentimental value. Worth almost nothing but well-worn. Comfortable. A staple of her wardrobe that she liked to drag out of the closet now and then. Remember how it felt. The years had put lines on his face and gray in his hair. Made him unattractive to others. Kept him hers. How many times had she sat with him in that bustling Costa on the Kings Road, surrounded by mums with prams and students with laptops, each too engulfed with themselves to notice this strange couple always teetering on the edge? He was her junior, but it was she who enjoyed these childish games, played with him as she had with her toys when she was a girl. Picking them apart and piecing them back together so that they were never quite the same. Never letting anyone else touch them.

"No, Gordon."

"But we—"

"No, I don't think it's appropriate that 'we'—you meant you, of course—see other people. You pursued me all those years ago, if you'll recall, knowing I was *married.*" She leaned in and whispered the word. "You wanted me. You have me. You should've thought of the long-term consequences if this wasn't what you wanted."

"I want something stable. Consistent. A relationship I can discuss openly. Not hide in the shadows."

"Lower your voice, darling. People might stare. Look, I can see you're upset. Why don't you take a deep breath and go fetch us some more coffees? And one of those pastries I like. The millionaire shortbread. Then, when you get back, we can continue to discuss this like rational adults." Her smile was like the snap of her fingers. He went from the table, and her eyes traced the familiar slouched lines of his figure.

The chime of her phone pulled her gaze away, which was when she first saw the message from the blocked number.

Would be a shame if your husband found out.

Ellie looked around the café, spotted Gordon in the queue but no sign of who texted her.

Keeping Gordon around after all this time.

And then came the picture. Her and Gordon in her car. The new car David had bought her last week.

Gordon remained in the queue, speaking to the barista. Her hands shook as she typed a reply. She took the time to go back and correct her mistakes.

What do you want?

She waited. The caffeine made her edgy. Her bouncing knee banged the underside of the table. Money, favors. What could she offer to keep this from getting out? Even her daughter's hand in marriage wasn't off the table at this point. But the words that popped up on the screen were the last she'd expected. She gripped the phone with two hands to be sure she was reading it right.

Caldwell Street.

Callum.

Wait for the email, princess.

A millionaire shortbread appeared on a plate. Gordon said something to her, but all she could see was her phone. Somehow, she had made it to her car before screaming.

How could a little decision she made years ago lead her here? If she had chosen to cut Gordon free when she was supposed to, would she even be here inside Wolfheather House now?

As they walked down the passage, Ellie pressed her hand against her thigh to keep it from shaking. It was adrenaline, she knew that, coursing through her body. The adrenaline from taking care of young Mr. Caskie. It had been the right choice. She knew that. He couldn't be allowed to get away from them. Not with what he said. Not with what he knew. She wished, though, that the adrenaline would hurry up and leave. It was the same way she reacted after a fight with David or after she smacked one of the children. This heat would linger inside her until she could go for a run or take a bubble bath or lock herself in the walk-in closet and scream until she ran out of breath.

Those options weren't on the table as she followed Oliver and Maeve up the steps at the end of the dark passage. She would have to hold it all in, hope her hand would stop shaking on its own.

Oliver and Maeve paused at the top of the short flight of steps. Lorna, unaware, bumped into the back of Ellie, mumbled something that might have been an apology. Ellie's glower went unacknowledged.

Oliver pushed the door open.

Peeling paint that might've been green but took on a bluish hue in the light from their phones covered the walls, except for places where door-frames had been bricked up long ago, the mortar chipped and gray. The windows at the front had been boarded up, like Maeve said, and those boards were covered—plastered—in photographs. Photos from their Caldwell Street days. Ones from earlier that year. Ellie even saw her decades-old engagement photo. She dug the nails of her shaking hand into her thigh.

"This is some serial killer shit, this is," Oliver said, startling her. He'd stuck close to her in the passage and remained close to her side now. She didn't like the way he looked at her. Like he was trying to see inside her head. Like he no longer completely trusted her.

"Yes. It's disturbing," she said, stepping away from him. He followed.

"There are some doors down here that aren't boarded up," Lorna said, making her way down the length of the ballroom.

Ellie's gaze focused on one picture. Oliver moved the light away.

"Hang on." She grabbed his wrist and pulled it back to that spot. "I recognize this picture."

"I recognize a whole fucking lot of them."

"No, not like that." She plucked it from the wall. The pin that had held it in place skittered to the floor. An adult couple in their forties, in a picture taken very much in the eighties, smiled in front of Wolfheather House.

"Why do they look familiar?" Oliver asked.

"Because Callum kept this picture stuck on the wall above his desk. I remember warning him that if he used Blu Tack it would ruin the walls and he might not get his security deposit back. Oliver, these are Callum's parents. Do you remember how he used to say he was from Inverness but that his family didn't live there anymore? That his dad had bought a place farther out?"

"You think this is Callum's house?"

"Leave me alone, Maeve!" Lorna's voice echoed to the back of the ballroom. Lorna waved her mobile. "Check over there for a way out."

"All right! I'm sorry." Maeve crossed to the other side of the room.

"We need to get out of here. Fast," Oliver whispered to Ellie. "Find anything, girls?" he called out.

As he moved down the other end of the ballroom, Ellie tried to return the photo to the wall but couldn't find the tack. It seemed important, somehow, to return the picture where she found it, like she had further upset some balance by removing it. That this was somehow a more grievous error then the death of the man in the study. She knelt on the floor and rifled through the rubbish and belongings there, searching for the tack, until her hands fell upon a stack of notebooks.

One stood out from the rest, squarer and fatter with a cloth cover.

Some daylight peeked through the boarded windows and she tilted the notebook to get a better look. The Cahill logo emblazoned the front, along with a familiar name written in fat permanent marker across the top: ELEANOR HUNT. Inside, some of the ink was smudged and water damage warped the pages, but she recognized her own handwriting. Certain pages were marked with little tabs. The dates were printed neatly in the upper right-hand corner: 14 September 1994, 2 December 1994, 6 May 1995. She snapped the diary shut.

She was stuffing it down the back of her waistband, underneath her jumper, when Lorna called out.

"Hey guys. I think I found—"

A door slammed, cutting her off.

"Lorna?"

"Lorna!"

Ellie ran down the ballroom to where Oliver and Maeve were tugging on the door that must have shut on Lorna.

"Lorna?" Maeve asked. "Are you okay?"

A scream echoed through the hollow ballroom.

Ellie could barely keep track of what was happening. Oliver and Maeve banged on the door, trying to open it. Lorna banged on the other side. They were screaming her name and she was just screaming. Ellie's hand shook again, and she covered her ears.

Like a rainstorm winding down, sounds faded away. First Lorna's screams. Then Oliver's banging and shouting. All that was left was a pitiful "Lorna?" from Maeve. Oliver leapt back and it took Ellie a moment to realize why. Something seeped under the doorframe. Oliver shone his light on it. Red.

·"Oh, my god, Lorna," Maeve spoke softly. Suddenly, she threw her body at the door. It didn't budge, and she backed up and tried again. "We have to get her out of there. We have to—"

Oliver took Maeve by the wrist and held her back. "Do you see that? Do you see it?" He pointed again at the wet stain. "We don't know who's in there."

"Lorna's in there!"

"And who else?"

"Does it matter?" Maeve asked.

"It does if you don't want to be next."

"She could be alive. Head wounds bleed a lot."

"Yeah," Oliver grunted. "Just ask Hollis."

Ellie slapped him. Not too hard but enough to hurt. Enough to make him shut up.

"Give me your light," Ellie said. He stared at her, and she didn't think he'd listen. Then he slapped his phone into her palm.

Oliver kept Maeve back as Ellie knelt down, careful to avoid the stream of blood. She shone the light in the crack between the floor and the door. Lorna's glassy eye stared back. Her head rested in a pool of blood, the wound obscured by her hair and her position on the floor. Her half-lidded eye did not blink; no breath from her gaping mouth rippled the blood that passed beneath.

"Lorna?" she whispered, but Lorna wouldn't answer.

Ellie sat up and handed Oliver his phone back. There was no need to tell them what she saw. Oliver kept looking at the door, then the floor, as if trying to figure out how they fit together.

"If we all try the door," Maeve said, tears glistening on her face, "if we all kick it together we can get it . . . we can open it . . . if we—"

"She's dead, Maeve!" Oliver clenched his fist, like he was ready to thump her, but he kept his hands at his sides. "There's no point in opening the door. She's dead. We lost her, okay? We . . . She was an idiot for wandering off like that anyway. She was an idiot."

First Hollis. Now Lorna. Another connection snapped. Another broken strand of a web. They were unmoored. Ellie could see them all drifting further apart when the three of them needed to remain closer than ever.

The diary dug into her back.

"She'll keep coming after us," Ellie said. "One by one. Until we're all gone. It doesn't matter if we get out of here. If we escape this island alive. If we return to our families. She knows where we live. She knows all about us.

And she'll keep coming until we're dead. We'll spend the rest of our lives looking over our shoulders."

"Then what are we supposed to do?" Maeve's voice was foggy with tears.

Ellie could keep them together. Keep them on her side. And, if not, at least keep them in sight.

"We stop her here," she said. "We stop her now."

Pp. 84–89

When they were so certain they'd figured it all out, it took every ounce of self-control I had not to laugh. That was their problem. They were always so sure of themselves. That they knew everything. That they were doing the right thing. Even when it was obvious to anyone else how wrong they were.

That April, the residents of 215 Caldwell Street moved like planets, large and foreboding but limited in their rotations, passing far enough apart to avoid disaster, waiting for some unknowable force to push them out of orbit. Hollis could be around any of the girls but never Oliver. Oliver could only be in the same room with Lorna. Maeve would not have minded Oliver, but he took exception to her. The possibility of Maeve and Lorna depended on Lorna's mood. Ellie, attempting invisibility, avoided all, drifting from room to room like a lost satellite. No one paid much attention to Callum. Like Pluto, he once existed as one of them but no longer.

Their lives continued in this way until the day they made the decision that would eventually result in their deaths.

It started—though she would never acknowledge it—with Ellie, who on this day sat alone in her room as the world fell apart around her.

The words on the letter in her hand swirled around the page, each understandable on its own, but when arranged together made little sense. A wild green parrot landed on her windowsill and looked at her through the glass. Ellie stared back.

"I think I'm failing out of university."

The bird cocked its head to the side; then flew away, disregarding her petty human complaints. Ellie tried again to read the letter in full but found that she could not and gave up. Daddy always said it was fine to give up some things if she found they didn't suit her, like field hockey or horseback riding, but she was fairly certain one of those things wasn't a university education. Daddy thought women should be strong, self-sufficient, educated, and with a good job. "Let a man marry you for your money," he would say, but now that she thought about it, she didn't think it was a joke at all.

She set the letter on her desk so the words could not be read, but the orange Cahill emblem burned from the page like the eye of Sauron on the cover of the *Lord of the Rings* book Callum had abandoned in the front room. She stood up, slid the letter into an empty A4 folder, and sat back down. Then she stood up again and put the folder into her desk drawer alongside her diary. But the letter could not live there forever. Someone else would have to see it. She tried to imagine what it would be like to sit down with Daddy and Mother in the living room, surrounded by photographs of herself and her accomplishments, and explain to them the contents of this letter. She found that she couldn't. So she tried to imagine what it would be like if she simply handed them the letter and watched them react to its contents. She found that she could not do that, either. She could not visualize them receiving the contents of that letter in any form because in no future was it possible for her to explain to her intelligent, well-educated, happily employed parents that their only daughter was failing out of school. It had been bad enough when she'd only managed to get into Cahill. She blamed it on clearing, that she'd got a bad operator at the other university who didn't get her the spot she wanted, but that hadn't been true, and she suspected her parents knew as much. They could not see the letter without their perceptions of her potential changing once again. Ergo, they could not see the letter.

A sharp knock interrupted her thoughts. She thought it was the letter attempting to escape.

"Hey," Hollis called. "*The letting agency's on the phone. They want to know if you want the room next year.*"

As with the letter, she had difficulty understanding him.

"Me?"

"*Yeah, they're asking each of us. I can give them your answer if you want.*"

"Yes. I mean no. I mean I'm not sure yet. I'm waiting to hear what some other friends are doing," she lied. "When do they need an answer by?"

"They said today. They need to start advertising it for the autumn term."

"Do you think they could wait until Friday?"

Hollis said he would ask, and it turned out that, yes, they could wait until Friday but no later. If she hadn't decided by then, they would assume the answer was no.

"Are you staying?" she asked. If Hollis was staying, that would be all right, wouldn't it? She liked living with Hollis. But then she looked at her desk drawer and remembered it wasn't up to her if she wanted to stay.

"Might as well. I mean I . . . Look, this is weird talking through the door. Can I open it?"

"What? Yes, sorry. Of course." She had a smile on her face by the time the door opened. "Sorry, I was studying."

She sat on the bed with no books or papers in sight.

"Right, well." He cleared his throat. "Anyway, I'm thinking I'll stay, then I can leave my stuff over the summer instead of—"

"Let's order from that Indian place on Sandal Road!"

"Let's what?"

"Take away. Let's all get take away. Have dinner together. Order me a chicken tikka masala. With jasmine rice. Oh, and naan bread."

"Okay. Chicken curry. Jasmine rice. Naan bread. Got it." He waited in the doorway. Her smile struggled to hold as she waited for him to leave. "So, uhm, are we all going to pay for ourselves this time, or . . ."

"Oh. Oh! Yes, I have cash. Hang on." She grabbed her handbag from the back of the chair. When she opened her wallet, she saw a twenty-pound note, some change, and the credit card Daddy gave her for emergencies.

"They take card over the phone, don't they?"

"Yeah, but they won't split orders. So if you want—"

"That's all right." She handed over the card. "I'll pay for everyone. My treat."

Hollis hesitated. "Seriously?"

"Mm-hm."

He took the card as if he were afraid it would run away before he could grab it.

"Okay. Cheers. I won't tell Oliver, though. He finds out it's free he'll—"

She waved him off. "I don't mind. Tell Oliver. Tell everyone."

Hollis looked at the card, then at her. "Right. Well, I'll let you know when the food's here so you can . . ." He glanced at her bare desk. "Keep studying."

Her smile lingered a few moments after he closed the door, like the after-image of a camera flash.

Though Indian from Sandal Road normally took over an hour, in what seemed like no time at all, Hollis was again knocking on her door. The letter's presence remained with Ellie as she walked down the stairs. The memory of its contents wrapped around her waist like an unwanted hug and held her back from the kitchen as her housemates unpacked the food. The smell of curry and spices covered the fetid stench coming from the bin no one had emptied in almost two weeks. Brown paper bags, Styrofoam, and plastic containers littered the countertop. Like foxes in a rubbish bin, her housemates picked and pulled at what they found and filled their plates.

The most Ellie had ever charged to the card was £15 for a train ticket home and that had been for an actual emergency when her grandmother fell ill, but there had to be at least £100 worth of food strewn across the counter. She knew her parents could afford it, but this was a wasteful expense. Daddy hated waste. Wasting money, wasting time, wasting education.

"Hey, take a plate." Hollis placed one in her hands.

As each person filed out, she wandered in and searched through the crumbled bags and containers with a delicate touch, afraid to move a single scrap unless necessary because if she moved something, she would start to tidy up, and if she started to tidy up, she would start to clean, and if she started to clean, it would be like when she had chicken pox and Daddy told her not to scratch or it would make the itch worse. If she scratched that itch now, she would never ever stop.

She found her curry and her naan bread, but the rice had already migrated to the front room, piled high on Maeve's and Oliver's plates. She said nothing as she squeezed her thin body onto the floor next to the armchair where Hollis sat.

"You can sit here if you want," he offered, already shifting, but Ellie shook her head. Oliver cracked open a can of Heineken. He raised it in a toast. To her. They were all looking at her and raising their drinks—Lorna a Diet Coke, Maeve a Heineken, Hollis a Foster's. Ellie hadn't brought anything to drink.

"To the founder of the feast! Our Princess Ellie!" said Oliver.

"Princess!" they cheered.

Ellie wondered if they expected her to say something, but her contribution was forgotten as soon as they lowered their drinks.

"You know your Dickens?" Lorna asked.

"Not really. But I played Tiny Tim in a panto."

Maeve snorted beer through her nose and covered her face in embarrassment.

"You did panto?" Lorna asked.

"When I was *seven*. Besides, I was pretty damn good, I'll have you know. Bernard Cribbins played Scrooge, and he told me so himself. Even offered to hook Mum up with his agent. Gave her his number."

Lorna tore off a piece of garlic naan from a large plate on the center of the floor and asked, "So what stopped your illustrious childhood acting career?"

"Mum crashed our car and . . ." He cleared his throat. "We had a car crash. Nothing serious, but it messed up my knee. I could've only played kids with bum legs and I'd already played Tiny Tim—*the* top bum leg role—so what was there to aspire to, eh?"

He laughed, and the room laughed with him. No one but Ellie noticed the shadow upon his face.

Even Maeve, usually so in tune with his emotions, had forgotten to pay attention to Oliver. Her guilt kept her glancing at the front door. She shouldn't be having a good time with them. But then again, why not? She hadn't really promised anything, and she hadn't had Indian in ages. Plus, Ellie was paying. Maeve was skint, and going out would've cost her at least ten quid, if not more. This was an economical decision. Everyone laughed, and she joined in even though she didn't know what they were laughing at.

The evening continued that way, Maeve clinging to the threads of their conversations, too afraid of being cast aside to contribute any worthwhile comments, willing herself to be content on the fringes of this group even though she could have been with Callum instead, where she would've been the center of attention. When she thought the others weren't looking, she'd look at the door, waiting for him to appear. How long would he wait until he realized she wasn't coming?

When they finished their beers, someone found an old bottle of white wine. Maeve drank it warm from a Hoegaarden glass stolen from the pub. Even after the food was gone and Maeve had resorted to licking her finger and pressing it into the crumbs for something more to eat, they remained together, talking and laughing as the rooms within Caldwell Street warmed for the first time that year. The night could have continued in this way and ended amicably if Oliver hadn't said, "We should have a party."

The buoyant mood deflated, but Oliver laughed away the silence. "Come on. It's been ages! We've not had one all term."

They shifted in their seats.

"I don't mean tonight, obviously. Next week, end of term. We can blow off some steam. Say goodbye to old Caldwell Street in style."

If someone had said no right away, before breath could blow life into the idea, Oliver's proposal would have withered and died. Maeve knew she could do it. Maeve who, unbeknownst to them, had saved them from parties so far this term, she could speak up, and she knew she would be heard because she held the words they wanted to hear.

"I think it's a wonderful idea."

Everyone turned to Ellie. Maeve swallowed the sentence she'd been forming.

"You do?" Lorna asked.

"It would be great fun to get lots of our friends together. And we could keep it a little more orderly than our other parties. For example, let's say we can only invite up to three friends each. And everyone has to bring their own drinks and food to share. And it has to end at one."

Oliver raised an eyebrow. "One?"

"Two, then."

"Two-thirty and it's a deal." He held out his hand. Ellie hesitated, then shook it. "Go on, then. What do the rest of you say? Party, Ellie's rules?"

Maeve fell back to the fringes. If she held out now, she'd be a spoil-sport.

"Ellie's rules." Maeve blurted it out so fast, she sprayed spit but pretended no one noticed and offered her hand to Oliver. He ignored her, and she resumed playing with the crumbs on her plate.

Hollis sighed. "Ellie's rules."

Lorna took the longest to reply. "If you say so."

The conversation picked up again with talk of dates, music choices, and bets on how long it would take the neighbors to complain about the noise, until the front door opened and Callum appeared, face red as if he'd been running.

"Do what you want then!" he shouted outside. A woman's voice shouted back, but Callum slammed the door, cutting her off. He turned around and stuttered to a stop, surprised to see them all gathered there.

"So you decided to eat in?" he asked Maeve, unable to catch his breath.

Maeve couldn't answer. Couldn't even look at him.

"Yeah." He barked a laugh that tore the awkward silence. "I'll be upstairs. Enjoy the rest of your night."

Maeve called after him but didn't follow, and he didn't answer.

Oliver whistled. "Ooo, trouble with your boyfriend there, love?"

"He's not my boyfriend." Maeve sucked the last crumb off her finger and carried her plate to the kitchen.

"Chill out! I'm only teasing."

Oliver finished off his beer and crushed the can in his fist. Lorna looked like she wanted to say something but she didn't, and soon she too was gone from the room. Hollis carried away as much rubbish as he could and did not return for more. Finally, Oliver thought, life was getting back to normal here. It might have been late into the term, but that was better than never.

"That was fun," he said without sarcasm. "Thanks for backing me up about the party."

"I need a favor."

The tone of Ellie's voice kept him from poking fun.

"You owe me a favor."

Her words crept over him like ants, and he weighed the consequences of saying no. She waited until he was finished.

"Yeah, all right then. What is it?"

"I need you to read a letter."

And on dancer's feet she rose and tiptoed around the mess of their meal.

The morning after that fucking party—Ellie's party—Hollis would be the first downstairs. He would come down to grab his orange juice and instead stand frozen by the armchair Ellie had used the previous night as her throne. He would remember finding his grandfather when he was eleven, looking to all the world as if he were asleep. But Grandad hadn't been sleeping. And, like the day he found his grandad, Hollis would shout and keep shouting until he heard his housemates' doors opening, their arrivals announced by the groans of their headaches and hangovers.

Lorna would be the next to arrive and the first to yell at Hollis for waking her and the first to realize why he had shouted. She would stop on the bottom stair and would move no closer.

Maeve and Ellie would come next, and they too would fling their questions into the air, only to have the answers boomerang back as they looked at the sofa.

Oliver would arrive last. The alcohol in his bloodstream would slow his reflexes so that he wouldn't understand what they were all staring at. It would gradually become clear, like fog lifting from the road.

They would see Callum's body but also the broken lamp and the phone off the hook and the notebook they didn't know Callum had kept, and they would know that whatever had happened had not been an accident and that what was written in that notebook would incriminate them all. They knew they could all say they hadn't done it, and they would all know that one of them was lying, and they would all know that—because of that notebook, because of the records he kept—it could be any one of them.

So for a very long time, no one would say anything. And although they would all think the same question, no one would remember who finally asked it.

"What do we do?"

They could never see past their own problems, their own false solutions. So they could never see what was wrong with Callum, or that they could've helped him. To him, they were his friends. But to them, he became the source of their problems, and his death, their solution.

9

Ellie

Ellie was ashamed of what she had written in the diary. What adult wouldn't be, looking back on what their teenaged-self had written? But it wasn't shame that kept making her slip her hand to her back, checking that the diary was still there, still hidden. She knew that if Oliver and Maeve were to read it, they wouldn't see it the way she wrote it. The way she felt it. They would only see the words and infer their own meaning. And she knew how those words might look to an outsider. So she had to keep them busy. Keep them occupied. The less they paid attention to her, the more time she had to think. The diary would have to be destroyed—at least certain pages of it if nothing else—but not while the other two were watching. The idea she'd devised on their short walk through the passage back to the study was perfect. She just had to convince them.

The shadows had grown in the study since they were last there as the unseen sun wound its way to the opposite side of the house. If she didn't look directly at Caskie's body, it was easy to imagine he was just asleep in the chair, although the growing dark couldn't conceal the strong metallic smell of blood.

Once Ellie laid out her plan, Oliver stared at her, slack-jawed. Maeve looked vacantly at the floor. They weren't on board, not yet. But Ellie had experience closing a sale, experience Oliver only wished he had.

"You both agreed we have to lure her out. This is the only leverage we have."

"Yeah, but—" Oliver started. Ellie cut him off.

"Her point is to remain hidden. Attack us from the shadows. Nothing we've done so far has provoked her into revealing herself. This is the only thing that will."

She waited for them to realize she was right, but it was taking longer than she'd hoped. Lorna's death had shaken their foundations. Next to Hollis, she had been the strongest stabilizing force in the group. One who was analytical, avoided hysterics, was able to reason. Lorna was tough and brusque and could easily make people dislike her, but she had no agenda. She hated everyone equally, and her honesty in all things hurt her friendships but allowed them to respect her decisions. It was not lost on Ellie that the three who were left were the three most prone to fighting and hysterics. She had no doubt this was by design.

But Ellie knew the power of silence. She knew not to oversell. And after a few seconds that felt like minutes, the tension in Oliver's body released. He stuck his hands in his pockets and turned to Maeve.

"Do you want the feet or the head?"

Maeve stopped chewing the cuff of her jumper and blinked. "Huh?"

"Have you heard anything we've been saying?" he asked.

She looked between Oliver and Maeve, a vacant expression in her watery eyes. "Sorry. No. Sorry." She wiped her eyes with the sleeve of her jumper. "What are we doing?"

Oliver huffed, flexing his fingers. "Ellie wants us to hide Caskie's body upstairs. She thinks doing, well, whatever it is she wants to do with this woman's son, is the only way to draw her out."

"What I want to do, as I've already explained, is to pretend he's still alive and hold him ransom for the keys to the house. Honestly, if you two would just listen." Ellie crossed her arms, felt the diary shift against her back, and quickly moved her hands there, pretending she was stretching.

Oliver and Maeve didn't seem to notice. Each was in a bubble—Oliver shrouded in a mist of anger, Maeve a cloud of grief. There was a delay between her words and their actions.

"But—but—" Maeve stammered. "Why not just put him in the cellar? Why do we have to carry him upstairs?"

Ellie's face got hot the way it did whenever the children were arguing and they wouldn't listen to her.

"Because," she snapped, storming around to the back of the bar and emerging with a small paring knife, "and I have already explained this as well, she has obviously been using that passage between the ballroom and the cellar, and the whole point of this endeavor is to put him somewhere he won't be found."

As she was talking, she started cutting. The cords that bound Caskie snapped as sharp as her voice. His body slumped forward, then toppled to the floor. The thump echoed in the study. Ellie set the knife on the counter.

"So go on then," she said. "Pick him up."

Oliver moved first. Ellie had to hide the smile that twitched at the corner of her mouth. He grabbed Caskie's shoulders and then Maeve went for his feet. Before they lifted him, Oliver glared up at Ellie.

"Aren't you going to help?"

"I'm going to get the door." Ellie marched ahead before he could say anything more and held the study door, which had already been half open to begin with.

Oliver at his head and Maeve at his feet, they carried Caskie face-down. His stomach sagged in the center as they struggled with the tall man's body. Gravity pulled blood from his open stomach wound onto the hardwood floor. That blood marked a path as they carried him toward the stairs, the sound of its dripping muffled by the carpet runner, then resuming again once they crossed it. Ellie remained by the study door, near the dying peat fire. That had been her plan. To burn the diary in the roaring fireplace while they weren't looking. But no one had stoked the fire since that morning. The peat bricks were nothing but embers. There were fresh bricks stacked to the side. If she could throw a few on, poke the fire and get the flames going again . . .

"Oi!"

Oliver shouted at her from the bottom of the stairs. He was panting. So was Maeve. Both of them out of shape and exhausted from carrying the body that short a distance.

"Get over here and lend us a hand," he said. Maeve used her dirty sleeve to wipe the sweat from her face.

"I thought I should get the fire restarted. It's going to be dark soon."

"This takes precedence, don't you think?"

"So is being able to see. Or do you want to be wandering around in the dark with a killer?"

"All right. Go on then. Fix the fire. We'll wait." He folded his arms. Maeve, who looked like she was barely aware of what was going on, mirrored his gesture unconsciously.

"We shouldn't delay," Ellie said. "You start taking the body up while I get the fire going and—"

"We stick together."

"I won't be long."

Oliver crossed the room and grabbed Ellie by the arm. She shouted, but he didn't let go as he dragged her over to the body. She felt the diary shift, slipping from her waistband. Before she could yank her arm free, Oliver let go of her with a shove.

"We stick together, princess. Now grab him in the middle, and help us carry him upstairs so we can get started on your plan."

Maeve had already taken up the feet again, following Oliver's commands without question, like one of the little dogs she so loved. Oliver lifted him up underneath the shoulders. They waited for Ellie. She glared at them both, then crouched down, the diary stiff against her back, and placed her arms underneath him. They immediately became cold and sticky as Caskie's still-drying blood adhered to her, like she'd laid her arms across wet paint.

On the count of three they lifted. Though Ellie used weights at the gym, her arms trembled from the effort. They moved slowly, one step at a time, Oliver at the head leading the pace. Maeve stumbled more than once, falling to her knees on the steps, dropping Caskie's feet. Each time she dropped him, more of the weight fell to Ellie. She gritted her teeth. Sweat beaded on her forehead, but she was unable to wipe it away. With every slow step, the diary shifted again. She could feel it working free from her waistband, but she couldn't stop to fix it. Oliver wouldn't stop staring at her.

He walked backward up the steps so that he could maintain a better grip on Caskie, but by walking backward, he could also watch her.

Princess, he'd said.

He knew how much she hated that word. She wasn't a princess. Princesses didn't have to work. Princesses didn't have to fight. Princesses didn't have to carry corpses. Princesses were saved.

The next time she looked up, she thought they were finally at the top, but they had four more steps to go. Her arms shook, her lungs burned. Sweat dripped from her armpits down along her sides. Oliver reached the top step first. As soon as Ellie got there, she let go, even though Maeve hadn't reached the top yet. The sudden loss of support caused Maeve to stumble and drop Caskie's feet.

Ellie staggered back, her muscles weak from the effort, and stared at the bloodstains on her arms. When Caskie died, she had only got a small stain on her hand. Now his blood was all over her forearms up to her elbows. Without a word, she started away from the group, but Oliver grabbed her before she could get too far.

"Let me go," she whispered.

"I told you we stick together."

"I need to change my shirt."

"Not now you don't."

Though her arms were tired, so were Oliver's, and this time she was able to pull herself away.

"You don't get to decide when I want to go to my room. You don't get to decide when I get to change."

"It's for your own good."

Ellie stared. Then she laughed. It was high and bitter, and it felt good and she couldn't stop.

"You're joking," she said between laughs. "My own good? My own good?" she repeated. "Since when is anything you do for my own good? Is it when you convinced me to try marijuana and I got so paranoid I cried all night because I thought there was a man hiding in the toilet? Or when you convinced me that cheating on my exams would be the best way to fix my grades? Or how about when you raped me, Oliver? Was that for my own good, too?"

He stepped back. Stunned. The word shocked him just as it shocked her. It tasted like fire on her tongue. She said it again.

"Go on. Say it. Rape. Not 'took advantage of.' Not 'I was pissed, too.' Call a spade a spade. I was passed out. You carried me to your bed and you raped me while I was unconscious. Say it, Oliver. Say it!"

She wasn't laughing now.

His expression was unreadable, but he was on the verge of something. The verge of finally confessing what he had done. Of apologizing and begging forgiveness. Or the verge of doubling down and smacking the word out of her mouth. She was prepared for either.

A thud sounded above.

They fell silent.

There came another. Maeve crouched as if the ceiling would cave in.

Fast footsteps sped away above their heads.

Oliver turned to run. But then a door slammed open behind them. A door at the end of the abandoned east wing. They grabbed their phones and cast circular pockets of light down the dark hall. It mirrored the one that housed their guest rooms but looked occupied by ghosts, the furniture pressed against the walls covered in white dust sheets, the shaking lights seeming to give them movement.

Oliver hesitated. With no further sound from the footsteps, he yanked the rope from the wall and headed for the open door. Ellie followed, turning when she heard someone behind her, but it was only Maeve hurrying to catch up.

The hallway ended in a wall. A dead end. And no windows meant no light, until Oliver shone the light from his phone into the open room.

A bare mattress lay on the floor. Light blue curtains made from old bedsheets covered the window. Posters of Pamela Anderson and Glimpse '91 and random *NME* covers were taped to the walls. A business ethics textbook on the floor bore the smiling penis Oliver had been prone to drawing on everything at the time. And, stuck in the book, a blue envelope with Oliver's name typed on the front. He unfolded the unsealed flap and read the note inside. The note fell from Oliver's shaking hand. Ellie caught it before it hit the floor.

```
There once was a cad name Ollie,
Who fucked up his life, by golly.
He thought he had won
When he decided to run
But turns out his thoughts were all folly.
```

She was about to comment on it when the footsteps again raced across the floor above. Oliver shoved Ellie out of the way and ran after them. Ellie lost her balance. Her shoulder caught the edge of the doorframe. She couldn't grab the wall in time and tumbled to the floor. Maeve stood over her, staring like a dumb cow, like she wasn't even sure where she was. She made no offer to help. With a growl, Ellie grabbed the doorframe and hoisted herself up, then ran after Oliver.

She caught up to him on the floor above just as he was about to run down the east wing. Anticipating his movement, she started after him, but he jerked to a stop and she ran into the back of him, falling again, this time into the hard corner of a sideboard. She looked up in time to glimpse a brown blur shoot around the corner of the hall.

"Did you see that? What the fuck was that? Was that her? Was she crawling like in the fucking *Exorcist*?" Oliver ranted, hands clasped behind his head. He turned back and forth as if expecting more things to start leaping out of the walls.

"I couldn't see because you were shoving me into a wall."

"I wasn't shoving you! It was an accident."

"Of course it was. Every horrible thing you do is accidental. None of it is ever your fault!"

And she could tell he had decided. He was going to strangle her. He came toward her with hate in his eyes.

This time it was Maeve's voice that stopped him.

"It's my fault."

A jolt passed through Ellie. From the shock in Oliver's eyes, she knew he felt it, too. Maeve was coming clean. About what she did to Mr. MacLeod. Her possible allegiance with Mr. Caskie. About everything. Ellie turned, ready to hear the rest of the confession, but then saw what Maeve was holding.

"'It's my fault,'" Maeve continued reading. "'It's all my fault. I did it.'"

Ellie pressed a hand to her back. There was nothing there.

"'I went downstairs for a glass of orange juice,'" Maeve read from the diary. "'I was so thirsty. And when I came out, there he was and the phone was in his hand. He was going to tell them everything.'" She read the next lines in silence, then looked up and met Ellie's eyes with her own. Maeve had given up when Lorna died, but Ellie could see what little strength she had return, hardened by twenty years of jealousy.

Maeve closed the diary. "You fucking bitch."

Ellie ran for her, but Oliver grabbed Ellie and pinned her in his arms.

"Get off me. Get off me! Let me go! Let me go, Oliver!" She kicked at air. Wriggled against a brick wall. "Don't touch me! I don't want you touching me!"

Maeve showed him the page, the page Ellie had known all along that they wouldn't understand.

"We don't need to pretend this woman's son is alive," Maeve said. "We just need to give her Ellie. Isn't that right, princess?"

Oliver

18 hours earlier

He knocked on her door. Three raps, then the drag of his knuckles down the wood. Just like he used to. He listened to her soft footsteps cross the room. Pictured her in slippers and a silk dressing gown, her hair braided and wrapped in a kerchief. It was prone to breakage, her hair. She thought he never listened, but he remembered some things, like their knock and the feel of her hair through his fingers.

"What do you want?" she whispered through the door. It pleased him that she remembered the knocks as well as he.

"I thought we should talk."

"What do we possibly have to talk about?"

"You can't be fucking serious."

"Language."

But he heard her hesitation, and then the door clicked open, just wide enough for him to enter.

"Quick. Before anyone sees you." Ellie closed it behind him, so quietly he never heard the door shut. She was dressed in a nightgown, her hair in a ponytail. In his mind's eye, he had pictured a golden glow about her, but the yellow lighting revealed the wrinkles around her eyes, the subtle sagging start of a turkey neck. She still had that figure, though. Oliver sat on the bed and stretched out his legs, flexing his knee to ease the subtle ache there. She remained standing, arms crossed at her chest, her body contained and bottled up.

"Go on then. What is it you wanted to say?"

"Hello."

Ellie rolled her eyes.

"No, really. We never said a proper hello. So, hello. Hi. How have you been?"

Her eyes darted to the desk, where the letter containing her blackmail lay, torn into pieces.

"I suppose that's a stupid question." He sighed, self-deprecating.

She lowered her arms. "Very."

"I know the circumstances are as far from ideal as they could possibly be. But I am glad to see you."

"Tell me what you want from me, Oliver. I've played enough games tonight."

"Fair enough. I want you on my team."

"Your team?"

"We know how this is going to play out tomorrow. We'll talk about Callum. And talk will shift to blame. Whoever gets the most blame will be the one at fault. And the one at fault will be the one turned over to our so-called benefactor. I don't want that to be me, and I don't want it to be you because we both know neither of us did anything wrong that night. But the odds are against us. Hollis sure as"—he moderated his language for her —"crap isn't going to admit to anything. And Lorna will be on his side, easy. She's never really liked either of us. Maeve—"

"Maeve is still infatuated with you," Ellie said. "Did you see how she kept looking at you tonight?"

"She's the wild card. But she and Lorna always got on. And Maeve tends to side with authority, which Hollis as a detective," he sneered, "has in spades."

"It would still be two against three."

"Which is better than four against one."

"And which of us would be the one?" she asked.

"Do you know why I came here? How I was tricked into coming here? I'm trying to get my life together, Ellie. I'm trying to be better. To be good again."

She looked him in the eye. "You were never good. You were never kind. You played at emotions like that, Oliver, but you never felt them. Not once."

He sat back, dropped his folded hands in his lap. "Want to hear about my little letter? This person knows I was stealing money from my ex-stepfather's company."

"Embezzling."

"If you prefer the proper term. And if my sister finds out about that . . ." He sighed. "Let's say I have very few positive things in my life right now, and if she knew, I would have zero."

Ellie walked to the desk and poured a glass of water from the carafe. The bed creaked as he rose. She tensed, but he took a deliberate step back and chose his next words very carefully.

"I was wrong that night. We were both pissed, but I still had enough of my wits to know better. And I wasn't ashamed then, you're right, but I am now. And I know my words won't mean much, so I want to prove it with my actions. Whatever happens tomorrow, I'm on your side."

She stared into her water glass. "So long as I'm on yours."

"I'll leave that up to you." He moved toward the door, not too fast but not too slow, giving her enough time to think and respond.

"Be nice to Maeve tomorrow," Ellie said. "Flatter her. Don't overdo it, but don't be cruel, like you were tonight. She'll have spent tonight, like we all are, thinking about Caldwell Street, so she'll be thinking about you. Play into her fantasy of you, her need for affection, and she'll bend your way. She can't help herself."

Oliver nodded and started to leave, but the hardness in Ellie's voice gave him pause.

"You didn't know we would be here, did you?" he asked. "You didn't know what you'd find."

She raised the glass to her lips. "I thought I won a contest."

He returned to his room then, knowing she was lying, but not why or to what extent. But he also knew it wouldn't matter, so long as he stayed in her good graces.

Present

Ellie kicked out and bit Oliver's arm, but even though Oliver wasn't as fit as he once was, he beat her in sheer weight and was able to keep her restrained.

"How about in here?" Maeve asked, holding open a door. Oliver nearly dropped Ellie when he saw the replica of Ellie's Caldwell Street bedroom. All that saved him was Ellie's own panic. She fell to her knees. Without her kicking, he was able to lift her up.

"Well, isn't this just perfect for you, you lying cunt?" He spat the word in her ear and threw her in. Maeve shoved the door shut and held the knob tight as Oliver dragged over an armchair. The dust sheet fell as he secured the chair beneath the doorknob. Ellie railed from the other side, no words, just shrieking and pounding her fists. Oliver, winded, leaned against the wall while Maeve cradled the diary against her chest. He had gone to Ellie's last night to gain an ally. He knew the others had always suspected him the most in Callum's death. He knew he would need someone on his side, someone to defend him if need be. He and Ellie were most often on the same wavelength back at university. She had seemed like the best choice. He hadn't realized Ellie had been his ticket out of here all along. If only he had known then what was in the diary Maeve held. He could've turned Ellie in last night. Maybe Hollis would still be alive, Lorna too. He could've headed off a disaster instead of trying to scrape together a meager stalemate.

Maeve paced back and forth, staring at the carpet. He couldn't even guess what she was thinking. He could count the number of times he and Maeve had been alone together on one hand. In those times, he'd either be sniping at her or they'd stand in awkward silence. Back then he would've ditched her as soon as possible. But things were different now. She was his only ally. The one holding the key to their escape.

"Can I?" he asked and held out his hand.

Maeve hesitated, then gave him the diary. He read the whole page again.

"You know, Ellie, if I would've found this back then, I would've just called the police and handed you over," Oliver called through the door.

"Would've saved us a lot of trouble," Maeve added. They smiled at one another.

He could hear Ellie breathing through the door. She must've been pressed against it, her fingers like claws digging into the wood.

"You did good, Maeve." He spoke loud enough so Ellie could hear him.

Maeve shrugged and examined a hangnail. "I only found it because she dropped it."

"But the old Maeve would've handed it back to her without thinking."

"I wasn't one of her lackeys."

"No, but you admired her." He stretched out his knee and heard it pop. "I'm not saying that's a bad thing. I did, too."

Maeve ran a hand through her hair. It tangled in the knots, her fingers getting stuck until she yanked them out.

"So what do we do now?" she asked. "Wait for this woman to show up and take her?"

"It would be nice to see her face to face. Maybe we should—" but he was interrupted.

Thump, thump, thump.

Oliver looked up and down the hall, expecting the woman to appear. But there was only carpet and antique furniture and Maeve, who heard it too, her head cocked toward the stairwell. A few seconds of silence and then a series of thumps.

He waited for more, but seconds passed without a sound. After checking that Ellie's door was secure, he guided Maeve toward the main staircase by her elbow.

There was no one there.

Not even Caskie's body.

"Where is he? Where is he?" Maeve asked and asked, her voice pitching higher each time. Oliver covered her mouth with his hand. They inched toward the top step. Though difficult to make out on the red carpet, wet splotches marked where Caskie's body had stained the steps. Oliver peered down, his eyes following the wet stains that appeared around every third step, expecting to see the body at the bottom.

But it wasn't there, either.

He looked at Maeve and lowered his hand from her mouth. Without either of them saying anything, she nodded and together they started down the steps. The house had fallen completely silent. Not even Ellie made any noise from behind her door.

Halfway down, they could follow the blood trail that led from the stairs around to the right. Three-quarters of the way, they could see James Caskie's body propped up against the reception desk. At the bottom, they could read the piece of paper propped in front of his bloody stomach.

No Deal

Maeve threw her arms around Oliver, and for the first time, he reciprocated. He needed warmth. Physical contact. And Maeve would suffice. He hugged her tight as she cried into his shoulder and placed the lightest of kisses on the top of her head.

"We'll give her Ellie," he whispered. "She won't hurt us if we give her—"

A crash sounded from the study.

"Go!" He pushed Maeve toward the stairs, but she tripped, banging her knee hard on the step. Oliver grabbed her underneath her armpits and hoisted her to her feet.

A glint of metal gleamed from the pocket of her jumper. He pulled it out before she saw what he was doing, and while Maeve continued up the stairs, Oliver stared at the ring of keys in his hand. Why did Maeve have the keys all this time?

"Oliver, hurry!"

She turned. And when she saw what he held, she patted her pockets.

Then she was coming down the stairs after him, and she no longer looked scared. Oliver ignored the stiffness in his knee and ran, trying to pick out the right key as he did so. There were only four but they all looked alike.

The first key didn't work.

Maeve reached the foyer, but slipped in a smear of Caskie's blood.

The second key didn't work.

As he inserted the third key, he looked over his shoulder and saw the study door open. The key turned in the lock. Oliver ran out in the cold, damp air and slammed the door behind him, cutting off Maeve's scream.

Pp. 92–96

Of course, I'd known all along it was Ellie. Ever since I'd found her old diary, I knew. I knew it was Ellie who had stepped out of the kitchen doorway with a glass of juice and saw Callum on the phone. It was Ellie who listened to Callum as he explained that he was going to call the university office and leave a message on the answering machine, explaining what he had done and who else was involved. It was Ellie who had begged Callum to put the phone down and, when he didn't, Ellie who had shoved him onto the couch, placed her hands over his mouth and nose, and held them there until he stopped breathing.

Look, I know what you're thinking. Why didn't I just go after Ellie? Because they were all at fault, you idiot, in one way or another, for what happened that night and the morning after. I couldn't just let the rest of them get off without any consequences. What kind of a person would that make me? But I admit, it was fun to watch them all suffer. To see them suspect one another and pass the blame back and forth. Fun to see how Ellie would react as she tried to hide her secret. And fun to see what she did after they knew.

Shit. I'm running out of time. I have to leave soon, and I can only write so fast. You want to know what happened that night. What the police never bothered to uncover. I guess it's time I told you the rest.

That afternoon, a delivery van rear-ended a two-door passenger vehicle on Griffin Road, which paralleled Caldwell Street along the back gardens of houses 217 through 209. The accident is documented in public records and consisted of no more than a minor tap. However, the incident escalated because the delivery van left a scrape on a car that happened to belong to the son of a junior MP who had both more money and more impatience than he knew what to do with. What could have been resolved civilly devolved into a battle of fisticuffs won by the van driver, who had a good three stone on the MP's son and significantly more experience in backroom brawling. The subsequent sound of police sirens as the son of the junior MP lay bleeding on the eastbound lane of Griffin Road was what woke Oliver that afternoon. He could have gone back to sleep, but the sun coming through the window made him sweat in his sheets and sparked the urge to urinate. He tripped over his business ethics textbook and stumbled into the bathroom, where he relieved himself with a low, satisfied groan.

"Good morning."

Oliver turned. Thankfully, he had finished urinating—otherwise he would have coated Maeve's leg in a stream of warm piss. She stood at the sink with toothpaste foaming around her lips.

"Door was open." He slipped himself back into his pajama trousers.

"Yep." She pulled the toothbrush from her mouth. "Didn't think I needed to close the door to brush my teeth." She laughed too hard and sprayed toothpaste foam on his cheek. "Oh god."

She spat into the sink as he wiped his face with the closest towel.

"I'm so sorry."

She spat again and wiped her mouth with her own towel. Oliver grunted and shuffled out of the bathroom.

"I'm really sorry! There's half a chicken sandwich left from my lunch, if you want it. I didn't bite off it or anything."

He waved his hand as he descended the stairs.

Maeve followed him into the hall. "And let me know if there's anything you want me to get for the party!"

"Party?"

Callum stood beside her. His eyes were bloodshot and his hair and skin had a greasy sheen as if he hadn't showered in several days.

"Yeah. The party. You know." She waved the foamy wet toothbrush as she spoke.

"No, actually I don't."

"We told you. We definitely told you. End of year bash. Final farewell to Caldwell Street. You must not remember." She poked him in the shoulder. Callum palmed the area as if wounded.

"No. Nobody told me. I would've remembered if Oliver was planning on throwing one of his stupid parties because I would've said no."

"It's not one of his parties. It's one of ours. We established rules and everything."

Callum frowned and turned to go back to his room, but Maeve caught his wrist and held it, his pulse thumping beneath her thumb.

"Callum, what is it? What's wrong?"

There were few times in Maeve's life where it could be said she was genuinely concerned for the welfare of another human being. Here, as she held Callum's wrist, was the first of these times. And everything might have turned out differently if Callum had been allowed to answer that question. But at the precise moment he spoke, Ellie appeared in the hall, shower caddy in hand.

"Oh hello! What are we all doing out here then?"

Maeve dropped Callum's wrist. "Nothing. Do you need the shower?"

"I do. Didn't have a chance to wash my hair this morning. Lorna took ages, and I want to look fresh for tonight. Aren't you excited for the party, Callum?"

It was then that Maeve performed the single bravest act she'd commit in her lifetime.

"Actually, Ellie, I was thinking maybe we should cancel the party."

"Cancel? But we set up rules and everything."

"I know, but Callum's feeling a bit under the weather, and it is finals week, after all. He needs rest. It would be rude of us, playing loud music, talking"—she lowered her voice—"smoking, when he's up here trying to get some rest."

"Oh, poppet." Ellie frowned. "Are you really that poorly?"

Callum looked stunned. Whether because of Maeve's actions or because he realized he had not yet escaped to his room, they would never know.

"Forget it, Maeve. It's fine," he said.

"Are you sure? It's no trouble."

"I said I'm fine! It's fine. It's all fine. You didn't ask me when you planned it. Why should you ask me to cancel it?" He vanished behind a slammed door.

Ellie folded her arms, her shower caddy dangling from her fingers. "Well, honestly, there was no reason to be so rude about it."

Maeve watched the closed door as if by staring hard enough she could get it to reveal the secrets within.

"Are you done yet? In there?" Ellie jerked her thumb toward the bathroom.

"Sorry. Yeah. Almost." She shuffled to the sink to rinse her tooth-brush while Ellie waited in the doorway.

"You know, if you wanted to cancel, we could," Ellie said.

"Really?"

"Of course. I know how nervous you get at these parties. If it makes you uncomfortable . . ."

Maeve snapped the toothbrush back into its yellow travel case. "I don't get nervous. I'm just concerned for Callum."

"Of course you are."

"Not like that!"

"I wasn't implying anything."

"Yeah, sure you weren't." Maeve shoved her toothbrush, paste, and tweezers into her toiletry bag, shaking it hard when it wouldn't all fit. Ellie's shower slippers flapped against the tiled bathroom floor.

"I'm sorry. I didn't mean to upset you."

"I'm not upset!" Maeve cleared her throat. "I'm not upset."

"Good, because the party really is going to be fun. I even bought some of those strawberry alcopops you like."

"You did?"

Ellie rested her caddy on the toilet and brushed out her hair. "I got something for everyone. And you know I heard Oliver saying he liked that little yellow dress you bought from Top Shop."

"The one with the buttons?"

"He saw it hanging on the closet door before you took it upstairs. He thought it was mine."

Maeve looked down at her waistline. "I have lost some weight."

"But it's up to you, of course. And if you want to cancel, I'll be behind you one hundred percent."

Maeve stared at herself in the mirror, smoothed the eyebrows she hadn't had a chance to pluck, teased her hair with her fingers. "No, you know, it's fine."

"Are you sure?"

"You already bought all that food. It would be a shame to waste it."

"Brilliant! So are you . . . I mean, I need to shower."

"Right, yeah. Sorry." Maeve gathered her towel and toiletry bag, then paused at the door. "Ellie, later, would you mind helping me with my hair? I can never do anything with it."

"Absolutely! It'll be fab. We can have a whole makeover session."

"Makeover?"

"Oh, the water's warm. Better get my shower before it runs out. Mind closing the door?"

Maeve remained alone in the hall for several minutes, staring at Callum's door. I don't know exactly what she was thinking, whether it was something to do with Ellie's makeover comment or learning Oliver liked her dress or Callum's attitude or how she hadn't even thanked him for helping her with that tricky maths exam. When I asked, she couldn't remember, like how she couldn't remember seeing me and saying "hi" before she went upstairs to hide in her room. That disappointed me, but I wasn't surprised. If there was anything consistent about their memories from that period, it was that they barely remembered me. Even if I didn't live there, I was around often enough. I knew all of their names, where they were from, what courses they were taking. I knew all their bad things and their secrets, and they couldn't even bother to remember my face.

10

Maeve

Maeve screamed and punched, desperate to get free from the hands trying to restrain her. Oliver had the keys. Oliver had found the keys. She needed to go after him. She needed to get them back. It was her job to keep the keys safe. She'd promised.

"Maeve. Maeve!"

She heard her name like a distant echo. A ghost calling to her.

"Maeve, stop. It's me! Look at me."

She hadn't realized she'd closed her eyes, and when she opened them, the ghost was there.

"It's okay. It's me. It's really me." Lorna held up her hands. "It's me."

Maeve saw the blood—or at least, in the fading light, what looked like blood—but the air didn't smell of it, not like when Hollis died.

"Paint? Is . . . is that paint?"

"I knocked over a can in that office. But I'm okay."

Maeve stepped forward, saw she was real, and the two women embraced. Maeve was crying before she could even think about stopping herself.

"What happened to you? I thought she killed you!"

"Nothing. Nothing happened. No one attacked me. I faked it." Lorna rubbed her back.

"Why would you do that? I thought you were gone. I thought I was on my own. I thought—"

"I know. And I'm sorry. But I needed to get away from you. I mean, not you, specifically, but the group. And there was no way to do that without drawing suspicion."

"But Lorna, why?" Maeve pulled back and wiped the tears from her eyes. "It's not safe to be on your own. Not with this crazy woman running around. She could've killed you for real."

Lorna rolled her eyes. "Right. And who is she? This crazy woman?"

"Callum's ex-girlfriend."

"The so-called ex-girlfriend none of us remember? The one Ellie conveniently recalled after she killed James Caskie?"

"But the ballroom. She's been sleeping in . . ."

Lorna went to sit down, but the nearest chair was the bloody one in which Caskie had died. She turned away from it and leaned back against the bar instead. The paint on her clothes had mostly dried, but the occasional patch glistened like a fresh wound.

"Callum never had a girlfriend," she said. "He cared about you. He wanted you. Ellie's story is bogus. A cover. Someone was camped out in the ballroom, but it's not any mythical ex. There isn't anyone else here. I think . . . I think it was just Ellie."

"That doesn't make any sense," Maeve said. "Why would Ellie be living here? Hiding here? How would she have even known . . ." She thought back on everything Ellie had done this weekend, every comment, every reaction. Had she known all along? How good an actress was she? It didn't seem possible. And yet, Maeve had been so hurt when Ellie mentioned a girlfriend. It would be just like Ellie to make up a story that would hurt Maeve the most.

"She looked right at me, Maeve. Ellie looked me right in the eye when she bent down to check that I was dead. She knew I was alive. She knew I was faking. She played along anyway, and the only reason she would do that would be to maintain her story that someone else is here."

"Is that why you did it? To see her reaction?"

"I did it so I could sneak around and see what proof I could find. I didn't know it would be her that checked on me. But turns out that's all I needed to see." Lorna pushed off the bar and paced the floor, carefully avoiding the blood soaked into the carpet. "When Caskie died, I couldn't stop asking myself, why would Ellie do that? She had no reason unless she knew he was working with us and she killed him to get back at us."

"But what was Caskie even doing here? He wasn't supposed to come back till tomorrow morning."

"I don't know. I never got the chance to ask him. But Ellie must've found out about our plan."

"*Princess*. God, I shouldn't have called her princess in the text." Maeve said. "She figured out it was us and then must've found out what we'd planned. But then why did she come at all? If she knew what we were going to do, why not stay home? Why risk hiding out in that other room if Caskie or even Mr. MacLeod could've found her? Why would she be camping out here at all? What was she doing all that time? And did she kill Mr. MacLeod?"

"Maybe. I don't know."

"She must've. And she could've slipped that twine into my pocket when we were searching the rooms together. But I still don't understand why Caskie returned early in the first place. He wasn't supposed to come back until Monday morning."

"I don't know. He said it's because MacLeod found out we were staying here, but Caskie had problems of his own. It's why we were able to convince him to let the house to us in the first place. He wouldn't have tried to defraud his employer if he was such an honest, upstanding young man, now would he?"

"So maybe Ellie turned him? Like a double agent?"

"I don't know."

"But then she killed him anyway? And what are we supposed to do on Monday?"

"I don't know."

"He was supposed to find the two of us hysterical, covered in blood, weeping over the nightmare weekend we only barely survived. The last ones standing. The final girls."

"I don't know!" Lorna pressed her palms against her eyes. "I don't know. I don't know! God, Maeve. I don't have all the answers! All I know is our plan's been fucked ever since MacLeod turned up. But Hollis is dead, and Oliver's too stupid to pull something like this off. Put tampons and a bra in with that camping stuff to throw us off his scent? Please. He couldn't even touch an empty box of tampons on our bathroom counter. It has to be Ellie. She killed Callum, and we're the only witnesses to what happened that night. You, me, Oliver, Hollis. For years, that's never been a problem. None of us was going to talk. But once we texted her about Caldwell Street, that looked like it was going to change. So she plays along and decides to take her chances. See if she can off us one by one. So we need to sort her out. Now. Like we always planned. And the rest we can figure out later."

Maeve looked up at the ceiling as if she could see through the floors and walls to the room where Ellie was trapped.

"Oliver!" Maeve remembered. "He took the keys, the diary . . ."

"And he can't get far. He won't know how to navigate Caskie's boat back to Skye, and the next ferry is over twenty-four hours away. Let him go for now, and we'll take care of Ellie first. Finish what we started." Lorna held out her hand.

Maeve took it.

Lorna

13 months prior

It had been the kind of Edinburgh day that taunted with the promise of blue skies and sun in the morning but drew clouds and temperature drops in the afternoon. She sat in a back booth against the large picture window in Black Medicine Coffee, nursing her second flat white while ignoring the pain au chocolat in front of her. Though the café was warm, she huddled in her oversized peacoat, a knit cap pulled down over her ears. Each time she checked her watch, she had to draw back the sleeve of her coat and the jumper underneath. The train had arrived twenty minutes ago, and Waverly was only an eight-minute walk away. She supposed she could've chosen a seat by the door. It would've made it easier to watch the people passing by, maybe pick her out from the crowd. But the table by the door felt too exposed. A back booth felt more suitable for their discussion. If she came, that was.

And come she did, bursting through the doorway in that clumsy manner of hers that hadn't changed in two decades, late as always, more frazzled than she was trying to appear. She looked for Lorna and, once spotting her, gave a big childish wave before ordering her coffee. She waited at the counter until it was done, even though they'd bring it to the table, and spilled some of the large, frothy cappuccino as she carried it over.

"Lorna, oh my god. It's so good to see you!"

Despite Lorna's reluctance, Maeve drew her into a hug before taking a seat.

"Did you get a pastry? Maybe I should get a pastry, too." She looked over at the counter. "I got food on the train, but dropped half my sandwich on the floor, spilled coffee on my lap, and the toddler next to me swiped my crisps. Although I suppose he wasn't a toddler. Maybe five or six? I'm terrible at judging ages. Do they have any danishes or scones?"

Lorna pushed the pain au chocolat across the table. "You can have this."

"Are you sure?" Maeve asked, already picking it up.

"I'm not as hungry as I thought."

"God, Lorna. Cheers. Thanks." She bit into it and spoke with her mouth full. "And thank you for all this. I can't remember the last time I had a holiday where I wasn't playing nanny to Max's kids. You remember my brother, Max, don't you?"

"I do." She looked at Maeve's frizzy hair, the bags under her eyes, the uneven lipstick. "You're exactly as I remember."

"You don't look too bad yourself. I love what you've done with your hair!"

"I'm trying something new."

The pain au chocolat was already gone—all that remained was a few flakes on the plate and a crumb stuck to Maeve's lower lip.

"I dropped my bag at the hotel before I came over. I hope you don't mind. That place is so cute! I would've never found it on my own. I usually end up at a Travelodge or, if I'm really lucky, a Jurys Inn." She rolled her eyes.

"Maeve, I don't want to be rude, but I'd like to get straight to the point."

Maeve paused with the oversized mug at her lips.

"About why I invited you up here."

"Oh! Yes! I'll be honest, I never really pictured myself working for a university, but to tell the truth, I could so do with a change of scenery. I've always liked the idea of Edinburgh, even if I struggle with the Scots accent. The poor conductor had to repeat himself four times before I figured out he only wanted to see my ticket. What? I'm rambling again, aren't I? Sorry. It's . . . I'm so excited to see you. To see anyone, really."

Lorna realized she'd been staring into her coffee cup, only half-listening.

"No, look. I'm sorry. I haven't been completely honest with you about why I asked you here."

Maeve sipped her coffee, smiling at a little terrier crossing the street with its owner, but the sadness in her eyes was clear. "There's no job, is there? Well that's all right. The chap at the unemployment office is lovely. I can at least tell him I tried to get an interview."

"Maeve . . ."

"No! It's fine. I'll make something up. I've got quite good at that, as it turns out. Besides, it's still a holiday, isn't it?" She finally noticed the crumb and brushed it away.

"There is . . . there is something I'd like you to do. Something I'd like us to do together. And I wasn't sure you'd come if I told you straightaway. Plus, it's not something I wanted to put in an email." She sipped her flat white. It had gone cold. "It's about Caldwell Street. About Callum."

Maeve pushed the plate to the end of the table, suddenly more interested in a loose thread on her coat than looking Lorna in the eye.

"Have you ever felt bad about what happened?"

The sound of milk being steamed drowned out Maeve's initial reply. She repeated herself.

"I don't like to think about it."

"But doesn't it bother you that Oliver and Ellie, even Hollis, have gone on with their lives like it never happened?"

"Oliver was on *Dragons' Den*. Did you see that? The cheek. Watching him get shot down by all four investors was the happiest I've been since . . . a long time." She folded her arms and watched out the window, doing what Lorna suspected she'd done for most of her adult life: trying not to think about Callum McAllister.

Lorna leaned across the table. "Callum loved you."

"Stop it. Just stop it." Maeve sat up straight, her hands clasped in her lap, out of sight, tears welling in her eyes. "If that's all you brought me up here for—to guilt-trip me—well, I don't need to be in Edinburgh for that. I'll go. And not just from this coffee shop. I'll get my bags and I'll figure out how to change my train ticket and—"

"Maeve, I'm sorry." She reached across the table, but Maeve remained unwavering.

"I thought you invited me because we're friends." She looked into her lap. "We were friends. Why does everything we do have to be . . . be tainted by what happened at Caldwell Street? Why can't we just talk about the weather or stupid coworkers or weird shit our family does? Why . . ." Her voice rose as she spoke, and a pair of backpacking tourists eyed her from the next table. Maeve grabbed her mug, coffee spilling over the side onto her hand. She raised the mug but didn't drink, using it to hide her face.

"Is that what you want?" Lorna whispered. "To forget him? Pretend he never existed? Write him out of history? Because I've tried that and it doesn't work. I've tried to live my life like none of it ever happened. And then I'll see an ad for Scottish Rugby. Or it'll be a Wednesday and for one second I'll think, 'What's he got for me today?' Or someone will show me a picture they took on their phone and I'll think, 'Callum would've framed that better.' And it might be one moment. Just one flash, and then for the rest of the day everything I see will remind me. Remind me of the one person who I didn't find constantly annoying. The one person other than my dog who didn't judge me for my sexuality. Who called out those idiots for heckling me during class. He stood up for me every time I needed him. And when he needed me, needed us, we turned our backs. If you want to keep looking the other way, I suppose I can't blame you. Honestly. It's not like I don't understand. But I'm too tired to keep turning."

Maeve shook her head before speaking. "No. I want . . ."

She laughed, once. A laugh tinged with so many years of sadness.

"What I want is a TARDIS. I'd go back in time and rescue him in a TARDIS. Can you imagine the look on his face? God, he loved *Doctor Who*. Don't you remember? I couldn't get him to shut up about it sometimes. When they started it back up again, every time I watched David Tennant, all I could think was how much Callum would've loved this. A tall, lanky Scotsman playing the Doctor. He'd be in heaven." Maeve wiped an errant tear from her cheek. "I buy the box sets every year. I tell myself they're for my niece and nephew, but really I imagine giving them to Callum. Pretend that one day he'll come by and we'll binge-watch them all together. And he'll tell me random facts about Daleks and I'll pretend to be interested and . . ."

Lorna handed her a tissue. Gave Maeve time to compose herself.

"I always thought *Doctor Who* was stupid," Lorna said.

"Well, nothing could compare to your beloved Hitchcock, could it?" Maeve blew her nose and folded the tissue into quarters. "It's more stupid for me to watch it. Because he's never going to come by. He's never going to call or text, and I won't need to wow him with all these random facts about the show. He won't friend me on Facebook or any of those other stupid things he never got to do. Because there's no such thing as a TARDIS. No time machine that can stop us from doing what we did."

Lorna rested her hand on Maeve's. "What they did. Hollis. Oliver. Ellie. Maeve, this was their fault. They took him from us. What happened at the party, we had nothing to do with it. Maybe we could've done more to stop them, but in the end, it was them. And they have faced zero consequences. I mean, look at this." Lorna pulled out her phone, showed the news article she'd found. David and Eleanor Landon, a picture-perfect couple being lauded at a gala for their charity work. Ellie beaming in an expensive gown, dripping in jewelry, on the arm of a handsome, well-dressed man. "Doesn't that make you sick? Princess Ellie and her perfect life. Hunt the Cunt getting her happy ending while Callum gets nothing. Not even the acknowledgment that he was murdered. Don't you think it's time they paid for it?"

"Pay for it how?"

"You know I love horror films, right? Have you ever heard of the Final Girl trope?"

Lorna leaned back in the chair, listened to milk being steamed, dishes clanking. People laughing. While Maeve stared at Ellie's picture on the phone. Maeve's face hardened.

She handed back the phone. "Let's order more coffee."

Present

The others never tried to hide the bad parts of themselves. Oliver was an arrogant ass. Maeve a cloying sycophant. Hollis a chummy conflict avoider. Lorna a people-hating bitch. They wore these traits like badges of honor. But not Ellie. Eleanor Hunt always had to pretend to be what she wasn't. Beautiful Ellie Hunt pretended to be kind. She pretended when she needed a cup of tea and got one of the others to make it for her. She pretended when she needed to borrow a fiver or a tenner and, in her silly lightheaded way, always forgot to pay it back. She pretended when she needed a good cry and arms to hold her. Over the months, the tally of things sweet, kind Ellie had needed increased, while those she had given in kind were nonexistent. Lorna was the first to notice, followed by Oliver. Maeve, for once, was not the last. Hollis took the longest. He might have continued to condone her to avoid stirring up conflict, but he noticed.

But Callum never did. Callum took people at their word. Whatever side you chose to show him, that was the person you were. Which is why, to Callum, Ellie was always kind. Until she wasn't. And then it was too late for him, for any of them, to do anything about it.

This was what Lorna wanted to say to Ellie before she killed her. As she and Maeve made their way up the main staircase, Lorna rehearsed it in her head, wanting to get every word right because she would only have one chance. She thought of villains in action movies. How their monologuing always got them in trouble. How if they would just shut up and kill the hero, they would win. She used to wonder why they fell into such a trap. Now she understood. She needed to say these things to Ellie. She needed to say them to her face because, if she didn't, they would build up inside her to a crescendo that would tear her apart. So she would say them, and then she would kill Ellie. And then she and Maeve would find Oliver and finish the job, quickly. There was nothing she needed to say to him.

They reached the top of the first landing and continued up the next.

"Do you think she rang Mr. MacLeod?" Maeve asked. Lorna had been so lost in thought, she couldn't understand the question. "Was it Ellie that got Mr. MacLeod to return to the house?" Maeve repeated.

"I already told you I don't know."

"But Ellie must know that we killed Hollis. What if she's found a way to call the police? She might go to the police. She might—"

"I think she cares more about the police not finding out what she did to Callum."

"And Caskie's body? That was you and not—"

"Yes, it was me. I used the passage we used to move Hollis's body to sneak upstairs and downstairs. I pushed the body downstairs to get your attention and keep up the ruse for Oliver."

"Did you know about that other passage? The one to the ballroom?"

"No. Caskie never told me about it. Maybe he didn't know."

"Or maybe he only told Ellie about it. She does have more money than us. The more I think about it, the more I'm convinced he was a double agent and she turned on him and . . ."

The conversation was drawing her attention away from Ellie, the words Lorna needed to say to her. She pressed her fingers against her forehead, trying to keep them in. She'd smacked her head harder on the ground in that utility room than she'd meant to and a headache had blossomed behind her eyes. But Maeve kept talking.

"Ellie could have tipped him off but—"

Lorna turned and placed her hand over Maeve's mouth. "Maeve. I understand you want to figure this all out, but right now MacLeod and Caskie are both dead, so for the moment, I'd rather focus on the people we came here to kill. Okay?"

"Right. Sorry."

At the top of the stairs, Lorna stepped around an armchair and continued down the hall, but Maeve stopped. Lorna was afraid she'd been too crass and prepared to backpedal until Maeve asked, "Where are you going?"

"It's down here, isn't it?"

"No." Maeve pointed. "It was this door."

"Are you sure?"

"Yes, because I put her in her staged room. It was already unlocked, so I didn't have to worry about Oliver seeing me with the keys out."

Lorna returned to Maeve's side. Stared at the chair angled awkwardly in the hall.

"But," Lorna said, "this door's open."

They looked into the room. It was empty.

The sound of breaking glass flooded their ears.

Oliver

3 months prior

The doctors had said she should've succumbed to the cirrhosis by now. Had promised she would. But each day she persevered. The smell bothered Oliver most. She'd lost control of her bladder and bowel movements a few months ago, a side effect of one of her many prescription drugs. Adult diapers wouldn't have been so bad, except most days she was too drunk to change them herself. He either had to let her sit in her own filth or clean her himself. So he bought boxes of latex gloves. Unable to carry her anymore, he laid the plastic sheet under her, changed the diaper, and wiped her down. Each day he told himself this was what children were meant to do. Parents changed nappies for years and then they got old, and the kid had to return the favor.

Except Oliver's mum wasn't that old. She was just an alcoholic. He was, too, but not like her. He'd never be as bad as her. He'd need a drink or two to get through the day, but he could get through the day. He found work, paid bills, took care of the house. She lay on her backside and watched daytime talk shows and *Antiques Roadshow*, her bedroom full of empty Carling cans and vodka bottles because he refused to take them out anymore. He'd buy them, but she had to clean. That was a woman's responsibility after all, wasn't it? He didn't care that he always kicked them when he entered her room, or that the drips of stale beer stained the carpet, so rough and brittle now. No, that he could handle. All that bothered him was the smell because now he smelled of it too. It was his sister who hadn't been afraid to tell him.

They sat across from one another at a Pizza Express behind Royal Festival Hall on the South Bank. He watched the feet of the people passing on the pavement outside and she watched him, her long brown hair flat-ironed to within an inch of its life, black liner lengthening her eyes so they resembled her father's side of the family more than their shared line.

"You're starting to look like her," she said.

"She's my mother. I've always looked like her."

"You know that's not what I meant."

The waiter approached and Oliver ordered a beer, but his sister kicked him under the table. He asked for a Coke Zero instead.

"You're starting to smell like her, too," she said when the waiter had gone.

"I shower every morning."

"It doesn't matter. Not with the state the house is in. It's in your clothes. Your hair. Your skin."

"How do you know what state the house is in? Not like you've seen it in years."

"Is it any better?"

He didn't answer.

"So I can only assume it's worse." She reached across the table and took his hand. He kept his eyes fixed on the menu. "You have to get out of there, Oliver. Come stay with me."

"You've said this before."

"She's killing you."

"And that."

"Well, I mean it!"

The couple next to them glanced their way then turned their heads. It was obvious what they were whispering about. Oliver lowered his voice.

"She's going to die soon."

"So will you." From her Marc Jacobs bag, she pulled out a brochure. The letters of Wolfheather House Rehabilitation decorated the front in an obnoxious cursive font. It looked shoddy. Slapped together. "Visit this place. They're having an open house. I'll cover the cost. Please."

The waiter returned with their drinks, and they ordered a pizza to share. Not another word was mentioned regarding their mother, but the brochure found its way into his coat pocket. He took the train and stopped at the pub for a few pints before going back to the house, where he found her passed out in her bed, bathed in the glow of the television. He pulled out the yellow paint sample from Homebase and compared it to the tint of her skin. Still 'Happy Daze' but moving closer to 'Lemon Punch.' He sighed and kicked a pile of cans, hoping the sound might wake her. It didn't. His sister was wrong, though. He was a survivor, and he could survive her. So he went to the front room to watch television with a beer but before he got too involved in *Top Gear* reruns, he found the brochure in his pocket and dialed the number.

Present

Oliver's breath clouded in front of his face, the cold air biting his cheeks as he shoved the quivering key into the door and locked it. He took a step back. Waited to hear someone pounding on the other side as Ellie had. But there was nothing. The sounds of the house were locked away. Whatever horror was happening inside could no longer reach him. He staggered into the gravel car park, clutching the diary with both hands. He didn't know what he was going to do with it. He only knew that he needed it. And that he needed to get it away from the house.

As he ran to the parked cars, his bad knee gave out and buckled underneath him. He fell hard, the gravel cutting his palms, the diary skidding out of his hands. He tried to stand but couldn't put any weight on his leg and crawled behind the nearest car instead, a Vauxhall, and collected the diary along the way. He sat with his back against a taillight, looking out at the loch in front of him. One hand clutched the diary, the other massaged his knee. All of these cars were about as useful as his own body. He could risk a rest—his knee gave him no choice—but what then?

As the rain speckled his clothes, he reached into the pocket and pulled up the near-ruined brochure his sister had given him at the Pizza Express. That had been the last time he'd seen her, but he hadn't thought it could be *the* very last time. *Wolfheather House Rehabilitation.* What a joke. Why hadn't he bothered to google the place first? A simple google search, and he would have realized this was all a lie. Why did he always have to be so fucking lazy? He crumpled up the fake brochure and tossed it toward the loch. When he got out of here, he was going to find a real rehab. And his sister would pay for it because she'd feel so guilty about leading him into this mess in the first place. Even if she did find out about the whole embezzling thing, she would still take care of him after this, especially if he did what she wanted and left Mum to her own devices. He snorted. Maybe Wolfheather House had rehabilitated him after all. Now he just needed to get out.

He waited until the pain in his knee had finally faded to a dull ache and hoisted himself up, using the boot of the Vauxhall, gently testing out his knee. It wouldn't take his full weight, but he wasn't falling over. He turned on the spot, taking in the useless cars, the house. A rancid smell reached his nose, as though a deer lay dead somewhere in the gorse. The gray gravel drive blended into the gray cloud-covered sky. He remembered his walk down that drive, how sore his knee had been by the end. He would barely make it back to the main road, let alone all the way to the quay.

Then he noticed the tire tracks in the car park. In the mud formed by the rain, a set of tracks wrapped around the house. Oliver followed them, dragging his leg, past the dining room windows, around the side of the boarded-up east wing. He thought the tracks stopped at a dumpster behind the house. And then he saw the old Land Rover behind it. He had to stop himself from shouting when he saw the keys hanging from the ignition.

Oliver climbed into the car and tossed the diary on the passenger seat. It smelled of wet dog and lager, but to Oliver the Land Rover was the most beautiful thing in the world. It must've been Caskie's or MacLeod's, but either way it didn't matter to him. A dead man's car had become his salvation. As he adjusted the seat, he noticed a sheet of paper plastered to the windshield. Hollis's handwriting, the ink wet and running from the rain. The jagged top of the page indicated it had been torn, maybe from the notebook Lorna had been looking for. And while Oliver couldn't make out most of Hollis's scrawl, he could tell it was a list of names, the one at the bottom double underlined.

Jen

Oliver turned the ignition key while still staring at the note, but when the engine started, the wipers immediately went into motion, and the paper was lost to the wind.

He managed to get the vehicle turned perpendicular to the dumpster, and that was when he saw Ellie, like a ghost appearing from nowhere. In the distance, he couldn't make out the details of her face, but her shoulders were hunched forward, a bull ready to charge. But he had a car. She had nothing. Oliver gave her a two-fingered salute, then threw the car into gear.

The windshield shattered. A brick lay on the hood. And Ellie was running at the car. He covered his face as a second brick penetrated the driver's side window, hitting him in the head. Shards of glass rained over him. Oliver lost the vision in his right eye. He tried to scramble into the passenger seat but had trouble getting over the gear box. His hand slipped on the diary. Ellie opened the door and clawed at his legs, trying to drag him out. He grabbed the diary and shoved it down his shirt, then stretched out an arm, fingers brushing against the passenger door handle. He almost had it when a sharp pain exploded in the back of his thigh.

Turning as far as he could, he saw the handle of the corkscrew protruding from his leg. Ellie ripped it out and stabbed his other leg. Oliver screamed and kicked, hitting her in the face with the heel of his boot, and felt something crunch. Ellie cupped her nose with an animalistic growl, giving him enough time to open the opposite car door and tumble to the ground, head first, like a child falling down a slide. The corkscrew remained in his leg and he instinctively pulled it out and dropped it in the mud.

"You fucking bitch! You weren't even that good a lay!"

He supported himself against the house as he tried to get to his feet, but as soon as he put weight on his left leg, it collapsed in pain. He tried the right. Even leaning was too much.

Ellie was coming for him, squeezing her thin body between the car and the dumpster. He found a rock on the ground and hurled it through the nearest window of the house. The glass shattered and he broke out the rest with his elbow and tried to hoist himself through. Hands grabbed him, helping, but when Lorna's face appeared, the shock caused him to let go.

"What the fuck?"

"Give me your hands!" she shouted.

With a shout of pain, Oliver obeyed and forced weight onto his feet so he could push himself up through the high window. Something pulled him from below. Ellie had latched on and was dragging him down. He wanted to kick but couldn't get his leg free.

"Don't let go," he said to Lorna. "Don't let go."

Lorna tugged at his arms, regaining ground lost to Ellie. His chest rested on the sharp edge of the windowsill, but he was almost there. A little farther and his center of gravity would tip him into the house. Lorna removed one hand, reached into his shirt.

"Lorna."

She removed the diary. Oliver met her eyes. He knew what she was about to do, but he didn't want to believe it. She would help him. Someone always helped him.

"Lorna. Please."

She let go.

Maeve

16 hours prior

The tire iron struck the back of Hollis's head with a sickening thwack. Whatever he'd been about to say never left his lips. One moment his eyes had been hazy and pained. The next they were lifeless. Maeve hadn't known the transition could be that quick. The tire iron trembled in Lorna's hand as the rest of his body hesitated, a belated shutdown of the system, like a computer powering down. Then he fell face down in the mud. Maeve imagined him breathing mud into his lungs, then blinked and remembered that wouldn't be a problem. Hollis wasn't breathing.

"We have to get him back to the house."

Maeve wasn't sure who had spoken, but she tasted rain on her tongue and realized it had been her.

"We have to get him back to the house," she repeated. "Before Oliver and Ellie see him. Lorna? Lorna."

Lorna finally looked up when Maeve touched her arm.

"This was step one, remember? We did it. Step one."

"We did it," Lorna said.

"Step one. For Callum."

"For Callum," Lorna repeated.

Together they looked down at Hollis's body. If only it could sink into the mud, Maeve had thought. Sink and disappear into the earth.

"We have to go through with the rest of it now, don't we?" Lorna asked. "It can't end here."

Maeve placed her hand on Lorna's shoulder. "Final girls, remember?"

"I'm sorry," Lorna whispered.

"Don't be."

"Hm?" Lorna looked up.

"You said you were sorry. Don't be. We owe this to Callum."

"Right." Lorna nodded and tucked the tire iron into her jacket. Then they dragged Hollis together, carrying him back to the house through the conservatory and into the study, where they were almost caught by Ellie. They'd had just enough time to hide behind the bar with Hollis's body as Ellie came in and fixed herself a drink. They hid right beneath her among clean glasses and bottles of tonic water, lying perfectly still on the rubber mats, Hollis between them, as she mumbled to herself. Maeve thought then that they were done. That Ellie would come behind the bar for a drink, or even gaze over the side, and spot them there. That months of careful planning would be over in an instant. Ruined, as so many things were, by Hunt the Cunt. But then Ellie walked into the conservatory and out again, leaving the study, ignorant of their presence. They hadn't been caught, and it had been that giddy exhalation that had pumped Maeve full of adrenaline and made her think they could do this after all.

Lorna, though, remained grim as they continued their journey upstairs. A reflection of the sullen, moody girl Maeve had first met decades ago. Maeve could see the doubts written across her face, and she had no words to make Lorna feel better. They positioned Hollis on the bed and shoved the bloody tire iron underneath it.

"Okay, okay," Maeve had sighed, looking everywhere but at Hollis's body. "What else do we have to do? I have to go fuck up the cars. You have to finish double-checking the other rooms. Caskie did a good job with Hollis's. God, I feel like I'm actually there. I can't believe that I saved that many pictures of Caldwell Street. Do you think I'll be able to get them back?"

Lorna remained silent, staring at Hollis's body. Maeve accidentally glanced at Hollis again and cringed, tasting vomit at the back of her throat.

"It was his fault as much as the others. All those drinks, remember? It's like you said. Hollis said he'd keep an eye on Callum. He didn't. Let's finish up and get to bed. Tomorrow's going to be a long day."

"You're right." Lorna nodded. "This is what I wanted. This is what I planned for. What we planned for." She squeezed Maeve's hand. But as

Maeve turned to lead Lorna from the room, ready to leave Hollis until they would "discover" him tomorrow, Lorna pulled away and returned to the body. Maeve thought she was praying over him until she reached into his jacket pocket and pulled something out: a small notebook. She started flipping through it.

"What's that?" Maeve asked.

Lorna paused, reading something. Her eyes went wide and she inhaled sharply. She tore out pages, ripped them in half. Then crossed to the room and hoisted the window.

"Shh!" Maeve hissed as the window creaked. "Lorna!"

She tossed paper down toward the dumpster below.

Maeve ran across the room and grabbed Lorna's wrist. "What are you doing? Lorna? Lorna!"

Lorna shuddered, her body relaxed, but she remained at the window, watching the pieces of paper disappearing into the darkness below.

"Just in case Oliver or Ellie decide to search the body. They don't need to find Hollis's notebook."

"You could've just burned them. What if Oliver or Ellie heard that?"

"Sorry." Lorna left the window open but drew the curtain. "I wasn't thinking. I just . . . wasn't thinking. Sorry."

"And that's why we both need to get some rest. Come on. Let's go do what we need to do." Maeve sighed and took one last look at the room before flicking off the light.

Present

Once they'd killed Hollis, Maeve thought it would be easy. Dragging his body through the house, positioning it on the sofa upstairs. She had made it through these actions without being sick. But the violence of that act had been hidden by the night. Two quick hits with a tire iron, and it had been over.

This was not quick. This seemed to have no end. Ellie kept bringing the brick down and down and down. The brown eyes Maeve had once so admired were gone. So were his cheekbones, his chin. His teeth. No one would ever see his face again because there was no face to see.

A red puddle formed around what remained of his head, mixing with the mud. Ellie stood over him, the blood and bone-spattered brick in her hand, fresh stains on her skin and clothes. A pause hung over them all, a vacuum created now that Oliver—this force that even in his absence had dominated much of their lives—had been eradicated for good. Maeve looked at his hand, which twitched as the nerves received their final signals from a brain that no longer existed. How long they all stood there, each adjusting to the vacuum in her own way, she would never know, but when she made eye contact with Ellie, the moment ended like the crash of a wave against the shore. Lorna took Maeve's hand.

"Run."

Pp. 98–120
not to get sidetracked, but all this took me years, you know. Years of tracking down their old diaries, old witnesses, old friends. Squeezing the truth out in droplets from the five themselves. And I've put it together as best I could. I admit some details may be wrong, but the key facts, the important facts, can all be verified. If anyone would care to bother.

So let's talk about that. Fucking. Party.

It should have been no different from any other party in the house's history. Remembrances of raucous nights were so ingrained in the muscle memory of 215 Caldwell Street's nicotine-stained walls that a pulsating heavy bass beat could sometimes be felt on quiet Sunday mornings. The house fed on empty glass bottles stashed in the mouth of its disconnected gas fireplace. It breathed clouds of cigarette and weed smoke. And, like the monster it was, it gorged on the numerous sweating bodies that lingered inside. Brief moments of tranquility could be found in the clear air of the back garden, but those who escaped would eventually return inside, driven by the need for another drink, another toke, another kiss.

It's easy to picture that night—the most beautiful night of 1995. Earlier in the evening, every pub with garden seating had been packed to capacity, the chatter and laughter of hardworking folk, students and regulars, mingling in the air like prayers to heaven. But after 11:30, the last straggler headed home or to a club while tired bar staff cleared sticky glasses from the picnic tables, able to enjoy the night's tranquility for the first time since they came on shift. If anyone was out in the garden of the Byeways pub, and it's likely there was, they would've heard the music drifting up from Caldwell Street, the bass thumping away even at that distance.

The sounds within the house were exponentially greater. A mate of Oliver's acted as DJ and kept the music flowing through a series of boom boxes hooked up to speakers the size of mini-fridges.

Maeve tripped over the cords as she maneuvered from room to

room, looking for some place or some group where she could fit in. She'd been left wandering ever since Lorna declared her night done and disappeared to her bedroom. Maeve muttered half-heard "pardon me's" as she walked through the crowd, the cheap white wine in her tumbler sloshing over her hand as she forced her way through the bodies that filled the kitchen. She glanced at the picked-over pizza boxes, but only a few gnawed pieces of crust remained. After an elbow to her breast, she stumbled into the back garden, where the music was muffled and the smoke less dense. She hadn't realized how dry her eyes had become until they watered in the fresh air. She pictured her mascara running down her cheeks; not wanting anyone to mistake her watery eyes for tears, she made her way through the high grass to the old chair by the fence. The green plastic bent under her weight, the legs sinking into the soft ground of the marshy corner. She tried to lean back but the chair tipped, so she settled for leaning forward, her glass cupped in both hands as the skirt of her sweat-stained yellow dress rode up her thighs.

From her position, she could watch the party unfold through the windows of the house. People she didn't recognize talked, smoked, and kissed. Backlit by the house lights, they looked like profiles in silhouette. A shatter of glass and burst of laughter made her wince.

"So much for your rules."

Maeve fell back. Her shoulder scraped the rough wood of the garden fence, but she managed to stay upright and save her drink.

"Jesus, Callum. Who said you could sneak up on people like that?"

"Sorry." He sat on the ground beside her. It must've been damp, but he didn't seem to mind.

"I thought you were upstairs."

"I was, but it's hard to think straight in there."

Maeve pretended not to know what he meant and sipped her warm wine, telling herself she didn't mind the taste.

"I thought Ellie got you some of those strawberry things you like?"

She shrugged. "I had one. Other people took the rest."

A new song came on, and those within the house cheered.

"Not what you expected, is it?" he asked.

She watched the people enjoying themselves so effortlessly. So unselfconsciously.

"It is," she said. "It really is."

Many seconds passed. In the course of an average moment on an average day, those seconds would've felt like the life of a fly, there and gone with hardly a passing thought. But this was not an average moment on an average day. Each second grew heavier than the last, weighing on each of them in different ways until even breathing became too painful.

"Maeve." His voice cracked the silence. She kept her eyes on the windows, pretending she was in there and not out here.

"Maeve, I wanted to talk to you about something. Something that's been on my mind. That's been bothering me for a while."

Oliver stepped in front of the window. Inside the house, Maeve had sweated terribly. Despite the amount of deodorant she'd sprayed on, her makeup ran and her armpits stank. But Oliver looked immune to the heat and smoke. His face glowed. Every time he smiled, Maeve hated herself.

"Maeve? Are you listening?"

She'd forgotten about Callum there on the ground, sinking in the mud. "I'm sorry."

"Right, but what I was saying was—"

"No, I mean I'm sorry if you ever thought I was flirting with you or if you thought I was leading you on." She fixed the strap of her bra. "You're a nice guy and all, and a really good friend, but I don't like you that way. I never have, and I don't think I ever could."

She didn't look at him. She couldn't. She wasn't sure if she could ever look at him again. But she heard him stand up. Heard him brush off his jeans. Heard him say, "This had nothing to do with you, actually? But fine. Whatever. It's fine."

She stared at the ground as he left. Listened as his feet stamped across the garden. When she could raise her head, the house had already absorbed him, the anonymous throng of bodies making him one of their own. Oliver's face, though, remained at the window, clear and bold. Brazen, as Lorna might say. He chatted up a girl while Maeve downed the rest of her warm wine and wondered how she might extract another bottle from within the house's depths.

In a comfortable corner of the downstairs spare room, cluttered with the useless junk left by previous tenants, Hollis was having no such problems while he chatted with a few of the lads from the nearby technical college.

"No, see, I wasn't arrested." He waved a can of Carling as he spoke. "It was a security guard that spotted me. He thought it were a real fox and the bloke panicked. Saying he couldn't believe someone would be so cruel to an animal. I tried to calm him down, but he was in such a state, I had to cut it down and show him it were fake. Well, taxidermied. And then I ended up admitting I'd nicked it from the science hall. And that's what got me in front of the dean."

"So they expelled you?" asked the lad with the buzz cut.

"That or get arrested, and I didn't want a record. Worst part is that the guard was so embarrassed, he spread this rumor that I'd gone and gutted a living fox and was thrashing it around like some sociopath."

"And you want to be a guard after all that?" Buzz Cut asked.

"Nah, mate. I want to be a real policeman. Help out kids like me that get the short end of the stick. 'Cause I was one of them right? I know how they think and . . . Callum. Hey, Callum!"

Hollis caught sight of his lanky housemate skulking past the door and waved him inside.

"Oi, this is my mate Callum. He lives here, but he's not like that wanker out there." He nodded toward the front room. "You had a drink yet?"

"I was actually going to bed."

"But I haven't seen you all night. Come on then. Have a seat. It's rough out there with that lot, aye, but we're all right in here, aren't we?"

He handed him a can of Strongbow. "Was keeping that for you from the rest of the vultures out there."

"Cheers." Callum took a seat with the unopened can, looking unsure what to do next.

"Here, mate. Let me help you with that." Hollis pulled the tab for him, then brought out a bottle of Smirnoff. "Add a bit of this. Give it a little kick." He poured a healthy shot into the can.

Callum hesitated and took a small, tentative sip. Then another. Then he chugged the rest while the room cheered. Hollis slapped him on the back.

"There you go! Told you he was tops, didn't I?"

Now that Callum seemed relaxed, Hollis handed him another can, and Callum drank that, too. They sat in the room swapping stories, and though Callum said very little, to Hollis he seemed content to sit there and absorb the atmosphere. He even smiled once or twice. When they ran out of alcohol in the spare room, they migrated to the kitchen, where, with their muscle, they secured a prime spot near the main drinks station. Whatever Hollis offered, Callum drank. When someone passed a joint around, Callum smoked that, too, even though in all the months they'd been living together, Callum had never shown any interest in marijuana.

When Buzz Cut went to relieve himself in the back garden, Callum wiped his mouth with the back of his hand and tried to speak. Each word seemed forced. Despite all the drinks, he hadn't consumed enough social lubricant to speak plainly.

"Hollis, I need to talk to you about . . . about the thing."

"The thing?" Hollis's brain worked slowly through the alcohol, trying to figure out what Callum was referencing.

"You know. The *thing*. The . . . exams. And everything." Callum shook his head, the unspoken words forming a backlog in his throat. Although unnecessary in the noise of the party, Hollis dropped his voice.

"Not really the time for it, mate."

Callum took a swig of his beer. "What did your family say when you were expelled?"

"To be honest, they weren't that surprised."

"And you were able to get into another uni?"

"Yeah, but we didn't, uhm, exactly broadcast why I left Exeter. I weren't officially expelled, like I told them. Just asked not to return . . . But look." He clamped a hand on Callum's shoulder. "No one's going to find out, okay? And it's not like you have to keep doing it. New year, new start this September, eh?"

Callum nodded, then continued to do so, like a bobble-headed dog, until he belched. It might have been the shoddy lighting, but he seemed to turn a bit green and left the beer on the counter, slipping out of the kitchen and into the crowd. Hollis watched him disappear, wondering if he should follow, then became distracted when Buzz Cut announced the start of an American-style drinking game in the back garden, shattering the fragile tranquility that had once existed there.

One floor up, the noises from below were somewhat muted. Lorna's room faced the front of the house, so she could not see the shenanigans taking place in the back garden. With her door locked, she knew little of what was going on downstairs either. She could only guess from the different noises and vibrations coming up through her floor. She sat cross-legged on her narrow bed in her pajamas with an open copy of Truffaut's *Hitchcock* in her lap. With the small electric kettle she kept in her room, she'd made herself a nice hot cup of tea and had a pack of Fox's custard creams open on the desk beside her. But instead of reading her book, drinking her tea, and eating her biscuits, her unfocused eyes stared at the same page as she tapped her bookmark into the spine.

She had tried tonight. She really had. This was to be the final party in Caldwell Street, and she'd wanted to make a go of it. Try to relax. Try to make friends. And it had started all right. Two of the girls from her film studies class had dropped by early, right at the start, bringing a bottle of wine and some nibbles for them to share, and the three of them had sat on the sofa by the front window with Maeve and drunk and chatted as more and more people arrived. It became clear within the second hour that the three guests per person rule wouldn't hold, but she, her friends, and Maeve had staked their spot, chatted in their little bubble, and Lorna—to her surprise —found herself enjoying their company even as the music and smoke intensified and the bodies multiplied around them.

But then her classmates had to leave. She went to the door to see them out, and when she turned back their spot on the sofa had already been reclaimed by Oliver and a ginger girl she didn't recognize, pawing each other and rubbing noses as Maeve sat on the opposite end trying to ignore them. Lorna wanted to hold onto that thin thread of enjoyment she had experienced earlier, so she and Maeve wandered between groups, trying to find a home within their home, but Lorna only grew more uncomfortable—and, though she didn't want to say it, anxious. Other than her housemates, she knew no one else here. She didn't like weed or cigarettes, and already felt sick from drinking. The music became too loud, and in every place she tried to stand, she felt awkward and in the way.

Reassuring herself that she'd given it her best shot, half an hour after her classmates left, she excused herself from Maeve's company and went upstairs, bypassing a couple smacking on the stairs and locking herself in her room. But even though she'd removed herself from the throng downstairs, invisible tendrils of the music's beating bass leached up through the floor, scraping against her skin as if trying to claw their way inside, the whole party an infection seeking a way into her body. On the outside, she knew she looked calm, tap-tap-tapping her bookmark, but on the inside a nervous storm raged.

A loud thump from Callum's room made her spill tea over her lap.

"Shit!"

The tea was lukewarm, but it seeped into her thin pajamas. She looked frantically for a towel or napkin, but there was nothing save her bedsheets. The single loud thump multiplied into a series of rhythmic ones.

"Glad someone's having a good time."

She set her mug on the edge of the desk, jabbed the bookmark into *Hitchcock* and gathered her strength for what she needed to do next. The wet tea chilled her, but with her hand on the doorknob she hesitated. Her toes curled into the carpet. Would she be able to hold in her rage, or would something snap? Would she unleash a torrent of hate and vitriol on all those in the house, a tirade she knew would only result in her ridicule? Or would she be able to hold it together? Could she grab a towel from the bathroom and return to her sanctuary unscathed?

The thumping in Callum's room continued. Tea dripped into her knickers. Holding her breath, Lorna opened the door, avoided eye contact with anyone who might've been in the hall, and took the two steps into the bathroom. She exhaled.

Then took a step back.

Callum, on his knees, was vomiting into the toilet. Whatever he had drunk came pouring out of him, splashing into the bowl like someone dumping a pot of soup. Her feet warmed the cold tile as she stood there, unsure of what to do. Callum, looking pale and worn, rested his head on the toilet seat, arms hanging slack at his sides.

Lorna took a step forward, grabbed the nearest towel off the rack, and retreated to her bedroom.

In Callum's room, the thumping couple laughed as she changed pajamas and wiped herself off. She opened her window, tossed the remainder of the cold tea into the hedges below, and boiled water for a fresh cup. She didn't leave the room for the rest of the night, not until she heard the shouting the next morning. But that came later.

As Lorna boiled water, Ellie held court in the front room, lounging in the brown armchair. Someone kept topping up her glass with nice cold white wine. All of her rules had been broken, except one—that the party would end at 2:30 a.m. According to her watch, it was 2:25, and the party looked like it wouldn't be over any time soon. Ellie found she didn't mind. She was having a splendid time. Everyone was. The music was good and people were dancing. Someone filled her glass again, and she thanked the person but couldn't remember his name. Or hers. It was hard to tell. The hair was short and her vision had gone a bit blurry, but it didn't matter. This party had become a celebration, and she didn't want it to end.

Then she saw Maeve alone, leaning against the closet under the stairs, an empty glass dangling from the fingers of her lowered arm. Her hair had given in to the humidity and frizzed in all directions like she had been electrocuted, and her makeup, which Ellie had so painstakingly applied, was smeared. A wine stain marred the hem of her yellow dress—a dress that was really a bit too small and cut into the flesh around her arms. No one else seemed to notice her, yet Ellie felt Maeve's misery spreading like the wine stain, touching everyone who passed. Ellie couldn't bear it any longer.

"Maeve. Maeve!" She waved her over. "Poppet, your glass is empty. What've you been drinking? Never mind. You must try this wine." She tapped her anonymous caretaker on the elbow. "Be a dear, would you, and fill my friend's glass? Cheers! You're ever so kind."

Maeve stood awkwardly before Ellie as both their glasses were filled.

"Here. Sit here." Ellie patted the armrest.

Maeve leaned against the edge, staring into her drink. "I really shouldn't. The wine's already going to my head."

"Well, that's the point, isn't it?" Ellie laughed. "Come on. Let's drink together."

They did.

"Now tell me. What's got you in the doldrums?"

Maeve looked at the people around them, the ones with whom Ellie had been chatting, the ones who were listening now.

"Give us some privacy, please. Housemates only!" Ellie shooed them away. "Go on then. You know you can tell me anything."

"I'm tired. That's all. It's been a long night." Maeve took another long sip of wine.

"You're not thinking of going to bed, are you? Oh, don't be like Lorna, please. You know, I didn't want to say this, but it is going to be so much nicer without her here next autumn, isn't it? She's such a wet blanket when it comes to these things."

"It has been a nice party. It has. I . . . ."

Ellie watched Maeve's gaze as she glanced across the room at Oliver flirting with a slutty ginger whose breasts threatened to escape her top.

"You know," Ellie said, "you just have to make him notice you, that's all."

"We've lived together almost a year."

"Nine months."

"That's almost a year. And if he hasn't noticed me by now . . ." Maeve let her sentence trail off and finished her glass. Ellie poured her a refill.

"Callum's noticed you."

"God! Could everyone shut up about Callum? I don't like him. He's tall and weird-looking and always has this stupid look on his face like someone's kicked his dog."

"Does he have a dog?"

"I don't know! And I don't care. I just want this year to be over so he can move out and I never have to see him again. He's so fucking annoying."

"Ellie."

Callum towered behind Maeve, his face cast in shadow. Maeve gasped and ran out of the room while Ellie tried not to laugh. His face remained neutral.

"Yes? What is it?" she asked.

"I was wondering if I could crash in your room tonight? There's these people in mine, and I can't shift them, so I was hoping . . ."

"Oh, Callum. You should've locked your door like the rest of us."

His hands turned to fists. "My door doesn't lock. I've said that almost every single day since we moved in, and I say it every single time you lot say you want to have a party. Don't you remember anything?"

Ellie despised aggression to begin with, but aggression on Callum looked unnatural.

"Sorry." She sipped her drink to avoid eye contact.

"So can I crash there or not?"

"Have you asked Hollis or Oliver?"

"Of course I did. You think I'd come to you first? But they're planning on having some girls spend the night." Ellie didn't like him like this. Had Callum always been an angry drunk? Had she ever even seen him drunk? She chewed on her lip and pictured the sanctity of her room spoiled by this drunken, angry, sweating boy.

"I really don't know."

"Seriously? You owe me, Ellie."

"Look, I'm not sure where my key is right now. I hid it somewhere to keep it safe, but when I find it—"

"Can you look for it now, please?"

She crossed her legs. "No, actually. I can't. I'm enjoying myself. When I feel like getting up, which means losing this chair, I'll look for it and let you in. All right?"

Callum shook his head, then swayed as if the motion made him ill. "You'd rather not lose a chair than help out a friend?"

"It's not—"

"Nope. I get it. I finally get it. You're only nice when you want something. Lorna's tried telling me that for months, but I wanted . . ." He shook his head and laughed. Then held up his hands and walked away, disappearing into the party. Ellie leaned back in the chair and waved her new friends back over. They filled her glass and they talked and they laughed and Ellie thought briefly of Callum and wondered what he would do if she continued to refuse his request. Then she drank more wine and let the thought float away.

Across the room on the sofa whose base was now so broken the cushions sank almost all the way to the floor, Oliver attempted to get into the ginger girl's knickers. Other than being ginger she was exactly his type: thin but big-chested, clear skin, someone he hadn't known before tonight. She was also, as he was learning, a terrible cock tease. Each time he dove in for a kiss, she turned her head or put her glass to her mouth. But then she'd place her hand on his thigh and squeeze. He'd groan, a little louder than needed, and try to kiss her again. Several times, he strongly indicated they should go upstairs to his quiet, private bedroom, but she wouldn't budge, even though the way she sat on his lap made him want to drag her upstairs like a Stone Age caveman. He thought if maybe he could remember her name, it might help to move things along.

Despite all this, he knew the party was a success. As he'd suspected, it hadn't taken much for Ellie to break her rules, and the rest, like the sheep they were, went along with it. With Lorna, the chief no-fun insti-gator, nowhere to be seen, he knew that meant she'd packed it in and would not be bothering them for the rest of the night. He'd managed to capture the corner of the ginger's mouth with his own when the music cut out, the sudden silence then replaced with a slow song. He rolled his eyes at first, but the ginger seemed to be into it, rolling her body in rhythm against his, lowering her head to his neck where she licked the sweat from his skin. He got lost in her touch. Until she burst out laugh-ing. Anger filled him like a flash flood and he was about to shove her off when he realized she wasn't laughing at him.

"What is she doing?" the ginger whispered.

Maeve—a very, very drunk Maeve—danced by herself in the center of the front room, doing what he thought she thought were seductive moves. A crowd gathered as she ran her arms over her body, the dress that made her look like an overstuffed banana. The fabric was riding up her crotch and sticking there, thanks to sweat and static electricity. When her hand reached her mouth and she sucked on a finger, Oli-ver smothered his laugh. He looked across the room at Ellie, and they shared a smile. They knew someone should stop her before she really embarrassed herself, but neither of them moved.

Maeve swayed as she undid the top button of her dress. Someone in the crowd shouted, "Oh shit!" and everyone laughed, but Maeve didn't notice. She undid the second button and someone else whistled.

Someone really, really needed to stop her.

Oliver held the ginger tighter on his lap. She whispered something in his ear that he didn't remember, but it made him laugh. The third button came undone and then the fourth, and Maeve started to work her shoulder free from the dress. People laughed harder when it was clear her fat arm got trapped in the sleeve.

Maeve let her stuck arm hang and undid the next button with her other hand, exposing the plain tan bra underneath. She looked at Oliver then as if he were the only one in the room, and he leaned back against the sofa with his arms over his head and the ginger nestled against his side. Maeve's strip halted as she attempted to remove her other arm, which had also become stuck. The entire party, having sniffed desperation like hounds on a fox hunt, was in the room now, excited to see what would happen next.

"What's going on?"

Callum burst through the crowd, hesitated, then stepped in front of Maeve to shield her.

"Maeve, stop. Stop. Come on. Put your clothes on," he whispered, trying to help her button her dress as her clumsy fingers fought to stop him.

"Aw, Callum." Oliver grinned. "I was enjoying the show!"

Callum glared but kept talking to Maeve. "Come on. That's enough now."

"But I want to be noticed," she slurred. "I want to be noticed!"

"Trust me. Everyone noticed. Let's get you to bed."

"No!" Maeve slapped him across the face. The crowd whooped and cheered. Ellie could no longer keep it together and laughed like a hyena.

"I don't want to go to bed. I'm at a party, and I want to have fun!" She raised her arms above her head and jumped, her tits popping out of the dress Callum had tried to close. The crowd cheered.

"Leave her be, Tripod." Oliver pushed himself up, ready to intervene. "She's having a good time, aren't you, Maeve?"

Callum shoved him away. Oliver staggered back, then punched Callum in the eye. The crowd gasped. Fists raised, Oliver turned to the ginger and smiled. He looked back at Callum. Callum punched him square in the jaw, sending him back onto the couch.

Fight, fight, fight . . . the crowd chanted.

With a growl, Oliver launched himself at Callum. The two little boys—for that was all they were at this point—collided and tumbled in a drunken heap. Both got their punches in as they rolled on the floor. Maeve, in an attempt to dodge the melee, smacked the back of her head against the mantel, toppling the empty bottles that had been left there. Indistinct whoops and cheers echoed from the crowd until Hollis muscled his way through.

"Oi. Oi! Break it up. Break it up!"

With help from Buzz Cut, Hollis split them apart. Oliver had a bloody lip. A bruise formed around Callum's eye. Maeve sat in front of the fireplace, dress undone and skirt riding up to expose her knickers. Hollis tried to ask what happened, but Callum shoved him away.

"You're all horrible people, you know that? You're . . . you're not nice and you fucking deserve each other." Callum grabbed a bottle of whiskey out of a bystander's hand and disappeared.

No one saw him for the rest of the night. Or so they said.

For years and years that's the story they clung to.

But they lied. You know they lied. And for years and years, I picked those lies apart until I finally got to the truth. They had not seen who had killed him, that was true, but they knew it hadn't been an accident. They knew it had been one of them.

But they didn't know what to do about it. This was so much worse than cheating on an exam, and they knew that, too. That morning, as they stood around their housemate—heads like cotton wool and stomachs hollow while the late morning sun inched its way into the room, heating the spilled cups, empty boxes of wine, Pringles cans, and plastic ashtrays filled with ashes and butts—they saw their futures fading in front of their eyes.

Unable to bear the sight any longer, though they bore it longer than any decent person would have, they moved to the kitchen and poured each other warm juice and munched on leftover crisps. They had no answer but decided it would be best if they talked about this before they rang anyone. They were all there last night, and they all remembered what happened. Didn't they?

And someone said it wasn't their fault, and someone else agreed, but, just in case, shouldn't they be absolutely certain no one would put the blame on them? After all, Hollis had given him the drinks and Maeve had insulted and slapped him and Lorna had ignored him and Oliver had fought him and Ellie had forgotten him. They didn't want anyone blamed for what was clearly an accident. Because it was an accident. It was an accident after they put the phone back on the hook and threw out the broken lamp and burned the notebook Callum had kept as a record of what exams he had sold and to whom he had sold them. It was nothing more than an accident. A party gone wrong.

So they told their story to one another. To ensure it made sense, they told it many times. Until it became their truth. They remembered that after the guests had left but before they had gone to bed, Callum had stormed out of the house. They never saw him again until this morning.

Then they called an ambulance. They cried and told the police that they would have checked on Callum if they had known he was there. And the police told them it was all right, there was nothing they could have done, and carted Callum away in a black plastic bag but left the pink sofa, which to them smelled of rot. They returned to their rooms and studied for their exams and waited for Callum's parents to come for his things. They made sure to express their condolences but were more grateful that his belongings, especially the camera, were gone.

But he wasn't gone. Not entirely. The smell of his body became their contribution to the house's growing inventory. Like the second broken microwave, it would never be removed, not until the fire years later.

All it would have taken was for one of them to tell the truth, just one, and their story would have fallen to pieces. But they were all so scared of what would happen to them if the truth came out. They'd be labeled as liars and cheaters. Disappointments. The truth was, they never told the truth because they were glad that he had died. Glad that their secrets were safe. Glad that they didn't have to face the consequences of their mistakes. Life was easier for them with Callum dead, so they didn't fear whoever had done it. They thanked them, and though they never spoke of Callum, even to the ones they loved, they never really forgot him.

But they never remembered me. Of course, why should they? I was part of Callum's life, so to them, I was nothing.

11

Ellie

Ellie whispered to what was left of Oliver.

"If you had really regretted it, you would have called it rape."

She knelt in the mud and the blood and ran her hands over his clothes.

"But you're not going to hurt me again."

She patted all of his pockets, put her hands down his shirt, but she couldn't find the diary. She had seen him put it down his shirt, but now it wasn't there.

"You won't do this to me. I won't let you do this to me! I didn't do anything wrong."

Then she heard the someone gasp and saw Maeve and Lorna staring at her from the broken window. And Lorna's presence didn't surprise her. Ellie knew what it was like to look into a dead man's eyes. Lorna's had been very much alive.

Ellie clambered through the broken window, ignoring the glass cutting her. She saw the blood running down her arms, staining her clothes, but felt nothing. Wasn't even sure what was hers or what belonged to the men of this house. She leaned once more on the windowpane and looked at what was left of Oliver.

"This was all your fault and you know it."

She smoothed back her hair, streaking it red, and adjusted her bracelet. And then she ran. Maeve and Lorna had taken off and were now out of sight, but she heard Maeve's heavy footsteps on the stairs. Ellie rounded into the lobby in time to see someone's legs disappearing around the corner on the first floor. She reached the upstairs landing and heard them continuing up to the next floor. Could even hear Maeve's wheezing breath. Then a blur dashed the opposite way—they must've split up. Ellie knew her chances were better with Maeve. She'd take care of Lorna later.

She wove her way to the top floor, and there at the end of the hall she saw it. The door to the attic.

Open. Waiting.

Ellie could no longer see those now old scratches, but she ran her fingers over where they had been and remembered she had a choice. She could go back the way she came, out the broken window, make her way to the quay. Play her part so well when the first ferryman came. Through tears, tell him of the monsters inside Wolfheather House.

Ellie pictured her children running up to her on Monday, telling her how much they missed her and how much they needed her and how thankful they were that she was alive. David could take her into his arms, hold her tight, and she could smile because everything would be perfect again. She could let Gordon go. Be done with him. And no one would begrudge her anything after all she'd been through.

Or she could go into the attic.

Ellie removed her shoes to silence her steps and made her way up the narrow staircase.

The rain fell like gunfire on the roof so close to her head. Her hand felt for the light switch but then she stopped, remembering it wouldn't work anyway. So she stood and let her eyes adjust to the darkness. The stillness seemed absolute. Even her breathing felt intrusive. Where would Maeve go? she wondered. Would she continue to hide like the coward she was, or would she come out and face her?

"I know what you did," Ellie said.

She walked through the stacks of boxes, listening for any noise behind her.

"You didn't need to trick me into coming here. You could've just asked."

A shadow moved in the corner of her eye. Ellie spun, but there was nothing in the darkness. She paused, then kept moving forward.

"I would've helped. I feel just as awful about Callum. And there's no reason we can't be friends after this. We can clean this all up together. No one will ever know."

She peeked around a mothballed rack of clothes. Nothing. Silence.

"You know, it's only fitting that we tore ourselves to pieces, isn't it? We didn't need anyone to help us along the way. It was inevitable that we'd be drawn back to each other. It's chemistry. Jilly was studying chemistry for her GCSEs, and she read all about how different elements are harmless on their own, but when put together they can be explosive. That's exactly what we are, isn't it?"

Back in the far corner, a shadow darker than the rest.

"But it's different now, with Hollis and Oliver gone. Especially Oliver. We don't need to destroy each other anymore. The three of us ladies, we can stick together. After all, what happened to Callum wasn't your fault, just like it wasn't mine."

A figure leaned against the attic eaves.

"It wasn't my fault at all."

She lunged and brought the corkscrew down again and again. She brought it down to smash the events of this weekend, to shatter the memory of Caldwell Street, to erase Callum from her mind. But it was only after several blows that she realized what she had been stabbing wasn't a person at all but pillows covered in a quilt. Wispy duck feathers floated in the air. One stuck to her lip. She brushed it away.

There hadn't been a person. Only pillows leaning up against the wall in a far corner of the attic, with the only path out behind her, where someone already stood.

Maeve

The tire iron struck Ellie in the back of the head, but unlike Hollis, Ellie didn't fall. She spun away, striking Maeve in the hand with the corkscrew. The sharp scratch stung, but Ellie hadn't been able to hit hard enough to do any real damage. Maeve swung again. A gash opened up on Ellie's cheek. She pressed her long fingers to the blood with a laugh.

"So this is how it's going to be," Ellie said. "I could've helped you. All girls together against Oliver and Hollis."

"This was never about them," Maeve said. "This was about justice for Callum."

"I wanted that, too." She staggered into a wall.

"No," Maeve said. "You wanted him dead."

Ellie sighed. It was the same sigh she made when someone hadn't flushed the toilet or the microwave hadn't been cleaned properly. The sound she'd made when Maeve had offered her the last Oreo on a cold day in January before everyone else had returned to the house for the new term.

"I didn't want Callum dead. He helped me. Why would I want him dead?"

"Because he was going to the dean. He was going to confess how he got you the test answers for your finals."

"He was selling answers to everyone. You and your maths test. Hollis. Oliver bought more than a few. Even Lorna after she had that woman-hating lecturer again. Why should I be any different?" She staggered back into the eaves.

"You took his money. Instead of leaving it for his parents, you took it."

"We all did!" Her knees bent, but she caught herself on the wall before she fell. "We all took some. For his sake. To cover for him. To protect his family from the truth. Don't you remember?"

"I remember you came home the next day with a new Fendi Baguette handbag."

"Callum helped me. He helped me! I would never hurt him."

"Then why did you?" Maeve whispered.

Ellie gave a half-smile. Blood trickled down her chin. "All I did was ask him not to pick up the phone. All he had to do was listen. Why doesn't anyone ever listen to me?"

Maeve dropped the tire iron and lunged, knocking Ellie to the ground. Her fingers tightened around Ellie's throat. Her skin was so soft. She really did moisturize well, and with that thought, Maeve detached. The hands squeezing Ellie's neck tight were not Maeve's hands. The rage forcing her to maintain the pressure was not Maeve's rage. She floated above it all. It was someone else doing what needed to be done.

When a hand lay on her shoulder, she lashed out in retaliation. But it was only Lorna kneeling beside her to tell her it was over, to tell her it was done. Lorna turned on the light from her phone and Maeve looked at the body beneath her. It no longer moved. The eyes remained open, the sclera lined red from burst capillaries. A glob of red drool trailed from her lower lip. It was over. And suddenly Maeve wanted it not to be. She wanted Ellie to get up.

"Fuck you," she said. "Did you hear me? Fuck you. Fuck you fuck you fuck you!" She slapped Ellie's face. "Aren't you going to scold me for my language? Go on then. Fuck you!"

No answer. So she slapped her.

"Fuck you!"

And again.

"Maeve."

"Wake up you stupid bitch and yell at me. Fuck you!"

And again.

"Wake up!"

"Maeve."

A hand tugged at her arm.

"It's over. Maeve, it's over. It's done. Let her go. Come on. Let her go."

Lorna guided her down through the house and back through the foyer. Maeve waited there, watching the flameless fireplace, feeling the presence of Caskie's body behind her, while Lorna went to retrieve the ring of keys from Oliver's body. She returned, picking broken glass from her jumper, and unlocked the front door.

They both sat on the ground just in front of the door, nestled between the two cracked urns, and listened to the wind. The clouds were finally beginning to clear, revealing the brilliant blue sky that had been hidden from them the entire weekend. Maeve tried to make shapes out of the remaining clouds, but nothing could distract her from the feel of Ellie's skin underneath her hands.

"I guess if we smoked," Lorna said, "now would be the time."

"I guess."

The air was cold, but Maeve still felt hot. She didn't know if she would ever be cool again, or if her skin would always feel like it was on fire.

"What are we supposed to do now?" she asked.

"Well," Lorna said. "We have about an hour and a half until sunset. We could go for a walk. Make something for dinner. I didn't eat lunch and it's almost three, so . . ."

"I mean James Caskie isn't coming back for us."

Lorna sighed. "I know."

"There's no one we can use as an alibi."

"It's only Saturday. We have a whole day before anyone starts to suspect something's wrong. We'll figure something out."

Rain dripped from the gutters, streamed into the car park. Maeve followed the trail with her eyes to her own car. She felt guilty for having vandalized it when she really had just paid it off. And then she felt guilty for feeling guilty about a car, when she had done so many other bad things in the last forty-eight hours.

"We don't smoke," Maeve said, "but what would you say to a drink?"

"I'd say it's an excellent idea." Lorna rose, but when Maeve moved to do the same, Lorna motioned for her to sit. "I'll get it. We both need some time out of this house."

Maeve looked at the open door. "But what if—"

Lorna placed a hand on her shoulder. "It's fine, Maeve. There's no one else in the house."

Maeve listened to Lorna's footsteps cross the foyer. Then she chewed on the cuff of her jumper, bounced her knee up and down, but it wasn't enough to dispel the energy within her. The tears came and she could not stop them. She thought she'd feel relief once the job was done. That her guilt over Callum would be assuaged. But it had only been replaced with guilt over Hollis and Oliver and Ellie. She didn't know if this guilt would ever leave her. Maybe it would. Maybe one day, its last vestiges would fade to nothing. But for now it remained wedged inside her, a weight in her chest. She wiped the tears away, but they kept rolling down her cheeks. She had no control over them, and sitting still was no longer helping.

"Lorna, I'm coming to help."

But when Maeve entered the study, Lorna wasn't there. She checked the conservatory, but this, too, was empty.

"Lorna?"

Her voice echoed in the lobby.

"Are you in the kitchen? Were you getting snacks, too?"

As Maeve moved toward the dining room, she heard a noise from the back hallway.

"Lorna? Stop being silly."

But there was no response. Maeve worried the cuff of her jumper. Lorna always shouted at the stupid people in horror films, the ones who followed strange noises instead of running away. But this wasn't a horror film. Lorna was fine. And if she wasn't, Maeve had seen enough pain to last the rest of her lifetime. Lorna was her friend. She wouldn't let any harm come to her.

Maeve stepped around MacLeod's body.

"Lorna?"

A scratching sounded to her left, around a corner that led to a narrow hall. Maeve followed the sound. Windows at the back of the house provided the little light that was left that day. The damp air made her cough, and she almost missed the bark. A small shadow scratched at a door on the left. Maeve held up the light on her phone.

A small dog with shaggy brown fur panted in the hall. It remained at the door as Maeve approached.

"Hello! What are you doing here, Gizmo?"

The dog's ears perked up at its name.

"Lorna? I thought you said you were leaving Gizmo with friends."

She bent down to pick him up, but he darted away. The door he'd been scratching at cracked open.

"Lorna, are you in here?" Maeve pushed it in and held up the light.

It must've been an optical illusion.

A double bed. A Take That poster. A crate of food with Oreos and tins of beans. It was all so familiar. But it couldn't be. Her Caldwell Street bedroom wasn't supposed to be here. Not hers or Lorna's. These weren't among the things Lorna said she took from the house before she set the fire.

Maeve felt the pain in her side before the warm breath on the back of her neck.

"I'm so sorry."

Maeve gasped as her side burned. She had been hurt so many times before, so many times just today, but this was different. She had never known pain like this.

"Shh, shh. It'll be all right. Here. I'll help you sit down."

One hand held the knife in place, while the other guided Maeve to the floor. Already, Maeve could not support her own head. It sank until it rested in Lorna's lap.

"Lorna . . ." Blood stained her lips.

"Shh." She stroked Maeve's hair. "Lorna's in the boot of my car. I killed her three days ago. You haven't spoken to the real Lorna since the day you all moved out of Caldwell Street."

"Who . . ."

"Look here. Look at my eyes. People said we had the same eyes." She held Maeve's head so Maeve could see. All these months, and she hadn't noticed. Hadn't suspected. But Maeve could finally see the truth as she died. She saw through the dyed hair, the clothes. "That's right. I wasn't Callum's girlfriend. He never had a girlfriend. It's me, Jen. Jennifer McAllister. Callum's sister."

Maeve tried to speak, but it hurt too much. She tasted more blood in her mouth.

"No, no. Don't strain yourself. It'll only make it hurt more."

Lorna—no, Jennifer—placed her arm around Maeve's shoulder, supported her.

"I'll talk. You can listen. I told you there wasn't anyone else in the house. Just me. It was me living in the ballroom. I didn't have anywhere else to stay the past few months. I've put all my money into this and my rent. Sorry. That's not your problem, is it? That's not what you want to know. You want to know about Lorna. I knew I wouldn't be able to do this all by myself. I needed one of you, and the best way to befriend one of you was to become one of you. So I picked Lorna, because she was the easiest to impersonate. Unmarried, not even a girlfriend, no children. She lived alone in a city distant from her immediate family. And she wasn't on social media. She didn't even have any old social media pages until I made that Facebook profile for you to find. She made it too easy, really. I had Callum's pictures of her. Of all of you. He took so many pictures. It was easy to match her hair and we already had the same bra size. But I did get my nose done. Got it to match Lorna's, best I could anyway. Amazing how adjusting something so small can change your face entirely."

Each time Maeve tried to pull in air, she got less and less into her lungs. Tears dropped from Lorna's—from Jen's—face onto Maeve's cheek. Jen's hands were shaking as she brushed Maeve's face.

"Does it hurt? I didn't want to hurt you. I looked up videos on where to stab where it would cause the least amount of pain. But maybe they were wrong. Or I got it wrong. I don't know. So much has gone tits-up today, ever since MacLeod showed up. And then James. It wasn't . . . They weren't . . . I've been scrambling."

Maeve coughed. Warm blood on her lips. Jen wiped it away.

"Shh. Okay. It's okay. You want to know the truth. I owe you that. You helped me so much, and I owe you that much. Let me start at the beginning. You rest. I'll tell you the story. I'll start here. With this house. Our dad bought it in 1982. He loved the outdoors, our dad, and he'd been itching for a place in the Highlands as long as we could remember. Mum always said we couldn't afford it, a second home, but one day he shows up with this ring of keys and says we're going for a drive. Mum thought, okay, it's probably a cottage or croft house or something, and then we reach the crest of the drive and there's Wolfheather House. Mum pitched a fit, but it was too late for her to do anything about it.

"It was completely uninhabitable. No one had lived in it since the fifties. Dad fixed it up in starts and stops for almost a decade. Every penny we had went to this house. No holidays. No big Christmases. Mum bought most of our clothes secondhand from charity shops. Callum and I hated it, but we never said. There was never any arguing with Dad. But every time he brought us up here, instead of helping, we'd run and hide. Sneak around the old servants' staircases. Sit up here in the attic and listen to the rain. We had more fun living in the walls of this house than in the house itself.

"It wasn't until '93 that Dad realized the only way he was going to get any return on his investment was if he turned the place into a bed and breakfast. He was furious with himself. Like somehow he'd failed as a father. I mean, he probably had, but none of us cared by that point. Mom was too tired, and Callum and I were going to university. Dad hated the English, and he hated London and anything near it, so Cahill was perfect. Callum and I were going to room together, but Mum really wanted us to try and live apart, be our own people, she said, so we did. For her sake. I found this house share with three other girls who seemed fairly nice, but I didn't know them all that well. I heard later they called me the Ghost because they only knew I'd been in the house if they saw my food disappear or if my coat had moved. Callum found Caldwell Street, obviously. He used to tell me about the fights in the house. How things seemed to be escalating. How little cliques kept being made then broken then remade, but he never seemed concerned. Part of the experience, he said, of going to uni."

Jen's warm tears continued to drop on Maeve's cheeks.

"Everything was normal until we went home for Christmas break. God, I wish we hadn't. We found out then that Dad had lost his job in November. His entire career at one company and he was the first let go when the layoffs started. And we didn't have any savings. It had all gone into this house. We thought that was why Mum looked so sick, but it wasn't. She looked sick because she was sick. Cancer. Started in her left breast and spread to her lungs, liver, and lymph nodes. Two years she'd been diagnosed and she'd hid it from us, Dad too. Do you know how strange it is to sit around the Christmas tree with your family, a hot cup of mulled wine in your hands and a fire crackling, and know that one of you won't be around the next Christmas? None of us mentioned it the next Christmas, the three of us sitting there, Mum knowing it should have been her and not Callum who was missing."

She paused to wipe her face. Maeve tried to speak, but Jen hushed her and stroked her hair.

"Don't try to talk. It will only make it hurt. I'm sorry. I'm almost done. So, when we went back to Cahill that January, Callum, being his noble self, wanted to help Mum and Dad out, so that's why he finally gave in to Oliver and agreed to use his part-time job in the uni office to steal test papers. He wanted to tell me about it, but I was too busy clubbing and drinking and sleeping around. God, I was such a cliché.

"Callum thought the pregnancy scare would change me. I showed up at Caldwell Street that morning crying, mascara all down my face, and Callum went out and bought the pregnancy test for me because I was so scared I could barely move. But as soon as I saw it was negative, it was like it never happened. I went back to partying. Which is how I ended up at your party in May. I ignored Callum the whole time, and, because I knew how angry it would make him, I flirted with Oliver. My hair was ginger then. My natural color. And after the fight, I went up to Oliver's room and we had sex while the rest of you were letting Callum drink himself to oblivion. Later, I was sleeping when Ellie put her hand over his nose and mouth and watched him die. Dad was the one who told me. After the police called him, he rang me and started crying. I thought Mum had died. I'd never heard him cry. I cried, too, but not because I was sad. Because I was angry.

"I lived with that anger for twenty years until I finally realized what I could do with it. Social media made it so easy to find all of you, except Lorna, like I said. I had to change my name and move to Edinburgh to befriend her in person. But I was most nervous when meeting you, Maeve. If I couldn't fool you, I knew I couldn't fool the others. But you believed me. Beautiful, wonderful Maeve, you fell for it all, and that's when I knew it could work. When we talked about Caldwell Street, I used what I knew from Callum—he used to tell me everything about all of you. God, I couldn't get him to shut up sometimes. And I used what I'd learned from Lorna to get you to tell me more. And I saved it all. Wrote it down in those notebooks you found so that I'd never forget.

"The only person who knew any of this was our younger cousin, James. God, James was supposed to set up the rooms for us and check us in, like I told you. I just never told you he was my cousin. But he wasn't supposed to be here. Stupid, stupid Jamie. He was only five when Callum died, but we were the only cousins each of us had. When Dad finally had to sell Wolfheather House, it was Jamie who got the idea to get a job with the new owner. MacLeod, what a pompous ass. But Jamie wasn't supposed to die. That was my fault. I underestimated Ellie. Underestimated the effect this house has on people. Do you know how hard it was not to cry when I saw him? How hard it was not to kill Ellie right then and there? But I couldn't. Because Lorna Torrington did not know that man and would not have cried, so neither could I."

Barking interrupted her. Maeve turned her head and, through clouded vision, saw the blurred outline of Gizmo in the doorway.

"Hello, Gizmo," Jen cooed. "Ellie let him out of the attic by accident. He's the one that scratched her and he's been running around here almost all day, probably looking for Lorna, poor thing. Lorna wouldn't go anywhere without him. She thought we were coming here together, you see. That's how I got her in the car. But she had to bring Gizmo, and I couldn't hurt him. Only a monster would hurt a dog. It's all right, Gizmo. I'm almost done here."

The dog. The dog could save her, Maeve thought, and she reached out her hand, hoping he would come near. Defend her from her attacker. Let her run her fingers through his soft fur and give her the strength to rise and run. He lay down in the doorway and rested his head between his paws.

Maeve wheezed. "Please ..."

"Gizmo and I have become good friends, haven't we? That's how Lorna and I first met. I befriended her at the dog park a couple years back, right after my nose job. Offered to watch him when she went on business trips."

Jen kissed her on the forehead.

"Everything was going so well. Until MacLeod returned. I'm sorry I set you up for his death, but I couldn't have Oliver or Ellie suspecting me, could I? I strangled him this morning before everyone else woke up. I came down first and saw the lit fire in the lobby and I knew there was someone else here. I found him back here, poking around the rooms. I pretended to be a confused guest and he led me back to the lobby. Then I strangled him while his back was turned. I put the twine in your pocket, Maeve. When Oliver was interrogating you. I'm sorry. It was between you and Ellie, and you were standing closer to me. And then to make matters worse, James showed up!" She shook her head. "I still don't know why. He chickened out, I think. Never left the island on Friday and hid in the house all morning. I wanted to ask him why, but thanks to Ellie I never got the chance. I don't know why he let us find him. Some things are always left unanswered, I suppose."

Maeve's vision grew darker. The sun was setting. It was about that time, wasn't it?

"My plan was always to kill you last, but when James died, I thought about letting you live. I really did. You're a cool person when you're not trying to impress other people. And it would be nice to have a friend after all this."

Blood dripped down the inside of Maeve's throat, and she coughed. Couldn't stop, gasped for mouthfuls of air.

"I'm so sorry, but I had to go through with it in the end. Because how could I let you live when you were the one that stopped them from calling the police in the first place?"

Jen stopped stroking her hair.

A memory came to Maeve. Bubbled to the surface like the blood at her lips. Standing around Callum's body, someone asking what they should do, and Oliver—Oliver reached for the phone on the wall, but Maeve had raised her arm and said, "No." Maeve said they should talk about this in the kitchen first and then decide what they should do. And for that one moment in her life, they had listened to her and followed her instruction rather than the other way around, and it had been so exhilarating that she forgot the reason they were all gathering in the kitchen in the first place.

"Do you even remember telling me that, that first night in Edinburgh? You were so drunk. I knew everyone had lied about something that night, but I never knew it was your fault that the police never suspected he'd been murdered. That it was because of you that Ellie got to walk away."

Jen rested her head on Maeve's shoulder.

"But I want you to know that it's not all your fault. We all did some bad things that year. Things we wish we could take back. Each of us is to blame. Just some more than most."

She adjusted her grip on the blade.

"I'm going to remove this now, and you're going to bleed out. But it'll be all right. I'll be here with you the whole time. I won't leave until you're gone. I promise."

The edge of the knife cut the inside of Maeve's body as Jen withdrew the blade. Blood spread down her belly, over her shirt, a blossoming stain like a flower in bloom. Her head went fuzzy. Jen helped her lie back and Maeve watched the water stains on the ceiling twisting into shapes. Into the picture of a grungy front room with a worn brown armchair and a sagging pink sofa. And she could hear music—Take That—and smell crisps and cigarette smoke. Hollis offered her an Oreo while Ellie gave her new dress a thumbs-up and Oliver glanced her way and smiled. And Lorna—the real Lorna—rolled her eyes with a smirk and a shrug and opened a book. And there in the back garden was Callum, sitting alone, looking up at the stars, and she sat beside him and took his hand in hers, and together they looked at the dark sky, and Maeve said, "I'm sorry."

And Callum looked at her with eyes she never thought she'd see again and said, "I know. But that's not enough."

Jen

The rising moon illuminated Wolfheather House like a picture on a post-card, the horrors that happened inside censored by brick walls. Several hours had passed since Maeve died, since she had killed her, and Jen wasn't entirely sure where all that time had gone. She remembered crying over Maeve's body, wishing Maeve hadn't needed to die. But the next thing she remembered was sitting in the attic where she and Callum had once hid as children, wrapped in the moth-eaten quilt of their mother's, a quilt now stained with Ellie's blood. She had lost so much time, and there was still so much work to do, work she had to complete on her own now that James, too, had been taken from her. That work was almost done now, but not quite.

Now she was outside. Jen looked down from the sky and into the trunk of the Vauxhall. Lorna's gray body lay curled in the fetal position. Thank god the trunk latch hadn't broken yesterday. The smell bothered her, but after everything she'd been through this weekend, this was a minor incon-venience. She hefted the body from the boot and dragged it into the house.

The generator was running now, and the lights hummed inside the house. Gizmo, tethered to the front desk, barked and growled, but she cooed to him and continued hefting the body up the stairs. Her arms were tired, her back sore. But this was important. This had to be done before she could finish the diary she planned to leave for the police. Because even-tually the police would come, and she wasn't going to be here to explain everything when they did. The diary would have to suffice.

She dragged Lorna to the room with all the rest. Sat her on the pink sofa between Hollis and Maeve. She stood back and examined the picture she had taken off Hollis's body, the one she'd accidentally dropped down the sofa cushions. A stupid mistake, but one that had given her an idea. Her brother had loved photographs, and what better way to document all that she had done for him than one last group picture of the residents of 215 Caldwell Street?

Pp. 122–123

Hollis told me last night that the end of the world is different for different people. He was right. It could be a reformed alcoholic giving in to a drink on a lonely New Year's Eve. Or wrecking your parents' Rolls-Royce when you weren't even supposed to be out. The loss of a job. A spouse discovering your lover. Failing an audition. A pet's death. A parent's rejection. A loved one moving out of the country. Shop security finding that pinched lipstick in your bag.

When I was five, the end of the world was not getting this final Happy Meal toy I needed to make the complete set. It was the thing I wanted most in the world, but it was also something that was denied me, for no reason I could see. I don't remember what that toy was, and if I had it now, it would only be packed in the basement or the attic of Wolfheather House with all of the other detritus from my and Callum's childhood. But I remember the feeling of how much I wanted it and how much it hurt not to have it.

But our end of the world changes as we age. In spring 1995, I didn't care about Happy Meal toys anymore. I was most afraid of becoming a disappointment. Disappointing myself and disappointing my parents. I know it was the same for Callum. We were twins, after all. And the same was true for the others. This is why I don't hate them for what they did, despite what you might think. Like most teens who grew up with school as the source of their biggest dreams and biggest fears—who were taught by society that if they failed school, they would fail life—failure was the end of the world. They had the tunnel vision that comes with adolescence. The belief that nothing in life would ever be more important than what they were experiencing right at that moment. Not even life itself.

So I don't want you to think it was stupid of them to let Callum die over something we adults view as silly as cheating on a few exams. Because to them it was what mattered most.

But that doesn't mean I was going to let them get away with it.

ONE MONTH LATER

12

Linda

Linda Drummond finished reading and slid the photocopied pages of the diary back across the table to DS Khan.

"I want to see the photo," she said.

"Linda, I don't think—"

"The detective from Scotland told me about the photo, so I want to see it. They said they sent you a copy."

"You don't want to see your father that way."

Linda could see how easy it was for DS Khan, with his calm, measured voice and deep brown eyes, to comfort victims. But Linda didn't want to be comforted. She didn't deserve it.

"I want to know what this psycho"—she shoved the pages again—"decided was a suitable punishment for a mistake my father made when he was nineteen. Show me the photo they found with the diary." She straightened her shoulders and stared DS Khan in the eye until he sagged and sighed.

"Wait here."

He returned two minutes later with a manila folder and took his seat across from her, but he didn't open the folder right away. He kept both hands on top as if preventing monsters from leaping out.

"The picture shows the bodies in the upstairs bedroom in the same positions the local police found them, but she had taken it days before the discovery, based on ..."

Linda crossed her arms. "Based on?"

"The state of decomposition." He hesitated, then pushed the folder forward.

Before DS Khan could warn her again, Linda opened the folder. At first glance, nothing seemed wrong. It was a normal Polaroid picture of a group of old friends gathered on a sofa. But then she noticed that the man on the end had no face. It had been crushed in. The others' eyes stared not at the camera but vacantly at blank space. Their skin varied in shades of gray, their mouths agape as if they forgot how to say "cheese." Blood in various patterns streaked their clothes.

Linda forced herself to look at her father. Dried blood covered most of the wound to his head, but she could see a concave shape to his skull where it should have been round. She closed the folder and slid it back to DS Khan.

"Do they have any idea where she is?"

He shook his head. "They're not even sure what she looks like. The fake Facebook page she created has been deactivated. They're working on getting a warrant to release the data. All the Caskie and remaining McAllister families had were some childhood pictures, nothing of her older than eight or nine years of age. It seems she managed to take any recent pictures they had of her out of the house weeks before the murders. She purposely left us that diary, but we have no idea how much of what she wrote is even accurate and how much was fabricated for the police's benefit. She could be anywhere. And, based on what she was able to pull off, she could be anyone."

Linda grabbed her old messenger bag off the floor and paused as she looked at the badges her dad had once helped her sew on. Then she threw the bag strap over her shoulder.

"I know who she is. She's the woman who murdered my father."

She left the interview room without saying goodbye and navigated the familiar halls of the Greater Manchester Police Headquarters alone, unsure where to go next even as she got on a bus to the city center. She thought this visit would help in some way. Assuage more of her guilt for not raising the alarm sooner when her father hadn't responded to her calls or texts. Make her feel like less of a fool for falling for that woman's stupid tricks in the first place. She felt none of this, though. Only a confused knot of guilt that she had done something she didn't know how to fix.

She hopped off the bus a half hour later, no less confused than before. As she waited to cross the street, a dog on a lead barked and snarled at her, the woman on the other end doing nothing to quiet it. When the light changed, the woman yanked on the dog's lead, dragging it across street and kicking its belly when it refused to walk. Linda watched the woman and reluctant dog until they were out of sight.

Linda changed direction.

Using the National Rail app on her phone, she bought a one-way ticket to Edinburgh. Then she scrolled through her contacts, found the number the police said they couldn't trace. The number of the woman who said she'd been a friend of her father's. Linda had read the diary cover to cover, had read her stupid ghost story, and asked herself the very question Jennifer McAllister had posed at the end of the obituary. Which one are you?

Linda sent a series of texts she wasn't sure would be read.

I'm not the laird. Or the guest. Or the pack.

I'm Hollis Drummond's daughter. And I'm going to find you.

An hour later, as she sat on a train at Manchester Piccadilly watching travelers race across the platform with their coffee, their luggage, their children, her phone dinged. There were no words, only a picture. A twin image of the one she had seen at the police station. The same people, decades younger, gathered on the couch and smiling up at the camera, arms around one another. Except in the foreground, at her father's feet, sat a tall young man with ginger-brown hair. And there, in the background, walking into the frame as if by accident, face blank as it recognized the camera, a young woman with long, ginger hair and pale eyes, unnoticed by everyone except this girl sitting on this train. A young woman waiting for her chance to do something very good, or something very bad.

ACKNOWLEDGMENTS

Thank you to Jannicke Bevan de Lange for reading the early chapters and helping me realize what wasn't working and fix it before it was too late. Also, thank you to Sandra Sawicka for helping me fix what I didn't even realize was wrong (but seems so obvious now!). Thank you to Cal Barksdale and the team at Arcade CrimeWise for turning this from a manuscript into a book.

As always, a big thank you to my family, especially Mom, Cherie, and Lindsey, for not always knowing what I'm doing when I'm locked away in my office but supporting me anyway, and to Harry and Gizmo, who don't mind hanging out with me in my locked office.

Finally, thank you to terrible house parties everywhere for reminding why I prefer to be locked in my office.